I0633527

AMONG THE
STARS

NICK TURMAN

Copyright © 2024 by Nick Turman.

All rights reserved. No part of this publication may be reproduced, distributed, or transmitted in any form or by any means, including photocopying, recording, or other electronic or mechanical methods, without the written consent of the publisher. The only exceptions are for brief quotations included in critical reviews and other noncommercial uses permitted by copyright law.

MILTON & HUGO L.L.C.
4407-11 Park Ave., Suite 5
Union City, NJ 07087, USA

Website: *www. miltonandhugo.com*
Hotline: *1- 888-778-0033*
Email: *info@miltonandhugo.com*

Ordering Information:
Quantity sales. Special discounts are granted to corporations, associations, and other organizations. For more information on these discounts, please reach out to the publisher using the contact information provided above.

Library of Congress Control Number: IN-PROCESS
ISBN-13:   979-8-89285-011-7   [Paperback Edition]
                  979-8-89285-012-4   [Digital Edition]

Rev. date: 02/28/2024

CONTENTS

PROLOGUE

Millions of light years away from the present day Milky Way, lost and endlessly floating through deep space in a beaten and battered starship, a group of Guardians recall the horrors they've just only moments ago escaped from. Their peace however, was short lived as the very evil that destroyed their assigned world, came jumping out of hyperspace to erase the last of The Order present in that part of the galaxy. A third-class Elder Guardian, with shoulder length blue hair, skin soft to the touch, and sunset colored eyes by the name of Luna Joyce, and a few other third-class Elite Guardians who didn't share the same beauty, with their last desperate action, performed a *Bonding Ritual*, allowing the bonded target to share memories and realities alike. Luna and her comrades hoped they could successfully warn the galaxy of the incoming fire long thought extinguished. The task proved most difficult because concentrating knowing death was around the corner was nerve racking to say the least. The three entities channeled the Source Energy of the cosmos, levitating and chanting confidently as if they knew their efforts would bear fruit. Alarms blared as their spaceship began to break apart, screaming in pain as the enemy forces bombarded it with Kinetic Energy. This massive spacecraft of Darkness and death towered over Luna's ship. The ship itself resembled an enormous black box, and had strange tentacles protruding from the bottom, slithering with a sense of hunger. Upon further inspection, the ship had no visible signs of propulsion, only mysterious cracks of red light that covered the entire outer shell. This massive ship was named: *The Obedience*. Time froze for Luna as she delivered the warning with the belief that she gave hope to the galaxy, or so she thought. The Elder felt a sense of peace and accomplishment rush over her as she closed her eyes accepting her fate…but suddenly, the bombardment stopped. The Guardians aboard the damaged spacecraft felt a sinister presence; an immobilizing Aura, as *Orion*, self-proclaimed God of Darkness, appeared before them. It was as if he was already onboard their crippled spacecraft, waiting for the perfect moment to reveal himself. He levitated effortlessly as his Black Aura, intoxicating and visible to the naked eye, dripped from his long dark colored robe like a water fossett struggling to close. His skin, dark red in coloration, was as cold and dead as deep space as his long black hair shined with beauty; his three black horns birthing mystery. His very presence commanded fear, his power could destroy entire cities, sucking the very lifeforce from every living thing, like a vampire feeding on the innocent. He looked down upon Luna, captivated by her beauty and saw the rebellious strength; the hope in her eyes. He knew of the pitiful last act she and her comrades committed, but it mattered none, for his power was inevitable; his revenge undeniable. Luna could feel him in her mind, invading, searching and dominating, like a terrible song that wouldn't leave. She screamed as she was helpless to Orion's influence, like a baby trying to swim in the ocean. Orion was intrigued by the will of the Elder and captured her, bringing her onboard his colossus sized ship, leaving the others onboard the broken ship. Orion forced Luna to watch as he destroyed her fellow Guardians, leaving what remained forever floating in deep space...

CHAPTER

ONE

WARNING

Two hundred thousand light years away from the capture of Luna, in the deep inner-portion of the **Myrmidon Galaxy**, on a luscious and lively planet named: **Journia**, the time was 9:35pm on a Saturday night. The city of **Mos-Dia** was calm and quiet…too quiet for a population of seventeen billion, second only to the capital city of **Sarvis** which had a population of twenty-four billion sentient beings of different species, shapes and sizes. Usually the capital city was extremely busy like a never ending flame. Citizens with jetpacks, hoverboards, and speeders traversed the city, going to and from stores and restaurants, attending festivals, and celebrating the galaxy's long found peace. Galactic crime was at an all time low thanks to the Guardians and inhabitants with some noble pedestrians refusing to even litter. The people of Journia and other key planets lived and protected each other under the **Law of One**, which acknowledges that an entity's soul is a unique portion of the Creator, and that one's soul is a single unit of consciousness that stems from the Creator's consciousness or the **One Infinite Creator**. This fact further represents the togetherness of beings on a spiritual level. Furthermore, it is through the Love and Light of the Creator that every living entity throughout the known Universe be intune with **Source Energy**. Source Energy being a field of vital Divine Energy which acts as the "breath of life" for living beings, as well as to provide a bridge to different powers and abilities. As a result, a Universe full of endless possibilities, both desired and undesired was born.

Two centuries ago, there was a devastating war which spread across the entire galaxy known appropriately as the *Galactic War*. This raging conflict lasted six long years, and saw hundreds of worlds and trillions of entities destroyed by a foul Darkness. Legend says one day, that same Darkness will return, seeking vengeance, and a burning drive to reclaim a power thought unreachable. If that happens, the galaxy will surely fall victim to a second Galactic War; an "Eternal Darkness", or so the legend says. To ensure the continuous survival of the galaxy and its inhabitants, the *Ashura Order* was formed and organized by *The Nine*. Nine of the strongest Source Energy wielders who were instrumental in the Galactic War. These beings now act as the "brains" of The Order, and were the first masters, practitioners and teachers of the Way of Ashla.

Currently on Journia and other key planets across the galaxy, The Order operates as peacekeepers. An army of skilled and powerful freedom fighters for galaxy scale threats, and the overall protection of the globe and its people. Most of these brave protectors were later named *Guardians*. The majority of these empowered entities found honor in such a title, but others found that serving the Creator was its own title and reward. Guardians, along with chosen alien races, possess their own unique connection to Source Energy. Moreover, through the teachings of *Ashla*, or the Light side of Source Energy, a Guardian is able to deepen their bond to Source Energy, enabling a level of enlightenment and tranquility within a Guardian's very soul. The Nine taught there was only the Way of Ashla, and to shy away from *Bogan* teachings or the Dark side of Source Energy, for within the Way of Bogan comes an extraordinarily powerful connection to the strength aspect of Source Energy. Though power stems from this path to Source Energy, the Way of Bogan is fueled by fear, hate, greed, jealousy, and sorrow. Emotions that blind one from the Love and Light gifted by the One Infinite Creator.

After completing basic combat, survival, medical, and pilot training, earning the rank of third-class Paladin, Guardians are split up into groups, depending on their Energy type, to begin their Ashla teachings.

Depending on their understanding of Source Energy through Ashla teachings, Guardians are given a classification ranging from third-class to first-class. A Guardian who has achieved first-class within a rank has the option to be promoted to the next Guardian rank. These ranks being **Elder, Elite, Acolyte**, and **Paladin** with first-class Elder being the highest achievable rank. A Guardian ranked first-class Elite or higher has the choice of joining a **Faction**, starting one, or continuing solo. A faction is a group of Guardians that receives its status based on two points. Firstly, the rank of the mission assigned (**Wolf, Bear, Dragon**, or **Demon** with Demon being the most challenging) and secondly, the success rate of each mission. The higher the status of a particular faction and/or Guardian, the more responsibility that is required, along with power, strength and the will to preserve what is right and just. One faction has the potential to hold up to a hundred thousand Guardians or more, but a lot of members doesn't make a faction more or less than any other. It's what is done when faced with impossible odds that determines true strength and resilience within an individual, Guardian, faction of Guardians, or grand faction of Guardians. There are currently over fourteen million active Guardians that are split up into ten thousand active duty factions to cover more ground, on and off world. Together this army of Guardians coordinate and work diligently and humbly to preserve the well-being of Myrmidon. You'll always have your "anti-this" and "anti-that", but one thing is certain, Myrmidon has seen an extensive period of peace, wealth and prosperity which can be a humble blessing and a weighing curse. Therefore when reality comes knocking, the galaxy will need the full might of the Ashura Order. Factions will undoubtedly sink or swim, and the Elder and Elite ranked Guardians will need to push past their limits to survive. So let's hope this time of peace and stagnation hasn't left The Order soft and out-of-shape.

Vinzent, a first-class Elder Guardian, currently rests in his place of residence on this lovely Saturday night, after he and his comrades completed their ninety-third Demon ranked mission, setting a new record. The six foot three, golden curly-haired, Aura-user, laid in bed, tossing and turning as he found it extremely difficult to enjoy the replenishing rest. Lost in REM sleep, the Guardian heard the unpleasant screams of men, women and children; screams that should never be heard from a living being. He looked within his dream in disbelief as he saw a horribly distorted, four-armed creature, covered in rotten black flesh. This disturbing entity tore the appendages off innocents with one set of hands, and used the other set to slice people in half with swords made from hellfire, sending its victims to the afterlife. Nothing was spared as the population of innocent pedestrians were wiped from the history books like erasing a mistake from a sheet of paper. He helplessly witnessed the horror unfold, but felt sinister eyes watching him, invading his subconscious mind. He felt this heavy presence of another as faint whispers glided past his ears.

Unknown voice: *whispers* "Revenge…"

Vinzent was overwhelmed and wished to escape such a nightmare, but before he could, he heard a soft angelic voice call to him. The Elder turned and saw a beautiful blue skinned woman, filled with distress and grief, but also with a sense of duty. She explained to the Aura-user that what he just witnessed was no mere dream, but a bonding ritual enabling him to temporarily peer into her memory so that her warning harbored truth.

Luna: "Vinzent! There isn't much time and I have no time to waste. There is a great evil that plagues Myrmidon and he will stop at nothing till this galaxy and everything in it are shrouded in death and Darkness. His name…is Orion. He and his followers are the embodiment of chaos and devastation. I warn you because I have faith that you and your faction will warn The Nine and mobilize The Order before it's too late. Cleanse this plane of existence of this wickedness once and for all, effectively saving the known galaxy and beyond. Please, you must avenge the fallen…avenge my comrades."

Vinzent suddenly woke up, covered in sweat as he was shaken by what he experienced. Thinking it was simply a crazy dream, he fell back asleep, brushing it off as merely a subconscious adventure, one he doesn't know if he would've survived. The Elder awakened the following morning to a strange and ominous feeling. The feeling of great distress, like an ancient evil marching near from the deepest darkest corner of the known galaxy. The sensation weighed down on him as if submerged under water. He was concerned by this feeling, this malicious presence. Driven with a sense of caution Vinzent sent three electromagnetic waves of Elemental Energy, powered by his **Blue Aura**, which allowed the Elder to alter the minds of weaker targets, and/or telepathically communicate with the right conditions. Vinzent's ability, **Aura Conversion**, allowed him to generate different colored Auras that independently affect the nature and properties of his lightning ability.

The Guardian sent the waves and requested the counsel of his faction members. Afterwards, Vinzent scurried to gather his essentials, dressing in his civilian attire. He looked in the mirror of his bathroom to take a few swift minutes to brush his shoulder length, golden brown curly hair, before putting it in a bun. He grabbed a fresh banana, gave thanks to the One Infinite Creator, then rushed outside to see his home city of Mos-Dia alive and jumping.

Vinzent's neighbor: "Hey, Vinzent! Thanks again for fixing my roof! I know an Elder Guardian like yourself has better things to do than be bothered by an old man like me."

Vinzent: "No worries! Always happy to lend a helping hand!"

The two waved and said their goodbyes as Vinzent turned to generate his **Red Aura**. This Aura enabled him to manifest lightning into physical weapons and objects. The Elder felt the life of the city around him as he saw aliens and humans living in complete harmony. The sight comforted him as he knew this world, this galaxy, was worth protecting. Vinzent put one hand toward the sky, feeling this immense Source Energy from the Creator as he concentrated that Energy to a single point on his raised hand. He began to feel the pulsating Aura of his soul through his hand as his Elemental Energy traveled down his arm, into his heart and up to his mind, giving him the means to manipulate the gifted Source Energy into an electric red glow. He then condensed and manifested the red glow into a surfboard made with red lightning. Flipping onto the board, he focused and used the electromagnetic waves of the planet as propulsion to fling himself at high speeds toward the faction's base of operations. A heavily armed fortress a hundred and thirteen miles Northwest of his current location, in the mountain lands of **Mara**. What would take a citizen roughly two hours to accomplish took Elder Vinzent mere minutes as he made quick work of the journey, gliding flawlessly as if he were one with the wind. The fluidity of his movements caught the eyes of the local children as they jumped and cheered with amazement.

Seventy-four miles true west from the base in Mara, a first-class Elder Guardian by the name of **Nico Tulex**, a six foot two dark-brown Taiyōnian male, with short black dreadlocks and brown eyes, sat in his home participating in a session of calisthenics. The up-side-down Elder possessed strange tattooed-markings that pulsated with a mysterious darkened marigold-orange glow that covered his entire body, leaving only his head and neck untouched. The markings showed a chaotic, yet orderly pattern of brilliantly placed lines, angles and curves, resembling a warrior's ritual.

Elder Nico sensed the intense bursts of electromagnetic waves from Vinzent, knowing a sudden burning urge for a faction meeting meant the situation was no ordinary walk in the park. With that in mind, the Elder finished his calisthenic workout before standing to give thanks to the One Infinite Creator. He dressed in his daily robes, stopping a moment to hold a picture of his deceased family from long ago. And another of him and his long time friends, Elder Rex, Elder Kicks, and Elder Casanova, who were all reported missing a year ago. After a moment of silence, he rushed outside, feeling the blessing ray of Source Energy from the Sun that pierced through the deep tree line. The streams of light shine gracefully on his forest home village of **Solla**. Nico breathed in, feeling the Sunshine around then within himself. He channeled the Source Energy of the Sun, allowing his **Solar Mutation** ability to take effect. An ability that allowed Nico to amplify, mutate, and regenerate his body on a muscular and cellular level. The rarity of Nico's power and Healing-Factor are thanks to the Solar Source Energy, gifted from the Sun and the Creator. Another rare trait that only allowed Nico to harness the power of Source Energy when under a Sun. Through this ability, the muscle-fibers in Nico's legs grew bigger and stronger as the texture of his flesh hardened, like cement drying. Stepping into the Sunlight, the Elder felt the surge of power in his legs as he fiercely propelled himself hundreds of feet in the air, bursting through the tree line. Because of the high altitude jump, Nico gained a sense of direction as gravity pulled the Elder down hard on his feet. Following this, Nico began his journey towards the base in Mara, parkouring through the giant trees and branches with ease.

Off in the distance, Vinzent arrived at the heavily guarded perimeter of the base in style, surfing the waves of Journia's electromagnetic Energy. The Elder flipped off his board before releasing the converted Elemental Energy into the atmosphere. From the rear, Nico landed hard from a previous high altitude leap before jumping fifteen feet in the air as if he were on a trampoline. The Guardian mutated his arm into one of his many mutations called: *Hari*, which allowed muscle-fibers to burst free then wrap around his arm. As a result, the Elder's arm mutated into an elongated limb which formed four small blades at the end, that acted as a potential grappling hook and/or a whip, hence the name.

While in mid-air, Nico wrapped his mutated arm around a sturdy tree branch and swung like a simian before somersaulting to land at the main entrance of the facility. Nico greeted his comrade before mutating his arm and leg fibers back to normal.

Nico: *cheerful tone* "Vinzent! Good to see you brotha. I pray all is well in Mos-Dia?"

Vinzent: *cheerful tone* "And you as well my friend. And yes, nothing but smiles and laughter fill the streets. Keeping the peace in Solla I hope?"

Nico: "Without a doubt. The One Infinite Creator is forever generous."

Vinzent: "That he is."

The two Guardians finished their greeting, then compared entrances, making a friendly, but competitive competition out of it with the loser buying the winner a drink. Returning to the serious nature of Vinzent's request, the two entered the facility by speaking a certain phrase known only by the faction members. After speaking the phrase *"in life there is purpose, in death there is freedom"*, an eighteen foot rock split open, giving way to two steel plated doors, sixteen feet in length which was reinforced by an energy shield, and engraved with the saying, *"For the Creator watches over the way of the Righteous"*. After spoken, the shield was temporarily deactivated as the doors opened, allowing Elders Nico and Vinzent to enter a hallway. Upon entering, the two were reunited with the base's internal beauty. Beautiful lite-brown wood covered the walls with gray colored stone covered by a rug, burgundy in color, which masked the floor. The base was also reinforced with a specially made steel which acted as a resilient exoskeleton.

As the Elders walked through their base, seven smaller doorways were shown. Three on the left, which contained the living quarters and kitchen as the first room, a state-of-the-art simulation training room or STR as the second. And thirdly a medical/rehab center. Three on the right, which housed the meditation chamber firstly. Secondly, the armory, which contained weapons, gadgets and a lab to improve those gadgets. And thirdly, the security/defense office, which also acted as the heart of the base so security there was tight. The final door offsetted to the rear of the fortress was the war room, which contained *Jasmine*, a personalized AI computer mind with feminine characteristics. A meeting table made with holographic technology, and an elevator formed from reversed engineered levitation technology. Furthermore, the elevator could either lead up towards the air-pad which contained the faction's starship, the *Hercules*, or could lead down to the underground hangar, where the multi-transport, all-terrain vehicle or *MT-AT* sat ready for deployment.

As the two Guardians made their way towards the war room, they were struck with a feeling of unease and worry. They extended the doors leading inside the war room to find first-class Elder Guardian, *Raito*, a six foot six, dark skinned, Mahōnian male, with black and lite-brown dreadlocks tied up in a ponytail, and dressed in his civilian clothes. Elder Raito anxiously worked through the master computer's files to find answers for the presence felt earlier that morning. It was to no surprise to Nico or Vinzent that Raito made it there first, despite being over four hundred miles away from the base, in the desert city of **Zotune**. After all, his super speed was unmatched.

With his Grimoire in hand, Raito greeted his fellow companions as he made his way towards the table in the middle of the room. He was joined by Vinzent then Nico as Vinzent informed both of them of his dream/vision...

Vinzent: "I've requested this counsel because I've had a disturbing vision, more like a warning from Elder Luna Joyce. This dream or vision, I don't really know what to call it, it felt so real. At first I didn't think anything of it, thinking it had to be a subconscious fear, or memories from a past mission, but when I awakened this morning, I felt this...this–"

Nico: "Malicious presence?"

Vinzent: "How did you know?"

Nico: "Because I felt it as well during one of my meditation sessions. Something powerful, something truly unholy is disrupting the very balance of the galaxy. There is more to us than we may know, spiritually and physically, and I fear this faction is more involved than we hoped to be. What kind of warning did Luna deliver?"

Vinzent: "She said there is an evil that plagues this plane of existence, corrupting and destroying. And that my faction and I shall, 'cleanse the galaxy of the Darkness', bringing forth the Light. She mentioned the name of 'Orion'? I don't know what to think about this, so I came to you guys for counsel and to see if you guys heard or felt the same, but it seems you have."

Raito: "Luna mentioned our faction specifically? What about the entirety of the Ashura Order?"

Vinzent: "I was curious about that too. She did mention it would be in the galaxy's best interest to inform The Nine right away. I have a bad feeling about all this…"

Nico: "Now that I think about it, the name Orion is vaguely familiar. I have read the manuscript from the Galactic War, y'all have read it as well, and it talked about a wicked group, the 'The Organics.' A dishonorable and sinister group of entities bent on conquest, enslavement, destruction and vengeance, and was the group that threw the galaxy into the War. It also talked about some kind of powerful 'horned race of people with red skin', but the information there has been locked in The Vault. This lone entity 'Orion', must be the head honcho said to return. However, I am unsure."

Raito: "We've also read the *Law of One*, stating that 'All are One and One is All, under the Love/Light and Light/Love of the One Infinite Creator', but to think this Orion entity could be so monstrous, hateful, and so close to home is utterly frightening, but nonetheless prophesied."

After Luna's warning, the Guardians made their way towards the meditation chamber just a few feet away as Nico pushed the wooden doors behind them shut. The wood inside was made from the *Tree of Protection* from Nico's hometown.

During a deep meditation session, the lite-brown wood walls form a bubble of transparent Source Energy around the entity, allowing the meditator to temporarily leave one's physical vessel in order to enter the different dimensions of space/time, as well as to provide protection to the astral body during the process. Leaving the physical body exposed to the elements was a great risk, but well worth it if what the meditator seeked was found, learned and accepted.

After Vinzent informed his comrades of the insightful warning, the three Guardians made a unanimous decision to find out exactly what the hell was going on, and what they were up against. Upon entering the chamber and lighting a few incense, the Elders sat in a triangular fashion as they began to chant the mantra, *"Energy flows through all things, and I am Energy"*, repeatedly as it is the foundation of The

Order's strength. The combined Ashla taught Source Energy could be felt off the planet as the Elders lifted a foot off the floor, lighting the engraved runes marked on the walls and ceiling in a Sunshine yellow hue. With the atmosphere set, and the pre-meditative preparations completed, the Guardians began a three day meditation session where they all channeled Source Energy to share a vision…

They saw a planet, a beautiful flourishing planet with an abundance of life. The Energy there was strong and loving as if the embodiment of love itself gifted them with the eyes to see, the heart to feel, and the mind to understand. These compassionate beings went about their daily lives. Growing food and caring for their livestock, when suddenly, the sky darkened and a massive storm approached, a storm powerful enough to blow the very light from the Sun. It brought with it a dark and thunderous cloud of the damned as an ungodly entity commanded this unnatural abomination. The storm was conscious as it looked down upon this innocent population and screamed… "FOR ORION!" in a hideously distorted tone. The storm then began destroying buildings, while tearing the very earth from the ground, leaving behind a trail of black flames. The experienced Guardians looked at the vision in horror as Orion himself descended to the planet's surface in his flying citadel, big enough to block out the Sun. The ship's beating red lights and atmospheric nature made it seem like its own individual planet; its tentacles slithering like worms. It felt…alive. The Obedience crashed down hard, sinking and embedding its tentacles into the soil of the planet, draining the very Source Energy from the planet's core. You felt the pain from the planet, the torture as if being burned alive from the inside out. The front of the devilish ship opened, releasing Orion's combined army of soldiers a.k.a *The Corrupted*. This group of corrupted beings included *Monos*, the same creatures in Vinzent's dream, *Corrupted Soldiers* and genetically modified beasts a.k.a *Walkers*. Behind Orion were three specialized warriors who stood aside merely watching the genocide unfold. The Guardians helplessly watched this army of demons demolish this peace loving world, its population and the Guardians protecting them, slaughtering the men, assaulting the women and enslaving the children, killing the kids too young to be of any service. **Shortly after, the vision came to an unexpected turn as the Elders saw a forest, an extremely recognizable forest, one right here on Journia...**

The vision faded and the Guardians were left with nothing, but rage, fear, compassion and the sense of honor and duty to help those in desperate need, and to put an end to such an atrocity.

Nico: "We will put an end to this once and for all! And I will personally put Orion's head on a spike!"

Raito: "We just can't go in swinging or else we'll suffer the same fate. We need a plan."

Vinzent: "I agree with Raito. We need to know our enemy, see how they move, think and attack. And most of all when and where they'll attack next. You know the standard procedure Nico. We understand how you feel, but you saw the power and loyalty of his followers alone, and those fighters at his back remain a mystery."

Raito: "Don't lose yourself to your emotions Nico. You know better than anyone what anger and hate can lead to."

Nico: "So we just sit and wait while innocent people are slaughtered and their planets destroyed because we don't have a plan?! On the battlefield, plans rarely go accordingly and y'all know this! To hell with this, I won't sit here and listen to these cowardly words!"

Raito turned to the infuriated Taiyōnian as he got up, severing the triangular space they once held. Blinded by emotions, Nico ferociously pulled both wooden doors open as they slammed against the wall before making his journey back to the facility's entrance, leaving Raito, Vinzent and the facility altogether as he disappeared into the surrounding forest.

Raito: "Nico!"

Vinzent landed a hand on Raito's shoulder, effectively stopping him from pursuing the angered Guardian.

Vinzent: "Let him go, he just needs time, he'll come around because we'll need him just like he'll need us. Right now we need to figure out our next move."

As Nico parkoured through the forest, swinging and flipping through the forest with his amplified leg muscles and Hari whip, he reflected back on the conversation between himself and his comrades, seeing and understanding both points that his friends made, but he was too blinded by his rage and anxiety. He retreated back to his homestead in Solla in order to meditate to calm his nerves, and to find balance within himself once again.

In the meantime, Elders Vinzent and Raito decided that now was the time to relay the shared vision, as well as Elder Luna's warning to The Nine. They both agreed that Raito, using his super speed, would race toward the capital to inform The Nine of the coming danger as soon as possible. Afterwards, he was to meet back with Vinzent who would venture ahead to the forest area witnessed in the shared vision.

In a blink of an eye, Raito shot off out of the base and into the forest, speeding across Journia at lightning speed to the capital city, Sarvis. Upon reaching the Ashura Order's headquarters, he pushed past the entrance before making his way to the grand office located at the heart of the enormous building. Elder Raito had been inside numerous times, but the inner beauty never ceased to catch his eye. The hallways were filled with a crisp tan stone which was complemented by white marble flooring. A rag, navy blue in coloration, made from the finest material, covered the floor. The walls were joined with holograms of the brave Heroes, sacrificed during the Galactic War, with the saying: "*Though Darkness Takes, in Light we Remain*", engraved above. A fire burned in Raito's heart as he found motivation to find and snuff out the rushing danger. He continued onward, and turned the final corner to see two massive white stone doors engraved with the saying: "*Though outwardly we are wasting away, yet inwardly we are being renewed day by day.*" He walked towards the massive doors before being granted permission to enter the Court Hall. A levitating table, fitted with nine chairs, floated gracefully as nine entities sat and patiently waited to hear Raito. The

Elder respectfully greeted The Nine and explained the warning, the shared vision, the mentioning of a horned race, and the mentioning of the name, Orion. After hearing Raito, The Nine, for the first time in a long time, were unsure and fearful, thinking "they" were defeated during the Galactic War two centuries ago. The fear resonating from The Nine greatly worried Raito.

Raito: "Greeting counsel, peace, Love and Light to you all. I've come bearing heavy news. I have reason to believe that the Darkness supposedly vanquished during the Galactic War has returned and is even stronger than before."

The Nine all looked towards each other as distress filled their very being. A brief moment of silence fell upon the group before one of The Nine members spoke out.

The Nine member #2: "We thank you for your helpful insight. However this is a grave situation you have brought to light. A situation that would require more than simply telling us. How can you be sure of these claims, Elder Raito?"

Raito: "Because my trusted comrade has had a warning, a vision from Elder Luna Joyce, and because I shared a vision between myself and fellow faction members, seeing the same sinful entity Orion and his forces slaughter innocents."

The Nine member #7: "And given that Elder Luna has been stationed near the edge of Myrmidon, her faction would be the first to report back to us if something were amiss without The Order's knowledge. However, why she contacted your faction first remains a mystery. If what you say is true, we'll need to mobilize the entire Ashura Order, sending out a Demon alert to all available Guardians, deeming this a priority one request."

Raito: "I agree. There's more…"

The room fell quiet as all attention shot to Elder Raito.

Raito: "At the end of our vision, we saw a forest area, right here on Journia. It had some strange tree formation."

The Nine member #1: "Ah! You must mean the forest of Nalmoth. The pure and untamed Source Energy in that region makes it difficult for one to stay there long, or risk suffering from unpredictable side effects. I wonder why you saw it… Who all shared this vision with you, Elder Raito?"

Raito: "Elder Vinzent, Elder Nico, and myself counselor. If I may, I also came here to request your permission to take those who shared the vision on a reconnaissance mission, with the hopes of seeing first hand what we're dealing with. We'll gain some intel, then return to report what we've learned."

The council negotiated amongst themselves before turning to the patient Guardian with their decision.

The Nine member #1: "Your Demon mission request is risky, but we grant you permission on two conditions… Do not engage until either you have concrete intel or until backup has arrived."

Raito: "That's the plan. Thank you, Counselor."

The Nine member #1: "Go forth then, my friend, rejoicing in the power and in the peace of the One Infinite Creator. Adonai."

Raito: "Adonai."

Just as fast as he got there, Raito zipped away in the blink of an eye. He rushed through the city, dodging traffic while stopping briefly to assist those in need with quickness and efficiency. After a short trip out of the city and through the neighboring forest, Raito regrouped with Elder Vinzent, who reached the area a few minutes before. After a fifty minute hike, the Aura-user came across a strange and mysterious formation of trees in the forest lands of *Nalmoth*. Three trees to the north and south along with three trees to the east and west. Each tree possessed leaves of every color, and each color affected Sunlight differently. In the middle of this superb formation of trees and leaves, Vinzent had a feeling, subconsciously knowing that this was the right spot. Raito communicated to Nico and Vinzent, using the telepathy established by Vinzent. He confirmed the permission granted by The Nine to move forward with the Demon ranked reconnaissance (only) mission. Calming his nerves, Nico headed for the spot in the forest that was revealed to the group. In the forest, Vinzent approached the strange Source Energy in the middle. He somehow resonated with the Source Energy and heard a voice call to him, a voice he didn't recognize...

Unknown: *whispering* "Vinzent.."

Vinzent: "Hello? Who's there??"

Vinzent looked around, unsure as to how or where he heard the voice. He moved towards the center of the trees, entering into the field of Source Energy. The wind blew, brushing the leaves together, forcing the branches to sway; the mystical area seemingly came alive as if the trees were bipedal beings.

Raito: "Hey Vinzent... What are you doing?! When do you ever see people move towards the spooky sound of their name? Let alone ominous Source Energy just floating about?"

Unknown: *mild whisper* "Vinzent..."

Vinzent: "Shhhhh. Did you hear that? It sounds like...it's coming from..."

Raito: "I didn't hear anything."

Vinzent: "Quiet your mind and you will hear."

Unknown: *loud whisper* "Come...."

Vinzent silenced his mind, sat on the ground, and began to meditate on the rainbow colored ground in order to feel the mysterious Source Energy being created by the trees and leaves. Suddenly, there was a flash of brilliant white light and just as fast as it appeared, it disappeared like a generous breeze kissing your skin as it passes by. After the flash of light, Raito was in disbelief as he saw nothing, but an empty space where Vinzent once stood. Elder Vinzent was nowhere to be found, sparking a heavy sense of restlessness within Elder Raito.

Raito: "Vinzent? VINZENT!!"

TWO

DEPARTURE

Animals roamed their natural habitat, birds sang a beautiful tune, and static could be heard deep within the forest of Nalmoth, on the planet of Journia. Raito, a first-class Elder Guardian, struggled relentlessly to reach his lost comrade through Vinzent's telepathy, then through his communications device, but all he was given was the electrical sound of disappointment. Raito refused to give up the search and anxiously sped through the entire forest region of Journia, but to no avail as his efforts bore only more disappointment. Raito was stuck with the overwhelming feeling of unease, but quickly discarded such an emotion, thinking to himself that his comrade was more than capable of handling himself, so he worried not, for he, Vinzent and Nico were among the strongest within the Ashura Order. But even with such power and resilience, the Guardians were not deaf to the calls of death therefore caution was warranted.

Running low on options, Raito casted a beacon spell called: *Guiding Light*, which acted as an distress beacon, sending forth a high altitude beam of Prana Energy, alerting his fast approaching comrade of his location. A short while after casting the signal spell, Raito began to hear rumbling in the leaves high above as Nico popped out of the trees like a lion pouncing on its prey. Nico flipped and landed on a sturdy tree branch a few feet from the ground. The Elder leaped down to confront his perturbed comrade, but as he drew near, Nico could feel the disharmonious nature of Raito's demeanor as he explained the situation.

Nico: "Raito,what is going on!? I can't sense Vinzent's Energy anywhere as if he vanished from the entire planet."

Raito: "I'm sure you felt the immense Source Energy as you drew closer, did you not?"

Nico: "I did, such a strange feeling, it disappeared as fast as it came."

Raito pointed to the strange field of Source Energy that flowed gracefully above the ground; flowing with both chaos and order.

Raito: "Vinzent has a special connection to pure Source Energy, specifically Aura based, more so than any other Guardian. He meditated on the ground, pouring his own Elemental Energy into it, moments later, after a blinding flash of light, he was gone. Maybe his Aura Conversion ability resonated with the Source Energy in a way unknown to us, maybe even to Vinzent as well."

Nico: "Hmm. First the vision now this. I don't like where this is going. Nonetheless, if it has something to do with Aura based Energy, Vinzent is in good shape. Still, I take your point."

Raito: "Perhaps Elder Luna teleported him directly to her. Can she do that? Perhaps this is something different altogether. I remember something about a bonding ritual performed by Luna? That doesn't fully explain what's going on, but at least we have a lead."

Nico: "Our best bet now is to head back to base, gear up, recover our comrade and complete this mission before we lose our window of time. I fear Luna's warning may soon come to fruition."

Raito: "Agreed."

After discussing their next move, the two Elders made their way through the forest, entering into a friendly race to see who was faster. Raito initiated the race by utilizing his super speed as he zoomed past trees and rocks at lightning speed. The Elder found a drip of complacency, thinking his victory was all but assured. But little did he know Nico, utilizing his Solar Mutation ability, was not far behind. After several moments of sprinting, and parkouring, the Elders reached the mountain region approximately fifty minutes away. Despite Nico's Solar Mutation amplifying his speed and agility, Raito's name as the fastest Guardian alive was shown, enabling him to win the race against his tattooed comrade.

Raito: "So, you thought just because you strengthened your body, you'd beat me at my own game? You may be the strongest, but I'm not the fastest for no reason brotha."

Nico: *laughs* "Didn't hurt to try. I know exactly how far ahead of me you truly are now. All I have to do is find that perfect momentum and victory is as good as mine."

Raito *chuckles* "Good grief."

Repeating the key phrase, the large rock blocking the main entrance split open as the two made haste, speeding towards the armory with renewed focus. Upon entering, Nico stepped into his section of the armory as he walked toward a large chest containing his gear. He unlocked the chest by injecting a tiny sphere of Solar Energy into the keyhole. After a moment of humming, the symbols engraved on the chest began glowing in a marigold-orange light. The container then opened as Elder Nico suited up, preparing himself for the coming journey. He strapped on armored tabi boots, equipped with a built in noise canceling feature, that raised up a few inches below his knees. The boots went over loosely fitting combat pants, which were held up by a utility belt and his people's flag. This utility belt was equipped with Solar Seeds and a communications device, as well as a pouch to place his wrist computer and earpiece. The Elder finished with a tight fitting, sleeveless combat vest that was made with special fabric to handle Nico's Solar type of Source Energy. Lastly, he flung on a short cloak which was engraved with a lightning bolt inside of a Sun that had been joined by a pair of wings. This symbol was represented as the faction's logo, and was shown in the middle of Nico's cloak. Several meters away, within his section of the armory, Raito proceeded with his choice of armor and gadgets fit for a true speedster and Prana wielder. He wasted little time gearing up in his charcoal black and apple red colored leather pants and long-sleeve. A thin layer of black armor covered his leather attire as the Elder pulled a long black cloak over himself. It was engraved with the faction's logo as well, filling the top half of Raito's cloak. His armor was made special with an extremely light and durable style of steel made in his hometown of Zotune. The armor had also been modified with a heat resistant finish to handle the friction caused from his super speed. Even though he was a Mahōnian, Raito possessed human-like stamina, which forced the Elder to take short, but inconvenient breaks in order to catch his breath. Raito had not found a spell to change this issue, so to compensate, Raito created **Stem Shots**, which were placed within his utility belt, along with his communications device, and a holster for his Grimoire.

Stem Shots were small syringes filled with a bioluminescent substance specific to Raito's genetic makeup. Upon injection, the glowing liquid gives Elder Raito a boost in stamina and strength, enabling the Guardian to push past his limit, and increase his speed. Along with possessing super speed, Elder Raito comes from a long and powerful line of mages, who utilized a specific form of Energy called **Prana**. This variation of Source Energy required the use of a **Grimoire**, a spell book containing spells and incantations, which was not only used for spells, but also works to filter the calm, yet chaotic nature of pure Prana Energy. Raito's most frequent use of the Light-bow spell. The longer it takes to cast a spell and/or incantation, the stronger the effect and the more taxing it was physically and mentally.

After a quick, but lengthy time gearing up, Nico walked out of the armory and towards the war room, pushing the door open just enough to comfortably walk through. He motioned towards the master computer before sitting down, letting out a focused deep breath as he and Jasmine accessed Vinzent's communication device. After a moment of pressing, searching and coding, Nico's expression showed a moment of relief and glee as he found a faint, but visible signal coming from Vinzent's comms. His joyous expression soon faded however, giving way to confusion as he didn't recognize the planet or its star system, but that didn't matter. His comrade was without backup, without his gear and in a completely foreign location. With these satisfying findings, Nico copied the coordinates to his wrist computer, and headed back to the armory where he found Elder Raito collecting Vinzent's battle gear, knowing he'll need it. Nico helped Raito gather Vinzent's gear, placing it in the cases laid before them. Raito then programmed the suitcases to follow behind them, opening the way for them to walk into the war room, making it the second time for Nico. They motioned towards the rear end of the room and entered into the spacious elevator; Vinzent's gear hot on their heels. Afterward, Nico pressed the 'down' key on the control pad, giving the elevator the means to create artificial gravity as it shot down at high speeds, rivaling Vinzent's surfing entrance a few days ago. After a brief trip, the two Elders found themselves in the hanger, a mile under the base's entrance, where the four wheeled MT-AT waited patiently to wreak havoc upon its enemies. Nico refueled and inspected the armored vehicle as Raito packed the needed equipment and Vinzent's gear, securing everything within the vehicle. During inspection, Nico did a rundown of the tank's interior and exterior parts and function.

Nico: "Okay. So upon inspection, the MT-AT has eight wheels that meet the required PSI, four primary wheels for mobility through all terrains, and four spare for unforeseen circumstances, as well as a five hundred horsepower V-eight engine. It's been built with an air tight hull, which is great because the tank can withstand the crushing pressure of deep sea travel, acting also as a submarine if need be. Let's see…it's protected by a 360 degree rotating repeating laser cannon on each side, an anti-air defense system, and an energy shield that disables all weapons when activated. We're in good hands with this vehicle."

After Nico finished the inspection, Raito fired up the engine, listening to the glorious sound of power and courage as it filled every corner of the hanger. "She's ready," Raito confidently confirmed in his mind. The back door to MT-AT was lowered as Nico hopped in, inspecting the inside.

Nico: "As for the inside. There are four seats to the left and four to the right with a comfortable walk space between. Storage areas above that are used for spare parts, medical supplies, Vinzent's gear, etc. Inside the cockpit are three seats, two pointed towards the inner-hull wall, with a control console in front of both seats, and of course the pilot's seat. That completes the inner and outer checklist for the MT-AT."

Nico completed both inspections before closing and securing the back door of the vehicle. He turned around to make his way to one of the control seats offsetted towards the wall before accessing the control console. The Elder keyed in his passcode, allowing him access to a number of weapon and defense systems. The pilot seat remained where Raito now sat, gaining control of the movement, tank-to-submarine transformation, as well as the weapons if need be. Raito commanded the hangar doors to open as the hangar door's shields were temporarily disabled. Sunlight shone through the opening hangar door where the Hercules was seen hovering a few feet off the ground, waiting for its passengers to board like a train at a stop. Raito wondered how the Hercules was ready to go as Nico explained that while at the master computer moments ago, he went ahead and requested that Jasmine prepare their starship, and keep it on standby by the hangar entrance for a quick "load and departure".

The AC-07, a.k.a *"Hercules"* was a cream-white starship with it being a hundred feet port side to starboard side and a hundred and forty-four feet bow to stern. Its medium-lightweight frame enabled the craft to take a punch and dish out twice as much, while maintaining its swiftness. The ship was equipped with two retractable, rapid fire cannons, placed on the wings for forward enemies, as well as two on its underbelly for enemies towards the rear. The craft was capable of land assaults by dropping bombs overhead, as well as possessing a retractable heavy beam cannon, placed at the bow which fired a focused laser that could pierce through almost any surface. For propulsion, the two main thrusters gave the craft a tremendous speed increase, with four smaller thrusters to assist with stability and acceleration. Entering the state-of-the-art spaceship, on the bottom level lay the cargo bay, which was big enough to hold the MT-AT. This lower level also contained a small room housing spacesuits, ship repair tools, security weapons for protection purposes, and an emergency airlock. The level above was the biggest level, containing the crew's quarters, a smaller war room, and a medical center, as well as airlocks placed on both sides of the spacecraft for quick deployments. The engine of the ship was granted fuel and Energy from the core of a Sun, and was protected by its own energy shield, restricting all access to non-faction personnel only; this room would also be housed on the biggest level. Lastly, on the bridge of the ship contained the control area, the cockpit, fitted with two seats for the pilot and co-pilot, and an emergency airlock located towards the very top of the ship.

After briefly checking the ship's status, Jasmine confirmed the MT-AT had been secured, giving Nico and Raito the green light to takeoff as Raito began the pre-flight checklist.

Raito: "Weapons and shields fully charged. All planet-side and space systems are green. MT-AT secure, we are good for space entry."

With all systems go, the Hercules, and its three-man crew shot off into the sky, leaving the atmosphere. The thrusters hummed harmoniously, like listening to a wondrous opera as they flared with power from its engine. Once in space, Jasmine activated the ship's life support system as Raito studied the plotted coordinates in confusion as he's never heard of the planet **Zora**.

Raito: "Zora?"

Nico: "Same expression I made my friend."

Raito: "Says here that the entire planet is covered in sand with days lasting two times as long, and an average temperature of a hundred and twenty degrees fahrenheit. The habitants, the Zoranians, are a four armed, hard shell skinned, reptilian alien species, being most recently made primitive? They worship two hundred foot worms they call *Dios de la Arena* which translates to 'Sand God'... Great."

Nico: "I'm surprised, I thought you'd like it because of the sand."

Raito: "Very funny Nico, but all sand isn't good sand."

Nico: "Good sand?"

Raito: *sigh* "Nevermind, can we focus on the task at hand?"

Nico warmed up the hyperdrive which took fifteen seconds, depending on the available energy. The ship sang as it charged...blasting into unknown space like a bullet leaving a handgun. The view from hyperspace never ceased to amaze the Guardians. The flow of colors, the dimension of light speed travel; it was truly a humbling experience. While submersed in light speed travel, the Elders prepared their minds, bodies and spirits as they raced through hyperspace to regroup with their lost comrade, speeding through the unpredictable yet wondrous cosmos...

Light years away on the massive worldship The Obedience, Orion showed his newly honored prisoner, third-class Elder Guardian Luna, the horrifying features hidden within the walls of his mountain sized ship. They examined the fortress as Luna was astonished by the frightening beauty of this vessel. It possessed its own ecosystem, its own natural way of life despite how dead inside its master was. Luna continued through this massive ship as anxiety turned her stomach in knots. She followed close behind Orion as they walked because that seemed to be the only way she'd go untouched. Orion's forces bent at the knee at the sight of their lord, but radiated harmful intent towards Luna. The Guardian tried to find beauty in the ship's ecosystem, but couldn't as the rivers brought peace yet worry as dead bodies floated about. And the waterfalls were beautiful at first glance, yet were masked by disparity as more corpses were thrown off the top like unwanted waste. Elder Luna walked further, hearing screams and cries with a smell that can only be described as the smell of dry blood and feces. Luna was demoralized and distraught by the horrors of Orion's ship, thinking to herself, "is everything on this ship a testament against the Love and Light blessed by the Creator?" The Elder continued behind Orion to the one area she thought showed love for life. A flower garden, which birthed a sense of care and compassion, but that feeling was quickly discarded as the flowers were picked ruthlessly, and used for a mysterious potion being crafted by a mysterious figure.

Upon further inspection, this being grabbed Luna's curiosity as she studied this distorted entity. This being had no skin, but bones that were as gray as cement. He had no mouth to speak, yet Luna heard a quiet mumble. No eyes to see, yet she felt the piercing glare as she walked by him. He levitated like Orion, but it's different, like someone having their legs amputated and being strung up like a piñata. His chipped and cracked boney body was covered by an aged, dry and stained purple robe with skulls, small skulls like those of children, embedded in its shoulders like trophies. A hood was pulled over, covering not a head, but a strange purple flame covered by a skull as his head. This figure had to be some kind of sorcerer, given his use of a Grimoire and talent for *Apana Energy*, which was Prana Energy's opposite. His name was *Makai* or simply known as *The Mind*.

After creating this mysterious potion, The Mind injected the thick red substance into an enslaved prisoner. The helpless entity began screaming in agony as he looked at Luna walk by. His eyes said it all as they whispered "kill me", before he burst into flames, dropping in a pile of death and ash. The Mind looked, wrote something in his Grimoire made from flesh and teeth, then turned to the next helpless prisoner to continue the experimental nightmare. Luna couldn't take anymore as she continued behind Orion. She was disgusted by the sight of enslaved children being tortured by Orion's minions. Their will broken; their individuality erased, while being turned into mindless, enslaved beings of death and obedience, standing ready to execute Orion's will to the letter with complete disregard for their own life or others. Those slaves, men and older male children, who showed promise are taken to be turned into the monstrous four armed Monos, the same four armed demons that haunted Vinzent's dream. After being mentally, spiritually and physically broken, the slaves were injected and dipped into a black goo; an *Accelerant*, which was Orion's blood mixed with less desirable ingredients. Upon contact, the chosen prisoner screamed out in unmeasurable pain as if having alcohol poured on a severed limb. The pain was unbearable as some test subjects died from shock, while others had the black goo reject their genetic makeup, causing the Accelerant inside their bloodstream to eat away at everything including organs, muscle-fibers, bones, and flesh, reducing them to nothing, but a pile of slime with a smell worse than a mountain of long forgotten corpses. Those who survived the initial stages of the Accelerant went through the same level of pain and distress, but the difference lay within the end results. Instead of the black goo destroying the body completely, the accelerant targeted the weak parts of that slave, breaking the entity apart in any way to build back up better in every way, like a successful workout at the gym, but on an unprecedentedly wicked scale. The rest of the male slaves were reconditioned into corrupted soldiers, and were equipped with an organic battle suit that provided the wearer with all their basic survival needs, an organic rifle, pistol, and knife. Aside from the men, the women and older girls were taken to the birthing chamber, down in the lower levels of the worldship. There they would spend the rest of their lives giving birth endlessly, never to lay eyes upon their freshly born as corrupted soldiers took the newborn babies to be enslaved, tortured and trained, with Orion's will being their sole purpose. Those women who couldn't give birth were tossed into the vacuum of space. Shortly after touring the hellish vessel, Orion and Luna made their way to Orion's personal quarters, where the Guardian voiced her disgust.

Luna: "Do you enjoy the suffering of others, you devil?"

Orion looked down at Luna. A twisted smile showed on Orion's chiseled face.

Orion: "Myrmidon is weak and blind. I am here to correct that weakness."

Luna: "You find correction in the murder of innocents? Have you no shame? No honor? No, you don't, and the Light will vanquish you, once and for all for what you've done!"

Orion picked the brave Guardian by the throat, choking her. His grip was as cold as ice and as firm as a screw too tight to move.

Orion: "The Way of Ashla is nothing more than someone too afraid to accept the Darkness around and within themselves, but I will show everyone the freedom that is the Way of Bogan. Let me ask you, m'lady. What was there before the creation of this Universe? What is there when rage or sorrow inevitably plague your heart? And what does Light give birth to?"

Orion dropped Luna as she fell to her hands and knees, coughing and gasping for air. He looked down at just how pitiful she was, and wondered where that same spark of hope went.

Orion: "So you see m'lady, no matter how bright your Ashla taught Source Energy shines, there will always be a greater Darkness that surrounds such a fragile disappointment. The Light has taken everything from me, so I will do the same."

Luna: "You'll never win. *cough* Your death is all, but assured."

Orion: "I've heard that before, but here I am, saving and liberating, in the name of myself. Did you enjoy it when I slaughtered that population and destroyed their planet? The world you and your Guardian comrades were supposed to protect? I certainly did. The sound of screams as they cried to their Creator to…'save them', was music to my ears. Perhaps you desire an encore!"

Orion smiled spitefully as he commanded his worldship pilots to orbit outside of the closest nearby planet, in the outer-portion of the galaxy. There lived a population of three billion, men, women and children. The Obedience's main weapon, *The Black Launcher*, which turns a planet's core into a black hole, sucking the planet into itself, was charged and ready to fire. Elder Luna begged for Orion to spare the lives of so many, but her plea fell on deaf ears, and with Orion's command, the corrupted soldiers in charge of The Black Launcher fired. Luna fell to her knees as she helplessly watched the planet of three billion fall victim to a violent internal black hole. The Guardian felt an ocean of hopelessness flood her heart as she watched Orion's forces capture and destroy any ships attempting to flee the planet's destruction. Orion simply laughed maniacally because death and suffering pleased him greatly.

Luna: "You're a horrible devilish creature that will meet a painful death."

Orion: "I like to think I'm a liberator of peace and weakness who will free this foolish galaxy of peace, Love and Light, for they are an abomination and a distasteful lie. You and every entity in the Universe will see the strength and truth in Bogan as I have."

The Orion Crusaders raided several other star systems, destroying and conquering dozens of worlds with some fighting back with help from the Ashura Order, but posing little to no threat outside of the Elder ranked Guardians. Some worlds surrendered at the very sight of The Obedience. Other planets willfully offered sacrifices, so as to avoid an extinction event. These scenarios humored Orion the most because planets, and their inhabitants offered their most beautiful or powerful or most important individuals as a way to "save" their home world, only to have it destroyed anyways. It only further proved Orion's point that Love, Light, hope, freedom, and loyalty were nothing but foolish ideals to help children sleep at night. This spree of death and Darkness would spread all across the outer portion of the galaxy and would last for several grueling weeks.

During the raiding of a planet, a neighboring planet within the same star system and within The Order's jurisdiction, bore witness to the massacre and requested help from The Order. Back on Journia, the Guardians, within the communications department, received the distress signal before deploying a small fleet of Paladin and Acolyte ranked Guardians, oblivious to the true danger level of the enemy. The small fleet consisted of one battleship having most of the firepower, and was equipped with a super heavy laser cannon, as well as a strong shield and multiple rapid-fire cannons. The battleship was accompanied by three starcraft carriers containing forty fighters in each, and two support cruisers that reinforced the fleet's overall energy spendage and shield strength. The commanding Guardian of the fleet, second-class Elite Guardian Basil Lawson, had received the deployment call from HQ. He accepted the Bear ranked mission before plotting the course, allowing his fleet to jump into hyperspace. Upon entering hyperspace, Basil felt a chill run down his spine, a feeling he hasn't felt since fighting Elder Nico one-on-one, during the Elite entry exam years ago. The feeling led him to command the fleet to gear up and charge the shields for a textbook rescue mission, or so he thought.

Basil: "Mission Log: Bear 3136-222. This is Elite Basil reporting. Our given Bear ranked mission is to investigate the area at the heart of the distress call, with the added task of search and rescue. We lost communications just as we entered hyperspace. There are seven hundred and fifty Guardians joined for this operation, with six hundred being of the Paladin rank and a hundred and fifty Acolytes which I've split among each ship as commanding Guardians. I have a bad feeling about this given The Nine's alert weeks ago, but I trust my comrades and they trust me. End Log."

The fleet jumped out of hyperspace, a few clicks from the targeted area. Despite it being a Bear ranked mission, Basil's instincts told him otherwise as he reminded the fleet to stay ready and armed. Tensions among the Guardians were high as they were hit with the feeling of despair. Confusion also found the fleet because upon arrival, the planet which had sent the distress call moments ago vanished, leaving nothing but a black hole and destroyed spacecrafts, both of Ashura Order and civilian origin. Confused and anxious, Basil made an attempt to reach

HQ, but his comms were jammed when suddenly, one of the support cruisers was blown to pieces like popping a balloon. The Obedience made the first move by ambushing the unexpected fleet. The situation seemed to have indeed risen to a Demon rank, warned by The Nine as the fleet and its commander sprung into action.

Basil: "All units! The mission has been raised to the Demon level! Take evasive action!!"

The three starcraft carriers made haste, releasing all the Ashura fighters like someone disturbing a beehive. Out of nowhere however, one of the starcraft carriers blew up without warning in a ball of fire from a Kinetic Energy blast shot by Orion's ship. The shot tore the ship's engine from the vessel, killing everyone on board instantly. The attacks afterwards only grew increasingly violent and ruthless as The Obedience grew several cannons from its outer shell like trees growing branches. On top of its ability to grow and retract weapons at will, the large craft of evil surprised the space battle by forming two large openings, which were five hundred feet in length and two hundred feet in width, giving way to hundreds of small meteor-sized fighters. These small spacecraft were seen to be ten feet across and twenty feet from end to end, making them extremely hard to hit, with the given name: *Ryū*. They moved and attacked like one mind looking through many eyes as they demonstrated the true strength of a collective mind.

Despite the fact that the Guardians were outnumbered and overwhelmed, the Guardian fighter pilots valiantly demonstrated their skill and resolve. But their courageous efforts fell short because of the enemy's numbers. Slowly, the Guardian fighter pilots met their demise one by one, though not before destroying at least four Ryū fighters per Ashura starfighter. However, it wasn't long before silence filled the space battle, leaving a sea of destroyed ships and dead bodies with not a single Ashura starfighter left operational. Elite Basil and his brave, but unexpecting fleet, were face to face with an enemy unlike anything they've experienced up until that point. A ship capable of growing weapons at will, the use of black hole technology, and the Ryū fighter fleet. It was as if the Orion Crusaders were from a different

Universe or time period. Were they the beings supposedly destroyed during the Galactic War? Basil thought to himself. Desperate, Basil's battleship and the support cruiser that survived the initial assault, made a last all-out attack against The Obedience. With no hope of escape, the intrepid Guardians converted all remaining power to the ship's weapon systems. And on Basil's command, the remaining ships opened fire against Orion's worldship, letting loose missiles, torpedoes, and anything with an explosive charge. The Guardian continued their assault, firing everything until the guns overheated. But when the smoke settled, despair plagued the hearts of every Guardian, followed by a decrease in morale, because of a mysterious Black Aura which protected The Obedience from all attacks against it, rendering the fleet's efforts fruitless. Only Basil, who, instead of fear, found only defiance and courage in the face of death.

Basil: "My brothers and sisters in arms. Today we find ourselves face to face with death itself. But do not fear, for even in death, the Creator stands with us. This is the moment where our faith is tested! Do not hide from this opportunity my fellow Guardians, but rather shine brightly, so that our enemy's wicked way may be brought to Light!"

After a brief moment of encouragement from the second-class Elite, the Guardians found that flame of valor and determination against impossible odds. But as the Guardians roared with strong purpose, the emergency alarms began to blare, when suddenly, the remaining fleet of Guardians felt a violent wave of gravity that shoved both ships, while simultaneously rendering both Ashura ships completely inoperational.

Basil: "Status report!"

Acolyte Pilot: "All the ship's systems have shut down, and I've lost contact with the support cruiser. It's only a matter of time before the oxygen levels zero out. It seems we've been hit with a large EMP blast, but in the form of a gravitational wave...We're dead in the water sir."

Dead in space like a car with a dead battery, Basil's battleship, floated helplessly through the void of space. The EMP shot by Orion's ship had cribbled Basil's ship, giving The Obedience the means to activate its use of black hole technology. Once activated, The Obedience dragged both the battleship and the support cruiser aboard like pulling a cow into a barn using a rope. Once secured, the platoon of Ryū fighters returned to Orion's ship which allowed The Obedience's crew to close both of its large openings, effectively imprisoning Basil and his fellow Guardians. Unfamiliar with the new landscape, Elite Basil commanded the remaining Guardians to secure both ships, given the loud thumping sounds that could be heard from outside the battleship. Upon noticing the thumping, two second-class Paladins, carefully walked towards the thumping sound as they readied their abilities for anything. But their preparations were in vain as the wall smashed open, giving way to an eleven foot hulking figure with navy blue stone like skin, a torn and tattered brown cloak, covering battle scarred armor, and blood stained hands added by a massive scar running across his face. This beast carried a one ton steel hammer, specially made to not only crush the unlucky victim, but to slowly drain an entity of their vital Source Energy. A gift from The Mind. Orion called this priced tool *Hando* or *The Hand*.

Hando forced his way through the outer hull of Basil's battleship with several swings from his hammer. The final impact was so powerful that the crashing force from the hit sent both Paladin Guardians flying as the two viciously crashed against the opposite wall, killing one as his neck snapped on impact, and paralyzing the other. Following this, Basil commanded the remaining Guardians to use their Ashla taught Source Energy abilities and training to bring Hando down, but their efforts were merely child's play to The Hand. With great strength and ferociousness, Hando swung his hammer, smacking one Guardian through three walls which ended her life. He then sent another brave Guardian to the afterlife with a devastating hammer upper-cut which tore the Guardian's head from his shoulders, allowing blood to gush out like a broken water fountain. Hando laid his hammer on his shoulder in order to grab another helpless Guardian by the ankle; the force of Hando's grip shattered the Guardian's ankle and shin bone. The Hand swung him around, hitting multiple Guardians like using a hand to swat flies away. Seeing these brutal feats, Basil knew this battle was completely one-sided as the Elite concluded that the Paladins never stood a chance, with the Acolytes proving just as vulnerable. The battle between The Hand and the outmatched Guardians raged on with a clear victor in sight. Elite Basil, bruised, bloodied and slow to his feet, made one last desperate attempt at victory over the hulking beast. Putting his life on the line, Basil channeled the Elemental Energy of his cells, giving him command over the element of water. Through the manipulation of this element, he used the moisture in the air to form a spear of water. Being surrounded by the enemy, Basil knew this act of hostile aggression would surely get him killed, but nonetheless he pushed forward. The Elite grabbed the spear, and with a glorious battle cry, the Guardian threw the weapon with great force and purpose. The spear flung through the air, killing several corrupted soldiers, and pierced the towering monster in the chest which sent Hando sliding backwards in pain. Gray blood ran down Hando's chest before the beast turned to look at the weakened Guardian with interest. Following this, The Hand proceeded to pull the water spear free from his chest, and returned the favor as he threw the spear back at Basil with greater force than the spear's originator. Before impact however, the Elite released the Elemental Energy that bonded the water molecules together as the Guardian received a splash to the face which temporarily blinded him. Basil was then suddenly met with a tremendous force as he was ferociously upper-cutted in the stomach by Hando's massive fist. The blow shattered the Guardian's ribcage and damaged several of his organs. Following this, Basil fell to the ground, coughing up blood as he was surrounded by his dead comrades. He found sorrow for leading his fallen comrades to their deaths and wished to join them in the afterlife. Soon after however, Basil's vision began to blur as he fell deeper into hopelessness, but before he could fully lose consciousness, Makai, who was sent by Orion, arrived to greet Hando. With a raspy tone, Makai commanded the colossal titan to bring the Guardian to his laboratory, afterwards, Elite Basil fainted due to exhaustion, pain, and stress, both physically, and mentally.

The Mind: "Bring…to…lab."

The Hand grunted compliantly, accepting Makai's command as he dragged the defeated Guardian to The Mind's lab. Upon arrival, The Hand threw Basil on the ground before leaving speechless. A few hours passed by as Basil woke up, sore and wounded as he found himself strapped to a table with nothing, but his underpants on and The Mind awkwardly floating beside him.

The Mind: "Wel..come...Ashla filth. My lord...need..important... information. You have...information in memory. I take...memory..."

Makai began to hum a disturbing rhythm before pulling a knife from his belt to carve symbols into Basil's flesh. The Guardian screamed in grimming pain as The Mind, using Bogan taught Apana Energy, casted a spell with his Grimoire called: ***Abusive Remembrance***, to forcefully pull the required information from Basil's mind with disregard for the damage done, like pulling teeth without the worry of gum and tissue damage. After several moments of complete torture, the spell faded and Basil was left mentally broken, forgetting his name, his faction, and even his loved ones. He was left a dejected mess as he sat lost, drooling and forgotten. Makai then took the much anticipated information to his lord.

The Mind: "My Lord...I have infor..mation. You will...be... pleeeeeeased."

Orion: "You have done well Makai. Go now and rejoice in my name."

The Mind bowed, showing gratitude for his lord's acknowledgment and took his leave. Orion studied the stolen memories and deciphered the needed information as he showed Luna her grave mistake. Orion's assumption was correct with him concluding The Nine were indeed behind the creation of the Ashura Order. Best of all, Luna made a direct connection to the planet's surface. In order to do so and being a Guardian herself, she must've known the exact location of Journia. With these juicy facts, Orion turned towards Luna.

Orion: "Well m'lady, I knew I picked you for a good reason. I'll ask you one time. Where's Journia?"

Luna spat on the ground under Orion.

Orion: *sigh* "You're too beautiful to brutally torture, so I'll spare you the pain and me the time... this time."

Orion opened his robe showing hundreds of trapped souls yelling and crying out in pain. The souls burst out flying and encircled the frightened Guardian as one by one they flew in and out of her body, like blowing a balloon up then releasing the air repeatedly. Their objective was to invade the mind and retrieve any and all information and memories Orion desired. It was like Makai's spell a moment ago, but perfected. Once completed, the souls returned to Orion as he closed his robe, leaving Luna laid out on the ground exhausted as if she's ran for days non-stop.

Orion: "How hard was that, and no one died."

Orion sent the information gathered to the pilots of his flying fortress. After receiving the info, the pilots immediately plotted in the coordinates before warming up the worm-drive. And with the charge of a small black hole, The Obedience blasted off deep into the inner-portion of the galaxy, into Ashura Order territory, and headed straight for Journia...

THREE

ZORA

Elder Vinzent laid on the soft warm sand, unsure as to where he was or how he got there. The last thing he remembered was a concerned Elder Raito and the mysterious voice calling to him. Knowing his best option was to keep moving forward, Vinzent got up from the sandy surface and thoroughly observed his surroundings, hoping to find… something or someone. The Elder raised a hand towards the blazing Sun, and headed to what he thought was North as he hopped on a manifested board of lightning. While gliding through the sandy world of Zora, Vinzent decided to test his communications device, but only received static as frustration entered his mind. Unsatisfied with that response, he used his Elemental Energy of lightning on the failing machine to boost the signal which gave life to the sand flooded device. Because of his efforts, the Guardian was able to produce a faint outgoing signal.

Vinzent: "Nothing but a bit of Elemental elbow grease to save the day."

The Elder continued to pour a bit of his Elemental Energy into the device to boost the signal, which for a time, filled Vinzent with the sense of accomplishment. But his positivity was darkened by the violent shaking of the ground behind him. Suddenly, two huge two hundred foot worm-like creatures burst from the sand as they roared savagely against Vinzent. The worms then dove back underground and pursued the electrical signal originating from Vinzent's communication device. The Elder was unsure at first how the creatures found him so quickly, but soon he put the pieces together as he sped away for dear life.

Vinzent: "Shit! How did they find me?...Unless they're attracted to this active device, and can trace bursts of electrical energy from machines. Great..."

The giant worms burst from the sandy ground once more with a giant boulder in one of their mouths. The beast blew the boulder free from its mouth like a cannon as it simultaneously dived back underground. Vinzent saw the life-threatening rock flying towards him, so without hesitation, the Elder demonstrated his combat experience and prowess. He hopped off his board of lightning to which he grabbed it, and with force and precision, flung it vertically towards the approaching boulder. The heat from the lightning board increased before splitting the rock in half which allowed Vinzent to dodge through the middle. After landing on his feet, Vinzent kept the first worm at bay with streams of lightning, but wondered where the other worm went, when suddenly, the sandy-floor opened like a trap door, revealing a massive mouth filled with thousands of razor-sharp teeth. Vinzent quickly reacted, enabling him to dodge the attack, front flip away and roll as he generated his *Orange Aura*. Vinzent formed several bolts of orange lightning that, on impact, exploded on the moist creature's body, stunning the building-sized animal. By the time the beast regained its composure, Vinzent was already on his newly manifested board of red lightning as he glided through the hostile sandy environment. The injured worm roared savagely as it quickly gained on Vinzent with a haunting sense of vengeance; the second creature hot on their heels. Following the chase, the Elder sent more Orange lightning explosions hurtling towards both worms which slowed them down, but ultimately failed to stop them completely. Vinzent realized that fighting the beasts two-on-one would be pointless and a waste of time and Elemental Energy. So instead he looked for an escape, and to his luck, he was blessed to see a collection of narrow rockways and a deep valley. The Guardian immediately turned and bolted straight for the naturally made maze with the worms following close behind. The Creator did not fail the Guardian though as Vinzent barely squeezed in safely. The greedy worms smashed head-first into the small entrance behind him, one after the other, screaming and roaring as they watched their missed meal look back and wink then glide away. Afterwards, Vinzent turned away, chuckling as he bragged about his narrow escape, thinking "Raito and Nico would have a hell of a time topping that."

After finalizing his safety, Elder Vinzent commanded the board to fade as he walked through the strange rockway. He heard grunting and running behind, then in front of him as he readied himself for what he thought was a fair fight. But that thought quickly disappeared as two, four armed reptilian alien beings, covered in a rocky layer of skin, appeared in front and behind him before speaking in an unfamiliar language.

Vinzent: "Who are yo–"

Zoranian Guard #1: "Shhh! Il dio verme è vicino."

The three took a moment to breathe as the giant worms slithered away, disappointed by the result of their chase. One of the Zoranian guards saw the lights flickering from the Guardian's communications device before snatching and smashing the box of electricity for obvious reasons. Though it was a necessary action for safety, the Elder still did not enjoy the destruction of his things, especially something that could've led to reinforcements.

Vinzent: *annoyed tone* "What the hell was that for?! I could've just turned the damn thing off!"

Zoranian Guard #2: "El gusano verá."

Vinzent: *sigh* "I knew I should've paid attention during our language training. I am a Guardian from the Ashura Order. Do you guys speak english?"

Zoranian Guard #1: "Ella te verá."

Vinzent: "I guess not."

The two grabbed the wildly confused Guardian by the arms as they traveled through the valley, making turn after turn before coming to a large opening that showed a lively, but fairly primitive way of life. These entities had no technology at all as if they were cavemen who never evolved. The sight was humbling, but odd as Vinzent and his comrades grew up in a technologically advanced society, besides the basic survival training required to be a Guardian.

Zoranian Guard #2: "Lo que buscas está ahí."

Vinzent was confused as he found no answer for who or what the Zoranian was talking about. Seeing the confusion on the Guardian's face, the guards pointed him in the direction of a large tent, brown in color with red and orange lines forming a triangle all around the top of the tent. Vinzent thanked the guards and entered as a mysterious figure was seen lurking in the shadows.

Mysterious figure: "Now what's The Order doing all the way out here on this ball of sand and heat? They haven't sent a rescue party have they?"

The mystery woman appeared from the shadows. Her long silky white hair flowing behind as she walked into the light. Her navy blue shoulderless dress carefully caressed her curvy athletic body which had been lightly armored. With her blue and white katana in hand, the light shined on her gorgeous soft powder-blue eyes. Her weapon was battle-scarred indicating many battles fought. Some won, some lost, something Vinzent could respect.

Vinzent: "Casanova Meyoki. The second-class Elder Guardian, Elemental Energy wielder of water and katana specialist."

Cass: "In the flesh. And you must be the first-class Elder Guardian Vinzent. Aura Conversion user; only one of its kind. What are you doing out here? I'm sure a dying planet could really use your help right now. Yet here you are on this rock of dust and worms."

Vinzent: "I could ask you the same thing. Where's the rest of your faction?"

Elder Cass looked down in sadness and anger as she emotionally replied.

Cass: "They're gone. Gone down fighting. Protecting this planet... or what's left of it anyways."

Vinzent apologized for her loss, but also for her having to relive the horror. Cass wasn't weak and knew loss came with being a Guardian, but loss wasn't always easy to get over. Realizing it could prove useful, Casanova explained the mission that led to her faction's ultimate annihilation...

Cass: "Rex, Kicks and I were given a Dragon ranked mission. We were tasked with helping the Zoranians build a relationship with the Way of Ashla, as well as the protection and training of Zora and its people until they were strong enough to protect themselves. We learned the language, the landscape, the people and came up with the best protection and training strategy, but as you know, plans rarely go accordingly. This world used to be a flourishing forest and ocean world with steady breakthroughs in advanced technology. Training was going well and showing promising potential, but that changed when the Orion Crusaders arrived. They popped out of hyperspace like the boogeyman jumping out of the closet. The locals, my faction and I thought we were ready, but this was no ordinary enemy. Their strange organic technology decimated the Zoranian space fleet of two hundred spacecraft, small and large, led by Kicks. Ruling space, the Orion Crusaders forced our remaining ships of eleven spacecraft to retreat within the planet's atmosphere. The enemy's fleet of course pursued, destroying more ships and bombarding the surface with attack after attack. Kicks in the chaos, with his ace flying skills and Cosmic Energy ability of Shapeshifting, managed to infiltrate that black box of death to find a weakness. His lone mission proved fruitful as he had discovered the ship's core, located at the very center of that planet-sized monstrosity. I assumed Kicks shifted into one of those corrupted soldiers. Doing so, he successfully sabotaged the systems to Orion's ship which temporarily disabled its weapons and the Ryū fighters. His efforts bought time for our ground forces to regroup and mobilize, though…it came at a high cost. Kicks was discovered and inevitably attacked, sending the intel just before losing communications. Rex and I assumed the worst, but we couldn't break down because of it. Through our will, shared strength and with the help of the local's planetary defense capabilities, Rex and I managed to protect Zora's capital from Orion's orbital attacks, forcing the enemy to commence a ground assault which gave us the home field advantage or so we assumed. The first wave contained about three thousand of those corrupted beings, a hundred of those four-armed demons, and a few of those big horned gorillas. It was unlike anything I've seen; they fought like souls of the damned longing to be freed. Our defense line of manned turrets, energy shields and brave men and women of the planet held the line, giving us a brief moment to tend to our wounded and recharge the shield, weapons and lost Energy. The second wave contained a less number of corrupted soldiers with the numbers in the low thousand, but what set this wave apart were the increased number of those hideous four-armed creatures led by **Ude** or **The Arm** they called him. An eight foot monster with a large pyramid helmet covering his head. He was also covered from waist to toe in a long bloodied robe, leaving his torso open for all to see the many deep cuts and battle scars. He wielded nothing, but a two-handed sword made from a dead star that had been infused with Apana Energy which could drain the Source Energy from its victims, specifically Ashla taught. He was accompanied by a taller warrior with a hammer; The Hand I believe. These two warriors charged at full speed, hammering and slicing away at the shield with their forces doing the same. We did the best we could with me utilizing the moisture in the air, creating dense bullets of water that managed to deplete a number of them, and Rex using his Cosmic Energy ability of Energy Transfer to reinforce the main shield. But even with a fearless band of locals Zoranians and two Elders, the Orion Crusaders broke through our defenses and slaughtered everyone. Our defense force didn't stand a chance once that shield broke...people were sliced in half, shot, and beheaded. Rex and I were foolish to think we could defend the entire planet by ourselves against an invasion force of that magnitude, something we picked up from Nico mistakenly. We charged head first at the two monsters hoping to sever the head of the snake, at least on the battlefield. I took the big one while Rex took the one with the scars. The big guy swung his hammer across, shifting his grip to bring it crashing down. I dodged both attempts on my life and countered with my agility and trusted katana, slicing at the beast's knees and torso before I hit him in the chest with a cannon of water. I knocked him down, so I did what any Guardian would do. I got in my stance and rushed the beast with my katana in hand, cutting his face wide open. Of course I thought he was dead so I mistakenly lowered my guard and turned my back, prematurely deciding my victory. I started slicing, stabbing, and blasting away at the incoming corrupted soldiers when suddenly I felt death creep against my skin like a strong cold chill rushing to greet you. I turned to see the monster swinging his hammer against me with murderous intent. I surely thought my life was over, but then I felt a forceful push. I turned to see Rex looking and smiling before taking the full force of The Hand's hammer which sent him flying. At that moment, I knew all was lost...So I ordered a full retreat within the forest surrounding the capital with me finding and picking up Rex, and covering our retreat, giving the enemy the means to do whatever they wanted to the planet."

Vinzent: "Wow, that's a hell of a Dragon mission. And The Hand and Ude...they must be two of the warriors we saw in the vision. How did Zora become a sandy wasteland? And what happened to Rex? If you don't mind sharing."

Cass: "The worms; they act as giant leeches. They sucked the planet dry of all its vegetation without completely draining Zora's core of all its vital Source Energy, like keeping the entire planet on life support. They hunted and destroyed anything electrical, preventing me from building a new ship. As for Rex, he died shortly after I found him. His last words were, 'you still have a chance.'"

Vinzent: "For what it's worth, I'm sorry, but that explains why I was attacked and followed earlier. I had an idea, but I wasn't completely sure. So Orion let you live? Why?"

Cass: "...O-Orion saw the strength and courage in Elder ranked Guardians and spared me and the remaining population to what you see now, no more than a few hundred. He killed my comrades and left this rotten planet to those Source Energy draining worms, calling it 'mercy'."

Zoranian survivor: "Vamos, la fiesta está por comenzar."

Cass: "Estaremos allí."

Vinzent: "You understand them?"

Cass: "When you've spent as much time on this planet as I, you pick up on a few things."

The two newly acquainted Guardians intended the small feast, resting in this special moment of peace and joy despite the present evil...

Meanwhile in outer space, the Hercules awakened with the ship's internal lights coming to life. Jasmine, the artificial intelligence, informed both Elder Nico and Elder Raito of their exiting from hyperspace. Upon receiving the update, Nico finished his meditation session as peace, Love and Light rushed throughout his body. And Raito finished improving his Stem Shots while also completing new spells within his Grimoire. Raito entered into the cockpit of the Hercules to take back control, and with a push of a lever, the Hercules popped out of hyperspace and approached the planet's orbit. A strange flow of Source Energy consumed the ship as Nico and Raito sensed the strong Energy originating from the planet, but they didn't know if that was a good thing or a bad one. The crew entered Zora's atmosphere, flying several thousand feet above the surface as they searched for a stronger signal, but to no avail. They couldn't find Vinzent's signal or any other electrical signal on the entire planet. It was as if the ruling force outlawed technology altogether. Although no electrical signals were picked up, Jasmine informed the Elders of several life forms, hundreds of feet in length that followed the ship from beneath the sandy surface.

Jasmine: "I did an initial scan of the planet as we approached Zora's orbit, and didn't find a single signal coming from any electrical source, worrying. However I did find several large organisms following the ship."

Raito: "Must be the Sand Gods. We can't land the ship or drive the MT-AT unless we want to fight some big ass worms."

Nico: "In that case, you'll have to use your super speed to cover ground and I'll pilot the ship close enough to keep the worms off your back. Be careful though Raito, Vinzent vanished here and the Source Energy is strong here. Our best bet is to head to the last place Vinzent's signal was picked up and move from there."

Raito: "Sounds good. I'll signal you from the ground when we're ready for extraction."

The two agreed on the plan as Nico flew the ship a few miles away from Vinzent's last known location. To avoid a confrontation with the Sand Gods, Nico swiftly approached the targeted area before drifting the Hercules as if he were gliding on ice. The Elder then opened the port side airlock, allowing Raito to leap then roll on the soft warm sand below. Soon after, Nico sped off to avoid unnecessary company. Elder Raito knew time was of the essence, so without wasting another moment, he sprinted through the sea of sand as he set out towards Vinzent's last known location. Upon arrival, Raito pulled out his Grimoire to cast a spell which enabled him to view past events of the targeted area called: ***Enlightened Past***. The spell revealed: *Vinzent waking up confused and lost. It showed him trying his communications device, but got nothing but static. Next it showed Vinzent manifesting a board of lightning to head North.* The spell faded as Raito gained a promising lead. The Elder then took off at full speed, sprinting several miles before stopping a moment to catch his breath.

Raito: *heavy breathing* "Who…in their right mind…would have a person…with super speed…take breaks after two minutes… of running."

After a short break, Raito's journey brought him to a large dip in the ground that had been filled with sand, and could make for a deadly sinkhole if not careful. He casted the same spell as before, showing the history of the targeted area. *It showed the humongous worms attacking Vinzent as he stunned the worms, and fled to the rocky valley a few miles to the Northeast.*

Raito: "And Nico said I'd like it here. At least I have a solid idea on where Vinzent is. I can't contact Nico though because that will draw attention to myself, and I don't have time to fight an oversized caterpillar."

Finding confidence in his choices thus far, Raito raced towards the mountain sized area of twists and turns, endless paths and dead ends. He ran through the entire maze before stopping to catch his breath when he suddenly felt eyes watching him like a silent owl watching the night sky. The Elder yelled for the perpetrators to show themselves, but got no response. Raito's hairs then stood on end as a spear was thrown from the shadow, forcing him to evade the life threatening weapon. Another was thrown which forced Raito to dodge to the left, but as he moved, a third annoying spear was thrown in his dodging path. With no other option, the Elder conjured a bubble of Prana Energy called: ***Forcefield***, that shielded him from the pending spear. He then spread his arms out and up, expanding the existing shield, which covered all lifeforms in the area. With the conditions met, Raito pulled his hands down into his chest, clapping as all three Zoranian guards came flying out of their positions, smacking the ground hard as if losing a game of tug-of-war.

Raito: "Now that I have your attention, I would like to know where my comrade is and I think you guys know. Start talking!"

Zoranian Guard #1: "Este perro se va a morir aquí!"

Zoranian Guard #3: "Él no tiene idea. estúpido hombre del espacio."

Raito: "Tus muertes llegarán antes si sigues haciéndome perder el tiempo."

The three four-armed guards turned to look at each other in utter disbelief and embarrassment.

Raito: "Didn't think I knew Spanish did you? Now, you three know why I'm here. Let's not make things ugly."

Annoyed by the four-armed entities who were wasting his time, Raito picked up one of the guards demanding that they show him to his friend. Realizing this was another Guardian, the Zoranian guards apologized and reluctantly agreed to show Raito to their hidden sanctuary within the confusing valley. After a short journey of twists and turns, the Zoranian guards approached the entrance which fueled Raito's anger. The Elder saw how the habitants of this world lived after the attack from Orion. Many women without their husbands and children without their fathers. Tents were made from sticks and covers with the only water resource being a dirty well which pumped out two gallons of water every four hours, and dried up bread being the only source of food. Raito's heart was struck as he found sorrow for the Zoranian population.

The guards pointed Raito in the direction of the same big tent with the red and orange design. Thanking the guards, Raito walked up to the hand-made structure, and pulled back the cover before entering the tent. Upon entering, the Elder was relieved to see Vinzent in one piece, but also surprised to see Casanova alive.

Vinzent: "Raito! About damn time you made it, and here I am thinking I'm faster than you."

Raito: "It's good to see you my friend, and in one piece after that game of tag with the worms."

Vinzent: "Oh you saw that. *hard chuckle* Anyways, Raito meet–"

Raito: "Elder Casanova Meyoki, second-class. The renowned water-bender and katana specialist."

Cass: "In the flesh. You're first-class Elder Raito, the Prana speedster right?"

Raito: "The one and only. Where's Elders Kicks and Rex? We could use the extra help."

Cass: "Gone…Killed by Orion's top demons."

Raito: "I-I'm sorry to hear that, and we will honor them appropriately… but right now we need to get off world and you need your gear, Vinzent."

Vinzent: "You're right about the gear, but wrong about leaving the planet."

Raito: "What are you talking about?!"

Vinzent: "I was called to this planet for a reason and I WILL see it through!"

Raito: "Vinzent we don't have time for this. We've lost too much time already and now you wanna chase a voice?! We have our mission and you're going to jeopardize it for some voice in your head?"

Vinzent: "To put it bluntly, yes. My intuition is telling me this is the way. Will you trust me?"

Raito: *sigh* "I will never understand you or Nico's blind trust in intuition, but I trust my faction."

Vinzent: "Will you join our faction Casanova and bring honor to Kicks and Rex?"

Cass: "Beats wasting away here. Just…let me say a few things to the locals."

Cass walked out of the tent and grabbed the attention of all the Zoranians as she delivered her message…

Cass: "Todos ustedes han sufrido mucho y han sobrevivido a lo imposible, enseñándome el verdadero coraje y la resiliencia frente al verdadero mal. Mi historia en este planeta termina aquí, pero la tuya apenas comienza. Toma lo que has aprendido, hazte más fuerte, próspera y recupera tu mundo de estos intrusos alimañas de una vez por todas!!!"

Vinzent: "Did you catch any of that?"

Raito: "She said their resilience and bravery has reignited her inner flame. And to let their experience guide them to a prosperous and protected future so they may take back their world from the worms."

Vinzent: "Well said Cass."

Following Cass's speech, there was a flow of sadness mixed with joy amongst the Zoranian people given the news of their hero's future departure. The people offered her the *Espada del Intrépido* (Sword of the Fearless). A sword made from the bones of one of the first worms killed not so long ago. The corrupted Source Energy was reversed, giving it the power to increase the morale of an individual or group of allies. Cass took the sword with great gratitude and honor as the Guardian exited the sanctuary. A Zoranian guide waited towards the entrance to show them the way out of the rocky maze. After a few moments of walking through the identical twists and turns, the Guardians arrived at an opening that led to a seemingly endless sea of sand and heat. Preparing themselves for a potentially blazing journey, the Guardians took their leave after waving to the guide and walked out into the overbearing Sun. Moments later, Raito casted the spell: Guiding Light, which released a beam of Prana Energy high in the air, allowing Nico to locate and pinpoint their current location. With Vinzent reunited with the faction, Nico telepathically warned Vinzent and Raito, telling them to "make it fast" as the worms had been stalking the Hercules since its arrival, waiting for one moment of error by the pilot. As Elder Nico closed in on Raito's Guiding Light spell, he saw Raito, Vinzent and…Cass? Nico was struck with a wave of anxiety as his hands began sweating and his nerves rushed to regain their composure. "Are you okay Nico? Your heart rate has increased exponentially", asked the curious AI. "Y-Yes. Just don't wanna be eaten by worms", replied the emotional Elder. Nico read the report and found that Cass's entire faction was wiped out, thankfully that data was somewhat wrong.

Zooming, descending then hovering, Nico gave the ship's controls to Jasmine and asked her to keep the ship as steady as possible, as well as to constantly check the scanners to alert them of any company. Jasmine agreed as the ship hovered several feet from the sandy ground, allowing the cargo doors towards the stern side of the starship to open wide. There Nico stood at the edge, searching and impatiently waiting for a visual on his comrades. In the horizon, Nico saw a strong Guardian covered in a blue combat-kimono and equipped with a katana as well as an exotic looking sword as he gave a sharp inhale. She was escorted by Elders Raito and Vinzent as they made haste towards the opened Hercules. Following this, the emergency alarms blared and Jasmine's voice could be heard all throughout the ship as she completed her given task.

Jasmine: "Uhhh, we have a problem…two large lifeforms detected, four hundred meters and closing. I advise immediate departure."

Nico: "We're not going anywhere. MOVE IT!!"

As Nico and Jasmine went back-n-forth, the ground began to shake as two giant worms drew closer with every passing moment. Raito, picking up speed, sprinted into the Hercules as he rushed past Nico and sat in one of the control room's chairs, readying the weapons. Vinzent knew time had run out, so the Elder concentrated on manifesting his Red Aura to make a pad of red lightning which resembled a mini trampoline. Both Cass and Vinzent leaped from the object and flew thirty feet in the air with their desired target being the opened doors of the Hercules. As they plummeted towards their starship, the ground buckled and split open, giving birth to two worms, two hundred and fifty feet from head to tail. The worm's sudden ascension from the sand reminded the faction of a jack-in-the-box toy, though that version was not kid-friendly . The Sand Gods roared and screamed, targeting the low hovering ship and forced Jasmine to take evasive actions. The worms lunged at the Hercules with Jasmine dodging left then vertically, barely evading the massive creature's attacks. Due to the Hercules's movement however, Vinzent and Cass were left free falling as their intended target moved out of danger's way. Seeing this, Nico sprung into action. The Elder amplified the muscle-fibers in his legs with his Solar Mutation ability, enabling him to dash from the Hercules with great force and velocity. The first worm chased after the Hercules and its electrical signal. But the second worm went for Vinzent personally. This particular worm remembered the hurtful explosions thrown by the Elder earlier as it elegantly moved through the sand like a snake through the jungle. It positioned itself to catch the two falling Guardians in its mouth as it opened wide like a patient getting a cleaning from a dentist. But before Vinzent and Cass could meet their end, Nico reached his target and violently kicked the worm on the side of its body, forcing the worm to crash into the sand below. This feat enabled Vinzent and Cass to land and tumble on the sand, saving them from the jaws of death. Jasmine and Raito, who were in control of the Hercules, brought the ship around to attack the worm that chased them. The AI headed straight for the worm's underbelly, which gave Raito the perfect moment to fire the repeating laser cannons into the monster as the worm collapsed hard, screeching in pain. Unfinished, the attacked worm submerged itself underground for another surprise attack before bursting out of the sandy surface which prevented the Hercules from successfully picking up Cass, Vinzent and now Nico. The Guardians found themselves in a pickle as they searched for a way around these two giant worms. Frustration found Elder Nico as he knew these simple worms couldn't possibly keep four Elder ranked Guardians from completing their task, so given the current situation, Nico came up with a plan.

Nico: "Raito, how long will it take you to conjure chains big and strong enough to hold these worms steady?"

Raito: "Two minutes."

Nico: "You have thirty seconds. Jazz, warm up the heavy laser cannon and wait for my signal. Vinzent, Cass, can you keep these things busy?"

Vinzent: "Felt like we've been doing that this whole time, but sure."

Raito jumped out of the ship and landed next to Nico, a few feet from the distracted worms. Vinzent's explosive Orange lightning and Cass's highly pressurized blasts of water successfully kept the worms occupied. The blazing Sun of Zora fueled Nico's cells, giving him a sense of confidence and courage as he and Raito showcased their abilities. Nico amplified then mutated both of his arms to utilize the Hari whip mutation, leaving Raito to begin casting his strongest binding spell yet. The two Guardians breathed in and out multiple times as they felt the strong Source Energy of the planet flow through them. Nico quickly opened his eyes and thrusted his arms forward, effectively wrapping both worms with the Hari whips. Nico's elongated arms enveloped both worms with a thick twenty foot rope of bladed muscle-fibers, the other being twelve feet, which led to the worms jerking in pain as the small blades dug into the flesh of the slithering animals, ripping and tearing away as blood showered the area. The task was most difficult however, because of the sheer size of both creatures. They lurched around violently, causing Nico's mutated grip to begin slipping. Ashla teachings alone did not possess Nico with the strength to hold them both completely steady for long, so in a rushed tone, he yelled for assistance.

Nico: *grunts* "Raito. I can't…hold them much longer…"

Raito: "I got you Nico, don't worry. Prana Energy: ***Binding Chains!***"

    With the call for help heard, Raito finished his spell preparation and casted four mighty chains of Prana Energy to help Nico restrain the Sand Gods. With the combined power of Nico's Solar Mutation and Raito's Prana magic, both worms were at a contested standstill. However, it didn't last long as Raito's chains began to crack and Nico's Hari whips began to loosen further. Knowing this could be extremely problematic, Nico gave Jasmine the signal, screaming, "Jasmine… NOW!!" Without hesitation, the AI fired the Hercules's heavy beam cannon which melted straight through both worms in a hefty blast of Kinetic Energy, like ice under the Sun. The blast carved a hole seven feet wide into the worms, effectively killing them as the slimy creatures collapsed against the ground in a cloud of sand. Nico fell to one knee gasping for air as his empowered muscle-fibers retreated back to normal while Raito hunched over his knees, panting heavily. Vinzent and Cass ran over to their exhausted comrades with Vinzent picking Raito up and Cass to Nico. They made their way to the ship as Jasmine was finally able to land. Upon entering the spacecraft however, Vinzent informed Nico of their need to stay on Zora.

Vinzent: "Hell of a job you two. Remind me to buy y'all a drink."

Nico: "You got yourself a deal. Now let's leave this place before anymore show up."

Vinzent: "About that, there's something we have to do."

Nico: "Did you not see what we just killed? And you want to stay?!"

Vinzent: "There's something strange about this place. I know you felt the Source Energy here, it's mysteriously strong."

Nico: "You aren't wrong, but—"

Vinzent: "Do you trust me?"

Nico: "With my life, but—"

Vinzent: "No more buts. Have my back on this..."

Nico ultimately agreed as he let out a deep sigh of acceptance. Raito then pointed Vinzent in the direction of his gear as the Guardian suited up in his black, white and gold, light-weight style of armor added by a medium sized cloak with a faction's logo engraved on the hood. Following Vinzent's wardrobe change, he instinctively plotted in the coordinates pointing to the source of the planet's Source Energy. While flying to the destination, Nico and Cass reunited.

Raito: "Nico, meet Cass. Cass meet—"

Nico respectfully interrupted Raito before embracing his long thought dead lover.

Nico: "I know who she is, we have...history. We...completed some basic combat and pilot training during our time as Paladins. Cass, I-I thought I lost you. Are you okay? What happened? Where's Rex and Kicks?"

Nico laid his hand on Cass's soft face as she embraced the touch she longed for.

Cass: "You'll never lose me and yes I'm fine. *smiles softly* Rex and Kicks...they were...killed by Orion and his soldiers protecting Zora and...me. We were attacked. I only made it out because Orion spared me..."

Nico fell silent as his raged filled heart was felt throughout the ship.

Nico: "I see. They will have a proper burial. At least you're still okay."

Nico kissed Cass on the forehead and walked down to the ship's cargo bay before shutting the door behind him.

Raito: "History huh? I understand your feelings, but why is he so uptight about it?"

Cass: "Besides the fact loss is never easy, when we were barely able to call ourselves Guardians back during basic Paladin training, Nico was reserved and isolated. A lot of young Guardians witnessed his ability, Solar Mutation, in fear and labeled him more or less a monster, even though his people helped stop the War. His power was so different from everyone else, and the rarity of his Healing-Factor caused a lot of jealousy and envy. So everyone avoided him, Rex and I regretfully avoided him as well. We were so close minded back then, but Kicks was different. He approached Nico and found he was just like us, a young Guardian trying to bring Light to a darkened galaxy. After getting to know Nico, we all trained together, ate together, essentially becoming family. Eventually Nico and I found something more than just a friendship, and here we are years later, and Nicos still as stubborn as they come. When he found out what happened to my faction, he never found closure. I never thought I'd see him again…b-but, nevertheless, fear keeps people from faith, I believe that wholeheartedly now. Loss is a hard pill to swallow, but as Guardians, we can't lose ourselves in grief or else our comrade's sacrifices would've been completely in vain."

Raito: "I understand and agree fully. Nico can be sensitive and blindfolded by his emotions to say the least."

Cass: "We all get a little blinded by our emotions, but action upon those emotions shows true character."

While Cass helped Raito to understand Nico's perspective, Vinzent informed the faction they were approaching the spot. However, they were aware as they all felt the strange Source Energy pulsating from the top of a pyramidal shaped building which was mysteriously surrounded by vegetation. Vinzent subconsciously knew this… pyramid brought him here, but for what reason, he had no idea. Vinzent asked Raito to join him inside the pyramid because of his magical background which gave Nico and Cass time to…catch up.

The Hercules hovered towards the entrance, allowing Vinzent and Raito to jump out of the lowered spacecraft and make their way inside the Source Energy rich structure. They stopped a moment, and turned back towards the entrance after realizing no worms had attacked them since their arrival. Raito believed this was due to the strong waves of pure Source Energy coming from the pyramid. Vinzent agreed, enabling them to continue into the mystical building. Upon entering, the pyramid reacted to their presence, shifting hallways and stairs, closing off one way to reveal another. The fluidity of the mystical structure reminded the Guardians of how flexible and submissive water was. Elders Vinzent and Raito basked in the presence of the gorgeous interior of the pyramid. Its flooring and walls were decorated with a beautiful emerald green marble added by three horizontal lines on both sides of the walls. The lines contained colors in order from red, orange, yellow, green, blue, indigo, and violet, the same pattern from the mysterious forest land of Nalmoth back on Journia, and the same order in which Elder Vinzent's Aura's fluctuated; this fact found internal curiosity within Vinzent. After journeying through the pyramid, the two Elders were led into some kind of chamber. In this chamber lay a large white, but aged cushion in the middle of the room, added by a circle around the cushion that held old dead grass. Vinzent opened his mind, and allowed his subconscious and instincts to take over as he sat, criss-cross, on the cushion before closing his eyes and breathing. Without a word being spoken between the two Elders, Raito activated a harmonizing spell which purged the room of any and all negative elements, while placing a Forcefield around Vinzent's physical body, protecting it as Vinzent's consciousness dove deeper into the meditative state. Raito meditated and focused on the present moment as he held the Forcefield, along with lending vital Ashla taught Prana Energy to Vinzent's soul. This added Prana Energy from Raito allowed Vinzent to dive even deeper into the spiritual realm. Here within the astral realm of consciousness, Vinzent was met by an masculine and feminine entity, completely covered in Source Energy by the name of Ra.

Ra: "We are Ra. We greet you brother, in the Love and in the Light of the One Infinite Creator. We have seen you and your other selves traverse this galaxy during this time/space nexus. Protecting the innocent and freeing worlds. With these actions, you all polarize towards service-to-others in the Love and in the Light of the One Infinite Creator, however, you fail to see the truth in Love and in Light."

Vinzent: "Greetings Ra. I'm honored to hear the Creator finds favor in us. But if I may, what did you mean by, 'failed to see the truth in Love and in Light'? Also, who are you and why have you brought me here?"

Ra: "We are, but a humble messenger for which the One Infinite Creator speaks through, and we have brought you here to learn/teach. Life was created by the Light, with Love for the purpose of learning and growing through experience, for within experience, lessons can be learned; karma can be erased. There are no good or evil things, nor beautiful or hideous actions. These are simply ideologies born from the ego, something your day and age takes too seriously my friend."

Vinzent: "I don't understand. When someone kills without remorse for the purpose of power and conquest, that's evil."

Ra: "And when Guardians kill without remorse for the purpose of protecting and peace, that makes it justified?"

Vinzent: "When it calls for it, yes."

Ra: "Then you are no better than the very evil you seek to vanquish my brother."

Vinzent: "I don't understand."

Ra: "And you won't until you see all living things as part of you, like pieces of a Universal puzzle. Until you see the divine Source Energy flowing through all things, you will continue to be enslaved by your own ideals and principles; what you deem is 'right'. Life is to be forgiven, understood, cherished and protected in the name of true Love/Light.

The Love to forgive lost entities such as Orion and the Light to show the way to an even greater power than that of you or your other-selves; that is the Law of One. Surrender yourself to Source Energy and become one, and when the time comes, free the galaxy from the cycle of untamed hatred, and master the Way of Bogan for it is you, and you are it."

Vinzent: "Forgive Orion?! How can I...how can you say that?! How can someone as vile as Orion be forgiven? How can you expect us not to give Orion and his army the same hell they've given the rest of Myrmidon?! And what's this you speak of? 'Master the Way of Bogan'? Just what kind of messenger are you?"

Ra: "The kind who loves and cherishes you my brother. Given time and experience, you and your brothers and sisters of this dimension will bring forth the correct justice, but not in the way you deem appropriate. We of the sixth dimension see the potential you, Nico and Raito hold. Continue down this path my friend, for the One Infinite Creator smiles upon those who believe in the wholeness of all creation. We leave you now my brother. Go forth, rejoicing in the power and in the peace of the One Infinite Creator. Adonai."

Vinzent: "Adonai..."

Vinzent's eyes opened as he was left confused and disappointed. He explained the Ra contact to Raito with the Elder sharing the same expression as Vinzent, befuddled and dissatisfied. They made their way out of the pyramid before signaling the Hercules for a pickup. They saw the cream colored spaceship come in for a quick load-n-go as the cargo doors opened, giving access to Vinzent and Raito. Following this, the ship shot off into space as Cass gave out a sigh of relief, showing her relieved expression and happiness to be off that graveyard despite the loving population.

All four of the Elder ranked Guardians sat in the ship's control room as Vinzent explained to Nico, Cass and Jasmine the conversation between himself and Ra. Afterwards, Nico took what Vinzent said to heart before asking for a private moment to meditate for a sign. The three other Guardians agreed as Nico left again, but with a different more focused attitude. He entered the crew's quarters and unstrapped his armored tabi boots before sitting crisscrossed on one of the beds. He began his session with the mantra, "Energy flows through all things, and I am Energy", repeated over and over until silence was his only company. Immediately he was struck with quick flashes of flames burning trees like a well lit fireplace. A large sword cutting innocents down, a red skinned entity, and what looked like the destruction of Journia. Nico opened his eyes with anguish and pain rushing through him. He swiftly pushed the door open, demanding Jasmine to give him the ship's controls as agitation penetrated his voice.

Cass: "Nico? What's wrong?"

Nico: "Journia's in trouble."

Vinzent: "What do you mean 'in trouble'?"

Nico: "During my meditation session, I saw fire and death and a red skinned entity I didn't recognize. And Journia was…destroyed…"

Nico, given the sense of discouragement added with a burning hatred for Orion, put in Journia's coordinates as the ship warmed up its hyperdrive. Soon after, a few moments passed before the Hercules blasted into hyperspace. Nico prayed to the Creator, hoping that his vision hadn't come to pass or with the hope that he'd be able to stomach what was yet to come…

CHAPTER

FOUR

ATTACK

The sky darkened and clouds, added by a cold breeze, filled Journia's air with sorrow and dejection. The Ashura Order and planet as a whole, honored the passing of the brave fleet of Guardians destroyed by the hands of the Orion Crusaders, as well as the billions of lives already lost. Banners were held high as citizens and Guardians walked the streets of Sarvis in unity. The capital city had seemingly paused its everyday activities to mourn the heavy loss. The annihilation of Elite Basil and his fleet cut deeply, like feeling the loss of a loved one. However, it also strengthened The Order's resolve and rallied the local population as the entire planet was put under a Demon alert. Spacecraft coming to or leaving from Journia were restricted to Guardian personnel only, the planet activated the protective shield, and *Bao* (Journia's moon) was fortified and armed to the teeth. A few Acolyte ranked Guardians in the communications department within The Order headquarters, contacted the Deep Space Radar space station or DSR, two AU's (astronomical unit) outside of Journia's star system. By doing so, they hoped the station would've perhaps picked up a signal from a surviving Guardian or Elite Basil, or if they had intel on the enemy that caused such a devastating blow, but all the communications department encountered was silence. No chatter, no cries for help, not even static. The Guardians were perplexed by the radio silence and did a full station sweep to find...

nothing, the station was completely destroyed, wiped clean from the face of the known galaxy like it wasn't even there in the first place. The head of the communications department, second-class Elite Guardian Jessie King, a short, purple-haired human woman, personally traveled to The Nine's courtroom and energetically informed them of the dire situation.

Jessie: "Council of The Nine, I've come with troubling news. We've lost connection with the DSR. It...was destroyed, along with all two hundred Acolytes aboard the station."

After a brief discussion between the members, The Nine took it as the final sign and wasted no time.

The Nine Member #4: "Thank you, Elite Jessie. We request you to send out a Demon alert to all Guardians, making this priority number one. We also request that you assist in coordinating a defensive perimeter around Journia's orbit as well as the ground, and to utilize Bao as a first line of defense. Once that is complete, mobilize your faction of Guardians and join the front."

Jessie: "As you command Counselor. If I may, what is going on? I've received multiple distress calls from numerous planets, all of which describing the same enemy, and now a destroyed Ashura fleet, and space station. The prophecy always said a foul evil would return seeking vengeance. There have also been rumors among the Guardians that we haven't been taught the entire truth. As head of communications, and a fellow Guardian, I humbly request the truth about this, Orion, so that I may complete my task as best I can."

The council members looked towards one another before one of the members explained the history behind the one known as Orion.

The Nine Member #1: "We knew this day would come, no sense in hiding it any longer. We accept your request, Elite Jessie... Orion, as you'll unfortunately find out, is an abomination to the very foundation of space/time and time/space. But to know Orion, you must know his past...... He and his kind, the *Asronians*, were a red skinned horned species who possessed an extraordinary connection to Source Energy. These horned individuals were ruled by their strong and proud Emperor, *Titus Ronan*, and his gentle wife and cunning Empress, *Athena Ronan*. Together they had three glorious and healthy children, a crafty first born son and heir to the Asronian throne, named *Theo*. A rowdy second born prince, named *Gabriel*, and a quiet baby princess, named *Rose*, all possessing two horns each, besides Rose who was born with one. The Ronan's ruled over their people with both esteem and fear, and their people loved them for it. Their technology was strange yet unique because it was alive. Even their starships, and houses. Back then, the Ashura Order was nothing more than a few entities, looking to spread the teachings and Oneness of the divine Energy Ashla practices. However, what made matters even stranger was their practice of Source Energy through the Way of Bogan or the Dark side, which empowered their Energy; that being Cosmic Energy. Bogan teachings are of course Ashla's polar opposite, and proved to strengthen one's abilities by far, but relied heavily on the use of emotions as motivation and fuel. However, when left unchecked, those emotions can and will lead a Guardian or entity down a path of evil and destruction. That is why we shy away from the Way of Bogan."

Jessie: "Why wouldn't the Way of Bogan be taught? I'm sure those within the Elder rank could handle the emotional turmoil."

The Nine Member #2: "Though Bogan teachings would prove beneficial power wise. The Way of Ashla doesn't just give one their gifts. It offers compassion, mindfulness, and Oneness. It offers an intimate bond with the Creator, if one accepts these gifts. However, Bogan, though exceedingly more powerful, draws from a dark place within an entity. A place of rage, grief, and envy. Through emotion, the Way of Bogan drastically increases one's potential, both physically and energetically, but prolonged exposure to these emotions can and will bring your soul down to a place you may not recover from."

Jessie: "I see why it wasn't taught. If I may, how does this correlate to Orion, Counselor?"

The Nine Member #1: "Things were peaceful during the initial stages. Though it was a major change for Titus, as well as us Ashla practitioners. It genuinely seemed like lasting peace and balance between the two paths would be our next move. But that all changed after the sudden death of his second born son, Gabriel. Afterwards, Titus fell into deep sorrow. He was consumed by grief, and started down a dark path, a path us teachers of Ashla refused to follow or accept. After a while, our relationship with the Asronians grew increasingly strained, especially as more entities across Myrmidon became followers of the Way of Ashla. Completely consumed by his unquenchable sadness and anger, Titus and his army of Red Nobles began destroying hundreds of planets, which was a sin we Ashla students refused to overlook; thus beginning the six year long Galactic War. Titus saw himself above others and didn't hesitate to sacrifice innocent lives to achieve his goals. During the sixth year of the War, which saw trillions of lives lost up until that point, the newly formed Ashura Order, along with the twenty surviving Senshi Warriors, combined their strength and formed a last strike against their home world, Asron, to end the bloody war. But this was their homeworld, and their use of organic technology made that task… nearly impossible. The Order and Senshi Warriors agreed to call them 'The Organics', because of their use of organic technology, and their gargantuan sized worldships. There were several of these ships, each a different shape; each with their own unique ability."

The Nine Member #9: "Can't forget about those pesky Ryū fighters and landers."

The Nine Member #1: "Ah yes, the Ryū fleet is forever burned in my memory… A lot of brave Guardians died that day, including thirteen of the twenty Senshi Warriors, but we achieved victory after destroying the remainder of their worldship fleet, allowing us to fight our way into Titus's worldship. There The Nine and the Senshi Warriors defeated Titus and his first born, Theo, taking them prisoner with a powerful binding spell called: ***Holy Chains***. Their remaining forces aboard the worldship engaged us in combat, hoping to free their Emperor. The rest fled to their planet's surface to reinforce Empress Athena. However, given all the galaxy had been subject to those last six years, we deemed it far too dangerous to leave Asron to recover or to let the soul of Titus live in this life or the afterlife. Upon this conclusion we...did what needed to be done.

The Nine members all looked in different directions with one member simply closing her eyes; another giving out a inhale of hesitation.

The Nine Member #2: "From the perspective of The Order, we were saving the galaxy. From the Senshi Warriors, 'life must be preserved, if able, no matter how evil.' But for Theo however, all he saw was his home planet, his family destroyed; it tore him apart. I could really feel the hatred and bloodlust coming from Theo as he watched his friends and family perish. I sensed something change dramatically in him at that moment. In his eyes, he saw why Bogan was the way; why conquest was a suitable replacement for peace. 'In this galaxy, those who are not strong, perish.' Theo saw the detestation, the deception, the separation, the pure blackness in a man's heart. He realized that Bogan was the true foundation, and that Ashla was a blinding way to fit in. The Darkness and death of everything he held dear, freed him from attachment, from Love and empty promises. That freedom allowed him to gain true strength and to utilize that earned strength at will regardless of morals; regardless of what was right and wrong. He realized the galaxy was caught in a never-ending cycle of hate, and the only way to save everyone from themselves was to destroy the cycle entirely. Theo, in that moment found complete peace, thinking to himself that everything he did, all the people he's killed for his father, had led him to that very moment, to 'save' Myrmidon. In that moment, pure darkened Source Energy offered itself to the young man, and Theo willingly and vengefully accepted it. Theo, realizing his new path, was stripped of his humanity, of any Love or compassion, but was instead gifted with power; unmeasurable power. The young man's body began to glow, and generate a menacing and intoxicating Black Aura, which had flooded the worldship and forced us off the ship. That Aura, it…it felt like inhaling toxic waste… After getting off the ship, the surviving Guardians witnessed Theo floating in space, outside of the last worldship, but he was now a three horned creation of blasphemy and revulsion. He thought himself a God, and for a second, we thought he was. It felt like he had the power and the authority to challenge the One Infinite Creator for all creation. In his eyes, he saw a new age, a hunting season, and the Universe was his prey. Upon this vision for revenge, for conquest, he thought it fitting to throw away his old identity, and name himself, *Orion*, after that of the Giant Hunter who ruled the skies. He then claimed and named his new worldship *The Obedience*, stating that 'his word is law, and this ship will obey that law.' He also claimed that 'the Coin of Life has been flipped, and Darkness will rise again', before disappearing into the void of space without a trace, until now."

Jessie: "There has to be a way to connect back to Theo. The Love from the Creator can't be extinguished so easily!"

The Nine Member #4: "Your optimism is welcoming, but Theo died hundreds of years ago with his people. All that remains is Orion, a blasphemer towards the Way of Ashla, bent on revenge. Now go forth now my friend, carry out this task rejoicing in the Love and the protection of the One Infinite Creator. Adonai."

Jessie: "Adonai."

As the doors shut behind the determined Guardian, the council members were left with fear, but renewed confidence as the Ashura Order was specifically established to protect Journia and Myrmidon, or so they thought.

The Nine Member #9: "We all know he has returned, but are we ready for him?"

The Nine Member #5: "I must concur, we have had hundreds of years of peace and prosperity. Are we and The Order strong enough to handle… Orion? Especially without the Senshi Warriors?"

The Nine Member #6: "How can you be so sure that it is Orion? For all we know it could be the return of the Asronians altogether...or something worse. Maybe the Kesshō Empire has found Myrmidon and come for the crystal..."

The courtroom fell utterly silent as if the room were empty. Soon after, a member broke the silence.

The Nine Member #7: "If the Kesshō Empire found this galaxy, we would've heard from the Star Hoppers. That aside, the Asronians were killed during the Galactic War. Do you not remember what we did to their planet? Besides, remember Elder Raito's warning. We should've prepared ourselves then. Now look at us, we've lost an entire fleet, a station and thousands of Guardians while our enemy toys with us."

The room was filled with panic and trepidation because of The Nine's inharmonious nature. The thought of the Asronian's return caused great unbalance within the council. They have lived each for hundreds of years, and though The Nine were powerful and well educated in the Way of Ashla, time had indeed aged the heroes of old...

Elsewhere in deep space, hundreds of kilometers away from Journia, The Obedience cloaked in Aka Energy sat patiently, watching their enemy mobilize and fortify as if preparing for a category five hurricane. Orion looked on at the unprepossessing planet in disgust, internally shaking with rage and hate, but with the added sense of pleasure as he too mobilized his forces. Elder Luna, a guest as much as a prisoner, looked at Orion's focused demeanor with a sense of nonplus as his normal calm and rational demeanor had suddenly been replaced with an unquenchable fury.

Luna: "The 'mighty' Orion, scared of Guardians...of the Way of Ashla?"

Orion: *sarcastic chuckle* "My dear Luna, this is merely excitement. I've waited for this moment for generations. You think I slaughtered and enslaved for amusement alone? No. Not only will the galaxy know

Darkness, but it will see the Light is a lie. Nothing more than a feeble candle light blown out by a winter breeze, and what are the Guardians without their power, their hope, their Ashla teachings? Nothing, but fragile and pitiful children playing with shadows."

The Orion Crusaders completed the mobilization of their forces as a hundred and fifty thousand corrupted soldiers, thirty thousand four armed creatures, and six Walkers stood ready to give their lives for their "god". Ude, Hando and Makai all approached Orion before bending their knees, readying themselves to die honorably for their lord. "Let us begin" said the sinister leader, the entire ship was flooded by the roars and resolution from his army. Hundreds of small Ryū fighters were deployed, surrounding a long cylinder shaped object which had grown from The Obedience and headed straight for Bao. The moon of Journia was heavily fortified with six bases spread out evenly among the entire moon, and tunnels underground which connected to the moon's core. Each base, in these desperate times, had a faction of two hundred Elite ranked Guardians, long-range artillery cannons, and manned energy turrets.

Elite Jessie had completed her requested task and had gathered her faction as they headed to reinforce the front line at base four on Bao. As they landed on air-pad number ten, Jessie noticed that pilots raced to their cockpits while the base initiated their defensive protocols. Jessie stopped one of the rushing pilots and asked for an update.

Jessie: "Guardian! What is going on?"

Guardian Pilot: "We spotted hundreds of small meteors sized craft guarding some kind of cylindrical object. They look to be in attack formation, so we're mobilizing all starfighters to intercept."

Jessie: "God's speed pilot. May the Light guard you."

The pilot nodded and the two parted ways not knowing that that would be the last time they'd ever speak. Because of the added fortification, the bases on Bao combined were able to deploy at least seven hundred Ashura starfighters. Each base was equipped with several anti-air energy cannons, as well as a "Code White" detonation, in case Bao fell to the enemy. With the added firepower to take out a fleet of ships, Bao was seen as a recognizable threat by Orion, but also a delightful warm-up.

Lucas: "Alright Guardians listen up! As you all know this is a Demon ranked priority one mission. This moon has been tasked with the protection of Journia, and the redirection of Orion's forces. Now the giant ship reported has yet to be seen, but we have reason to believe that these small rocky starfighters are a part of his army. They're guarding some kind of organic object, an object that we will NOT allow to pass our blockage. Journia is OUR home, and we Guardians must protect it with our lives if need be. That being said, do not fear the end, for death is merely a necessary process for growth. Now to your ships, and may the One Infinite Creator guide your path. Adonai!"

The Guardians organized as they received their Demon ranked mission, which was to "protect Journia and halt the Orion Crusader's advance". Shortly after the mission briefing, all seven hundred Ashura fighters deployed, zooming straight for the Ryū fighters. The two opposing forces clashed, firing weapons and missiles as multiple explosions, both sizable and miniature, filled the space battle. The Obedience deactivated its cloaking technology, revealing its hellish design of death and horror. "It's him," said Jessie as she was struck with fear. Orion's ship was available for all to see, striking fear in the hearts of the Guardians, the civilian population, as well as The Nine. Orion could feel the fear; the hate, it fed him; fueled him.

The Ashura pilots were extremely skilled and managed to hold the first wave of Ryū starfighters, thus keeping the mysterious cylindrical object at bay while sustaining minimal casualties. Orion grew weary of the Ryū pilot's incompetence, and commanded Makai to take action. Following his master's command, The Mind casted a Apana Energy spell called: ***Mind Paralysis***, which allowed Makai to enter into the minds of several Guardian pilots, paralyzing them for a short time. With the spell activated, The Mind also rallied a third of the Ryū starfighters which enabled Makai to destroy a large portion of the Guardian pilots. The heavy loss by Makai forced the Guardians to fall back closer to Bao, while unintentionally clearing a path for the strange cylindrical object to advance with The Obedience fairly close behind. Following the Guardian's retreat back to Bao's outer-orbit, the moon fortress helped lighten the load by supporting the Guardian pilots with anti-air missiles, as well as providing extra energy shields to the remaining pilots. Blessed with the timely assistance, the Guardian pilots held the line and managed to deal damage to the strange object. But suddenly a strong gravitational force, fired in the middle of the space battle, pulled both Ashura and Ryū fighters into a small black hole, crushing and killing all who fell victim. The weapon, fired by The Obedience, was a tide changer and added another deadly loss. With fewer numbers, the remaining Guardian pilots retreated to Bao's surface to help defend the moon from a ground invasion. The pilots landed as the Guardians in charge completed a headcount. "Seven hundred brave Guardians were deployed to fight the Ryū fleet, only twenty-two returned" said one discouraged Guardian. Orion had no need for a quick victory and wished to make The Nine and their pets of Ashla suffer. Orion sent Ude, a.k.a The Arm, down to Bao's surface, along with five thousand corrupted soldiers and sixty four-armed Monos. The Obedience flew close to Bao's orbit, blocking the Sunlight as darkness covered the moon's surface. Because of The Obedience's close proximity, the Orion Crusaders took heavy losses from the moon base's ground-to-air missiles as small Ryū lander crafts were destroyed in the air or before they had a chance to deploy the loaded soldiers. Not all of the Ryū landers were destroyed as some made it through the heavy flak and landed, deploying the corrupted soldiers and Monos, but the Guardians were well prepared. Groups of corrupted soldiers were slain by Ashura heavy artillery as the shells of Kinetic Energy decimated The Corrupted Army, forcing the Orion Crusaders to require reinforcements. More and more corrupted soldiers poured in like a broken water dam, and after a while, their numbers eventually overwhelmed The Order's heavy artillery, rendering the long-ranged weaponry ineffective. Still the Guardians did not fold, but yet buckled down and began their ground counterattack. The Guardians of the Ashura Order charged the corrupted soldiers, shooting, slicing and blasting away, showing not fear, but determination, courage and resilience against the overwhelming numbers in a deadly game of attrition. For every Guardian, fifty corrupted soldiers were killed and the number steadily increased as the Elite ranked Guardians were no pushovers. The coordinated teamwork from each Guardian caused excitement to flood through Ude's body. Seeing that the battle had dragged on long enough, Ude joined the fight and leaped from one of the Ryū landers just as it was blown away by The Order's anti-air weapons. Ude landed against the ground with a heavy thud, creating a shockwave that pushed others aside. When he saw the chaos and death taking place around him, his muscles tensed up, his grip tightened, and his lust for blood skyrocketed. The evil warrior ran for the nearest base, commanding his soldiers to follow his command or die. As The Arm led his troops through the thickness of battle, he entered the fight, slashing Guardians in half with his two handed sword as he spearheaded the opposition, leading his small army of corrupted soldiers to victory in Orion's name. Covered in Guardian blood, Ude made his way towards base number one located fifteen miles North, at the top of the moon. As Ude continued killing all who stood in his way, he was stopped in his pursuit by the third-class Elder Guardian, named *Lucas King*. A eight foot, three hundred and eighty pound purple haired mountain of flesh and blood. His armor was aged and battle-scarred, but resilient nonetheless. He wielded a two-handed sword made from stardust and gold, which shined with power and glory. Although Lucas did not possess a strong connection to Source Energy, his incredible willpower and mental stability made him the ideal leader on the battlefield, one that was desperately needed in that crucial moment.

A few miles from base number one, Elder Lucas led his faction of a hundred and fifty Guardians against The Arm and his two thousand corrupted soldiers. The two opposing sides engaged in a bloody fight for base number one. The fight was insane as blaster bolts incinerated organs, swords cut off appendages, hammers met their targets and Energy blasts flashed like fireworks on the fourth of July. Ude was bathed in the blood of fallen Guardians as he brought his sword down upon a Guardian, splitting her in half. He proceeded to kick another Guardian hard in the chest before swinging his sword around in a crossing motion to decapitate a different Guardian. As Ude's sword came rushing to meet the next victim like a stolen car, it was met with another sword of equal size with the wielder equally matched with Ude in size and strength.

Lucas: "Woah there beast. I am Elder Lucas of the Ashura Order, and you my friend, shall prove quite the challenge. I look forward to testing my stren–"

Ude head butted Lucas, cutting his face as The Arm's sword came in swiftly and forcefully. Elder Lucas blocked the life ending blow with The Arm interrupting Lucas's humble praise.

Lucas: "I see, not much for words. Fine then.."

After blocking Ude's attack, Lucas returned by swinging his sword in an upward motion, hoping to slice the unforgivable beast, but his hopes were shattered as The Arm blocked, followed by a powerful kick to Lucas's stomach forcing the Elder to block with his sword before sliding backwards. Lucas leaped off the ground with his sword, but missed the elusive beast. Lucas returned with a horizontal swing, however the attack was blocked as The Arm counterattacked with a forward thrust motion, aimed at his opponent's chest. Lucas quickly responded by swinging his sword at a downward angle, which deflected the death-bringing blow. Seeing an opening, Lucas severed Ude's left arm, then kicked him hard in the face, ultimately cracking his pyramidal shaped helmet which forced The Arm to tumble against the ground. Following this, Ude got up to stab his large sword into the ground as a way to keep it stationary. Time seemingly froze around the two, as Ude used his one good arm to remove his damaged helmet that revealed a horribly scarred head with no eyes, but a blooded mouth masked by an electrifying grin. "You are…worrrrthyyy", said Ude in a deep tone. The two continued their duel as blows were traded, and the battle for Bao raged on with the Orion Crusaders gaining ground little by little. Ude and Elder Lucas continued their intense duel for Bao with neither side slowing down. However, despite his unshakeable willpower, Elder Lucas's body could not keep up with Ude's demonic vessel. So he reevaluated his resolve and fought till the very end.

Lucas: *panting heavily* "You are a stubborn beast, but a glorious end. TO THE DEATH THEN?!"

The Arm: *roars savagely*

Knowing Orion was watching, The Arm pounded his chest as he roared a battlecry before charging at Lucas like a furious bull. Lucas, knowing this may be the end, grabbed his sword with a tight grip, and charged straight for the scarred monster. The two clashed as a heavy shockwave shoved Guardians and corrupted soldiers aside like blowing dust off an old table. Shortly after, the dust settled, and the two warriors stood there quietly as blood dripped on the moon's surface. Ude grunted as he found Lucas's sword lodged in his side. Lucas smiled, but suddenly felt cold as he looked down to see The Arm's sword impaled in his chest; blood flowing from Lucas's mouth like a red river. Afterwards, Ude proceeded to ruthlessly pull his sword from Lucas's chest as the Elder Guardian fell to his knees. The thrilled beast looked, and pulled Lucas's sword free from his torso as he roared in pain. The Arm then raised the sword high one last time as Lucas closed his eyes and muttered the words, "in Love we come, to Light we return", before Ude brought the weapon down on Lucas's neck, decapitating the brave Elder. Soon after, Ude stabbed the sword into the ground before moving to pick up Lucas's head as he held it up high, blood dripping on Ude's chest as he began roaring at the other Guardians as a sign of weakness and disrespect before proceeding to throw it aside like unwanted trash. The remaining Guardians retreated to moon base number one located at the top of Bao to initiate Code White. This action following their retreat, allowed Orion's forces to easily advance and destroy bases one, two, and three. The Arm picked up the defeated Elder's sword as he made his way to the other bases to complete the first step in Orion's plan to destroy the Ashura Order.

The Arm: *Deep menacing voice* "Souveniiiirrrrrr."

The emergency protocol was put into action across the entire moon as bases were destroyed, Guardians were killed and Bao was at risk. Bases four and six initiated Code White shortly after base five went dark. Following the disastrous reality, the Guardians setup perimeters as the defensive type Guardians covered the front, and the hard-hitters behind them for reinforcement. Every last Guardian on Bao prepared themselves to fight to the last man, woman and alien as some found peace with the inevitable, others cried, others showed fear. Elite Jessie, knowing death was fast approaching, contacted the forces on Journia to warn them.

Jessie: "This is second-class Elite Guardian Jessie reporting from base four. We've lost contact with bases two, three, and five with the most recent loss being base one after the confirmed death of Elder Lucas. Our front line managed to deplete most of their forces both in space and the ones on Bao's surface, but there's no telling the true magnitude of their army. Their organic based technology is terrifying to say the least, but not invincible. Their commanding officer has moved to base six and his forces split off to make their way to this base. I believe they're already here, melting down the doors. Orion's forces resemble The Organics from the Galactic War, which means their technology is unique and difficult to combat against, but not impossible. Bao will soon fall, but not before we defend it with our lives and relay this message. Don't lose hope, for in Darkness, Light shines brightest. Elite Jessie out."

Death, an inescapable fact and the ugly truth. It reminds one of just how fragile life truly was, and how the goodness and beauty of life must be protected, no matter the cost. The defiant Guardians knew the end was near, but this did not deflate their will to protect the Light of life. The last remaining Guardians initiated their counterattack against the outnumbering Orion Crusaders. They made good use of mounted turrets and medium-ranged explosives to draw in the persistent threat. The enemy pushed the Guardians back into their bases with complete ease as if the Guardians purposely let them through the front door; it was all going according to plan. The Arm pushed the attack further, killing several Elite Guardians, when suddenly he was struck with an odd feeling. He was a vicious animal, who only found joy in serving Orion and combat, but he was not stupid as he knew first hand what the enemy was capable of, and for them to welcome him and his forces openly into the base spelled suspicion. After disposing of the last Guardians protecting base number six, Ude entered into the main control area where he saw and heard red and white lights flashing, added by a worrisome countdown. After a moment of thought, The Arm put the pieces together and rushed for base six's exit, pushing and shoving his soldiers aside as they mindlessly awaited new orders. He communicated the situation to The Mind demanding for him to perform a teleportation ritual to get himself away from the moon.

The Arm: *deep tone* "Makai? The Guardians have something planned. Remove me from this moon at once!"

The Mind: "Hmmm… if I let you die… that will be… one less obstacle… keeping me from my lord… Orion…"

The Arm: "This isn't the time for your games Makai. Bring me back!"

The Mind: "And if… I don't? What… will you do? You'll…be dead!" *laughs*

The Arm: "Orion will wonder what happened…what will be your answer?"

Makai paused for a moment and wondered if he could get away with murdering Ude, but after contemplating the consequences of being caught, he decided against letting Ude die.

The Mind: "It would seem… lord Orion… still has use for your…skills. Wait a moment…"

The Mind rebelliously agreed and used the blood of his test subjects to draw a circle on a rough and moist platform. Next, with a dab of Apana Energy, the portal opened showing a distorted battlefield. In all the chaos, Jessie saw The Arm making a run for some kind of portal as she feared he knew about the timed danger. She bravely fought through the grotesque four armed creatures, determined to stop The Arm from escaping his fate and to avenge Elder Lucas. Jessie hopped on one of the hover bikes and zoomed towards the fleeing monster. She fired the built-in guns mounted on the bike as several bolts of Kinetic Energy punctured Ude's left leg and stomach. The monster was brought to one knee as he roared in pain before throwing Lucas's sword at Jessie like a deadly frisbee. Jessie dived off the bike and rolled away as the convenient vehicle was obliterated by the stolen weapon. Jessie then rolled to the left, dodging another attempt on her life by the angered killer. The Elite put up a good fight as she dodged, cut and stabbed Ude, however the Guardian knew this fight, this monstrous opponent was beyond her, but still she bravely fought on. Having had enough of the games, Ude threw his own sword at Jessie, forcing her to dodge, but Ude caught the Guardian and picked her up by the throat before slamming her viciously against Bao's rocky surface, completely knocking the breath out of her and breaking her spine. Elite Jessie searched desperately for air as she ran out of options against the overpowered entity. With Jessie held high in his hand once again, Ude slammed Jessie against the ground once more before picking up his sword and savagely running the large weapon clean through Jessie's torso. Blood spilled out of her mouth and wound as Ude smiled at her in a last act of defiance.

Jessie: *coughing* " Damn, you must be…one of Orion's top pets. *coughing mixed with laughter* You wouldn't mind sticking around would you? Don't want you to miss all the 'fun'."

The Arm threw Jessie aside like a used stuffed animal as she landed by Lucas's sword. Jessie, with her last bit of strength, grabbed the sword and held it close as she took her last moments. Shortly after, Ude, bloodied and injured, limped into Makai's portal.

Jessie: *cough* "Who would've thought I'd…die here. *cough* Everything is so…quiet…now. *cough* Hopefully I *coughs* bought enough time to…to avenge…Lucas…m-my brother…"

Elite Jessie stared off into space, laying down on the moon's rocky surface with her older brother Lucas's sword in hand. Blood leaked continuously from her stomach as her body fought desperately to keep the wounded Guardian alive, but to no avail. Jessie closed her eyes and took her last breath as the remaining bases exploded around her corpse. The explosions had set off a chain reaction, which led to the moon's core, causing the entire moon to explode in a violent blast of Kinetic Energy. As a result, the detonation killed all of Orion's forces as well as every Guardian present on Bao. The shockwave from the blast sent thousands of pieces of the moon, both a threatening size and laughable pebble, hurdling in every direction with planet-destroying velocity, including towards Journia and The Obedience. The planet's shields however, held strong as chunks of Bao crashed against the shield before breaking into smaller pieces like throwing glass against a stone wall. The people and Guardians of Journia mourned and commended the courageous sacrifice of the Guardians on Bao, hoping that Orion and The Obedience were caught in the blast and destroyed. Following the flash of light from Bao's detonation, the planet prematurely celebrated their victory and honored the lives lost to achieve it, but the time of happiness was short lived as the strange cylinder shaped object protected by the Ryū starfighters worked as a maneuverable shield generator, which protected The Obedience from such a devastating and destructive blow. It almost felt like Orion knew about the possibility of Bao being used as a giant bomb to stop him from reaching the planet's surface.

"Now then, shall we have some fun", said the arrogant entity. The Obedience engaged its gravity thrusters, flying towards Journia like an unstoppable train. Guardians on the surface geared up and readied several star cruisers for planetary evacuation, while brave civilians helped to mitigate mass hysteria among the majority. They led other civilians to safe waiting areas, effectively clearing the population, but people were scared and tension was high. Sarvis and Mos-Dia were cleared out, locked down and made into battlegrounds with hidden explosives planted within the outer towns, and gates were closed with energy turrets charged, and shields generated to protect the inner cities. Most of Journia's population were put into refugee camps hidden within the desert region housing Raito's hometown of Zotune, and within the mountain terrain of Mara as "waiting areas", while other civilians were already evacuated off-world. Each camp had a small army of Paladin ranked Guardians with five hundred personnel on watch, and one hundred Acolyte ranked Guardians stationed at each camp to reinforce and to act as leadership. In terms of experienced manpower, Journia was severely lacking because ninety-eight percent of all Elder ranked Guardians were off world protecting key regions of the galaxy or died fighting the Orion Crusaders on other planets, and all Elite ranked Guardians were either on the surface reinforcing the battlefront, off-world racing back to Journia or died fighting in the battle of Bao. Despite the early warning but late preparation, The Order's time of successful peace and blissful stagnation had indeed left the organization soft and out-of-shape. They were not prepared for Orion's return; for his power, or his army of corrupted beings, but that didn't halt Orion's advance as his worldship approached Journia's outer-orbit, where it seemed the Orion Crusaders would be met with more resistance.

Upon reaching the outskirts of Journia's outer-orbit, The Obedience was met by third-class Elder Guardian **Rachel Rose**, a five-foot five red skinned alien female with human features, golden yellow eyes, shiny soft skin and short dark red-colored hair that had been put in a pony-tail, along with a small red and black horn protruding from her forehead. She utilized support magic and protection spells fueled by Cosmic Energy. She was joined by her faction leader, first-class Elder Guardian **Matthew McCorvin**, a tall and skinny human male who was mentally gifted by Cosmic Energy, making him a strategic genius. Together, the Elders formed The Order's second blockade of starcraft carriers, support cruisers, battleships and two enormous dreadnoughts which acted as the Elder's individual flag ships. The fleet was massive as combined they deployed over twelve hundred spacecraft, both large and small, manned by ten thousand Guardians, mostly of the Paladin and Acolyte rank. The young Guardians looked on at the gigantic enemy worldship with fear penetrating their hearts, but suddenly a voice could be heard through all radio channels as Elder Rachel enlightened the fleet.

Rachel: "Steady your hearts and calm your nerves my fellow Guardians. The enemy may be powerful, but they lack compassion and the burning motivation to protect what they Love. We don't fight for ourselves, but for our fallen, for our comrades, our families, OUR PLANET! We will NOT be so easily defeated for we embody the teachings of Source Energy through the discipline of Ashla. Now, with me Guardians! And let us serve the Creator with Love and courage!"

Elder Rachel's words sparked a fire under the fleet with even Matthew feeling a sudden burst of determination. Elder Matt took the lead and sent twenty battleships in first to draw in most of the damage, which provided cover to the smaller starfighters as they flew in and attacked The Obedience directly. Matt followed behind the attack with his dreadnought and support cruisers offsetted on both sides of his command ship. These medium-sized craft acted as support spacecraft, providing extra shield strength and faster weapon cool downs. Elder Rachel, using her command of Cosmic Energy, performed a support spell called: *Battle Meditation*, which granted an increase in focus and calmness throughout the entire fleet, as well as allowing Elder Matthew to make more precise and calculated decisions under pressure. Rachel's spell proved fruitful as the fleet managed to hold Orion's Ryū fleet while keeping casualties at a hurtful minimum losing only eight battleships, but an undesired two-thirds of their starfighters to the enemy.

Orion: *sigh* "These Elder ranked Guardians are proving quite tiresome. I see now to break the Ashura Order of today, we must eliminate these...Elders.

Despite the damage to The Obedience, Orion pushed straight for Journia while taking the heat from the fleet, but dishing out its own damage as well. As the false god drew closer to Rachel's command vessel, he felt a strangely familiar Energy signature... one he hasn't felt since becoming Orion. He was shocked, and took a moment to summon Makai to his chamber.

The Mind: "Yes...my lord?"

Orion: "I have a task for you. You are to infiltrate that dreadnought and capture anyone with red skin and a horn. Bring them aboard my ship and do not delay. Do this and you'll have proven yourself once again. Take Hando with you, he's rested long enough."

The Mind: "As you command…my master…"

The Obedience used its black hole technology as a tractor beam to pull Rachel's massive dreadnought closer in order for Makai and Hando to enter. As that happened, Elder Matt saw and understood Orion's target. The Guardian quickly requested nine battleships to fire their heavy cannons at the enemy ship which, on impact, disrupted The Obedience's connection to Elder Rachel's dreadnought, preventing Makai and Hando from boarding. Orion grew weary of the constant delays, so the false god used his own Black Aura to empower The Obedience's weapons. Shortly after, Orion commanded the pilots of his ship to fire The Black Launcher to which they happily obeyed. The Ashura Order fleet began receiving warnings, indicating a spike in Energy from the enemy. This fact was further confirmed after the Guardians witnessed The Obedience fire a focused black beam which birthed a small visible sphere of gravity. This small rotating ball of violent Kinetic Energy expanded before gaining enough mass and gravity, which pulled and crushed all Ashura spacecraft and Ryū fighters within its radius. This weaponized black hole destroyed almost the entirety of the Guardian's fleet in an instant, but left The Obedience in a state of exhaustion due to Orion overwhelming his ship's energy regulators. When the smoke cleared, only seven battleships and two support cruisers remained operational, as well as both Elder Matt and Elder Rachel's dreadnoughts. However, every starfighter perished which in turn forced Matt to rethink his entire strategy.

Matt: "Damn it. We lost most of our entire fleet and all of our starfighters from just one of the Orion Crusaders' attack runs. How can one entity; one ship, possess this much power? I have to find a way to permanently disabled his ship and fast……That's it! Orion's arrogance and greed will be his downfall."

Elder Matt contacted three of the seven remaining battleships and Elder Rachel with his risky plan. With it, he hoped it would provide time and space to regroup and to recover, while also forcing the enemy to go on the defensive. He requested Rachel to act as bait, and gain the attention of Orion so he'd pursue her without delay. At the same time, Matt orchestrated the evacuation of one of the three selected battleships involved with the plan. Rachel was unsure as to what Matt was thinking, but nonetheless agreed as she trusted her comrade. Rachel's command ship took a few shots at The Obedience, taunting the huge worldship and its captain. Blinded by this familiar sensation, Orion followed Rachel oblivious to the trap set before him. The Obedience once again activated the tractor beam to commence the capture of the mystery entity that had Orion's attention. But suddenly his ship was attacked and heavily bombarded by two battleships as they unloaded everything from heavy laser cannons to ballistic energy missiles. They were also joined by the firepower of Elder Matt's dreadnought. The Guardians spared no weaponized Kinetic Energy as they wish to end this monstrosity. Orion was surprised by the Elder Guardian's plan and returned fire, destroying one of the two battleships and heavily damaging the other before he felt an odd sensation. "Somethings wrong," said the self-proclaimed god as the third battleship came in at full speed before colliding directly into the underbelly of The Obedience in a ginormous explosion. The ship was crippled and temporarily disabled as a crater, thirty feet wide, revealed the inside of the hellish spacecraft, while also damaging the ship's underbelly tentacles. The vacuum of space sucked out corrupted soldiers by the thousands, leaving Orion with a broken ship, without Rachel and with fury pulsating like waves constantly crashing against a mountain.

Luna: "Doesn't feel good, does it? Your downfall is only just beginning, you monster."

Orion was not in the mood for Elder Luna's slimy comments and slapped the Guardian hard across the face.

Luna: *grunts and spits out blood* "Well someone's angry."

The battered fleet used this opportunity to return closer to Journia's orbit in order to regroup and to allow Matt to mentally regroup so as to formulate another plan.

Matt: "Rachel's dreadnought, two support cruisers, and four battleships, with one badly damaged. The casualties are too high, but we managed to cripple the enemy ship, hopefully permanently, and buy more time for the ground forces to complete their fortification, as well as to increase the window of time for other Elders and Elites to arrive. Should we wait for backup or should we take the forces present and pursue the already damaged ship?"

Elder Matt's mind raced uncontrollably as he assessed the critical situation, but his attention suddenly focused as the recently thought crippled worldship sped towards the planet. With no time to think, Matt ordered all remaining ships to unload every weapon they had and asked Rachel to perform her Battle Meditation spell, but nothing seemed to be working as the enemy's ship fought through the weaponized Kinetic Energy. The Ashura fleet continued to fire, but after a powerful series of attacks and explosions, the ship's weapons overheated and energy among the fleet was low. However, that didn't stop The Obedience from gaining space. Upon further inspection, the Guardians witnessed a dense Black Aura protecting the ship as well as giving it propulsion. Unsatisfied with his reality, Elder Matthew realized what he must do; what he must sacrifice to protect his home of Journia.

Matt: "Rachel, I need you to take our remaining forces and return to the surface."

Rachel: "This isn't the time to be heroic."

Matt: *soft chuckle* "You belong on the ground where your support and protection spells can be used properly. Your story cannot and will not end here. Besides, everyone knows I'm not the best with physical battles. My talent lies up here, among the stars."

Rachel: "Matt we need your—"

Matt: "I'm not going to let this asshole kill us both, now GO!"

Following Elder Matthew's heroism, Rachel was seen combatively flying back to the surface alone as the surviving fleet stayed behind to further defend the planet.

Matt: "If anyone wants to return, now's your chance because this is a one way trip."

Acolyte Pilot: "We're with you to the end commander."

Matt: "Well alright. Let's shine some Light on this cockroach!"

Elder Matt and the fleet headed straight for the incoming worldship as they diverted the remaining energy to the weapons and thrusters, using everything to further damage the massive vessel before them. The Obedience, still aimed towards Journia, returned fire destroying both support craft, leaving only four battleships and Matt's dreadnought operational.

Orion: "I've had enough of these petty space confrontations and this inferior fleet. You cannot stop the unstoppable!!"

The two sides closed in on each other with Orion destroying one more battleship and crippling Matt's dreadnought vessel. Though draining even for Orion, the false god kept up the Black protective Aura around The Obedience, enabling the worldship and its crew to continue firing upon The Order. As Elder Matt drew closer to The Obedience, he began reminiscing, and wished he could see Journia's beautiful green forest and lively cities one last time. The smell of grilled food; the sight of the beautiful colors as one flew over the cities at night. The calmness of the forest regions and the vastness of Journia's mighty oceans. He wished to see his wife, Sarah, one more time, but despite these wishes, Elder Matthew found peace with his reality and whispered under his breath… "forgive me Sarah", before crashing his ship nose first straight into The

Obedience with the surviving battleships adding to the tremendous explosion. The shockwave pushed Bao's rocky remains deeper into space as the blinding light could be mistaken for the Sun. Elder Rachel landed on the surface before looking to see the massive explosion. She proceeded to close her eyes as rage fueled her determination. The people and Guardians all stopped what they were doing to witness what they thought was finally the end, but their hopes were shattered by a loud and deep humming sound. A young child pointed towards the sky, grabbing the attention of most adults and Guardians in the area. "Look, it's a flaming box in the sky," said the child. Though correct, this was no ordinary flaming box, for it was The Obedience penetrating the atmosphere. The ship broke through the sound barrier and came down hard on Journia's damaged inner-planetary shield, cracking it before shattering it as the ship crashed down on Journia's surface in a forest close to Nalmoth. The population screamed in utter fear as some people took their own life's, while others broke down and cried out for the Creator. "The end is here and we've been judged!" Said one man. "How could one ship destroy the entire Ashura fleet?! We're all going to die!" Said another. The Guardians were beginning to lose control of the situation as the population panicked.

Over by Nalmoth, the forest was completely destroyed and burned by The Obedience's crash landing. The massive vessel was left smoking and heavily damaged from the Ashura Order's fleet, and Elder Matt's plan which made Orion command a status report.

Orion: "Pilot. What is the status of my ship?"

Obedience pilot: "My lord, the outer-hull's integrity has been compromised which will make space travel difficult. The weapon systems, detention level, birthing chamber, and the underbelly tentacles have all been damaged. With the vital Source Energy levels of this planet, repairs should be completed in a few hours my lord."

Orion: "Very good. You may proceed."

Obedience pilot: "By your command my lord."

An opening was created to which Orion levitated out of the ship gracefully before brushing off the dust present on his shoulder. Shortly after, The Obedience embedded itself into the surface of Journia with its damaged tentacles before stealing, and utilizing the vital Source Energy of the planet to repair the damage done. Hando, Ude and Makai exited the recovering vessel and kneeled before their lord, awaiting his command.

Orion: "If that intel was correct, Ude you will venture to Solla. Burn it down and bring back any who you deem worthy to serve me. Do not delay. Hando, you will travel to Mos-Dia, destroy it and kill any Guardians you see, Elders especially. And Makai, You and I will leave for Sarvis, I wish to be reunited with the Council of The Nine."

All three warriors bowed with tremendous respect before splitting off to complete their tasks. Makai and Hando commanded twenty-five thousand corrupted soldiers, two Walkers and a hundred four-armed Monos each, while Ude commanded only a few hundred corrupted soldiers and a hundred Monos. Though a small fraction of the Orion Crusaders' true might, to Orion, it was more than enough to conquer the planet and put an end to the Ashura Order, and to the Way of Ashla forever...

FIVE

JOURNIA

Anxiety and gloom overflowed the Hercules as the faction of Elders prepared to exit hyperspace. Elders Vinzent and Nico sat within the crew's quarters, participating in a calming meditation session while Elders Raito and Cass, against their best efforts, failed to contact Journia after receiving a Demon mission alert from the head of the department of communication, Elite Jessie. However, it seemed as if communications incoming and out-going from the planet had completely ceased. Believing in Raito's technical skills, Elder Cass left Raito to continue searching for some sort of signal. She headed down to the bottom level of the Hercules to complete a maintenance checklist on the MT-AT. She managed to rotate all four tires, check the MT-AT's outer-armor integrity and update all the computer systems before completing the checklist. Afterwards, the Elder took a minute to herself to reminisce about her past, about her life with Nico, about her time as a Paladin. A time when Rex, Kicks, Nico and herself trained together. A relatively peaceful time where Kicks and Nico fought for the number one spot within the Guardian academy. Cass was lost within her daydream, wishing it to be her reality, but her fairytale from the past was cut short as Jasmine, the AI, alerted the faction of their exiting from hyperspace.

Jasmine: "Guardians, we are coming out of hyperspace. This would be a pretty good time to prepare yourselves. I haven't been able to make contact with the DSR, Bao or Journia. This isn't looking good…"

Following Jasmine's warning, the Hercules popped out of lightspeed like a speeding car coming to a sudden stop. Traversing their home planet's star system, the Elders were traumatized by the destruction of Bao. The disastrously distorted moon was left in ruin with millions of pieces scattered across space, like a glass vase shattering never to be the same again. With Nico in control of the ship, he carefully navigated through thousands of dead Guardians and corrupted soldiers, searching for Guardian survivors while maintaining defense protocols in case of lurking enemies. The experienced faction moved closer to Journia's outer-orbit as they pushed past a starship graveyard, filled with Ashura ships torn apart and destroyed. Elders Vinzent, Cass, Raito and Nico observed a blue and silver eagle and recognized it as Elder Matt's faction symbol. A chunk of his ship's underbelly floating through the cold and endless sea of space and time. The Guardians knew what had happened; who had come.

As the Elders assessed the situation, they were interrupted by three faint, but clear distress calls originating from Sarvis, Mos-Dia and Solla. Without delay, Nico punched the thrusters and sped past the horrifying battle scene. The high speed spacecraft raced towards Journia's orbit, entering the atmosphere before breaking through the stratosphere. Pushing past the unsettling black clouds, a massive forest fire was seen from twenty-two kilometers in the air. Smoke covered the sky like putting up a blanket to block the Sunlight, giving way to incredulity from the trained Elders. Disgusted and enraged by what he saw, Nico relinquished the ship's controls to Jasmine before telling her to drop him off, but his demand was met with resistance.

Nico: "Jasmine, I need you to drop me off at Solla."

Raito: "Don't lose yourself Nico. We are stronger together and right now, Sarvis is our priority."

Nico: "With respect Raito, it wasn't a request."

Refusing to lose anymore comrades; anymore cherished friends or loved ones, Cass grabbed Nico in her attempts to show him the value in togetherness and the strength of unity, but her reasonable words fell short.

Cass: "Nico calm yourself and think about this. Orion and his goons have had the upper-hand because of our separation. Kicks, Rex, Lucas, Matt, they were alone because they had to be, but we're strongest together and you know that! Don't be so easily swayed by your emotions! I can't lose you too."

Nico: "Thank you for your concern and I hear you, but Cass, who would've thought it'd get this far? Who would've thought The Order would be brought to its knees in such a way? Even after the Galactic War. And now my home burns, my village…burns. I can't sit here and consciously watch my adopted home set ablaze, knowing I have the strength and experience now to do something about it. You of all people should know how I feel about this; how I feel about losing a home. The Love and the Light from the One Infinite Creator hasn't failed us yet, and I believe my path continues this way. Don't worry my love, if the Creator wills it so, we shall meet again."

The two shared a loving embrace before breaking away to save their world.

Nico: "Meet you on the other side?"

Vinzent: "I'll be waiting for ya."

Raito: "Don't be stupid."

Nico: "Well if I am, just know I got it from you. Override code: T Nico 04."

Elder Nico stared down at an injured Journia through the opened airlock on the starboard side of the ship. He leaped outside as he dove from the Hercules, seventeen kilometers in the air, heading straight for his hometown. Cass attached a water-made parachute to him as he shot through the thick ash like a comet rushing through the sky. The Elder used the parachute to slow his descent before the water evaporated, allowing the Guardian to flip off trees in order to cushion the speeding impact. He landed on the ground, causing a small shockwave before sprinting and leaping great bounds towards Solla…

Meanwhile aboard The Hercules, Elders Vinzent and Raito came up with a plan to secure the other distress calls.

Vinzent: "With Nico gone to handle the Solla call, that leaves Sarvis and Mos-Dia."

Raito: "We all agree that Sarvis is still priority number one right? We can't afford to lose anyone else to their 'paths'."

Vinzent: "We can't allow Mos-Dia to fall…I can't allow that. Say what you want Raito, but Nico had a point. To just let my home perish without even trying…I'd have no right to call myself a Guardian. Besides, we received word that Sarvis and Mos-Dia were being turned into battlegrounds. It's only natural that we or I, go and reinforce."

Raito: *sigh* "I respect your point of view, I would feel the same if it were Zotune or Mahō. So what's the plan?"

Vinzent: "I will go to Mos-Dia to ensure that the evacuation is completed and to provide backup against the enemy. That leaves Sarvis for you two. Secure the city, then regroup with me in Mos-Dia. We must not let the Ashura Order fall. For the galaxy, for the Universe."

With their plan in motion, the three Elders flew for Mos-Dia. Upon entering the low atmosphere of the battleground, the Elders were surprised by shots from The Hand's forces which had already gained a worrisome amount of terrain against the defending Guardians. Hando's force rallied behind two large war-beasts which acted as walls of complete chaos.

These beasts were a genetic combination between a rhino and a gorilla; an experiment by Makai. These walking piles of carnage stood sixty-five feet tall, and weighed two tons of muscle. Their maroon red, stone-like skin protected them from most Kinetic Energy based attacks, and their ability to project balls of gravity made them a formidable long-ranged foe. When these gravity-based attacks met with its intended target, it released a burst of gravity that pushed then pulled, crushing anything within the blast radius which in turn made them the ideal tool for anti-ground assaults. They were given the name **Walkers**, because of their habit of walking straight through any and all who opposed Orion.

These Walkers looked to the skies as they took aim at the Hercules, firing with the intent to kill. The Hercules quickly responded by barrel rolling to the right before flying over the two assaulting war-beasts. Raito commenced a ground assault against the Walkers, dropping bombs on top of them which injured one of the beasts. The blast radius also took out a few hundred of the invading corrupted soldiers, easing the burden for the Elite Guardians on the ground. Hando was unfazed by the loss of his forces, and pushed onward towards the city of Mos-Dia to complete the given task by his master. The Hand's forces however, were met by more hidden explosives planted within the outer cities that damaged the previously injured walker, forcing it to the ground as it roared in pain. With a break in the enemy's formation, the Guardians on the ground pushed the enemy front, blasting and coordinating their attacks as they killed the second Walker and decimated thousands of Hando's soldiers. Following The Order's push, the Hercules doubled back, firing multiple shots into the first downed Walker's chest with the violent Kinetic Energy blasts breaching the stone-like skin, killing it. After the death of both Walkers, the Hercules descended safely behind Guardian lines allowing Elder Raito to perform a quick land-n-go. The Guardians, with the help of the Hercules, were successful in protecting the second largest city from the first wave of evil that invaded their homeworld. With The Hand's forces temporarily halted, the ship landed to drop off Elder Vinzent as Elders Raito and Casanova peeled off to protect Sarvis...

A few hundred miles away, just outside the forest village of Solla, Nico squatted in a tree undetected as a platoon of corrupted soldiers walked the forest trails, searching and killing anything that moved. The ten soldiers were unaware and ignorant of the lurking Elder high up in the trees above. Following their movement, Nico found a sturdy tree branch and crafted three sharp wooden sticks from it before throwing them with force and precision. The coarse blades pierced the heads of the three intended targets, cutting their enslaved life short. Confused and on alert, the seven remaining soldiers formed a circular shape to cover all points but one. Nico leaped in the air and utilized his Solar Mutation ability as the marigold-orange color of his mutated markings brightened.

Upon activation, the muscle-fibers in Nico's right arm amplified and strengthened, allowing multiple fibers to burst free from his body's opened pores and overlap his arm, like a snake wrapping and squeezing its prey. This allowed his amplified arm to mutate and form an elongated double-ended blade below the elbow. This sharp and deadly mutation would be called: Jūken. The Elder could also dual-wield this ability, which formed single-ended blades that mutate, replacing both hands a few inches above the wrist.

The Elder brought the Jūken blade down, splitting one corrupted soldier clean down the middle as blood gushed from the opened corpse. Shortly after, Nico kicked another soldier hard through a tree, breaking its spine before slicing a different soldier across the torso, killing it. The four remaining corrupted soldiers fired their organic rifles, but the Guardian instinctively responded by amplifying, then mutating his left arm into a thick medium-sized shield of hardened muscle-fibers. This collection of, harder than steel, muscle-fibers would be called: *Mamoru*. With the Mamoru shield active, all incoming blaster bolts were blocked and absorbed. Realizing their efforts were in vain, they ceased fire, giving Nico the opportunity to swiftly thrust one soldier in the chest with his Jūken blade before bashing his protective Mamoru shield into another soldier, ending both of their lives. Following this,

Elder Nico quickly mutated both amplified arms into the Hari whip to catch and choke the two remaining soldiers, closing the gap as the grip from the whips snapped and crushed their necks. Dropping their lifeless corpses like a bad habit, the enraged Taiyōnian released the Hari whips and retracted the visible muscle-fibers back into his pores, enabling his appendages to revert back to normal. Nico then found and approached the defeated corrupted soldier he kicked through a tree moments ago. Walking towards the enslaved being, the Elder used his bare hand to lift and choke the last remaining soldier with ease as a way of interrogation.

Nico: "Why have you come?! What is your objective?! Speak!"

The corrupted individual gave the Guardian a twisted grin and yelled, "FOR ORION", before glowing in a beautiful yellow glow, exploding in Nico's face. The blast could be seen from a mile away as it caught the attention of The Arm who in return, commanded forty of his four-armed Monos to investigate. At that range, the blast would've killed most Guardians, but Nico wasn't "most" Guardians as he lifted rocks and broken trees off of himself. He then reverted his left arm back to normal, releasing the Mamoru shield as his muscle-fibers softened and retracted back into his pores, like a sponge soaking up water. "A second later and that would've taken forever to regenerate from. The Creator is generous and will guide me", said the cautious Guardian. With his new found alertness, Nico pushed on to Solla to help in any way he could…

As Nico continued his lone mission, Raito, Cass and Jasmine approached Sarvis to help push back Orion and his forces of death and Darkness. The Elders flew the Hercules closer to the battle, but were under attack by two Walkers as they shot balls of visible gravity at the elusive spacecraft. Those aboard the Hercules were now confident against the slow and bulky Walkers, however, that feeling was short-lived after the Hercules violently buckled, leading to the ship's monitors being filled with damage alerts. After taking a closer look, Raito realized that they were hit with a hefty blast of Apana Energy, but not from the Walkers. Following this realization, Elder Raito was forced to dodged two more blasts of destructive Apana Energy. Raito's quick reaction saved the ship from total destruction, but didn't seem to help them escape unharmed as the stabilizing thrusters were critically damaged from the first attack. With two thrusters completely inoperable, and another barely able to hold a flame, the ship was seen struggling to stay afloat as a trail of smoke and fire followed the ship like baby ducks following their mother. Raito told Cass to prepare the MT-AT for an emergency departure, and for Jasmine to initiate back-to-home protocols which granted Jasmine access to fly the ship, if able, back to the faction's base in Mara. The two reluctantly complied as Elder Cass stumbled to the MT-AT for a quick activation, while Jasmine converted the emergency power to the shields and operable thrusters. At the same moment, Raito gave the controls to Jasmine and rushed to join Casanova aboard the MT-AT. Secured and ready, Jasmine kept the ship steady as best she could before quickly opening the Hercules's cargo bay. Following this, Cass and Raito promptly drove the MT-AT from the Hercules in mid-air, giving Jasmine the greenlight to fly the broken ship back to the base for repairs.

Descending from the sky, Cass used the land tank's weapons to fire against the Orion Crusaders which destroyed a few chunks of corrupted soldiers, while simultaneously using the anti-air missiles against the Walkers, obliterating one along with more of Orion's soldiers. The enemy pointed up towards the falling tank, blasting their organic rifles against the armored vehicle, but their shots bounced off like tennis balls ricocheting off a wall. The MT-AT then activated the outer-shields to lessen the damage taken before slamming against the planet's surface. Afterwards, the two Elders gathered themselves and traveled a very short distance to reinforce the battlefront. Once there, they took the lead and provided much needed cover to the Guardians on the ground. Jasmine informed the faction the ship could be fixed back at their main base in the mountain lands of Mara. However, with Nico radio silent and Vinzent protecting Mos-Dia from Hando's second wave, that left Raito and Cass, but they were busy helping repel the enemy in Sarvis. Raito quickly confirmed the ship's situation, but couldn't afford to waste anymore time as they were engaged in a deadly firefight. As the Ashura Order fought to protect Sarvis, they looked at their opposition with a disturbing sensation as they saw the number of corrupted soldiers pouring in, along with one hundred four-armed demons who fought without remorse. One walker was protected from the MT-AT by an awkward floating, skull face being given the name Makai, but there was another entity towards the rear, levitating gracefully like a leaf flowing with the wind. His Black Aura penetrated and burned the lungs of the weak, his three red and black horns commanded mystery, and his heavy noticeable presence bred a sense of dismay. This being…was Orion, the self-proclaimed "God of Darkness".

Back in the city of Mos-Dia, the ground began to rumble as the second wave of enemies marched towards the inner city gates. As Hando led his reinforcements straight for the Guardians, Elder Vinzent used the opportunity to concentrate and generate his Red Aura. The dense flow of red mist empowered Vinzent's Elemental Energy, permitting the Elder to manifest a tangible bolt of lightning. Vinzent grabbed hold of the bolt and added the explosive nature of his Orange Aura. The bolt popped and crackled with power, catching the attention of Hando.

Vinzent: "Come Guardians. Let us protect our home. Elemental Energy: *Explosive Bolt!*"

Elder Vinzent threw the bolt directly for The Hand which on impact, caused a massive explosion, as well as bursts of lightning that temporarily paralyzed groups of corrupted soldiers. The fellow Guardians by Vinzent's side were amazed by the power a single Elder possessed, and found solace in Elder Vinzent's strength and calmness. Following Vinzent's attack, Hando managed to survive, but not unscathed as the blast threw him into a building; smoke leaving his body like burnt buns from the oven. The strike from Vinzent proved too much for the eleven foot giant, but nonetheless, he recovered and pushed forward with his remaining forces, sprinting towards the Guardian's line of defense.

Vinzent: "I see he's gonna need a little bit more persuading. Guardians form up! The enemy approaches!"

Unwilling to bend to Orion's will, the Guardians formed up under Elder Vinzent's command to repel the enemy. Offensive Guardians took to the rear behind the defensive Guardians. Shields were charged and Energy levels were stable. Following the enemy passing the point of no return, blaster rifles were fired and more explosions tore through the battlefield. The enemy soldiers continuously shot and sprinted towards victory, screaming and roaring like entities with nothing to lose. The shields of the defense-style Guardians held strong against the Orion Crusaders as they used their combined Ashla teachings and willpower to strengthen the shield. The offense-style Guardians sent forth massive blasts of Elemental, Cosmic, and Kinetic Energy, which were greatly reinforced by Vinzent's Elemental Energy.

Vinzent: "Let us show these demons the strength of Guardians!"

Following the Guardians utilizing their individual Energy types, Vinzent orchestrated the combination of all the Energy types present, thus creating an enormous blast of Ashla fueled Source Energy. With the combined power of the Elite Guardians and Elder Vinzent, they successfully annihilated the rest of The Hand's assigned Walkers, as well as two-thirds of his corrupted soldiers. The blast of Ashla based Source Energy was so pure and incredible that it laid waste to thousands of soldiers like a blanket of Light, covering a Dark and bristly bed. The attack demolished most of the soldiers and outer city buildings, leaving nothing, but rubble from destroyed buildings and melted bodies of the enemy. Given the devastating blow, Hando's troops seemingly halted their advance as the Guardians began forming another major blast, when suddenly a heavy THOOM shook the battleground and interrupted their concentration. A flood of unrest rushed through the Guardians like a flash flood. The attack ultimately caught the Guardians off guard, and as the dust settled, The Hand's giant hammer was seen embedded in the ground as several Guardians laid dead under or beside it. Blood was everywhere as some Guardians laid there with their limbs crushed, others killed by the shockwave. Vinzent however, recovered and kept a leveled head through the chaos. The Elder proceeded to generate his soft and steady *Green Aura* to heal and stabilize those he could. However, without time to thoroughly process the damage, the Guardians were flanked from the sides and rear by the grotesque four-armed Monos. As a result, the Monos slaughtered a respectable chunk of the Elites due to their well-timed attack, empowered Bogan bodies and Hando's leadership.

Elite Guardian: "Elder Vinzent, there are too many of them and too many injured Guardians. At this rate, we'll be overrun!"

Unwilling to let his city fall, Vinzent dug deep within himself, and reevaluated his resolve. In a powerful show of determination and Elemental Energy, the Elder generated a powerful field of *Violet Aura* around himself before sending a dominant burst of Violet lightning rushing into the ground, which disintegrated all of the flanking enemy units. The save by Vinzent allowed the remaining Guardians left alive to retreat into the center of the city for a last stand as Vinzent covered the retreat by firing streams of lightning. With some distance between them and the enemy, Elder Vinzent took charge once again and bravely readied and led his fellow Guardian comrades to what may be their last service to the Creator.

Vinzent: "This is it. This is our last chance to defend Mos-Dia and secure this region of the world. We have lost many brothers and sisters to get to this moment, but there is still hope while we breathe; while we stand with the Creator, here and now!"

Off in the distance The Hand walked through the smoke and fire, dragging his large hammer as he approached Elder Vinzent and his brave Guardians. Six Monos and several hundred corrupted soldiers followed behind Hando, but the Guardians did not show fear nor intimidation as they, led by first-class Elder Guardian Vinzent, stood ready to achieve victory or join the Creator...

Elsewhere deep in Solla's local forest, Elder Nico heard multiple life forms close to his position. With too many to count, he leaped high in the trees and onto a branch. The enemy revealed themselves as multiple grotesque Monos as they searched the area of the explosion and the surrounding area, passing under the Guardian. Nico calmed his nerves and realized that attacking the enemy head on again, while they've been alerted, wasn't smart; he needed more information. So he waited for the four-armed, charcoal colored monsters to report back to their leader, and as they did so, Nico followed several feet away, hopping and flipping from tree branch to tree branch, hoping to get answers. His solo reconnaissance mission led him to the heart of Solla as Nico looked at his burning village with fury and horror. His nightmare from his previous meditation session undesirably came into reality. His hometown was in flames, buildings were either completely destroyed or had been ransacked. Bodies of the villagers were scattered across the ground like spilled cereal covering the kitchen floor. Nico saw a being, a towering figure with scars all over his body. The corrupted soldiers called him "The Arm". Against his better judgment, Nico stood on the tree branch before amplifying his body, and mutating both arms into dual Jūken blades. The Elder readied himself to recklessly risk it all, but got a well-timed transmission from an unexpected intelligence.

Jasmine: "I know what you're thinking and it's not a good idea…"

Nico: "I can't just let them burn my home and slaughter the people of Solla without even fighting Jazz! Not again!"

Jasmine: "So what are you gonna do? Fight off hundreds of Orion's bootlickers and one nasty looking ass-kisser? What if you're captured? Or you run out of Solar Energy? I don't know if you noticed, but the Sun is covered ya know. Stop, breathe and think. You're always jumping into situations either without thinking or without backup, and one day you'll find yourself in a situation you can't regenerate from. You will have your chance Nico, but right now Vinzent needs your help."

Nico: *deep breath* "You're right Jazz, I-I'm sorry. When the time comes, The Arm will pay for his transgressions."

Jasmine: "And I won't stop you. Just be ready and clear Nico."

With Jasmine's words of wisdom, Nico made for Mos-Dia as fast as he could, but not before bowing one last time to his people in respect for those he's lost. Shortly after bowing, Elder Nico channeled the Solar Energy from within his cells to a single point on both hands. The heated Solar Energy swirled in his hands, becoming increasingly dense and solid and formed two solar powered explosives. These two grapefruit-sized, sticky piles of pure Solar Energy, glowed brilliantly despite the blazing Sun currently covered by a sea of ash. This ability would be known as: ***Bakudan***. With time of the essence, the Guardian swiftly threw both bombs, sticking them on trees that surrounded the invading force. Afterwards, Nico amplified the muscle strength of his legs and dashed into the forest with great velocity, detonating the Bakudan bombs. Two large explosions caused several large trees to fall on The Arm, his soldiers, and the already destroyed village of Solla, crushing roughly three hundred and fifty-two of his small army of six hundred. Jasmine replied by saying "really" as Nico smiled while swinging and parkouring from branch to branch with his Hari whip mutation, and towards his overwhelmed comrade…

Elsewhere at Journia's capital city, the battle was bloody and full of Source Energy as Elder Raito and Elder Casanova, backed by Elder Rachel, and the remaining Elite Guardians, fought valiantly to protect Sarvis and The Order's HQ from Makai and his army. Orion merely watched the carnage in amusement. Cass led the Elites as they were caught in a brutal firefight against the persistent corrupted soldiers. Elder Cass sliced and diced with power, focus and precision, using both her katana and her gifted sword from Zora. She then used her katana and command of Elemental Energy to carve a symbol in the ground which then lit up in a sky-blue hue. Shortly after, a water gate opened which unleashed a ten foot octopus, made from water and ice, that wreaked havoc upon the Orion Crusaders. Guardians beside her admired the Source Energy of an Elder and followed suit, blasting, slicing and laying down their life's for the Light without fear, remorse, or hesitation.

Explosions filled the battleground like sand in the desert as Elder Raito fired the MT-AT's heavy cannons, blowing up pockets of enemies and chipping away at the Walkers. Annoyed, The Mind casted a small purple flame that seeked and attached itself to the outer-shell of the MT-AT's shield. Moments passed before a clamorous BOOM shook the battleground and the surrounding area around Sarvis. Makai's explosive of Apana Energy caused a colossal sized explosion that erased half of the Guardians protecting Sarvis, melted Cass's water octopus, and tremendously damaged the beloved MT-AT. However, Raito stumbled out of the wreckage miraculously uninjured as he casted his protective Forcefield of Prana Energy around himself, and activated the MT-AT's shield right before the eruption. Guardians laid dead and corrupted soldiers were, in return, exterminated as the battle raged on. Elder Rachel started to float from the ground, her eyes glowed in a gorgeous Sunset yellow as she used her Ashla taught support and protective magic, as well as her spell of Battle Meditation to drastically reinforce the Guardian army, enabling them to not only hold the enemy, but slowly push them back with great fortitude despite the devastating explosion born from The Mind.

Orion: "That red skinned Guardian has been my curious issue since that vexatious space confrontation. Bring her to me and do not fail me again."

The Mind: "Y-Yes my lord... as you command... Apana... Energy: *Shadow Hand*."

Makai used his Grimoire to cast a giant shadow hand that darted straight for Rachel who was unaware, but suddenly that hand was severed at the wrist by Raito and his conjured Light-sword.

Raito: *internal thought* "His use of Apana Energy... Could he be... Impossible, he was lost to the void of space long ago." *out loud* "Are you perhaps the fallen Prana Master, Simon Gato? One of the founders of the School of Prana?"

Makai grew quiet after hearing the name he long forgot. However, Simon was dead, and only Makai, The Mind and devoted follower of Orion's will remained.

The Mind: "A name… long forgotten… Now… only Makai… remains…"

Raito: "It would seem you have found your way to Darkness. Simon then is truly gone."

The Mind: "You are… in my way… Guardian. I will…kill…youuu… complete my task… and take your…Grimoire."

Raito: "Prana ain't the only trick up my sleeve hotshot. You'll also find that killing me can be quite… troublesome."

The Mind: "Your efforts… are in vain… Guardian. Be gone."

Raito, using his super speed, evaded multiple Apana Energy blasts from Makai with fluidity and proficiency. The Elder then conjured the Light-bow spell as a way to release several arrows against his Bogan fueled master of old. The Mind countered the white arrows of death by casting several shadow hands to negate and catch the arrows.

The Mind: *disrespectful laugh* "Your… Prana magic… is weak. I will…take your–"

The arrows exploded in The Mind's face, causing him to slam into a group of vehicles as he grunted in embarrassment and defiance. Raito smiled confidently before zipping towards Makai with blinding velocity. Elder Raito caught Makai off guard with his speed, and used The Mind's hesitation to strike The Mind's body a few hundred times a minute. The Elder then jumped away to conjure the Light-bow spell, allowing Raito to pierce the evil magician with a binding arrow and restrict Makai's movement. The Mind struggled to free himself, but only found further embarrassment. The Prana user saw one of Orion's warriors struggle and comment on how elementary the fight with Makai was.

Raito: "Well, that was…easy. If all of the others fight like you, this will be a piece of cake. Maybe you should—"

The Mind: "Unforgivable!… Unpardonable!… Inexcusable! You shall pay dearly GUARDIAAAAAANN!"

Unfinished, The Mind forced one hand free and pulled out a small bottle of a strange black substance, peaking the interest of Orion. Without hesitation, Makai smashed the bottle against his body, and poured the remains inside his hood. In a burst of Apana Energy, Makai broke free from his bondage, screaming in pain as his body tore itself apart to create something…horrible, yet magnificent. His body turned a mahogany red as his arms and chest burst into flames, and engulfed his Grimoire in flames. His head morphed into a palpitating fire pit, and burned off his hood showing glowing red eyes and mouth. This… monster was a walking volcano.

Rachel: "What the… I'm sensing some dangerous Apana Energy coming from him."

Raito: "As do I. Guardians, fall back!"

Makai turned his attention towards the Elder Guardian that humiliated him in front of Orion, and charged up a massive amount of heated Apana Energy into one enormous sphere of Energy. It was so bright and big that it could've been mistaken for a miniature Sun. The Mind screamed "DIE", as he released that massive blast of Apana Energy, hurtling towards Elder Raito and the raging battlefield behind him. With only a split second to think, Raito sprinted as fast as he could, grabbing as many Guardians as he could to one point on the battlefield before casting a powerful Forcefield around the ones he collected. Elder Raito yelled as he valiantly struggled against Makai's Bogan empowered attack, holding the shield up, and protecting himself and the Guardians under his care. But the amount of Apana Energy Makai gained from the strange black substance was too much for Raito. The shield that guarded Raito and the others shattered, leaving one piece standing as a blinding light from the attack made it difficult to see. The blast consumed everyone, making everything a victim as a huge explosion hushed the fight. Shortly after, the battleground grew silent as Orion, The Mind and fifty-five remaining corrupted soldiers were left standing.

Orion: "What an entertaining show, and I see your DNA was compatible enough for the Accelerant, how quaint. Too bad the Elder parished. She had a strangely familiar Energy to her. Thinking about it now, she was possibly going to be your replacement, but you'll do until I find a suitable subject or until you have served your purpose. How…disenchanting."

The Mind: "Thank you…for your mercy and gift…my lord."

Orion: "Indeed, come now. I have a council to interrupt."

They motioned towards The Order HQ, killing any Guardians who stood in their way. The Orion Crusaders basked in their victory over the Guardians as the remaining soldiers roared, raising their weapons high in a show of strength over the weak. They advanced to The Order's HQ, falsely believing that all of the Guardians present were killed. The sound of their footsteps grew increasingly faint, completely leaving the battlefield which had been filled with death and destruction. Miraculously, Elder Raito regained consciousness, slowly opening his eyes before feeling a sharp and agonizing pain from his left arm. He looked over in shock to see that half of his arm was completely gone, burned away from The Mind's Bogan fueled Apana Energy blast. Raito calmed himself before panic had a chance to creep in. He looked around to see if there were any survivors. To his joy, he was exceedingly relieved to see Elder Cass, Elder Rachel and at least four Elite Guardians alive and breathing. Raito woke up Cass, then Rachel to confirm their survival.

Raito: *grunting in pain* "Cass…Rachel. I'm *grunt* glad you guys are okay. We…we have a big problem."

Cass: "Raito your arm!"

Raito: "Oh this. *painful chuckles* This is…nothing." *grunt*

Raito fell to one knee as he scuffled to keep his balance. Rachel took and laid Raito on his back to utilize her support abilities.

Rachel: "Lay down bigshot, you've lost a lot of blood. Here, this should stop the bleeding and ease the pain. Cosmic Energy: ***Healing Hands***."

Raito: "You're a life…saver…"

With Elder Rachel stopping the bleeding, easing Raito's pain and relaxing his body, the Elder passed out as his body worked tirelessly to repair the damage, and to close the wound in order to replenish lost Prana Energy. Out of options, Elder Cass carried Raito on her back while following Rachel as she reformed the remaining Guardians, regrouping them. Rachel radioed for backup while formulating a plan with Casanova to take back Sarvis from Orion and his depleted forces. But as the two rehearsed their situation, things didn't look promising, and options were few to none. The two found they've lost contact with Solla, and hopelessly assumed the Guardians protecting Mos-Dia had sustained heavy casualties.

Rachel: "This isn't looking good Cass. We lost contact with Solla and the situation at Mos-Dia seemed to have only gotten worse I assume. Our forces here were completely destroyed by some ace-in-the-hole, Orion is currently storming the HQ and Raito isn't waking up anytime soon. We don't have many options, so I'll take the Guardians left and–"

Cass: "Stay here and Guard Raito."

Rachel: "What?"

Cass: "You are the only true healer here. Why would we sacrifice our only medic? Plus, I noticed that Orion was after you. I don't know what that's about, but my intuition tells me you should stay here."

Rachel: "You're more capable of actually Guarding him, plus I have to get payback for Elder Matthew."

Cass: "Believe me, I know how you feel, but acting on your emotions at a time like this will only get you killed or worse. I've been trying to teach Nico that for years. The Creator will always provide a way that's best for your mind, body and spirit. Plus, I hate to admit it, but without reinforcements, we don't have the necessary firepower to go toe-to-toe again, especially if Orion wants in on the action this time."

Rachel: *irritated tone* "So we just wait for Sarvis to fall? For The Order and the Light to fade?"

Cass: "As long as we live, as long as our will and Light as Guardians never dims nor changes, the Way of Ashla will never fade. The One Infinite Creator will see us through. *whispers* I know it."

As the two Elder Guardians weighed their options and formulated a plan, the Orion Crusaders pushed their way through The Order HQ guards, slaughtering and moving towards The Nine's courtroom as they created a trail of blood and death in their wake. The Nine sat in their floating table and chairs, going over the current situation, when suddenly they heard grunting, blasting, then eventually screams added by banging against the large white stone doors. Shortly after, silence fell before the doors were knocked down, giving way to the volcano-like monster holding the door Guardians by the throat. On Orion's command, Makai burned their necks, killing them as their necks and heads melted like hot butter. Orion followed behind, smiling as he's waited for this moment since that day.

Orion: "Well if it isn't the ones who destroyed my home. Time has not been kind to you. I sense the weakened state of your Source Energies. It would seem the Creator has abandoned you all."

The Nine Member #6: "Oh how far you've fallen young Theo. You won't succeed in your quest, and you'll NEVER become a god! What happened that day was brought upon Titus and your entire species because of their actions."

Orion: *sigh* "Makai..."

The Mind: "As...you wish... my lord."

The distorted entity fired a concentrated beam of heated Apana Energy that hit the speaking counsel member between the eyes, killing him instantly as he fell from his levitating seat.

Orion: "Anyone else?"

All remaining members leaped high in the room, combining their Source Energy into one blast of Light before shooting it directly towards Orion like a newly fired missile, but before the beam of Light and hope reached its target, Makai jumped in front of it, taking the full blast to the chest which critically injured the monster. The remaining council members surrounded Orion and readied themselves to end the age of Darkness before a second Galactic War could take full shape, though they feared it already had.

The Nine Member #5: "It's over Orion. You have lost and now you shall join your ancestors in the afterlife."

Orion: "Am I not worthy enough to be tethered like my father? *laughs hysterically* I have transcended beyond the fragile teachings of Ashla, beyond the lie you call...'Love' and beyond Theo! You don't realize that you've been lied to for centuries? That you all have been walking into a blinding Light, praying for...salvation, but I know the truth. I see the blackness in all living things. The hatred; the abhorrence. You cannot escape the immoral void that plagues your hearts, so you hide behind your...Light; your Guardians; your Creator. And hunt those who see the galaxy outside of the view you've all fabricated."

The Nine Member #1: "You've got it all wrong my lost child. The Light provides warmth during the harshest winters, the Love to forgive the unforgivable, and the bravery to protect those you cherish most against impossible odds. The Light and the Love of the One Infinite Creator isn't fragile nor a lie, but flows in all living things, including yourself. You're only hiding and suppressing what's already fundamentally there due to hatred, rage, and grief. In fact it shines brightest in the darkest of times like a self-sustaining flame that keeps away the coldness of spiritual isolation and overwhelming depression."

Orion: "And what do you think taught you that? As long as there's Light showing the ugliness of Myrmidon, the cycle of hatred will never cease and peace will never be realized."

The Nine Member #4: "And you have a way to solve this Universal issue?"

Orion: "It's mildly irritating to explain myself to such…out-dated beings such as yourselves, but as my father's old allies, I'll grant you this last wish… At the center of this galaxy sits five planets filled to their core with pure Source Energy, and exotic life; my mother talked about them constantly. Among this star system sits a small planet which contains a special tree that gives life to an extremely powerful and rare fruit. I will travel to the center of this pitiful galaxy, and attain this fruit to drastically increase the Cosmic Energy gifted from my father. Thus, I will destroy this galaxy and create a new one, bringing forth a period of peace and Darkness, governed by I, Orion. No more will the Light take, no more will the strong be hunted because of their power. I will become a God and rule over my new galaxy, and I will end this cycle of hatred for good! As of now I declare the start of the Second Galactic War!"

The Nine Member #3: "You imbecile! If you destroy Myrmidon and everything in it, who will you rule? If you bring an end to the galaxy, you will be destroyed along with it!"

Orion: *chuckles* "You are a bigger fool if you believe the Darkness is subject to your laws of the Light. You have no idea the potential pure Source Energy possesses when under the teachings of Bogan."

The Nine Member #1: "And you're the biggest fool if you think we're gonna sit and watch you destroy an entire galaxy full of possibilities."

Orion: *smiles heinously* "You'll all be dead before then."

The Nine combined their Ashla taught Source Energy into another powerful blast as Orion picked up the critically wounded Makai by the throat, draining him of his life and Source Energy, and killing the monster as the flames of his body extinguished.

Orion: "You have played your part exceptionally well Makai and I must show gratitude. Now, serve me beyond the grave."

Following this, The Mind faintly mumbled his last words, "for… Orion", before turning into nothing, but a pile of dried up rocks and ash. The Nine used this opportunity to unleash a massive blast of Source Energy from all directions at the god of Darkness, finding confidence in their combined ability to end it once and for all.

The Nine: "Source Energy: *Cosmic Judgment!*"

The blast was bright and huge as the shockwave blew the roof completely off the HQ building, catching the attention of Elders Rachel and Cass. However, as the light faded and the smoke settled, they looked in disbelief as Orion, covered by a broken shield made from The Mind's stolen Source Energy and reinforced by his own Black Aura, was protected from The Nine's trump card attack.

Orion: "I hate to admit it, but despite the age, you all still possess great power. I shall take it for myself… Cosmic Energy: *Snake Grip.*"

With those words, Orion utilized his Cosmic ability called: *Dorein*, which allowed the false god to drain the Source Energy of his victims, slowly killing them. As a result, Orion could use the stolen Source Energy to further empower himself and his Black Aura.

Following the utilization of Dorein, the Asronian spread out his arms as several snakes made from Cosmic Energy emerged from his sleeves, and swathed all remaining council members up, squeezing them tight as they helplessly struggled to break free. The snakes then slithered into the nose, mouths, and ears of all eight members before internally biting and sucking the Source Energy from them. Orion felt and bathed in the anguish from The Nine, laughing as they all passed into the afterlife one at a time.

The Nine Member #1: *weakened tone* "E-Even with…our deaths… the Light WILL prevail… just like… with your… people…"

Orion: "Shhhhh. Join your worthless Creator quietly."

With the deaths of The Nine, Orion felt a weight lifted from his shoulders. He felt as if he avenged his home and his family, but it wasn't enough. He desired to become The God and to end the cycle of hatred and strength related discrimination. Following this life mission, Orion fully accepted his role, becoming Orion "The Almighty God of Darkness" fully and wholeheartedly.

Shortly after his mental confirmation, Orion tossed the last council member against the wall like a used towel. He felt the stolen power of The Nine, coursing through his veins as he turned that Ashla taught Source Energy into pure Darkness. Concentrating the increase in Cosmic Energy, he caused a massive explosion of lava that shot through the large opening caused by The Nine's attack. The flow of Darkness and lava fired upward with tremendous power and force like the Mount Tambora volcano erupting on present day Earth. The towering stream of lava could be seen from space, like black paint splattered against an empty canvas. The lava fell from the sky in thick rain drops resembling a threatening thunderstorm as Orion flew high above the devastation, raising both hands in delight as he watched Journia burn. Elders Rachel and Cass took cover from the lava drops as they fell from the sky. Witnessing the horrifying scene, Rachel mumbled under her breath and said to herself, "this is hell, and Orion is satan"…

CHAPTER

SIX

DEFEAT

Journia, a once powerful, beautiful and peaceful world, now sat in the never ending cosmos engulfed in flames and full of death and chaos. First-class Elder Guardian Nico continuously jumped, flipped and swung from tree to tree as he leaped from the last tree to release the Hari whip mutation. The Elder exited the deep forest region and continued on foot towards Mos-Dia an hour away. After several amplified leaps, he approached the city's border, running past craters and cold bodies. The teachings of Bogan that were brought by the Orion Crusaders started to cloud Nico's mind, and began getting thicker as he traversed deeper into the devastated city. The Darkness weighed on him like gravity pushing down on one's chest; it made it hard for the Elder to breathe. He feared for his adopted homeworld, for his brothers and sisters of the Ashura Order, for Vinzent, Raito, Jasmine and for Cass. This level of mental conflict bred doubt and fear in the Elder, but then his mind was cleared by the loving and wise words of his long gone mother.

LaWan Tulex: "My son. Sometimes the Creator puts us through hard times to show us our true potential. Sometimes you must realize you are a sinner in need of forgiveness, of redemption, of a savior. Own your sins my son. Close your mouth and open your heart to the Creator's Love and Light, and you will see just how powerful you truly are. The path to righteousness is not one for everyone to follow, but nothing great comes easy."

Nico's fear subsided as his mind cleared and his nerves steadied, finding confidence and mental stillness once again. Just fifteen minutes from Mos-Dia, Elder Nico closed in on the battle between The Order and the Orion Crusaders…

Relentless in his attempt to fully destroy the second largest city, The Hand's army slowly closed in on Elder Vinzent, and his surviving Elites as blaster bolts and Energy beams were shot from the valorous Guardians. The corrupted soldiers surrounded the surviving Guardians, giving Vinzent the golden opportunity to enact his plan. Giving the greenlight, Vinzent used his ability of Aura Conversion to send a manifested red sphere of lightning high above the battlefield which expanded, changing from red to yellow and blinding Hando and his army. The attack was named: *Lightning Flash*. The soldiers roared in pain like dogs caught in a bear trap as their eyes dried out, and burned from the immense heat generated from Vinzent's Lightning Flash attack. With the critical moment at hand, the Guardians launched a devastating counter-attack that eliminated large masses of corrupted soldiers with quick, precise, and calculated strikes, orchestrated and executed with the help and leadership from Elder Vinzent himself. Refusing to be humiliated by such insubstantial mortals, Hando took matters into his own hands as he hopped in the battle, shielding his eyes with his hood while swinging his heavy hammer into groups of both Guardians and his forces, disregarding the friendly-fire by his hands. Hando's hammer was a lone force as it launched Guardians high in the sky like fresh popcorn. Hando then demonstrated his strength by bringing the hammer down, cracking the ground which sent shockwaves through the earth, changing the geography of the battleground with ease. Vinzent saw the carnage from The Hand, and bravely rushed in to take him on one-on-one. The Elder remembered what Elder Cass said earlier about fighting one of Orion's top goons alone, but what choice was left. Coming to peace with the inevitable, Vinzent relaxed his anxiety and concentrated on the present moment as he found the courage within to fight against this towering behemoth.

Vinzent: "It would seem fate has pinned me against you beast. If Mos-Dia is to be free of this Darkness, I must put you down."

Following Vinzent's resolve, the Guardian sent forth a bolt of lightning, hitting the beast in the back, followed by several orange lightning bombs that sent The Hand off his feet. Angered, Hando threw his hammer hard and fast towards the Elder at incredible speeds, forcing Vinzent to flip over the large weapon. While in mid-air Vinzent simultaneously threw axes made with red lightning that cut deep into Hando's thigh and torso. With the monster stunned, Vinzent channeled his Red Aura once more, allowing his lightning to feed and react as he converted the wild lightning into manifested and concentrated gloves of red lightning called: *Fists of Thunder*. With this ability active, the Elder dashed for The Hand as lightning crackled from behind. Upon reaching his target, Elder Vinzent performed a calculated series of punches, hitting his target with a left jab to the face, followed by a right then left hook, finishing his attack with a hard right upper-cut, with each strike clapping like thunder. Vinzent also added a blast of lightning to The Hand's chest, which sent him flying into a truck. Fueled by rage and Orion's approval, The Hand pulled himself out of the broken vehicle, bloodied and injured from Vinzent's Elemental Energy.

Vinzent: "Ready to give up beast?"

The Hand: *deep voice* "You are no match for Orion. You will fall like the rest."

Vinzent: "We'll let the Creator decide."

The Hand: *deep chuckle* "Your Creator is fleeting, just like your LIFE!"

Elder Guardian Vinzent grew tired of his opponent's doubt in the Creator, so he geared up and charged in for another series of thunder strikes, but as Elder Vinzent swung, Hando grabbed The Elder's forearm, and threw him into a nearby building before taking a car and throwing it into the same building, causing the vehicle to explode and the structure to collapse on Vinzent. With a premature victory, The Hand retrieved his hammer before making his way towards the raging battle to complete his task.

Luna: "Vinzent, Vinzent…VINZENT!"

The internal voice of Elder Luna shook Vinzent awake like receiving a splash of cold water. He regained his consciousness before picking himself up to brush off the dust from the collapsed building. He held his side due to the broken ribs received from Hando, but nonetheless readied himself for round two. "Don't underestimate a Guardian asshole", said the pissed off Elder as he climbed his way out of the torn down house. With his target thirty feet away, Vinzent closed his eyes, spreading his legs shoulder width apart with his fists to his side and bent at the knees. He gradually yelled, getting louder as his Violet Aura surrounded his body. He felt the power increase of his lightning as it resonated with his Violet Aura in a beautiful balance between lightning and Source Energy. The newly formed Violet lightning danced in Vinzent's hands. It flowed with the Guardian like a leaf moving downstream, even Hando knew this could be trouble. With Violet lightning crackling from his hands, Vinzent yelled, "This is for Rex and Kicks. Elemental Energy: *Lion's Roar*!", as he thrusted his hand violently towards Hando. The Elder released the attack in the form of a blast of Violet lightning that, before impact, took the shape of a Lion as it tore through The Hand, like a wild animal ripping through flesh. The Violet Lion carried Hando through multiple buildings before finally coming to a stop. As a result, The Hand laid against a broken wall, fried, gravely wounded and unconscious. The attack was witnessed by the surviving Elite Guardians fighting by Vinzent's side which boosted their morale, enabling them to quickly clean up the remaining corrupted soldiers as only twenty

Guardians remained standing. Two Guardians helped the recovering Elder up to his feet as he assessed the situation.

Vinzent: "Thank you my brothers and sisters. The enemy is defeated, but do not lower your guard. If Orion's top goons are anything close to him, that blast won't be enough. I need a minute to recover so stay vigilant, Guardians."

With the Elder's warning heard among all the remaining Elite Guardians, they took the necessary precautions and split up into groups to search the battlefield for survivors, both friendly and non-friendly. During the search, a group of four Guardians found The Hand unconscious with the lower half of his body torn away, added by a smelly gray liquid flowing from his body like a cracked pot of water. Two Guardians moved in closer to check for signs of life, but before they could react, with speed and anger, Hando suddenly grabbed both Guardians by the throat, snapping their neck like a twig before throwing their lifeless bodies into the other two Guardians guarding the entrance. The Hand dug his hand into his large wound to grab a small bottle of a black substance. With desperation, the injured monster opened and dug the entire bottle containing the Accelerant back into his large open wound. Grunting in torment, the monstrous monstrosity twitched, beating at the ground as he underwent some sort of transformation like that of Makai, but this was different...it was revolutionary. The Hand's body grew, getting larger and stronger than before as a thick hot steam engulfed him. His lower half grew back in a pool of hot dark-gray liquid, as well as being granted two extra arms. Hando's body turned to a dark green and gray, and was filled with strange and unfamiliar navy blue symbols which covered his entire body. Hando's once large two-handed hammer underwent a transformation as well as it became alive, splitting into four solid hammers that comfortably fit in all four hands. The hammers also had the ability to return to his hands if thrown. The change was complete as Hando smashed through the wall of the broken building, and stood ready and very much able to carry out Orion's will to remove Mos-Dia from history, and to personally thank Elder Vinzent for a golden opportunity to use Orion's gift.

Vinzent sat on a stone brick still recovering the loss of Elemental Energy from the fight, when he heard fighting off in the distance... but it sounded to Vinzent to be more of a slaughter. The Elder, slow to get up, witnessed blood squirting in the air like a busted fire hydrant; body parts from the Guardians sprung up like fresh popcorn being made. The scene was horrifying and sent a chill down Vinzent's spine, but he did not fear, for he knew this was no walk in the park from the start. The Hand walked closer to his main target, hammers in hand as blood dripped from them, anxious to taste the blood of an Elder ranked Guardian.

Vinzent: "What? How did you..."

The Hand: *monstrous tone* "My lord is a generous one. Blessing and gifting me with such...POWER! You will die here, but rejoice, for your life shall be taken by Orion's glory..."

With no Guardians left alive, Elder Vinzent prepared himself for the fight of his life. He felt the heated breeze from the surrounding flames, the smell of blood filling his nose, the sea of dead Guardians laid before him. The Elder converted his Ashla fueled Elemental Energy into a Red Aura, via his Aura Conversion ability. Doing so allowed Vinzent to manifest a red lightning sword and shield before entering his fighting stance. Without delay, Hando leaped for the Elder as the two clashed, causing a shock wave of Elemental and Kinetic Energy. The Hand freed one hammer, swinging it wishing to implode Vinzent's skull, but his efforts were in vain as the Guardian jumped backwards, dodging the attack before landing on a red surfboard. Unwilling to let his prey escape, The Hand threw two of his hammers at Vinzent with the Guardian responding by blocking the attack with his shield, canceling one hammer. Vinzent blocked the second hammer with his shield once again, but was also thrown from his board by the brute force of The Hand's empowered strength. This caused Vinzent to crash down onto a car and roll on the street as he struggled to his feet, his golden curly hair a total mess. Seeing his chance, Hando leaped once again at the Guardian, prepared to end the fight, but was blasted by

Vinzent's orange explosive lightning which knocked the beast to the ground. Vinzent then put both hands on the ground, sending a charge of lightning towards his enemy. Refusing to be caught again, Hando threw a third hammer at the Guardian, forcing the elusive Elder to dodge which disrupted the ground attack. Hando, using his newly given strength, dashed for Vinzent with impressive speeds, and uppercutted Vinzent in the stomach which lifted him from the ground. The Hand added to his attack by swinging his hammer, but the attack was blocked with a quickly manifested lightning sword. Although the attempt was blocked, the brute force of the swing sent the Guardian hurdling into a nearby vehicle. Seeing the Elder down, Hando grabbed the injured Guardian by his hair and lifted him up to show Vinzent his home in flames which reduced to nothing but a sad memory.

The Hand: *deep tone* "Witness the destruction of your home, your people. Everything you hold dear, gone. *laughter* Though you were strong, you weren't strong enough to save your city. And soon, your world will follow."

Vinzent tried to shock the beast, but his body started to overheat, making his lightning too weak from constantly fighting the Orion Crusaders and The Hand. With the Elder held high, Hando used the handle of his last hammer to break a few more of Vinzent's ribs before breaking his left arm to repay him for the attack earlier. Beaten and bloodied, the Elder ranked Guardian showed no fear, no pain, no submission.

Vinzent: *spits blood in Hando's face* "Is that all you got you four-armed ugly piece of shi–"

Hando punched the disrespectful Elder in the stomach once more before he could finish his insult. Tired of the lack of respect, Hando raised one of his free hands to summon one of his hammers. Receiving the weapon, The Hand pulled both hammers back, and readied himself to smash open the Guardian's skull. Vinzent closed his eyes to breathe in deeply, meeting his death with open arms...but the deed was halted by a double-ended blade. The blade came flying in at blinding speeds and severed Hando's top sets of hands off, effectively saving Vinzent and causing The Hand to drop his hammers. Gray blood spilled as Hando stumbled backward roaring in agony. The injured beast turned to see another Guardian with a large blade deriving out of what seemed to be a muscle-fiber covered arm. With the crucial moment at hand, Elder Nico quickly dashed and kicked Hando in the chest, sending him flying down the street and into a building. Nico then mutated, releasing the Jūken blade which returned his arm back to normal. Shortly after, with his legs still amplified, Nico hastily dashed for Vinzent as he grabbed his wounded faction member. He then forcibly leaped far away, leaving behind a small shockwave in the wake of his escape. The two Elders retreated to a battle-wounded house a few kilometers away to regroup, which presented Vinzent with a needed moment of rest and recovery.

Vinzent: *grunts* "About damn time. I was starting to think you'd gotten yourself captured."

Nico: "They'll need an army for that. Don't tell me that fart-catcher actually beat you…"

Vinzent: "No, he didn't as a matter of fact. *grunts* He was beaten, then decided to cheat using some strange black substance."

Nico: "I see. He really did a number on you. This should help your recovery process for the time being."

Nico reached into his utility belt to retrieve a glowing yellow seed called a *Solar Seed*, which cuts the consumer's recovery time in half. **Ex. If a Guardian receives a cut that takes four days to completely heal, the Solar Seed cuts it down to a day in a half. The seed can also greatly slow the blood flow of a wound.** After taking the seed, Vinzent's broken arm and ribs were healed. He also received an acceptable decent chunk of Elemental Energy.

Vinzent: *deep breath* "I appreciate that, I'm gaining my strength back."

With Elder Vinzent's strength slowly returning, he generated his Green Aura around himself, allowing him to heal some of his wounds as his lightning reacted to the Aura, becoming passive and yielding. But not all wounds were healed because of the overall loss of Elemental Energy due to the constant fighting.

Vinzent: "Were you able to save Solla?"

Nico: *sigh* "Unfortunately I wasn't. Everyone was...dead when I arrived."

Vinzent: "I'm sorry to hear that. As you can see, we're in the same boat. I just hope Cass and Raito have had better luck."

Nico: "Knowing Raito, they're probably already on their way here.

As Vinzent continued to rest, loud thuds and crashes could be heard outside as Hando vengefully drew near, and didn't come to Mos-Dia to play hide-in-seek. He smashed through buildings and flipped cars, leaving no stone unturned as he searched for his prey. Elders Nico and Vinzent, two of the greatest and strongest Guardians within the Ashura Order's history, formulated a plan best suited for the current circumstance.

Nico: "It didn't take him long to find us. I realize fighting alone all the time, especially against the Orion Crusaders isn't the best thing, so I'm here to back you up. Plus you need to recover."

Vinzent: "Ahhh don't treat me like a Paladin. I'm an Elder just like you. I managed just fine and even brought the beast to his knees before the bastard decided to level up."

Nico: *chuckles quietly* "I hear you. Then our best bet is to regroup with the others and talk to The Nine to figure out The Order's next move."

Vinzent: "I agree, but the only thing is, we lost contact with Sarvis after a massive spike in Energy which fried communications in and out of the city."

Nico: "Then we better go back them up."

With an escape plan set in motion, Nico walked out of the building to gain the wanted attention of Hando. "Hey! We don't have time for you, so we'll be leaving" said the confident Guardian.

The Hand: "Come now Guardian, my hammers yearn for an Elder's blood!"

Blinded by his need for blood and vengeance, The Hand rushed for Nico with the Elder responding by amplifying the muscle-fibers of his arms, allowing the loose fibers to wrap then tighten around Nico's awaiting limbs. Following the amplification technique, Elder Nico mutated and formed a single-ended blade from his wrists. "Guess he didn't get the hint." With dual Jūken blades mutated, the two clashed as Nico was surprised by the beast's speed. However, despite the need to bring down the beast, time was of the essence and defeating Hando was reserved for Elder Vinzent, just as Ude was for Elder Nico.

The duel was back-n-forth as Elder Nico deflected and dodged most of The Hand's attacks as if the Elder were merely stalling. Enraged by the Guardian's underestimation, Hando increased the speed and strength of his attacks, and managed to smash into Nico's chest before bringing another hammer down on his shoulder. Hando then quickly grabbed Nico by the face and slammed him into the ground, cracking the pavement underneath. Unsatisfied, The Hand lifted Nico up and ferociously threw him through several buildings. Hando beat his chest and briefly celebrated his victory, but his moment of triumph was masked by the eerie sensation of danger. He looked off in the distance and saw Elder Vinzent charging up a massive amount of orange Elemental

Energy. It was too late however, as Vinzent fired concentrated bolts of orange lightning at the stupefied monster, exploding and stunning him once again. Nico got up from the rubble as his broken bones, shattered arm, and damaged organs self-regenerated in moments. Empowered by Solar Energy from a Sun, Nico manipulated the cells of his body to regenerate all of his wounds in mere moments, showcasing the amazing rarity of his **Healing-Factor**. With Nico's wounds completely healed, he took a breath and saw that The Hand was recovering from Vinzent's counterattack. Reluctant to waste anymore time, the Elder once again, amplified the muscle-fibers of his legs to increase his speed which he used to dash for The Hand, rapidly closing the distance. Following this, Elder Nico simultaneously mutated as loose muscle-fibers burst from his pores to wrap and tighten around his arms and hands. His knuckles hardened and also grew in size. Nico felt the dramatic increase in strength and knew that the mutation would deliver the necessary power needed to send The Hand flying.

The Elder smiled due to this mutation being one of his more favorable mutations because of the skill and power he possessed while using it; he also preferred hand-to-hand combat. The mutation was given the name: **Ken**.

With the plan going as intended, surprisingly, Nico ceased the moment and dashed towards Hando, reaching him in seconds as the Elder dragged his Ken fists against the ground. With hardly any time to defend, Nico reached his target, punching The Hand in the chin with a left hook, then returning with a powerful right hook before intensely uppercutting the beast in the chin with the left fist, sending Hando flying high in the air. This gave Vinzent a clear shot as the Elder fired a large bolt of Violet lightning, hitting Hando directly in the torso. The bolt delivered a loud clap that was mistaken for thunder that sent the beast blasting through the sea of ash above, and out of the inner city of Mos-Dia before crashing down in a ball of fire resembling a meteor. Hando then came tumbling through numerous buildings as battle-torn structures came collapsing down, burying The Hand in a mountain of rubble like a failed game of Jenga.

Vinzent: "Great plan, now let's move before we have to waste more time on the fool."

With the escape plan successful and The Hand buried, the two Elder Guardians made haste to Sarvis, hoping for the best, but preparing for the worst.

Meanwhile at the capital city of Journia, Elders Rachel, Cass, along with an unconscious Elder Raito, and the four surviving Elite ranked Guardians, watched in dread as Orion floated above the burning capital city, basking in his victory over the weak and disappointing teachings of Ashla. Because of his self-glory, Orion was oblivious to the hidden vault underneath the courtroom, as well as the surviving Guardians taking shelter from the rain of fire. Fearing that Orion might sense their presence eventually, the group of Guardians moved away from The Order's HQ with extreme caution. They motioned out of range of the burning rainfall and under a flipped over Ashura vehicle, blessing themselves with some sort of safety despite the Orion Crusaders's head honcho close by.

Rachel: "We need to get Raito to a medical facility. Is there any way you can contact anyone for reinforcements?"

Cass: "I've been trying to reach Elders Nico and Vinzent, but my comms are being jammed. The blast of Apana Energy earlier must have fried everything."

The two Elders conversed between themselves, hoping to find a way out of the dire situation, but no idea seemed to work without an all-out battle with Orion himself. However, their attention was suddenly redirected by two beings off in the distance. Cass, Rachel and the other surviving Guardians, saved by Raito, prepared themselves for battle, but Cass sensed a familiar flow of Solar Energy as she put away her katana.

Rachel: "Cass this isn't the time to get cold feet."

Cass: "Relax you guys. It's Nico and Vinzent."

Relieved by the refreshing news, Elder Rachel relaxed her mind as her Cosmic Energy faded. Nico and Vinzent regrouped with Cass and the others, catching up and explaining the current situation.

Nico: "Cass! I'm glad you're okay."

Cass: "I'm glad you are as well Nico." *with concerned smile*

Rachel: "We're okay too…"

Nico: "O-Of course. I didn't mean to–"

Rachel: "It's fine, I know your heart is in the right place."

Elders Vinzent and Nico looked over and saw Raito unconscious with a missing arm. They ran over to their brother with great distress penetrating their hearts.

Nico: "Raito!"

Vinzent: "What the hell happened?! Is this all that remains of the army of four thousand Elites??"

Rachel: "I'm afraid so, Vinzent. We were heavily engaged with the enemy which was led by a being called The Mind. Raito saved me and saw an opportunity to destroy or capture one of Orion's top goons. The battle was fierce with Raito gaining the upper hand, but…"

Vinzent: "But what?"

Cass: "But The Mind had an ace up his sleeve."

Vinzent: "What do you mean an 'ace'?"

Rachel: "The Mind ingested some strange black substance which boosted the strength of his Energy ten times over."

Vinzent: "The same thing happened to The Hand. That's no coincidence."

Rachel: "The Hand?

Vinzent: "Yes. Another one of Orion's top goons."

Cass: "Did you guys finish him off?"

Nico: "We're not sure. We didn't have time to check."

Cass: "So you left him possibly alive!?"

Nico: "We made the decision to yes. In order to back you guys up which it seems you needed."

As the Guardians discuss the next course of action, Nico, Vinzent and Rachel all sensed a powerful burst from a heavy Black Aura zooming towards them. The attack hit its target, exploding violently against the Guardians. When the smoke cleared, Nico stood firm with his protective Mamoru shield active, along with Vinzent who manifested a red shield as well. Together they protected Cass, Rachel and Raito, but unfortunately failed to protect the four Elite ranked Guardians who were killed in the blast. The two standing Guardians looked out into the distance to see who fired upon them, but upon further inspection, their answer was as clear as the Darkness that plagued their world. Something terrible; a completely sinister presence, floating in front of them. Orion, self-proclaimed god of Darkness himself.

Orion: "So, not only did you defeat Makai and Hando, but you all managed to get them to use the Accelerant? You Elders are quite impressive, I'll give you that."

Vinzent: "Accelerant?.."

Nico: "Orion!"

Orion: "You forgot God of Darkness."

Without wasting another moment, Elder Nico quickly amplified and flared his muscle-fibers as they wrapped and tightened around his right arm and legs. Shortly after, Nico's double-ended Jūken blade formed from his arm, giving the Elder the means to dash straight for the false god. Nico mercilessly swung his Jūken blade for Orion's neck with Vinzent following the attack with a sword of red lightning pointed for Orion's heart. Though their speed and reaction time were remarkable, the attacks were easily halted by Orion's mysterious Black Aura as the field of intoxicating black mist stopped the Guardian's assault dead in their tracks as if they meant nothing.

Orion: "Maybe you all will be a better challenge than those nine feeble disappointments."

Nico: "What are you talking about? What have you done!?"

Orion: *laughs disrespectfully* "Let's just say their Source Energy won't be wasted."

With those words of discouragement, the two Elder ranked Guardians backed off their meaningless attack to regroup with the others. With his wound closed, Elder Raito woke up to find Elders Vinzent, Nico and Cass standing in front of him with Elder Rachel by his side.

Raito: "W-What's going on? Vinzent? Nico? When did you guys get here?"

Rachel: "I'm glad you're awake. Can you move?"

Raito: "Y-Yeah I can move."

Rachel: "Can you fight? Nico and Vinzent will need your assistance."

Raito: "They need my...I see, Orion. Give me a moment, this guy deserves both arms. Prana Energy: *Graceful Replacement*."

Raito rose to his feet and used his Grimoire to cast a spell that gave him a temporary arm made from Prana Energy, replacing the one burned away by The Mind. With Elder Raito as ready as he'll ever be in that moment, the Guardian stepped in front of Cass and Rachel, joining Nico and Vinzent as the three strongest Guardians readied themselves to fight Orion, god of Darkness.

Vinzent: "Glad to see you're okay for the most part."

Raito: "A trip to the medical center back at the base and I'll be good as new."

Nico: "Good. Let's finish this so we can get you right."

Orion: "Such confidence. I'd expect nothing less from the three 'strongest' Guardians. Fine, entertain me Elders!!"

The burning rain stopped as the ocean of ash and lightning plagued the once open sky. Orion, the self-proclaimed god, revealed his strong dark red colored legs, planting his feet against the ground as the weight of his presence cracked the cement. Orion then reached his hands inside his robe to pull out swords made from his menacing Black Aura. With speed greater than Raito's current top speed, Orion dashed straight for Nico as the false god kicked the Taiyōnian. The Elder quickly responded by blocking with his Mamoru shield. "So...heavy" said Nico undoubtedly. Despite his amplified strength from his Solar Mutation ability, Elder Nico struggled under the weight of Orion's leg.

Orion: "You're strong, Taiyōnian. But you are far from your Senshi brethren."

Nico grunted as he struggled to push Orion's leg off of himself, but just then Orion used the other leg to strike Nico in the face which broke his jaw and knocked him hard into the ground as he tumbled away. Refusing to see their comrade beaten, Vinzent and Raito jumped into action with Cass as backup and Rachel performing the Battle Meditation spell. Raito used his speed and Vinzent used his lightning ability to increase his speed as the two Guardians combined their assault. Their movements were so fast that to the naked untrained eye, there was nothing but streams of light resembling a shooting star as shockwaves were generated from the two opposing sides colliding. The fight was intense, but Orion merely toyed with the Guardians as he grinned, smashing Raito into the ground from his sword swing, leaving Vinzent to face the false god himself. Orion swung both swords, intending to dismember the Guardian, but he was unsuccessful as Nico quickly regenerated his broken jaw and dashed in the way, blocking the attack with his Mamoru shield. The force and power behind Orion's might sent the two Elders flying like a leaf blower performing its duty. Cass used her Elemental Energy abilities to construct several water walls that slowed and eventually caught the speeding Guardians.

Nico: "Thank you Cass."

Cass: "No need to thank me. This guy is insane. How do we... Aughhhh!!!"

Nico: "CASS!!!"

After saving Elders Nico and Vinzent, Orion used their distraction against them as he appeared behind Cass in a field of black mist, resulting in the false god stabbing her through the stomach as he smiled boorishly at Nico. Vinzent and Raito dashed for Orion, giving the saddened Elder time to run for Cass as she fell in his arms. Fueled by nothing but rage and grief, Nico gave Rachel a Solar Seed before forming his Ken fists. Afterwards, he leaped back in the fight, joining Elders Raito and Vinzent in the destruction of Orion.

Orion: "YESSS!! Show me the blackness of mankind's heart. Show me your hate, your pain!! Let the Way of Bogan fuel you!"

Rachel swiftly rushed over to Cass and gave her the Solar Seed before performing her strongest Cosmic Energy support magic on Cass's injury.

Cass: *cough* "Don't let...them fall to their emotions. H-Help them."

Rachel: "Don't worry, those three aren't the strongest Elders for no reason. Rest assured."

Rachel comforted Cass with a gentle smile as Cass briefly passed out from Rachel's relaxing support magic and the seed. Rachel shielded her comrade from flying rocks produced by craters made from the persisting battle. Solar punches were swung, lightning was struck, and Prana magic found its target as the fight was nearly impossible to see with the naked eye. Elders Nico, Vinzent and Raito battled against the false god of Darkness, however, against their best efforts, it seemed completely one-sided, and in Orion's favor. Elder Nico stood exhausted from the accelerated depletion of his Solar Energy and lack of direct Sunlight. Vinzent's body was overworked from constant battle as steam flowed from his body with him still feeling the effects from his battle with Hando. And Raito searched for air as he worked to catch his breath, taking a moment to charge his Prana Energy. The three strongest Guardians were stuck between a rock and a hard place as fatigue began to creep in.

Orion: "Tired already Guardians? How upsetting. You're supposed to be the strongest, but it seems even the best of The Order has their limits, what a shame. Has the Creator abandoned you all? Are you to be consumed by Darkness like those before you? *chuckles* Let us find out..."

Raito: "Here he comes..."

Orion, the god of death and Darkness vanished from sight without a trace due to his unbeatable speed, not even Raito could match his moves. Orion increased his assault against the Elders, showing zero signs of slowing down. The false god utterly overwhelmed the Elders as they desperately defended against Orion's physical attacks, and boundless power granted from his Black Aura. After somehow managing to survive a deadly series of attacks, the Guardians struggled, gasping for air as they perilously searched for an answer for Orion's might. Following this, the false god stood before the Elders with a final message.

Orion: "It's never too late to let go of the teachings of Ashla, Guardians. Why fight against something that resides within you? Why run away from your inner-Darkness? Embrace your right to power and join me as my prized disciples."

Vinzent: *breathing heavily* "And be what? A ruthless band of murderers; your tools?"

Orion: "To let go of what holds you to this reality. Attachments, possessions, friends, family, Love. These things keep you from truly knowing the Self. In Bogan there is silence...no expectations, no opinions, no reality besides the one you create. Not everyone is chosen for this path, but you three show promise. It would be a shame to kill you all and waste such... hidden talent."

Nico: "What you seek is impossible even without The Order! Friends and family are what help shape one into who they are! The environment, the experience from that environment, and the Love one feels thereafter. To cut yourself from what makes you, YOU, is ludicrous!"

Orion: *laughs maniacally* "For you mortals yes, but I am a god who has bear witness to the Darkness of this galaxy, and embraced the true lessons Bogan has to offer. My will is JUST!"

With more words of discouragement, Orion put away his swords inside his black robe while simultaneously floating once again. The

Elders sensed trouble as they felt Orion's power increase further, as if he wasn't strong enough already. He proceeded to use the mysterious Black Aura that surrounded him to forcefully shove away Raito and Vinzent as they crashed hard into nearby buildings. Because of all the fighting before, the impact from Orion rendered Vinzent unconscious as his body refused to move. However Raito, slow to move, watched as Orion beat Elder Nico down with miraculous speed and power. Orion's speed outmatched Elder Nico's Healing-Factor, and as Nico laid before Orion utterly beaten, the false god mercilessly ripped the Elder's arms from his torso, and burned them into ash, leaving him armless, bloodied and beaten.

Rachel: "Nico! What is he doing? Why doesn't he regenerate his arms and fight back?"

The weakened Casanova, who had regained consciousness, found the strength to answer Rachel's curiosity.

Cass: *weakened tone* "He can't right now."

Rachel: "What do you mean 'he can't'?"

Cass: *grunts* "When away from the Sun, he has a set amount of Solar Energy given from the Sun before needing to recharge. Every time he amplifies and mutates, he uses a small amount of that stored energy. *grunts* However, his Healing-Factor is different because each time he regenerates a lost limp or fatal wound, it uses a ginormous amount of that stored energy…"

Rachel: "And when Nico uses all of his Solar Energy, it causes his powers to weaken and his Healing-Factor to almost cease, it also doesn't help that the Sun is currently blocked. This is bad. What about Vinzent and Raito?"

Cass: "Vinzent's body can only withstand a certain amount of lightning before his body overheats. I assume in this case, because of the constant fighting, his body reached its limit. And Raito was already severely injured, so for him to be fighting the way he is against Orion is incredible, but it seems Raito is reaching his limit as well…" *grunts*

Elder Rachel continued to stabilize Cass's wound, but knew she would need real medical attention. A few meters away, Nico laid on the ground beaten and armless as Orion used his Black Aura to create a field of gravity that weighed down on Nico, pinning the weakened Guardian to the ground as the weight broke several bones. The screams from Nico's pain fueled Raito's resolve and courage. Following this, the Elder reached into his utility belt and grabbed one of his Stem Shots. Shortly after, the Elder stuck himself with the empowering liquid and instantly felt the effects. In a burst of speed, pushing far beyond his normal speed, Raito rushed for Nico and Orion in a blink of an eye, hoping to save his brother from the leader of the Orion Crusaders. However Orion, in all his might, saw the Guardian speeding towards him, and with one swift motion, the false god caught Elder Raito dead in his tracks before slamming the speedster hard into the ground, thus creating a shockwave as the ground buckled under Raito and Nico's back. The pitiless god of Darkness saw a golden opportunity to consume the Source Energy of some of the strongest Guardians the Ashura Order had to offer; the thought pleased him greatly. Soon after, Orion picked both Elder Nico and Elder Raito up by the throat and proceeded to use his Dorein ability to drain their Solar, and Prana Energies and lifeforce from their very souls. The two Elders screamed in misery as they could feel their Energies being ripped from their bodies like a horrible stomach ache that leaves one physically paralyzed with pain. Raito's levitating Grimoire dropped to the ground as his vision began to blur, and Nico's glowing Taiyōnian markings began to cool down and dim as the two were too fatigued to resist the jaws of death set before them by Orion. The two Elders were knocking at death's door, but before they joined the Creator in the afterlife, an unexpected turn of events occurred.

Rachel: "WAIT! Wait…almighty Orion, God of Darkness. Please, spare their lives."

Orion stopped the utilization of his Dorein ability, but still held the two Elders as he turned to this weirdly familiar entity.

Orion: "And what do you have in place of their lives?"

Rachel: "I give you…my life. You hunted me for sometime now. I don't know why or how, but my Cosmic Energy; my vital Source Energy, somehow recognizes you. Please take me. Just…just spare their lives."

Orion: "Oh? Mmmmm, that horn… could it be? *grins wickedly* I accept."

With the agreement established, Orion tossed Raito and Nico as their enervated bodies hit the ground.

Orion: "You are mine now."

Raito: *weakened tone* "N-No. You don't have…to do this!"

Rachel: "Don't worry about me Raito. Live to fight another day."

Rachel found acceptance with her decision as Orion waved his hand over her face, effectively putting her to sleep as she fell into his arms. Orion then vanished from view without a trace in a cloud of black mist, finally getting his hands on the curious woman. Raito found the strength to stand as he struggled to keep his balance. His temporary replacement arm of Prana Energy faded as he looked beside him to see Nico unconscious with both arms torn off. Soon after, he looked off in the distance and saw Vinzent unconscious against a wall with steam intensely originating from his body, resembling the burning buildings that surrounded them. And to the right of him to see Cass laying on the ground as she held her wound while utilizing her Elemental Energy to keep her vital signs steady, along with the help of the Solar Seed which slowed the bleeding. "Did we…just lose?" said the only Guardian left standing. Raito looked up towards the ash covered sky, accepting this moment as a true defeat…

CHAPTER

SEVEN

ROSE

Ash and lightning plagued the sky as black ashfall covered the destroyed capital city, Sarvis, on the planet Journia. First-class Elder Raito laid the unconscious first-class Elder Vinzent next to the unconscious and armless first-class Elder Nico, with second-class Elder Cass awake, but dangerously slow to move due to her injuries. Thinking about the defeat by Orion wouldn't change the outcome so instead, Raito focused on the present moment and the actions that followed. He used his communications device to contact Jasmine, the AI, but his efforts were hindered because of the high levels of Bogan fueled Apana Energy surrounding the area. As a result, communications in and out of the ruined capital were disrupted. Raito looked next to him once more to see his comrades in need of medical attention which gave him the determination needed to find another way. The Elder casted a Forcefield around his friends and set out to search for some way to contact help or to find transportation. The magical Elder searched and searched, finding nothing, but burned bodies of both Guardian and Crusader origin, and distorted buildings of the once great city of Sarvis; it was a tragic sight. After a while, his hope began to dwindle, but before he lost hope completely, he saw the MT-AT critically damaged, but intact nonetheless. Raito entered the defaced tank as he, with his newly conjured prosthetic Prana arm, worked tirelessly to get the main systems online long enough to get them to their base in Mara, seventy-six kilometers away. Sparks flashed as Raito attached wires to energy capacitors, power cords to heat regulators, and activated the spare wheels. He then poured some of his own Prana Energy into the engine for extra horsepower. Afterwards, Raito snapped his fingers, sending out a wave of Prana Energy which jolted the damaged engine alive. Raito's repairs and technical skills bore fruit.

Raito: "Ha! The Creator provides and we're not dead yet. Now, let's take her nice and steady— woah!"

The MT-AT shook and buckled, moving violently as Raito drove closer to his injured comrades. He drew near to see the protective bubble containing three beings as Raito gave out a sigh of relief. He brought the tank to a halt just a few feet away from the downed Elders as Raito opened the horizontal back door. Because of Makai's explosive attack, the damaged door malfunctioned, only opening partially. Frustrated, Elder Raito stomped on the door, breaking the loosened and damaged parts as the door broke and slammed open. "It'll be alright," said Raito mentally. With his Grimoire in hand, he conjured a large hand of Prana Energy that he used to carefully put under Cass which enabled him to lift, and carry her into the pending vehicle. With no open wounds besides Nico, Raito carried Vinzent, then Nico, on his shoulders and into the land tank. Soon after, he entered into the MT-AT's cockpit and drove out of Sarvis's destroyed inner-cities, the broken back door flapping against the ground.

Raito: "I don't know if y'all can hear me, but y'all are gonna owe me big time for this."

Cass: *smiles* "I'm sure they'll happily agree to your terms."

Raito: "They don't have a choice either way. How are you feeling though? That wound looked pretty nasty."

Cass: "It hurts, but thanks to Rachel's Cosmic Energy and Nico's Solar Seed, I'll make it, thank you. What about you and your arm? Keeping up that Graceful Replacement spell must be tiring."

Raito: "I appreciate the concern, and I'll manage. I'm sure Nico will be relieved to see you're okay...once he wakes up... *internal thought* How could one entity do all this?"

The MT-AT was heavily damaged with the weapon and shield systems offline, but that didn't stop the armored vehicle as it surprisingly sped its way out of Sarvis completely, and towards the base in Mara...

Elsewhere in the destroyed forest land of Nalmoth, Orion suddenly appeared before the ginormous ship that was The Obedience. As the cloud of black mist dispersed, he held Rachel in his arms. Recognizing their undisputed master, the pilots of the worldship welcomed their lord back with them opening up, revealing the ship's beautiful yet terrifyingly hellish features.

Obedience Pilot: "My lord, the repairs are complete. We are ready for departure on your command."

Orion: "Very good. Prepare for immediate departure, we have work to do."

The pilots obeyed their master's command and warmed up the built-in gravity thrusters at the bottom of the cubed vessel. Upon activation of the thrusters, The Obedience gave off a deep, bone-shaking humming sound that began shaking the forest area surrounding the ship. As this went on, Orion saw Ude coming out of the woods with freshened cuts and burn marks from Elder Nico's attack, and a missing left arm taken by Elder Lucas. A good chunk of his forces were missing, however the surviving soldiers carried groups of prisoners unseen by Elder Nico.

Orion: "Good, you have done well my friend. I trust you had no issue obtaining these beings?"

The Arm: *deep tone* "No my Lord. The village burns…and the people lay dead in your name. The rest will serve you as all entities must."

Orion: "Well done indeed. Have the men be reconditioned, and deliver the women to the birthing chamber. Also, escort this one to the lab. Restrain and guard her, I shall join in a moment."

The Arm: "As you command, my Lord."

Receiving Orion's praise with open arms, Ude grabbed Elder Rachel from his master before throwing her unconscious body over his shoulder, and continued inside the massive worldship with the prisoners. Hando was seen coming out of the woods moments after, bloodied and exhausted as he held his handless arms. He returned with nothing, but the cutup skin on his back and four hammers as Orion grew curious.

Orion: "The. Hand. I see you used the Accelerant, and they still managed to elude you? Did the Guardians push you so far? And have you none of the soldiers I blessed you with?"

The Hand: "M-My Lord, forgive me. I-I…"

Orion: "Shhhhh. No need for excuses. The city lies in ruin, you did what I asked so you are forgiven…"

Orion placed a hand on Hando's shoulder as he whispered ever so softly in his ear.

Orion: "Your God is merciful so just like The Mind, I will give you a second chance at redemption, but heed my warning. If you fail me again, you'll have proven to me that you're of no use, and I have no glory to spare for such…futile creatures."

With Orion's warning established, the false god motioned for The Hand to get aboard The Obedience and get cleaned up as the Orion Crusaders prepared to depart. The ginormous worldship fired up its thrusters in a violent burst of gravity which created a mile deep crater within Journia's surface. The Obedience pulled itself out of the self-made crater, like pulling a deeply rooted tree from the ground, as the sheer force from the ship sent a violent rumble rippling through the entire planet, imitating a planetary earthquake...

Several meters from the base in Mara, the ground shook and buckled underneath the wheels of the MT-AT as the damaged tank rushed for the Elder's base. Raito used his superb driving skills to carefully maneuver his way past falling trees, crumbling mountains and massive cracks in the ground giving way to a seemingly endless fall. He briefly looked back at his injured comrades which gave him the confidence, and the calmness to move through the chaos with ease and focus. A few moments passed and Raito saw the familiar mountains that contained their base as he initiated the emergency protocols. With the protocols started, the base quickly lowered the hanger shields, allowing the MT-AT to speedily enter before coming to a disrupted halt. Once the Elders were secured, Raito told Jasmine to put the base under a full protective lockdown via his override code.

Jasmine: "Raito! I lost communications with you guys and I feared the worst. Where are the others? And what happened to your arm!?"

Raito: "I'll explain later, right now I need you to lockdown the base. Anyone who enters the perimeter and doesn't register as a Guardian, erase them. Override code: Raito-08."

Jasmine: "Done, but what's this all about? I felt a tremendous shake in the ground and heard several distress calls all over Journia. I saw Solla's terrible fate, and Sarvis before the blackout. What happened out there?!"

Raito: *vengeful tone* "We lost."

Even though Jasmine was an artificial intelligence, she expressed emotions as if she were a human which is what made her part of the faction; of the family.

Jasmine: "What do you mean lost?! The Ashura Order, the Guardians of the Way of Ashla, and The Nine, don't just 'lose' Raito!"

Raito: "Orion humbled us. The bastard came to our planet and had his way with The Order."

Jasmine: "Are you saying that The Order... is gone?"

Raito: *humiliating chuckle* "To say gone is an understatement, but yes. The DSR, Bao, The Nine, Sarvis, and most of the Guardians in orbit and planet side, all gone. I don't even know if the refugee camps still stand, or if the population evacuated off world..."

The massive shaking of the planet ceased as Raito managed to get Vinzent, Nico and Cass into the medical center inside the base. He then asked Jasmine to warm up the surgery table for Cass, juice up the rehabilitation tank for Vinzent and to prepare artificial Solar Energy for Nico to bathe in.

Jasmine: "Done, done and done. That just leaves you and that arm."

Raito: "I appreciate the concern, but I have to make sure these guys recover and help you protect the facility. Besides, I'm sure you could use the company."

Jasmine: "Well it sure was lonely and nerve racking to be unable to hear from you guys. Thank you Raito."

Raito: "No need to thank me. I hope you didn't have too much fun while we were getting our asses kicked." *soft laugh*

Jasmine: "Actually, a few groups of those corrupted soldiers stumbled into the base's perimeter. It was pretty great to try out the new weapon systems."

Raito: "So that's where those craters came from. I was hoping that was you."

Jasmine: "Care to explain what happened to your arm now?"

Raito explained the battle between himself and The Mind, bonding while also protecting the base in the small window of calmness before the storm. The other Guardians recovered and healed from their one-sided confrontation with Orion…

Meanwhile floating in space just outside of Journia's orbit, The Obedience sat in the graveyard of the first-class Elder Guardian, Matthew, and his brave fleet of starships. In the ship's laboratory, Orion floated in front of the unconscious Elder Rachel as she slowly woke up to see a powerful being elegantly levitating before her.

Rachel: *sluggish tone* "W-Where am I? What did you do to me?"

Orion: "You are aboard my ship, and I injected you with a small amount of the Accelerant and blocked your connection to Source Energy associated with the teachings of Ashla, but don't worry, the effects are minor."

Rachel felt her body numbing as she tried to utilize her Cosmic Energy, but to no avail. Orion watched in amusement as the Elder struggled to move her own body. Soon after, she stopped struggling and came to terms with her reality as Orion conversed with her.

Orion: "That was quite amusing to say the least. Now, Guardian, at first glance there was nothing special about you. You were but a side character to someone else's story. Your courage was quite…admirable, but the horn you possess saved your friends, not your sacrifice. You all would've died if it wasn't for my curiosity and our deal. But now as I float here observing your features, I am sure I've seen you before. What is your full name? Who is your father? Speak."

Rachel: "You really think I'd tell you anything after what you've done monster?"

Orion: "You have the same fiery spirit as that Elder Luna, I'll give you that. Tell you what, because I am merciful *sarcastic chuckle* I'll give you a choice. Spare me the time it would take to invade your mind and tell me what I want to know, or be consumed by your own Darkness."

Rachel: *under her breath* "Though outwardly we are wasting away, yet inwardly we are being renewed day by day."

Orion: *sigh* "It seems like everyone in this story is so stubborn. No matter."

Orion floated closer to Rachel before pressing his cold thumb against her forehead, in between her eyebrows, silencing her futile chant as he whispered, "show me", ever so quietly. Rachel's eyes lit up as she yelled, and her mind invaded, laying all of her memories out. Her life, from birth to that point, laid out for Orion to see like a movie. He ran through her memories like flipping pages in a good book before finding what he sought after, Rachel's significance and her familiarity.......... After a deep moment of silence, Orion released Rachel as she leaned forward gasping for air with the god of Darkness simply, and utterly caught off guard for the first time since becoming Orion.

Orion: "Who would've thought you'd survive that day. After all this time..."

Rachel: "W-What are you t-talking about?"

Orion: "Of course you wouldn't know, you were but an infant. You are my sister. I thought you died that day with everyone else, but it seemed our mother saved you…"

Rachel: "You are my… Not possible. I can't be related to someone like you!"

Orion: "Your name is Rachel Rose is it not? I had an infant sister named Rose with the same red skin as your own and a scar on her left leg."

Rachel looked down towards her left leg where sure enough, she had a scar she received as a baby, marked across her thigh. This hard truth left the Elder speechless.

Orion: "Why did you think your teachings of Ashla felt so abnormal? Or why no matter how hard you try to deny it, the Way of Bogan seemed to feel more natural? The horn you possess, or the fact that you're over two hundred years old? Your time in the Light has stripped you from your true power; your true nature. You are a member of the most powerful family of our species, the glorious Asronian race. Stop playing pretend with those… Ashla blinded Guardians. They are nothing, but murderous manipulators who destroyed our homeworld and decimated our species out of fear. However fate has brought you to me. Join me sister, and together we will avenge our family, our planet, and rid the galaxy of the Light."

Rachel: "Even if what you say is true. The Order, the Light, they are my home. And IF what you say is true, then 'our' mother abandoned me and The Order saved me. You expect me to turn against them for something as trivial as revenge?"

Orion: *angered tone* "How dare you speak about our mother in that manner?! She risked everything for your survival! For your safety! The Light has not only weakened you, but blinded YOU as well! *deep calming breath* It would seem that my little sister is unworthy of the power she possesses, how disappointing. No matter, if this is a path I must walk alone, so be it. I will not harm you sister, but I will be using your Energy for myself. Rest now. Black Aura: ***Subconscious Slumber.***"

After using his Black Aura to cast a spell, the god of Darkness proceeded to corrupt Rachel's conscious mind by shielding her from the One Infinite Creator's Love and Light spiritually, as well as from the teachings of Ashla with his Black Aura. Orion showed her the Darkness within herself as he pressed both of his thumbs against her eyes and said, "see what you are". Elder Rachel, against her best efforts, fell victim to the rage and blood thirsty nature of her powerful ancestors. The voice of Orion in her mind proved too strong for her weakened Ashla blinded state, like attempting to complete a push-up after an arm workout. Rachel's body subconsciously stood up, twisting and turning, forcing her eyes to roll as she unwillingly connected with the Bogan side of her being. Her hair turned white as snow with her eyes matching the black and coldness of space. The Elder's skin morphed into a dark red complexion as bright yellow markings covered her body. She stood before Orion, powerful and free as she took on the true appearance of a raged fueled Asronian fighter.

Orion: "From this day forward, you are ***Rose***, a.k.a, *The Eye*. Now kneel before your master."

The corrupted Rachel Rose continued to stand, ignoring Orion's command as Rachel fought hard to gain control over her vessel.

Orion: "I said KNEEEEEL!!!"

With Orion's angered tone, he used his Black Aura to create a field of gravity, used to pin Nico, to pin the newly formed Rachel to the ground, but the Asronian was strong in her true form and could possibly go toe-to-toe with Orion himself; brother versus sister. She resisted Orion's power, refusing to bend her knee, but her defiance would not last as the false god, who was more experienced with the teachings of Bogan, used it to eventually overpower her. Shortly after, Rose was seen on her hands and knees, bending to Orion. The false god then pressed his thumb against her forehead, reverting Rachel back to her normal form as she fell against the floor.

Orion: *outrageously evil laugh* "Your power is absolutely remarkable! You could possibly be stronger than our mother! *maniacal laughter* We will plunge this Universe into Darkness and soon, I will be the ONE Infinite Creator! Maybe you can join me and ascend with me, my sister. Ude..."

Orion summoned his second in command as he showed up to the ship's laboratory in moments.

The Arm: "Yes my lord?"

Orion: "Take The Eye to my quarters with Luna. Restrain her and inject her with this. This will further solidify her puppet state and remove the teachings she received from The Nine."

Orion handed Ude a needle filled with the Accelerant before turning towards The Eye as she, and The Arm exited his quarters.

The Arm: "As you command my lord."

After Rose and Ude left the room, Orion took a moment and thought upon his actions thus far, basking in his glorious ascension into Godliness from his once mortal self. The false god did not feel the need to rush anything because who could stop him now. Who could stand up to the almighty Orion, god of Darkness? And now with Rose under his thumb, his goals were all but assured. He wanted to enjoy the suffering of others, the destruction of the galaxy; of the Omniverse. He wished to prolong the second Galactic War, all for revenge, and something more... Orion finished his moment of self-reflection and praise, and flew to his quarters, looking around his ship and its gorgeous planet-like features before entering his quarters to see Luna and Rose.

Luna: *sarcastic tone* "I see you have a new toy. You're not replacing me are you? Wait…Rachel?!"

Orion: "Your beauty could never be matched. However, she plays a more important role. Be patient, you'll see."

Orion pressed his thumb against her head, activating Rachel's transformation as if he had direct control over his own sister. The Elder however, tried to resist, but the feeling of Bogan, power and freedom felt too good as her consciousness was set aside to become Rose, or The Eye, the embodiment of chaos. Though to Orion's disappointment, it wasn't truly his sister, but merely a puppet with his sister's face. Nonetheless the false god used her accordingly.

Luna: "Rachel! What did you do to her?!"

Orion: "Simply reclaimed my sibling. Now Rose, show me your power and loyalty, destroy your adopted homeworld and show the Ashura Order why Asronians should be feared."

Luna: *internal thought* "Sibling?!…"

Elder Rachel fought subconsciously with her destructive self, but again her efforts were in vain as The Eye disappeared in a red mist before being seen floating outside of The Obedience, surrounded by a transparent bubble. Luna was in a state of doubt as she did not recognize this boundless being as Elder Rachel, but as a fearsome Goddess floating in space. With The Eye in front of Journia, the Asronian princess raised her hand as it glowed in a reddish-black hue. She then brought that hand down in one swift motion as if cutting through space. The mysterious glow faded from her hand followed by silence, but after several passing moments, nothing seemed out of place.

Luna: "It seems your influence wasn't as strong as you hoped for, devil. Rachel is still in there, fighting–"

Elder Luna's comment was suddenly interrupted as she looked out from the large worldship to see a bright vertical red line perfectly positioned down the middle of Journia as it circled the entire globe. The line began to get brighter and brighter until a light flashed, blinding all but Orion and Rose. When Luna recovered her sight, she looked back out from the opening in complete disbelief as the once dominant planet was split in half like cutting a stick of butter with a hot knife. No explosion, no pieces of earth sent flying like Bao, just two halves of a planet steadily floating away from each other, revealing the core of the planet like someone perfectly pulling apart a boiled egg, revealing the yolk inside. With Journia's core exposed, The Eye finished her given task and fired a red beam of Bogan fueled Cosmic Energy into the planet's core. Shortly after, the core began pulling the two halves together, gaining strength with every passing moment. Seeing that her task had been completed, Rose appeared aboard The Obedience in a field of red mist as Orion showed a level of praise towards The Eye.

Orion: "Magnificent! Splendiferous! Marvelous! You have indeed proven your worth, Rose."

Luna: "What have you DONE!"

Orion: "I liberated this world from the cycle of hate and saved them from themselves! I have revived my sister's true nature, and now I wield even greater power. This galaxy shall know Darkness as I have."

Orion was completely satisfied by the results and pressed his thumb against Rose's head once again, reverting The Eye back to her old weak self. Though locked away in her own subconscious mind, Elder Rachel could see, hear and feel everything as if she were in control, like watching one's life through their own eyes, yet helpless to influence any thought or action. Due to this, after Orion allowed her to gain control of her body, Rachel saw the destruction caused by her hidden power.

Rachel: *saddened tone* "W-What have I done…Cass, Nico, Vinzent… Raito. I'm sorry. If I just would've died with Matthew…none of this would've happened…"

Rachel fell to the floor, completely discouraged and spiritually defeated. She believed that she killed the galaxy's only saviors and with such a loss of hope, Rachel fell deep into depression, fully giving in to The Eye as the Darkness rose and vanquished the last of her Love and Light and stripped her of her Ashla teachings. Fully consumed by her regret and grief, Rachel transformed independently into The Eye before consciously kneeling before Orion.

Orion: "Welcome home Rose."

EIGHT

TAIYŌ

On Journia, a few hours before The Eye's attack, Raito and Jasmine finished their refreshing conversation as Raito walked into the medical/rehab room to check on the faction's recovery progress. After a successful surgery done by Elder Raito with guidance from Jasmine, Elder Casanova laid sleeping in bed, recovering her strength and Elemental Energy. Elder Vinzent was seen floating in a rehabilitation tank. The Elder was also hooked up to an oxygen mask, and had several monitors checking his vitals. The liquid that submerged and healed his body was powered by the healing properties of his Green Aura, and special liquid that was created by the knowledge of Jasmine. The seafoam green substance thoroughly healed Vinzent's wounds, as well as replenished all of his lost Elemental Energy. A few feet away, Elder Nico laid in a bed powered by artificial Solar Energy, also designed by Jasmine and Raito. His body resonated with the energy, allowing his Healing-Factor to take effect. Muscle-fibers slithered from Nico's open wounds, reconstructing what was lost like a salamander healing its limbs. The fibers twisted and turned, merging to regenerate his biceps and triceps, then forearms, then hands before coating his healed arms with chocolate brown flesh. With the artificial Solar Light dripping Energy into his cells, the Elder frantically woke up with his eyes wide open as he yelled "CASS", as if stuck in a nightmare.

Raito: "Don't worry, she's alive and well."

Nico: *sigh of relief* "What happened? The last thing I remember was getting beat down by that false god and my Solar Energy drained for my very body, now we're back at the base. Did you…"

Raito: "I wish, but no. Rachel sacrificed her life for ours."

Nico: "She isn't…"

Raito: "No thank the Creator, well at least I hope she isn't. Orion captured her and vanished, just like that."

Nico: "We have to get her back, there's no way we'd leave a comrade in the hands of Orion. Where's Vinzent?"

Nico rushed out of bed, but suddenly his body went numb, causing him to fall against the facility floor. Raito helped Nico back on the bed and advised him to rest.

Raito: "Woah Nico. I understand where you're coming from. I was tempted to go get her myself, but that wouldn't be using her sacrifice to the fullest. You and everyone else need to be one hundred percent if we're gonna defeat Orion."

With Raito's words of wisdom, Nico laid back, allowing Raito to reactivate the Solar bed's systems. Shortly after, Raito's curiosity involving the Taiyōnian race pushed over the edge.

Raito: "You know. We've been partners for quite sometime now. And I gotta say, that Healing-Factor of yours is an amazing ability. I just witnessed you regenerate from wounds that would otherwise be fatal in mere moments. I gotta ask, what's the deal?"

Nico: "What do you mean?"

Raito: "Cmon now Nico. Under the Sun, you're practically immortal. Cass told me about your guy's history. And I also know a little about the Taiyōnian race because of their part during the first Galactic War, but the Guardian side of you doesn't explain who YOU are, who the Taiyōnian are or what Solar Mutation is and came from. What's your story? Who were the Taiyōnians before the Ashura Order; before the first War? If I'm in your bubble just let me know."

Nico sat up in bed, surprised to find Raito's curiosity. The Elder nonetheless explained his people's history as best he could.

Nico: "Not at all brotha. To understand the gift that is Solar Mutation, you'll need to understand the history of my people."

Raito: "Enlighten me."

Nico: "If you're really that curious… As you know, Journia is my adopted home. My homeworld was called *Taiyō*, a few million light years away from here. We were, of course, called the *Taiyōnians*. During the earlier generations of my race, on our planet there was hardly any vegetation due to the blazing environment produced from the Three Suns. *Helios*, the Father, *Surya*, the Mother, and *Apollo*, the Spirit. The trio constantly baked everything from plants, to animals, to even its population. Because of the nonstop shine, every Taiyōnian on the planet had incredible amounts of melanin in their system. Everyone was either black, chocolate brown or golden tan. The unbeatable heat also made growing anything damn near impossible. For hundreds of years the Three Suns blazed the ground they shined on. And for hundreds of years countless lives were lost because of it, dying from dehydration, starvation, heat exhaustion, and by the hands of other Taiyōnians trying to survive. It was truly a horrible time back then, but we never lost faith in the Creator or his timing. However, at the beginning of a seven hundred year period, Taiyō was blessed with a turning point that would change everything forever."

Raito: "I could only imagine what the summers were like. But a turning point?"

Nico: "Yes. These facts came from the oldest Rekishi Scrolls, which were our history books. Plus my mother wanted my brother and I to know our story and would always teach us before…they came. Our turning point came after the King, King Lui the First, received a visit from a mysterious figure, dressed in a white robe with a yellow crystal embedded in his forehead, who claimed to be a 'prophet from the Creator'. This being went by the name *Lotus*."

Raito: "A prophet from the Creator. That's a bold claim. Did this Lotus entity give King Lui a reason to trust him?"

Nico: "None, but our King had an open mind and heart, and our world was in dire need of the Creator's Love and Light."

Raito: "Sounds like King Lui the First took a gamble."

Nico: "He did, but Taiyō had nothing to lose. Lotus came to King Lui with a prophecy. His prophecy was stated as follows: '*Great power will be bestowed upon the entities of Taiyō. No longer will Helios, Surya or Apollo inflict hardship, but instead grant spiritual evolution, physical strength, mental wisdom and global advancement. The Creator's Love will be fostered through the Light from the Sun, but be warned, for those who shield themselves from the Creator's Love, will find themselves in a Dark place from which the Light of the Sun does not reach. In due time, Taiyō will produce mighty warriors. Have faith, for the Creator works in mysterious ways.*'"

Raito: "That's a hell of a prophecy. It's almost like Lotus handed King Lui the key to salvation."

Nico: "My thoughts exactly. What made Lotus even stranger was just as mysteriously as he appeared, he disappeared without a trace, leading some to believe his claim as a prophet from the Creator."

Raito: "Do you believe he was?"

Nico: "I do. A few months after Lotus's disappearance, King Lui noticed the Three Suns began strengthening the people of Taiyō, which marked the beginning of our seven hundred year rise to prominence. Several more months passed and Taiyōnians began demonstrating extraordinary feats of strength, speed, agility and durability. Feats that seemed impossible for our people. Because of the newly discovered resilience to the Three Suns, Taiyōnians came together and built great villages and temples in honor of the One Infinite Creator and of Lotus."

Raito: "So the Taiyōnian race practiced the Law of One?"

Nico: "Oh yeah, completely and wholeheartedly. After all, it was the One Infinite Creator who formed the Universe and everything in it, including the Three Suns. It was also the Creator who saw the strength in the Taiyōnians and gifted us with the Solar Energy I'm blessed to display. Why us? That I do not know."

Raito: "Happy to hear you all followed the Light and Love of the Creator. Please continue."

Nico: "Two hundred years had passed since Lotus disappeared, and during that time, Taiyō evolved mentally and physically, just like Lotus prophesied. By this time, Taiyō made some incredible advancements in technology, like the creation of spacecrafts or the Dyson spheres created to prolong the life of our Suns. Through these technological advancements, research and blood testing, it was discovered that after hundreds of years of bathing underneath the Three Suns, our DNA mutated, enabling our cells to take in Solar Energy which became the root of our power. Upon this discovery, many people began to notice the muscle-fibers of their bodies strengthen beyond what was thought possible, enabling greater feats of strength, speed, agility and durability. Later on, this process would be called the technique of *Muscular Amplification*."

Raito: "That's where your muscle-fibers flow freely from your skin?"

Nico: "Yes and no. To push the muscle-fibers past the skin's capacity takes practice and muscle endurance, but it is the easiest step to master. Another two hundred years had gone by, and once again we had reached another milestone in our evolution. While some found satisfaction with the Muscular Amplification process, many pushed the technique further, finding that, with discipline and good overall knowledge on amplifying, a Taiyōnian could release free flowing fibers through the pores of the skin. As a result, Taiyōnians found they could manipulate their cells to repurpose those loose flowing fibers, and form different kinds of tools and weapons, similar to how I use the Jūken blade or Ken fists. This would be called the technique of *Cellular Mutation*. However, in order to form mutations effectively, a Taiyōnian must train and master the Amplification technique. This is because when one produces enough free flowing muscle fibers, it enables a mutation. Once a Taiyōnian has achieved the desired mutation, they must hold the cells and amplified muscle-fibers in place while completing the necessary task. This process is most troublesome as it acquired the complete mastery of amplifying, especially if one wished to further solidify those fibers to form sharp blades or a strong shield. These gifts, when combined, would be called *Solar Mutation*."

Raito: "So the Amplification technique strengthens and adds muscle-fibers to the body, while the technique of mutating repurposes those leftover fibers?"

Nico: "In a nutshell. Hundreds of years under the Three Suns mutated our DNA and blessed us with a special connection to Source Energy through Solar Energy. We gave all the glory to the One Infinite Creator, and to Lotus for delivering his message. As we grew and developed the gift of Solar Mutation, over time Taiyōnians all over Taiyō grew exponentially stronger, and our planet as a whole grew increasingly advanced, spiritually, physically, and mentally. We hit a point in our society where crimes and violent acts were a thing of the past. This level of global tranquility helped raise the frequency of our consciousness further, and that's when it happened, the return of Lotus four hundred years later. By this time, King Lui the First joined the Creator in the afterlife, leaving his descendent, King Lui the Forth, to receive Lotus's prophecy which was as follows: *'The life of the physical body is finite, but the Love and the Light of the Creator last for eternity. So long as the Light from the Sun shines, so will the life of Taiyō. But take heed, even though the Creator offers the fruit of immortality, the body will be taken by death if left untouched by the Creator's Light. These are the words spoken through me from the One Infinite Creator. And should be regarded as truth, for the Creator is the Alpha and the Omega. Adonai.'* After Lotus's final prophecy, he levitated high above Taiyō and burst into billions of marigold-orange orbs. These orbs then flew down to the surface of Taiyō, and merged themselves with every Taiyōnian alive, infants included. However, nothing seemed out of the ordinary, well besides the fact that at that moment, every Taiyōnian, man, woman, and child, received their mutated markings specific to their Solar Mutation, like the ones you see here..."

Nico stretched out his regenerated arms, showing the dimmed pulsating Solar Energy of his mutated markings.

Nico: "Afterwards, people went about their business, using their Solar Mutation for everyday life, and trained to master the Muscular Amplification technique, as well as the Cellular Mutation technique. By this time, six hundred years had gone by, but what stood out was the reality that not a single Taiyōnian, after receiving their mutated markings, passed into the afterlife, as if we really were immortal. And that's when it happened, the first ever reported case of someone using their Solar Mutation to regenerate a severe injury. An Amplification expert named Dr. Axle Wade. He was researching the effects of the body during prolonged amplification, when his research tool malfunctioned and blew his arm off."

Raito: "Ouch! You Taiyōnians seem to always receive such fatal injuries."

Nico: "Curse of being Taiyōnian. *chuckle* Dr. Wade reported that he managed to combine the techniques of both the amplifying process and the process of Cellular Mutation to stop the bleeding and regenerate his bicep and tricep. News of Dr. Wade's discovery spread like wildfire, and explained why no Taiyōnian passed away since Lotus's last appearance. After that, people all over the world began learning the gift that would be later called the ***Healing-Factor*** technique. This seemed like the final piece for our world because shortly after, we found complete world peace. The Healing-Factor technique was the final and hardest process to use, let alone master. It took even the most seasoned Taiyōnian decades to master, and required one to know the external and internal functions of the body to effectively replace what was damaged, as well as mastery over the other two techniques. However, those who obtained relative mastery over all three techniques were given the title ***Senshi***, meaning 'Warrior', thus forming the Senshi Warriors who fought in the first Galactic War."

Raito: "So Solar Mutation was a gift from the Creator, cultivated from hundreds of years submerged in complete Sunshine from the Three Suns, Helios, Surya, and Apollo. The Healing-Factor technique then came about after the mastery of the other two techniques?"

Nico: "Exactly. Solar Mutation consists of three fundamental building blocks. Firstly, the Amplification of the muscular system to increase one's physical prowess. Secondly, the ability to mutate one's limbs at will through Cellular Mutation. And lastly, the Healing-Factor, which is the combination between the two."

Raito: "Well what's next?"

Nico: "What do you mean?"

Raito: "How did you become the last of your kind when your people possessed God-like power?"

Nico: "Why do you wanna know all this?"

Raito: "Because ever since we've known each other, I truly never got to know you. Plus, I noticed Orion calls you Taiyōnian. I've heard of them, but never actually knew who they were or their downfall."

Nico: "If you insist. As you're well aware, there was a six year conflict, the Galactic, well first Galactic War, which saw the deaths of hundreds of planets. My homeworld was one of the first planets which had been invaded before the Guardians at the time, ended the war. I was just a teen back then, barely able to use my Healing-Factor efficiently, when they came. The Asronians... Though they possessed boundless power and wielded Bogan fueled Cosmic Energy, they attacked us at the peak of our civilization, and at the end of our seven hundred years of prominence. The Senshi Warriors, which was now a formidable force, had a hundred years to fully master the Healing-Factor technique. Because of this, the Red Nobles spent two of those six years fighting the Senshi Warriors on Taiyō. And for those two years we halted their advance against Myrmidon, and almost managed to defeat them entirely. Titus and his army of Bogan wielding Nobles had no answer for our Solar Mutation gift, or for the issues their organic technology faced from the blazing heat of our Three Suns. There weren't many who could stop a race of super powered self-healers, and for two long years the Senshi Warriors held them to little to no gain, shoot we almost pushed them off our planet altogether. However, due to our own complacency and obliviousness, we didn't realize our own weakness till it was too late..."

Raito: "This must be when it all went down hill..."

Nico: "Indeed. We always had our Suns, always, even before Lotus. We didn't think about the possibility of ever losing them or the effect on our physiology if we did. The enemy however, exploited this theory. With the gravity-based Energy of their worldships, they managed to destroy our Dyson spheres and extinguish all three of our Suns, though to me, after wasting two years trying to conquer Taiyō, I don't see why they didn't pursue our Suns sooner. I guess they thought we'd surrender... Without the Solar Energy of Helios, Surya or Apollo, or of any Sun for that matter, Taiyō grew dark and cold. We got desperately weaker, and dramatically slower like how we were before the Creator's gift; it was a nightmare. After that, the Asronian's attacks increased exponentially which eventually wore us, and the Senshi Warriors out. As a result, we… didn't have enough Solar Energy to keep up the Amplification technique, mutations or our Healing-Factors. Because of our weakened state, death became an ongoing phenomenon, thus pushing the process of *Saibō Shi* among us. One by one my people were killed, and so was my family. I assume my father and older brother died protecting Taiyō, they were both Senshi Warriors, and my mother died protecting me. Sword through the chest, right in front of me. She… she couldn't use her Healing-Factor… If only I was stronger, I could've saved her…"

Raito: "Don't blame yourself Nico. Your mother gave her life so that you could have yours. Use it for good, in service to the galaxy and to the Creator."

Nico: *deep breath* "Thank you Raito. After seeing the death of my mother and my people, something awakened within me. A blackness, a Darkness. I felt power coursing through me like I had never felt before. In that window of time, I no longer needed the constant shine of the Three Suns, because in that moment of desperation and grief, I pushed past my limits and utilized the reserved pockets of Solar Energy within my cells, and I was able to use my Solar Mutation fully, and without restriction. In all the chaos, I fought my way to a starfighter and escaped the invasion of my homeworld… And I watched as half of Taiyō disappeared into an internal black hole…"

Raito: "They didn't even spare your homeworld?!"

Nico: "For good reason. The Red Nobles couldn't spare the chance of a Taiyōnian surviving, but they failed because as my damaged ship flew away from Taiyō, I saw others who escaped Taiyō's fate, and rallied with The Nine to help end the war, or so I assume based on The Order's history. I was defeated, mentally, physically, and spiritually. I lost my family, my home, and my purpose. To make matters worse, the starfighter I took was damaged from my escape, rendering it basically useless, but I couldn't talk much though. That burst of Energy used up all my Solar Energy so I was basically useless too. Me and this Senshi starfighter, floating through the endless void, useless. I blacked out shortly after crash landing on a planet untouched by the Asronians. Next thing I knew, I woke up on a farm on a planet a good ways away from Taiyō. An older man and his grandson found my crashed ship in pieces with me still inside, and my legs crushed. Thanks to that planet's Sun however, my Healing-Factor took effect, which frightened the old man, but amazed the young boy. *soft chuckle* I spent years on that planet, helping them where I could, but also providing protection for them. It was the least I could do ya know? It was a peaceful time for me. I was able to honor my family, my people, and fully master my Solar Mutation. By that time, the first Galactic War ended, and the old man passed away due to old age. The young boy, who was now a man, started his family and found his purpose. I, on the other hand, struggled to find meaning, but that's when the Ashura Order came to that planet to spread the Law of One and teachings of Source Energy through Ashla practices. They found me, and witnessed my use of Solar Mutation in disbelief as it was thought the Senshi Warriors were wiped out, and they were, for I was no Senshi Warrior. I was asked to become a Guardian, but I initially declined. But then the young man helped me realize that becoming a Guardian could be my way of honoring my family and people. So I joined The Order and came to Journia, finding meaning once again, and the rest... well that's history."

Raito: "That's just, wow Nico. I never knew how deep your story went, or how powerful your species was."

Nico: "You wanted to know. But I'll never know how truly strong we were."

Raito: "How come?"

Nico: "Because I don't bathe under Helios, Surya or Apollo. I am grateful for the Sun I have the pleasure of experiencing now, here on Journia. But still, to feel those Three Suns again while I've mastered my Solar Mutation. *sigh*...Enough about me, what's your history Raito?"

Raito: "Story for another time my friend."

154

Nico: "I understand brotha, whenever you're ready. Thank you for listening to my story though. I know it was long, but I really appreciate the time you gave. Also I'm grateful for you for saving us back there and bringing us to safety. I owe you one."

Raito: "Of course Nico. Thanks for sharing, and to be honest, Rachel played a big part, but the One Infinite Creator did more of the saving. I just picked up the pieces."

The two shared brotherly Love as Raito left Nico to rest while moving to wake up Vinzent because of the completion of his healing. The Elder walked up to the tank's control panel before pressing key buttons to drain the green liquid. Shortly after, Vinzent awakened and released himself from the oxygen mask and monitors. Raito took the arm of the waking Guardian as he helped him to the nearby bed a few feet from the tank.

Raito: "Slow and steady. Your body has to adjust to the gravity. You may feel dizzy. Besides that, are you alright?"

Vinzent: *waking tone* "Y-Yeah. I feel…replenished, I need a moment to wake up my body, but I'm okay. How is everyone else?"

Raito: "Cass is recovering from her surgery done by Jasmine and yours truly, and Nico is awake. Did you know his homeworld had Three Suns? And that a prophet from the Creator came to his world?"

Vinzent: "Relatively good news, and no. How do you know?"

Raito: "He shared his life story. It's pretty interesting. That aside, Rachel… she sacrificed her life to spare ours…"

Vinzent: "Don't tell me she's…dead?"

Raito: "Same thing Nico said. I can't say for certain. Orion seemed like he needed her for something, but I don't know what."

Jasmine: "I may be able to help with that."

Vinzent: "I'd expect nothing less from you Jazz. Listen, Raito, you've done more than enough for us all and Nico and I owe you BIG time."

Raito: "Oh yeah, that's a given."

Vinzent: *soft chuckle* "Rest my friend. I'll reactivate the rehab tank so we can get that arm fixed."

Raito: "That would be lovely. Keeping up Graceful Replacement is exhausting, especially after our last fight. Unlike you guys, I haven't rested."

Elder Vinzent was healed and combat ready as he placed Raito in the rehab tank and handed him the cleaned oxygen mask. Vinzent locked and sealed Elder Raito away before filling it with the same seafoam green liquid. The warmth of the liquid massaged and relaxed Raito, putting the Elder to sleep while slowly regenerating his arm. Vinzent exited the medical/rehab center, leaving his faction members to recover. Later he joined Jasmine in the war room offsetted at the end of the base's hallway. He accessed the master computer, with the help of Jazz, to find out why exactly the most evil person in the Universe spared their lives for Rachel's. After Jasmine hacked and broke through The Vault's firewalls, Rachel's Guardian file was opened. However, the information available truly disturbed Elder Vinzent...**Rachel belonged to an extremely rare and powerful horned-humanoid species called, The *Asronians*. When they're connected to their natural power, Cosmic Energy through the Way of Bogan, the Asronians have the potential to harness an unlimited amount of Source Energy to then use as they please, thus making them mortal deities in a sense. The species as a whole however, was wiped out because of their ignoble-like nature which made their existence extremely dangerous and unpredictable. These beings wiped out entire star systems as their hunger for blood and vengeance increased. This ultimately brought about the first Galactic War. A devastating event that saw trillions** perish and lasted six years, thus creating the Ashura Order, the fall of the Asronian species and the creation of Orion. Furthermore, an infant girl by the name of Rose was found abandoned in deep space, during the early years of post-war Journia and The Order, and was found, accepted and cared for by the villagers. She would later be accepted and practiced the Way of Ashla as a Guardian and was given the name Rachel. She fought hard to achieve the rank of third-class Elder, and to shine some Light on her Dark ancestral history.

Vinzent: "The fall of the Asronian race by the early Ashura Order and Senshi Warriors caused the rise of Orion. Could Orion be getting revenge against The Order? Could Orion be an Asronian? What caused the first war to start in the first place? That aside, based on this hidden file, Rachel is an Asronian. This is extremely bad. If this file is true, we could possibly have two adult Asronians. As if Orion wasn't bad enough. How did we not know about this? How could The Nine keep something like this hidden?!"

Jasmine: "Maybe to protect Rachel? Or maybe to hide a terrible truth? Whatever the case may be, I hope it helped. I had to jump through hundreds of firewalls just to get Rachel's Guardian file. The Vault seems to have been completely locked after The Nine's death."

Vinzent: "We'll deal with The Vault later. Asronian. I've never heard of that species, and it says here that their home planet is called *Asron*? Jazz, any ideas?"

Jasmine ran through the heavily guarded data of The Vault and found more useful information.

Jasmine: "Hmmm. Oh, here it is! It says Asron was once a world filled with beauty and vegetation, but now it's a world filled head to toe with water? Looks like the Senshi Warriors and the Guardians from the early Ashura Order really wanted them completely gone. They straight up changed the elemental nature of the entire planet. Just who are these Asronians?"

Vinzent: "A formidable race that caused the first Galactic War, or so we've been made to believe."

As Vinzent and Jazz researched this old dangerous threat, alarms blared and an enormous red light blinded the Guardian as a Demon ranked alert filled the computer screens.

Vinzent: "What the? Jasmine what's happening?"

Jasmine: "It appears to..."

Vinzent: "Appears to what? Talk to me!"

Jasmine: "The planet's core is unstable..."

Vinzent: "What do you mean 'unstable'? I need more than that."

Jasmine: "An unfamiliar Energy source has split the planet's crust in half, and destabilized Journia's core causing massive amounts of heat and gravitational Energy to fluctuate uncontrollably. The split is causing the tectonic plates to shift all at once causing catastrophic disasters like massive earthquakes, tsunamis, gravitational unbalances, etc. The planet is literally tearing itself apart both externally and internally."

As Jasmine explained the dire situation, the base began to shake violently as historic earthquakes were felt throughout the entire planet. The nerve racking rambling woke Elder Cass up and caused Elder Nico to get up and stumble out of bed. He slowly regained enough Solar Energy to move on his own, thanks to the artificial Solar bed. Nico made his way to the war room and asked for an update.

Nico: "Jazz, Vinzent, what is going on?"

Vinzent: "Long story short, the world is ending..."

And with those heart crushing words, the two Elders found themselves floating as if submerged under water.

Nico: "Jasmine?"

Jasmine: "It appears Journia's gravity is fluctuating at an alarming rate. Everything is in free-float mode now. Based on these readings, the planet's core will generate enough gravity and will bring the two split halves together violently like smashing two eggs together."

Vinzent: "Then that's our queue, it's time to go. Nico, are you good?"

Nico: "I need the Sun to fully recover, but thanks to the loss of gravity, yeah. I'm good."

Vinzent: "Okay, I need you to get Raito and Cass to the Hercules and prepare it for launch. I'm gonna head to the MT-AT."

Nico: "Got it. Jasmine, what's the status of the Hercules and the MT-AT?"

Jasmine: "The Hercules is ready to go, but the MT-AT needs extensive repairs."

Vinzent: "We'll manage the rest of the repairs on the Hercules."

Vinzent, Nico and Jasmine worked vigorously to secure their faction's safety. Elder Nico drained the green liquid that submerged Raito which allowed him to carry both Cass and Raito thanks to the fluctuating gravity. Going down the elevator, Vinzent entered the lower levels of the base to prepare the MT-AT for departure. However due to the excessive shaking, pieces of rock fell from the ceiling and threatened the integrity of the damaged MT-AT. That was when Elder Vinzent sprung into action. The Elder generated his Red Aura, enabling him to manifest a bow and four bright red arrows. Without hesitation, the Elder shot all four arrows above the MT-AT. They fused together before bursting into a large fish net, which caught the falling rock. Following this, Jasmine informed both Nico and Vinzent of the status of the planet.

Jasmine: "We're in trouble here. The core's gravity is getting stronger, and pulling the halves together at an increased rate. I detect multiple meteors heading towards our direction."

Nico: "Activate the base's defenses. Buy us some time."

Jasmine: "Way ahead of you."

Jasmine took control of the weapon systems as the feminine artificial intelligence used the base's heavy energy cannons to blow several meteors out of the sky, allowing the two Elders to load everyone and everything necessary into the vehicles. Nico strapped Cass and Raito into the seats before taking command of the Hercules. Shortly after, Raito regained consciousness as the waking Guardian asked what was going on. In a hastened tone, Nico quickly responded by saying, "the world is ending." Elders Raito and Cass looked at each other in utter incredulity. The engines of the Hercules roared like a healthy lion as Nico abruptly took off, dodging floating rocks and trees. The lack of gravity gave the ship an extra push which Nico took full advantage of. Shortly after, Elder Nico used the ship's communications to contact his comrade.

Nico: "Vinzent where are you? It's time to go."

But just as he finished his statement, Elder Vinzent was seen bursting out of the base's lower hunger doors with the feat catching the attention of Nico. Vinzent drove the MT-AT like a professional as he fearlessly traversed the dangerous gravity-less area of Mara. He knew he needed to get aboard the Hercules, but he also knew Nico couldn't afford to land in such unpredictable conditions. So he thought as an Elder and used his Elemental Energy to boost the speed of the tank as he drove off a fallen tree. The jump propelled him high in the sky because of the loss of gravity, enabling the damaged tank to otherwise fly. With these abnormal turns of events, Nico ceased the present moment as he positioned the Hercules in the path of the floating MT-AT, allowing for an easy grab-n-go, but before the deed was achieved, a giant rock floated directly in the MT-AT's path, blocking the catch. With the weapons down, the MT-AT was helpless as it drew near, but suddenly the rock was split in half by a swift katana slice performed by Elder Cass as the two halves floated away. Cass saved the faction from devastation and allowed the MT-AT to safely land inside the Hercules's cargo area. After securing and exiting the tank, Vinzent joined Nico in the cockpit as the Elders escaped Journia's end, flying farther from their base. Raito looked back out the window towards the base in dejection.

Raito: "It's crazy how unprepared we were. We as The Order, as Elders, thought we were the best and strongest, and that no one would dare. Oh how wrong we were. How entitled we were, how comfortable we became…Orion took everything from us, and now we flee from our planet, barely escaping with our lives. Sounds familiar Nico?"

Cass: "Sometimes that's all we need. As long as there are Guardians who'll fight the good fight, the Light isn't lost. We faced Orion head on and lived to tell about it because of the One Infinite Creator. Regardless of how you look at it, fate has spared us. That counts for something."

Raito agreed as the two Elders joined Elders Nico and Vinzent in the cockpit. The Hercules flew deeper into space, outside of Journia's orbit as the spacecraft flew further and further away. The team looked at their planet in dispiritedness and sorrow. They watched as their once beautiful world collided in on itself, sending a huge shockwave that temporarily threw the Hercules to the side. That day, Journia became nothing more than a wound in deep space, joining the long list of worlds forever cursed by the Orion Crusaders…

NINE

ENLIGHTENMENT

The Ashura Order, a once untouchable force which protected the galaxy for centuries after the first Galactic War, now crushed under the weight of Orion's might. Journia was defiled and distorted as the small faction of Elders took their last look at their homeworld. Orion's worldship pilots informed their master of multiple spacecraft attempting to leave the star system. They also reported identifying a specific ship as the Hercules. Without a word, The Obedience opened fire upon the vessel, ignoring the other spacecraft attempting to escape. Elder Nico utilized his piloting skills to maneuver his way around cannon fire and leftover pieces of Journia's moon, Bao. The Elder performed timely barrel rolls, turns and twists while utilizing the pieces of the moon as cover, making it seemingly impossible for The Obedience to hit its target. But the battle was far from over as the giant planet-killer launched a small squad of Ryū fighters. These ships were smaller than the Hercules which enabled the vessels to close the distance between themselves and their target. With few options, Elders Vinzent and Cass manned the ship's turrets as the Elders engaged in a space dogfight.

Nico: "Coming up on our six! I'll get you in position…"

Nico abruptly cut the engines which forced the Ryū fighters to zip past the Hercules. Elder Nico then punched the thrusters, but not without getting Vinzent and Cass in position. With a clear shot, the Elders fired the Hercules's turrets, destroying several enemy fighters.

Cass: "Now that's what I call ace shooting!"

Vinzent: "We're not out of the fog yet."

Nico showcased more of his flying skills, out maneuvering the enemy fighters, and allowing Elder Vinzent and Elder Cass to destroy the rest with haste. Following the destruction of the enemy pursuers, the Hercules effectively cleared a path for them to make their escape. Jasmine warmed up the hyperdrive as the faction found an opening out of the astro belt made from Bao's destruction. They then cleared the thick field of debris before Nico and Vinzent coordinated the faction's escape route.

Nico: "That was close, but we should be clear. Jazz…"

Jasmine: "Already on it."

The Hercules began to hum gloriously with Energy from the core as the thrusters glowed with power. With the coordinates plotted, the Hercules blasted into hyperspace, leaving behind a trail of sky blue streaks as several reinforcing Ryū ships were left behind. The Obedience pilots begged for forgiveness for the Guardian's escape, but Orion simply reassured them of their important role.

Orion: "I see your sorrow my friends, all is well. You, my pilots, are important tools. Let them go, they couldn't defeat me before and now that I have Rose, I am inevitable."

The Obedience pilots roared in glee and newly found confidence. They then continued their onslaught as the Orion Crusaders finished destroying Journia's entire star system of nine planets, leaving only the

Sun. Six hundred and eighty four billion men, women, and children perished that day. With The Order in ruins, and all other major forces to oppose Orion's conquest destroyed, the Orion Crusaders took their time moving from planet to planet, killing, enslaving and destroying while abusing the Asronian Cosmic Energy found within Orion and The Eye, commanding her to commit mass genocide on a galactic scale. Orion spread his influence of death and Darkness throughout Myrmidon, moving all the while closer to his true goal...

Meanwhile in hyperspace, Nico gave Jasmine the controls as he and Elder Raito helped each other out of the cockpit; their recovery still incomplete. They entered the living quarters of the smoothly crafted starship and were joined by Elders Vinzent and Cass to discuss their next course of action.

Raito: "So, what now? It's not like we can just wait and call for backup. I hate to bring up the obvious, but we're kinda on our own here."

Vinzent: "You're right, Journia is gone. For all we know, we could be the last Guardians left which is all the more reason why we shouldn't give up. We came this far, survived impossible odds. I for one refuse to wait until we or the galaxy falls victim to this Darkness."

Nico: "Though I agree with you both, what's our next course of action? Because it kinda seems like we're the galaxy's last spark of hope. The thin line between life and death... no pressure."

Vinzent: "About that...Jazz and I found some rather...disturbing data, and it explains why Orion spared us for Rachel. It's not a solid path to victory against Orion, but at least we have somewhat of a lead. If you all would direct your attention to the hologram."

With the faction's undivided attention, Vinzent requested Jazz to share the data on the Asronian race...The Guardians looked at the information with wide eyes and edginess as Casanova started to put pieces together.

Cass: "So that's what he meant…"

Nico: "What do you mean?"

Cass: "When I was a girl, the village monk would share stories about the first Galactic War. About how these horned entities gave the galaxy nothing, but death and annihilation, and how The Organics was just a coverup to hide The Order's 'Dark side'. I always wondered why his stories never matched up with The Order's history. After a while, I assumed he was a crazy old man, but now I see why…These beings, they're complete monsters and to find out Rachel is one of them… it…it–"

Raito: "Doesn't change anything! We fought alongside Rachel. Yes she may be an Asronian, but she isn't one of these monsters. She is an amazing Guardian and is the reason we're all here now! She wouldn't be corrupted so easily."

Nico: "I get your frustration Raito, but–"

Raito: "You don't get anything! None of you do!"

Nico placed a hand on Raito's shoulder to comfort his brother, while looking him in the eyes.

Nico: "Then when shit hits the fan, and we're put up against Rachel on the battlefield, will you have what it takes to do what needs to be done?"

Raito: "What are you trying to say Nico?"

Nico: "I'm saying emotions play a big role in the midst of battle. Don't let them cloud your judgment. Take these words from someone who struggles with their emotions…"

Nico's words cut deep into the mind of Raito as he was left temporarily speechless. Given the silence, Vinzent took the spotlight once more, pulling the focus back to the present moment.

Vinzent: "Emotions are high, I get that, but we can't save Rachel nor the galaxy if we're emotionally and mentally divided."

Raito: "You're right. I'm sorry for losing my cool, I just...care about Rachel."

Vinzent: "We all want her back safe. It's safe to say that she's alive at least."

The Elders found peace amongst themselves before Jazz alerted the faction of their exiting from hyperspace. After a few short moments of the peaceful sound of space and the ship's engines, the Hercules popped out of hyperspace and approached a world completely covered with water. Cass being an elemental manipulator of water, felt excitement rush over her like a child in a candy store.

Jasmine: "Now approaching Asron."

Raito: "As- what now?"

Jasmine: "Once a gorgeous world filled with life and power, and home to the Asronian race. Now it floats in space as a wet disaster and a reminder that all things change in one way or another. Vinzent and I found some information as well as the location of the planet. And with, ya know, the Ashura Order gone and zero leads, why not start here!"

Nico: "Great. A water world..."

Raito: "What's wrong with that Mr, "all sand is good sand?""

Nico: *soft chuckle* "Let's just say I don't do well away from the Sun. Plus, I have sort of a weakness to water. It's kinda dumb, so I'm not gonna talk about it."

Raito: "It can't be that dumb. What could you say? You can't swim..."

Nico fell quiet and closed his eyes in embarrassment. Raito and Cass both let out a giggle, allowing Vinzent's grin to go unnoticed.

Raito: *chuckles* "I got the Sun part, but I didn't know about the water. But wait, Cass is a user of water, how does that…"

Nico: "She's different. Her water is…loving, gentle and beautiful, yet tight, strong and—"

Cass suddenly formed a water bubble over Nico's head, filling his mouth with water. Nico began desperately pulling away at the bubble, but with no luck due to the bubble being ungrabbable… She then grabbed the attention of her faction members to look at the planet as the faction entered the atmosphere.

Cass: "Ahem…hemm. Well, doesn't this planet look peaceful guys?…"

Vinzent, Jasmine and Raito all shared a laugh as Nico fell to his knees, knowing he was gonna die. The Hercules entered the planet's lower atmosphere as Jasmine, still in control, searched for a place to land. The AI continued to fly when suddenly, the cream colored ship paused in the sky as if it were caught in a spiderweb. The ship's systems began to shut down as the shields lowered, the weapons deactivated and the thrusters cooled down. The Elders were left floating and confused as they all worked to see what was wrong. But before any progress was made, the ship began a high speed nose dive towards the endless sea, several thousand meters below as if someone dropped a rock from a skyscraper.

Jasmine: "At this rate without the shields, the impact with the water will tear the ship apart! We need to stop this somehow!"

With Jazz's worry felt throughout the ship, Elders Nico and Cass looked at each other as the couple sprung into action. Cass hopped on Nico's back as the two Elders found one of the ship's airlocks. Nico forced the hatch open before feeling the blessing shine from this planet's

Sun as he said joyfully, "finally, the Sun". With his cells charged, Nico leaped from the Hercules's outer-shell with great force, pushing the ship upward which gave Nico and Cass a major boost in speed. The two plummeted straight towards the sea surface as Cass formed a board made from the planet's water, and a waterslide that Nico used to help smooth the landing to the ocean's surface. With no physical land, Cass enjoyed her time on the planet and placed her hand on the ocean surface, creating a solid foundation of dense water made from her Elemental Energy. With solid ground, Nico firmly planted both feet before forming his Ken fists, while amplifying the fibers of his legs and chest. Cass also added to Nico's efforts by forming two large hands of water above the Taiyōnian, which acted as cushions. Seconds passed and the once tiny ship began to grow in size as the Hercules descended closer and closer, forcing Jazz to advise Vinzent and Raito to get seated and buckled. The two Elders inside the Hercules hurried to their seats before feeling and hearing several splashes, then a deep THUD as the ship crashed into the sea, sending shockwaves rippling through the ocean. Moments passed and silence fell upon the single body ocean; an eerie silence as souls of the Asronian people whispered in the wind. Suddenly, the Hercules burst through the ocean's surface, showcasing its ability to float. Elders Nico and Cass were seen on the hood of the ship as Nico struggled to catch his breath.

Cass: "Good catch love."

Nico: *breathing heavily* "I couldn't... have done it... without you... milady." *coughs*

Cass leans over and kisses Nico on the cheek before patting his other cheek. Afterwards she made her way to the opened hatch Elders Vinzent and Raito were seen coming out of.

Vinzent: "We appreciate the save you two."

Raito: "Yeah, thank you. Don't think that counts as your favor to me by the way..."

Cass: "You both owe me one now."

Cass patted both Vinzent and Raito on the shoulder before heading back into the ship to check the systems, leaving the three Guardians to assess the situation. Nico caught his breath shortly after.

Nico: "She's amazing…that aside, it's not desirable, but we landed the ship. A lot better than the alternative. Now we need to find the habitants."

Raito: "Leave that to me."

Elder Raito took on the task, used one of his Stem Shots and sped off, using his empowered super speed to run on water and search the entire planet for…something and/or someone. Meanwhile, Elders Nico and Vinzent re-entered into the floating ship to find out what exactly caused the ship's sudden shut down. They, with the help of Jasmine and Elder Cass, completed a full diagnostics of the ship and MT-AT twice, but found nothing out of the ordinary besides minor damages from the impact, which bred more questions than answers.

Jasmine: "Strange. No system malfunctions, no major damages, no core issues. We did a full sweep twice and found only minor external damages. This day just keeps on giving."

Nico: "Maybe it's something unseen and unheard. Maybe we'll find what we seek if we dive into the spiritual realm."

Vinzent agreed with Cass joining them as well. Nico then tasked Jasmine with a submarine pre-launch assignment.

Nico: "In the meantime Jazz, could you prepare the MT-AT for submarine deployment?"

Jasmine: "You can count on me!"

Jasmine, the AI, prepared the MT-AT while the three Elders entered into the ship's living quarters before sitting in a triangular fashion. They began to chant their mantra, *"Energy flows through all things, and I am Energy"*, over and over. The mantra proved fruitful as it deepened their focus and helped connect them to a single lifeforce deep within the planet's core, however this lifeform's Energy seemed far greater and more controlled than most. With enough to go on for the time being, the Elders finished their meditation session while at the same time, Raito sped back to the group and into the ship. His face was blank like a piece of fresh paper, as out of breath, the Guardian informed Nico and Vinzent that there's, "nothing, but water, in every direction". Unsatisfied, Vinzent asked Jazz to do a full sweep of the sea floor below and what she found took her by surprise.

Vinzent: "What is it Jazz?"

Jasmine: "It's amazing and mysterious, and quite old. I would tell you, but there's no adventure in that. Go down and see!"

Vinzent: "You always know how to keep someone on edge. *soft chuckle* How are the preparations going with the MT-AT?"

Jasmine: "Because of the system shutdown, I couldn't finish repairing the weapon systems, but everything else is good as new and ready for conversion."

Vinzent: "Unfortunate, but doable nonetheless. Thank you for your effort Jazz."

Jasmine accepted the gratitude with open arms as she and Cass prepared the MT-AT for a deep sea dive. With Vinzent entering the tank's cockpit, he pressed a few buttons before pressing a pulsating green button with the word "convert" printed in black. He told the faction to make haste as Elders Nico and Raito traveled down to the MT-AT to help with preparations. Raito joined Vinzent in the cockpit to help complete any last minute tasks and repairs, giving Nico and Cass the appropriate time to secure the equipment. A moment of privacy welcomed Cass and Nico as the Elder asked for Cass to stay behind with the ship to protect it, and to be available if they needed a quick extraction. Cass agreed, wishing luck to the group of Elders before sharing a loving embrace with Nico.

With everything secured, Nico gave the "all clear" to Vinzent which he confirmed and pressed, holding the convert button. The Hercules hummed alive with water and Sunlight piercing through the opening cargo door. With Elder Vinzent in command, the Guardian drove into the ocean as the MT-AT transformed into a submarine, allowing the faction to descend deeper into the sea, reaching hundreds, then thousands of feet below the sea's surface. Nico noticed the increasing lack of Sunlight and gave out an accepting sigh. The Elders continued to dive, wondering what Jazz scanned when Raito looked out in the distance in complete amazement. The newly formed MT-AT submarine approached a massive underwater city, old and battle-scarred as it sat on the ocean floor, illuminated by the struggling Sunlight and glowing sea creatures. Sea mammals, large and small, found curiosity with the Elders and bumped into their vessel. Vinzent moved the submarine in closer, entering the city's perimeter to provide cover as Jasmine picked up a strange Energy source a few hundred meters straight ahead. Filled with the sense of duty and purpose, the faction of Elders proceeded without delay towards the beacon of Energy. But suddenly and without warning, the MT-AT's systems began to shut down, and Jazz was temporarily cut off from the MT-AT. At the same time, Vinzent lost all control of the submarine. Despite the current circumstances, level heads prevailed as the group worked to reestablish control over the sub and connection with Elder Casanova and Jasmine. However, their efforts were hampered by the mysterious Energy which had taken control of the sub. Shortly after, the water-vehicle was maneuvered into a large swirling pool of red liquid. Once submerged into the liquid, the submarine forcibly twisted, flipped and resurfaced, not back to the top of Asron's ocean, but in a different location completely, a location filled with grass, trees, and a mysterious, but enormous castle.

Raito: "Any idea where we are?"

Nico: "Hollow Asron? A planet within a planet?"

Vinzent: "It looks like we went through some sort of portal. None of our technology seems to be operational either, not broken, but turned off…what a strange planet."

The faction exited the submarine with the Elders setting foot on dry land. The Guardians turned and all expressed a sense of awe as they're towered by a ruined castle with Nico adding, "damn". The massive castle was ginormous with two statues, one male and the other female, in front of the main entrance, a hundred feet in height. The sheer size of the estate competed with The Castle of the Teutonic Order in Malbork, on present day Earth. The Elders proceeded into the unknown castle in a line formation with Nico taking point, Raito covering the left and right flank, leaving Vinzent to cover the rear. They reached the entrance as Nico amplified his arm's strength to push the massive stone doors open. As they explored this unfamiliar plane of existence, the Elders noticed heavily distorted, yet intact portraits of red-skin horned individuals that shared Rachel's distinct features. Some female; some male. Some with long horns; some with short horns. Some with two horns; others with one. The Guardians continued forward, passing by more paintings and unkept rooms filled with old remnants from a lost species as they're only met with emptiness and forgotten history. But that emptiness soon faded as Nico noticed a shadowy figure off in the distance. He signaled the faction to halt and prepare themselves as the figure's deep and powerful voice filled the ears of all three Elders.

Mysterious figure: "Who are you? Why have you come here?"

The Guardians were hesitant to speak, but the silence was broken by Elder Nico.

Nico: "We are Guardians of the Ashura Order. We noticed the entities on the walls and how they possess the horns of the Asronian race. We seek knowledge about the race and how–"

Mysterious figure: "What you seek is lost, Guardians. A race forgotten by history and scarred from the past. You all must leave this place. There's nothing here for you."

Vinzent: "With all due respect, I'm afraid we can't do that. You see, there's a war going on and the knowledge here may be our only chance in putting an end to it."

The mysterious man responded by giving out an amused, "oh?" before suddenly appearing right in front of Nico in a cloud of red mist. The figure was old with pasty red skin covered by a raggedy hood and robe as he stood, using his cane as support. The Guardians stood ready with Elder Nico amplifying and mutating into the Jūken blade. Elder Vinzent generated his Red Aura to manifest a red lightning sword and Elder Raito conjured a battle-axe of Prana Energy.

Mysterious figure: "You must've misheard me. I do not find interest in your galaxy nor your war. Get out."

The Guardians readied themselves as they sensed dense Bogan fueled Source Energy flowing from the being.

Mysterious figure: "You Guardians think you can enter someone's establishment and do as you please? Very well. I see this generation is in need of manners."

The mysterious man, with acknowledgeable speed and power, used his cane to strike Nico which threw him through a wall. The old man then traded a few blows with Vinzent's lightning sword to Vinzent's surprise, because of his wooden cane blocking a heated sword made from lightning. Seeing an opening, Raito stepped in to assist Vinzent with them combining their strikes, but the old man managed to successfully defend himself while occasionally attacking. Vinzent and Raito both jumped backwards, surprising the old man as Nico came in fast, slamming his Ken fists against the ground which barely missed the mysterious man as he dodged backwards. With the mystery being in the air, Nico dashed, appearing directly in front of the old man as the Elder quickly mutated his amplified arm and swung his Jūken blade in a downward motion, wishing to cut through the man. The elderly man reacted just in time to block the attack but was then blasted in the side by Raito, sending the old man flying into a wall. He leaned against the cracked wall as three Elder ranked Guardians stood before him, weapons trained and ready. Shortly after, the Sunlight shined on the figure, forcing utter silence among the Elders as they saw the man's rough and scarred red skin, long gray hair and beard, and torn off horns as he looked at Guardians with one good eye with an empty space in place of the other. Using that moment of hesitation, the old man quickly slammed the end of his cane against the ground, causing a shockwave that threw the Guardians off balance. And without a wasted motion, the old man swiftly reached into his pocket and pulled out a pile of blue dust before blowing it in the faces of all three Guardians, knocking them out. Nico's Healing-Factor worked to fight against the powerful sedative, but the Elder began to lose consciousness as he looked beside him to see both of his comrades unconscious and unresponsive. His vision further blurred, getting darker and darker as he witnessed the old man's mouth moving. Because of the dust, Nico had a hard time hearing the man, but could make out two words, "trust me", before collapsing on the floor.

Time passed as the ocean covered planet brushed its currents in the direction of the wind, as if being directed by gravity. Deep within the core of Asron, thanks to time and patience, Elder Nico was the first to awaken as he, along with Vinzent and Raito, all laid in separate beds. Elder Raito awakened next, curious as to what was going on, with Elder Vinzent regaining his consciousness lastly. All three Guardians were awake and relatively alert, but something was wrong. Soon after, the old man entered the room and properly introduced himself.

Titus: "Allow me to introduce myself. My name is Titus Ronan, once Emperor of the Red Nobles and great Asronian race. I formally welcome you all to my old estate, *Castle Pandous*, where I now spend my days walking the halls of this castle enlightened, yet prisoner."

Nico: "Emperor…wait, you caused the first Galactic War? You destroyed my home and caused the birth of Orion?!"

Titus: "The first? I assumed it was the only one. But, to put it bluntly, yes, no sense in lying. Though this Orion entity is news to me. Regrettably, I've destroyed countless worlds in my time. So do forgive me if I've forgotten your planet."

Wanting to punish the ex-Emperor, Nico charged at Titus, but nothing happened…Nico couldn't utilize his Solar Mutation, nor could Vinzent generate any of his Auras, and Raito's Grimoire wasn't responding to his Prana Energy.

Vinzent: "What have you done to us?"

Titus: "I blocked your flow to Source Energy associated with Ashla techniques and teachings, temporarily stripping you from your powers and abilities, for three reasons. Firstly, to train you, secondly, to enlighten you, and thirdly, to open your minds to the Way of Bogan. I wish to help you all build the correct relationship between the mind, body, spirit and Source Energy. And to prove that Bogan teachings can work in harmony with Ashla teachings, side by side."

Nico: "What do YOU know of enlightenment? Of balance? Was it not you who took all those lives, seeking vengeance against the entirety of Myrmidon?"

Titus: *sigh* "You three and the Guardians before you use the Source Energy flowing through you as a tool. As a kind of 'fuel'. In my time, I've found that raw Source Energy, without the teachings of either Ashla or Bogan, can be categorized into the four main forms: Cosmic, Solar, Elemental, and Kinetic. Cosmic Energy users are those who possess unorthodox abilities, such as gravity manipulation, Prana conjuration and/or enhanced mental capabilities, just to name a few. Solar Energy users are those who find power through Sunlight. Prime example would be the Taiyōnians and their Solar Mutation ability. Elemental

Energy users are entities who command one of the five elements: fire, water, earth, air and ether. Within these elements are sub-elements like Vinzent's lightning; this style of Source Energy is among the most common within Myrmidon. And lastly we have Kinetic Energy. These are beings who possess a noticeably weak connection to Source Energy, thus forcing them to use external means to match those who command great power. The Way of Ashla is only a means to use such Energies for the betterment of the galaxy in line with the will of the Creator; more of a set of morals and ideals. I'm sure The Nine has taught you this. But what happens when you infuse Bogan teachings in a way that harmonizes with the principles of Ashla? I wish to introduce you to a world not just in black and white, but of colors you thought were unseeable. I wish to show you all that, with a strong mind, the Way of Bogan can be used to further strengthen one's bond with the Creator, for it was he who created Source Energy and the paths of Ashla and Bogan. You all need to connect with your inner-Bogan in order to see the beauty of true power. Do not worry, like I said this is only temporary if you learn to flow with, then through the block, accepting what is and what can be."

Vinzent: "And why should we trust you?"

Nico: "I think we should hear him out...right before we passed out, he whispered 'trust me' and thinking about it now, he could've killed us while we were unconscious and even now as we sit here powerless."

Titus: "Wise words from a Guardian such as yourself. Your abilities from before are quite familiar. Who are you, Guardian? Where are you from?"

Nico: "My name is Nico Tulex. I am a Taiyōnian from the planet Taiyō."

Titus: "Ah yes! The Taiyōnians. I've destroyed hundreds of worlds, too many to count, but Taiyō… How could I forget the Senshi Warriors of the Three Suns. A population who formed their own Energy category, and that nearly ruined everything. Your people possessed incredible power, Solar Mutation was it?"

Nico: "Yes…"

Titus: "Even though your planet was destroyed, your species still managed to survive and help put an end to the war; resilient indeed. And I see your markings, you must have mastered your Solar Mutation fully, becoming a Senshi Warrior yourself."

Nico: "Yes. Took me a while to master my Healing-Factor without proper guidance, but the Creator provides. However, Taiyō was destroyed before I could earn the title of Senshi."

Titus: "I see. For what it's worth, I'm deeply sorry for what I did to your Suns, your people and homeworld. As you can see, we now share the same fate."

Nico: "I forgive you for what you took from me. And for the sake of my family, I accept your apology."

Titus: "Thank you Nico. Earlier you asked why I caused the Galactic War, the answer was quite simple. I wanted revenge for my son, and eventually dominion over all. I wanted all the power despite being the king among my Asronian bloodline, and to show the Universe the might of the Asronian race. Obviously it didn't work and instead of bringing glory to my people, and avenging my son, I brought the extinction and the destruction of my home to what you see now, a moist graveyard. And as for Taiyō. I saw the power of the Senshi Warriors and wanted their skills within my ranks. I asked your king, King Lui the Forth, to surrender and join my cause or die with the rest of the galaxy. I'm sure you know the rest, Taiyōnian."

Nico: "Didn't give us much of an option. How were you and the Asronians defeated?"

Titus: *soft chuckle* "A history lesson aye? Very well......As I assume, The Nine managed to keep my race from your history. They kept the true war from you all and decided to hide my people under the name 'The Organics'; what a degrading title. It started after a small group of Ashla taught entities, called, what you know as The Nine, came to my planet to spread the teachings of Source Energy through Ashla means. We Asronians knew only of the Way of Bogan, so it was weirdly intriguing to witness the other side of Source Energy in action. I found it amusing, so did my wife and most of my elected officials, but my oldest son Theo however, found the Way of Ashla disgusting and repulsive. It was a learning curve for all of us, The Nine included, however Theo did not accept these teachings and after a while, he started to resent me for befriending, and accepting The Nine and their ways. I was clouded by my curiosity in the Way of Ashla which dulled my senses. As a result, I could not see the plot being forged in the shadows. One night I heard screams from within my second oldest son's room. I rushed to his room, but I was too late. I found my beloved son, Gabriel... murdered by what felt to be Ashla taught Source Energy. I lost myself in confusion and grief. Darkness flowed through me like never before and everyone on Asron could feel my rage, my hate, my pain. I didn't kill the Ashla teachers then because of my wife who also ruled Asron beside me as its Empress. She convinced me they should be put on trial. I disagreed, but nonetheless they went on trial and went free due to inconclusive evidence. This enraged the majority of my people, and I was forced to make a choice. Do nothing or do something. I chose to do something, I chose to spread the Asronian name throughout the galaxy with fear as the main motivation and message. I chose this so that no one else among my people would feel the level of grief my wife and I felt, and that the galaxy would think twice before crossing the Asronian people. As a result, I started the Galactic War and killed trillions for the sake of my son Gabriel. Theo was my second-in-command, and gladly did everything I commanded without question. We fought and fought and fought, against The Order, the Senshi Warriors, and any other armed force who opposed us. It was a bloody time back then, but eventually, karma caught back up with me. Towards the end of the sixth year, The Nine fully formed their Ashura Order, and allied with the surviving Senshi Warriors. By this time, my forces were outnumbered and overwhelmed. This was partially due to spending two years worth of manpower and resources invading Taiyō. But also due to The Order's increasing numbers. Because of these undesirable truths, I was forced to command a full retreat back to Asron, where our enemies commenced an all-out strike to end the war. With the combined strength of the Senshi Warriors, and the thousands of Ashla followers from across the galaxy, they cornered us and destroyed the remainder of my worldship fleet, eventually coming aboard my own worldship, where Theo and I fought the enemy. It was a hard fought battle indeed, and many loyal Red Nobles died defending the bridge; necessary sacrifices for the greater good, or so I thought at the time. After The Nine managed to defeat and capture my son Theo, I surrendered, fearing they would kill him too. Theo called me a coward, and said I was 'unfit to lead the fearless Asronian people'. There was some truth to what he said however. I instilled fearlessness in Theo and my people, so for him to see his father, the one he admired most, surrender in fear, regardless of who's life was at stake, deeply discombobulated him."

Nico: "Was that the only reason why you surrendered?"

Titus: "No. The Nine taught us that forgiveness was highly valued within the Way of Ashla. So I tested that fact, and surrendered believing that I, and my planet, would be shown mercy and forgiveness."

Nico: "You really thought after everything you put the galaxy through, there wouldn't be any consequences?"

Titus: "I am no child Taiyōnian. I was aware that my actions would bring judgment and I was fully prepared to die because of them. However, I was not prepared for the judgment set before me. Even though I surrendered, my people and their Empress had not, and continued to fire upon The Order from Asron's surface. Shortly after, The Nine combined their Source Energies and formed a spell which altered the position of Asron's twin moons; that Energy felt like a step below the Creator himself. Theo and I helplessly witnessed this pure Source

Energy manipulate our moon's position towards Asron, which altered the stability of our planet's oceans; all six of them. The manipulation birthed supermassive tsunami's from all directions that engulfed the entire planet, drowning everyone and flooding everything from the tallest mountains to the widest structures. Anyone who managed to survive the initial flooding were mercilessly killed on site on The Nine's orders, innocent women and children included. I could only imagine the fear in those children's hearts as they were consumed and tossed by the tsunami's, like clothes in a washer. That day was named 'Day of the Angry Seas', and would be the day I lost everything. Shortly after, I was forced to agree to The Nine's ridiculous conditions and regulations. And banished to Castle Pandous, which had been pulled into the sea, and into what I assumed to be a planet within a planet."

After hearing Titus's side of the war, the Guardians were downright perplexed, and felt a storm of doubt and anxiety rush over them as Elder Raito spoke out.

Raito: "That's not true! There's no way Guardians of Ashla, let alone The Nine would kill innocent women and children...right?"

Titus: "Judging from your expressions, you all, and I assume most of the present day Guardians, had no idea that the Way of Ashla could be just as cruel as the Way of Bogan when not conscious of it. How does it feel knowing there's no true difference between Ashla and Bogan; good and evil; the strong and the weak; the righteous and the damned?"

Vinzent: "The difference is within the individual. Every entity has free will. A choice to follow whatever path they see fit to follow, regardless of what's right or wrong."

Titus: "Interesting. You think my son had a choice when he was killed in cold blood? Or my people had a choice when you Guardians slaughtered them and destroyed my planet?"

Nico: "You decided for them the moment you caused the war. When you sought vengeance over Love, peace and acceptance."

Titus: "It sounds like you found peace with what happened to Taiyō and its people."

Nico: "I was in a dark place, but the Creator gifted me with good people, a new home, new friends and family, a new purpose."

Titus: "Then you are among the lucky ones who found themselves in Darkness, but were shown a different way by the Creator."

Nico: "The Creator offers himself to any who find themselves in a Dark place. It's up to that individual to follow the Love and Light of the Creator, or shy away. That's the power of free will, like Vinzent mentioned before."

Titus: "Interesting."

Raito: "These conditions, I assume breaking your horns were one of them?"

Titus: "Very perceptive of you, yes. Along with killing the rest of my species, leaving me as the last of my kind, and banishing me to this castle, forever stuck within the core of this sunken world. For centuries I sought revenge, a hate as pure and potent as the Sun, but while in complete solitude, I found a sense of peace and absolute tranquility. I lost my influence, my world, my people, my family, but instead found enlightenment, peace, Love, and forgiveness. I was shown the One Infinite Creator, not directly, but his grace and absoluteness. I've learned that revenge is just another way to run from the issue. Truly I don't forgive myself for what I've done; my embarrassing lack of emotional control. However, being the last one of a species tends to open one's eye to the fragile nature of the cosmos, and how grateful we must be for every blessing and lesson."

Raito: "You're not the last of your kind Titus. Rachel survived…"

As Raito revealed the news to Titus, Raito showed the old man a picture of Rachel as Titus initially looked on in confusion at the unfamiliar name, but could never forget his daughter's face, regardless of her age.

Titus: "She's alive! I see she goes by Rachel Rose. *soft smile* It is indeed a beautiful name. Thank you for showing me. Despite all that I've done, all the blood on my hands, the Creator still smiles upon me. I am grateful to the One Infinite Creator."

Raito: "How exactly do you know Rachel?"

Titus: "Well…she's my daughter of course."

The room was silent as the Guardians were not so surprised that he's her father, but more so at the fact her father was the Emperor who orchestrated the first Galactic War.

Titus: "Her mother must've saved her before Asron was completely submerged. That woman adored Rose. I feared I'd never see or hear of her survival, but that's not the case today."

Vinzent: "A local village at the time found and cared for her. Later on, when she became of age, she joined The Order and became a powerful Guardian. She was given a chance to live, as you hoped, despite her… family's history."

Titus: "Ironic. The very force I wanted to destroy ended up saving my daughter. The Creator works in mysterious ways does he not? Being my child, I'm sure she's survived up until this point, where is she?"

Raito: *sigh* "Orion found out about her secret and has corrupted her soul, or so we think. She sacrificed herself so that we may live to fight another day."

Titus: "So that's who I've been feeling all this time, such a familiar Energy to that entity. So much pain, so much death caused by one being. And he seems to have destroyed The Order." *chuckles*

With a sense of disrespect, the powerless Elder ranked Guardian Raito stepped up to Titus before grabbing his robe with violence and rage.

Raito: "I'm glad you think this is amusing. Too many good people died fighting Orion and all you can do is laugh?! Even when he has your daughter?! I may be powerless, but I can STILL whoop your ass old man!"

Emotions were high for Raito as Vinzent got up to lay his hand on Raito's shoulder in an attempt to calm him down.

Vinzent: "Calm your mind and steady your heart Guardian. Now is not the time to let your emotions dictate your actions."

With his words of wisdom resonating with Raito. He unhanded Titus before apologizing to which Titus accepted and praised Vinzent.

Titus: "Your Love for your comrades reminds me of my wife. She always knew how to calm me down and despite my wicked nature, she was the most beautiful and loving woman I've ever met. It's because of how she lived her life that I was able to find balance within myself now. She was the only one among the Asronian people who could fully harmonize the Way of Ashla with Bogan teachings easily, and yet, she died because of my actions… Still to this day, I have no idea what she saw in me."

Vinzent: "If you don't mind me asking what her name was?"

Titus: *saddened sigh* "Her name was Athena. She perished during the Day of the Angry Seas. I didn't even get to say goodbye."

Despite his sinister past actions, the Guardians felt a splash of sorrow for Titus and his wounded life, but that moment was quickly dismissed as Raito asked for the Emperor's help.

Raito: "I understand you've been through a lot and caused a lot, but here's a golden opportunity to right as many wrongs as you can. Help us defeat Orion and save your daughter…"

Titus: "Unfortunately my fighting days are behind me, plus even if I wanted to, I can't leave this castle. As punishment for my transgressions, along with imprisoning me deep within Asron, The Nine formed a powerful prison ritual called: *Soul Tether*. It was taught by Asronians and is fueled by the Way of Bogan. This ritual tethers the mind, body, and spirit of the targeted entity to a magical barrier or inside a structure, forever imprisoning them. In my case, The Nine used both a magical barrier and the entirety of Castle Pandous. I will never be freed nor can I join my wife and son in the afterlife. However, that won't stop me from helping you Guardians unlock your true power."

Nico: "Why would the Emperor of the Asronian race, the man behind the first Galactic War, go so far for us Guardians of the Ashura Order?"

Titus: "Because the Universe should be left with a fighting chance against the Darkness I unleashed. Because it's my chance to right some of these wrongs as your friend put it. Because my little girl is in trouble. And because it's what Athena would want…You three are unique among all the Guardians I've faced, even you, Taiyōnian. I felt it when your ship entered the atmosphere. You all have a destiny to fulfill. Now get some rest, you'll need it."

Titus left the Guardians to rest and to think about everything that had transpired only moments ago. With nothing left to do or say, the Guardians continued their rest as they began their path to true balance.

Blood and cold bodies surrounded Vinzent as he sat on the floor of The Obedience. He held Nico's lifeless body in his arms, and saw Raito dead on the ground as Rose stood beside Orion. The God of Darkness showed Vinzent the destruction and rebirth of the galaxy as hundreds of trillions of entities and thousands of planets bent the knee to Orion.

Helpless, Vinzent simply lowered his head before The Arm executed the Elder, decapitating the defeated Guardian...

Vinzent violently woke up in a pool of sweat as he was relieved that it was a dream. However, it also somewhat frightened him due to the possibility of that outcome coming to fruition. Worried about his brother, the awakened Nico asked Vinzent about his dream and wondered if it could be another warning from Elder Luna, but they were both unsure. The Elders knew they needed to learn what Titus had to teach them, and unlock their true potential in order to save the galaxy, for it seemed like their best shot.

Moments passed and Raito awakened as all three Guardians rose from their beds, and traversed the massive castle. Turning the corner, the Guardians saw the old man standing at the end of a hallway with two large doors towering behind him. Titus opened the doors to show a huge opening resembling a battlefield.

Titus: "This is the training arena. Here you all will train to strengthen and master the techniques of Bogan, or fall victim to the overwhelming nature of your own Darkness."

Raito: "Not much of an option..."

Titus: "Being that your opponents are Orion, my daughter and his army, there's not much room for anything less."

Nico: "That aside, who are we training against?"

Titus: *chuckle* "Me."

Nico: "Didn't we already settle that?"

Titus: "The past is only for teaching and learning, not living. The blue dust I used to knock you all out, and halt your abilities should've worn off by now. If any one of you can defeat me in combat, then there will be nothing for me to teach you and you'll have shown me that you're ready to face the one called Orion. You're free to use any means necessary to achieve this goal."

Nico: "Easy enough."

Titus: *chuckles*

Titus walked towards the center of the training arena before taking off his robe, revealing his red skin and muscular physique. He proceeded to crack his knuckles and back while getting a quick stretch in as the old Emperor got in his fighting stance. With a thrust of the chest, a wave of intense Source Energy brushed against the Guardians, forcing them to defend. The Energy from Titus felt overwhelming, as if being towered by a tsunami. A shockwave was created as Titus crouched before saying "here I come". With amazing speed, the old man vanished from view as the Guardians were caught off guard by his increased speed; he was not the same as before. The Guardians readied themselves for battle, but despite their Elder training and experience, their lack of Bogan-discipline made them easy prey for the old man. Titus appeared before Vinzent first, striking him three times with power and precision, sending him tumbling across the ground. Nico and Raito quickly responded by throwing synchronized punches at Titus which were easily caught. "Weak", said the assured Emperor as he threw Nico and Raito against opposite walls. Nico picked himself from the rubble and yelled "ENOUGH" as he charged at Titus, amplified and with his Ken fists.

Titus: "Been a while since defeating a Senshi Warrior. Give me a challenge like your ancestors."

The two collided, trading punches and kicks as they were locked in hand-to-hand combat. The Elder, however, was overwhelmed by Titus's speed and combat experience which gave him the advantage over Nico. As a result, the Emperor broke through the Elder's defense, allowing Titus to uppercut Nico with a fist of Source Energy. This sent the Taiyōnian flying high above the training arena before crashing down, creating a shockwave and temporarily knocking him out. Seeing this, Raito and Vinzent combined their assault with perfectly timed Prana and Elemental blasts and strikes which for a little while, forced Titus to go on the defensive, but that advantage quickly faded as Raito and Vinzent both fell short from Titus's combat prowess, thus tasting Emperor Titus's might first hand. Raito, using his super speed, zoomed in, with a Light sword in hand to deal a fatal blow to Titus. However, the old man saw and caught Raito by the arm and face before slamming him into the ground, to which he punched the Guardian one good time in the chin, knocking him out cold in a shockwave of power. Titus then threw Raito's unconscious body at Vinzent as a way to distract and close the distance between them. Following this, Vinzent caught his comrade, but doing so caused him to lower his guard, giving Titus the opening he planned for. Wanting to end the training lesson, Titus proceeded to close-line Vinzent before catching the Elder by the ankles and slamming him into the ground forcefully as the ground beneath the Elder cracked and buckled. Vinzent wasn't done yet as he fired off a blast of lightning towards Titus, but to Vinzent's surprise, the Emperor caught the stream of lightning with one hand, allowing the Elemental Energy to flow through his body and out from his other hand, as if becoming one with lightning itself.

Titus: "Your weak Elemental Energy has no place here Guardian."

Vinzent: *grunts* "H-How?"

Titus: "When you find true balance between Ashla and Bogan, there isn't anything you can't achieve."

Vinzent hesitated because he's never seen an entity perform such a feat. Afterwards, Titus walked up to the downed Guardian as Vinzent passed out due to the concussion provided by Titus's slam. With all three Elders knocked out with ease, Titus looked around and realized that the Way of Ashla had softened and spoiled the Guardians of this generation.

Later the next morning, in the Guardian's room, Raito woke up with a massive headache as his painful body struggled to sit up. Titus, already in the room, stood with his robe back on and cane in hand.

Raito: *grant* "Damn. Feels like I got hit by a train. What was that? Such power."

Titus: "My horns may be broken, but I am still the Emperor, fallen kingdom or not. That aside, are you starting to understand why I wanted your minds to be open to the Darkness as well? You Guardians use Ashla taught Source Energy given to you as fuel, but what happens when it's not enough? If you want a chance at defeating Orion, you all must learn to go beyond your limits, beyond the Light, and become one with divine power from both sides of Source Energy."

Nico: "How would you know if we did or not?"

Titus: "Because of what happened on the training field. Because if I were an enemy, you all would be dead. You Guardians work well-ish as a team, but yet hide so much more. I sensed it the moment you entered the atmosphere up above."

Vinzent: "So that was you after all. I thought your prison was in this castle?"

Titus: "Physically yes. I still can't leave these haunting walls behind, but my influence extends to every corner of this planet. Now, if we're done with the idle talk, your enemies wreak havoc across the galaxy. Let us continue..."

Three months have passed since the faction's arrival to Castle Pandous as the Elders continued their rigorous training towards enlightenment and balance. Time after time, the Guardians would rely on the teachings provided by Ashla, rarely tapping into the Way of Bogan buried within. And time after time they would return from their training exhausted, bloodied and bruised, but a little stronger than before; they put trust in the process. The Emperor was a resolute and stalwart teacher, and didn't show sympathy or solicitude toward the Elders. Along with combat training, Titus would send the Elders to different parts of the castle for Bogan training to improve upon their weaknesses, and to overcome the emotional turmoil of Bogan.

In Raito's case, every spell casted would not only deplete his Prana Energy, but would also drain him physically, in addition to his human-like stamina. To improve upon this, Raito was trained to cast spells one after another until his body was left without any strength or Prana Energy. Moreover, Raito was forced to push his super speed to the max, sprinting throughout the entirety of Castle Pandous, which was roughly twenty acres, until he collapsed from exhaustion. Every time Elder Raito finished a lap around the castle, Titus would add a hundred pounds to Raito's body, while telling the Elder to increase his speed. Raito fought against the screams of his body; against the need to black out. The Emperor kept this up for weeks, and pressured Elder Raito into drawing strength from a different source. In Vinzent's case, constant use of his lightning ability would overheat the Elder's body, which disrupted his Aura Conversion concentration. To increase the amount of lightning Vinzent's body could dish out before overheating, while also maintaining laser focus, Titus tasked the Elder with the continuous blast of lightning, while balancing on a bamboo stick that was held up by two tree trunks. Titus would simultaneously strike him with another bamboo stick for physical and mental toughness. Vinzent was to keep this up for six days nonstop, and if the Guardian lost balance or overheated, he was to start over again. The Elder spent hours, fighting the fatigue that covered his body, the burning of his leg muscles, and the pain from Titus's swings. Time and time again his body would fail, forcing him to collapse against the ground a few feet below. However, Vinzent was determined, and did not let his failure hinder his efforts. In Nico's case, without the Sun, he had to rely on his reserved Solar Energy within his cells, in order to utilize and use his Solar Mutation. This was unfortunate because once depleted of all Solar Energy, Nico was just another powerless entity. To improve upon this weakness, Titus brought Nico down to the castle's lower levels where the Sun couldn't reach. There he fought against Nico until the Elder couldn't utilize his Solar Mutation by any means. Afterwards, with no Sun to draw

Solar Energy from, Titus would press his attacks against Nico, cutting, breaking, and piercing the Elder's body. Once Nico was brought to death's door, the Asronian Emperor would leave Nico to survive without the Sun; without Solar Energy. Every time the Elder would fight the pain that consumed his body, the dizziness from the blood loss. And every time, Nico would hear the footsteps of Titus grow faint as the Emperor left the powerless Taiyōnian to find his own way back to the Sun or die alone in Darkness. Titus did this to help Nico survive and thrive without relying on his Solar Mutation ability.

After multiple combat and Bogan training sessions a day, that used up all of the Guardian's Source Energy, Titus forced the Guardians to draw Energy from a different and Darker source. A source that could only be drawn out when the Way of Ashla proved inefficient. This was shown by relentless combat, and near-death experiences that pushed the Guardians past their limits and into new territory. But because of their weak and wounded relationship with the Dark side, Titus feared their unwillingness to find peace with Darkness may be their one downfall and ultimate destruction.

Within the training arena, Titus and the Elders continued with their second combat session of the day, as Nico was seen pinned to the ground by two swords in his chest and the Emperor's foot placed on his neck. Vinzent and Raito stood a few meters away, bloodied and fatigued. Titus looked around and spoke out.

Titus: "How do you expect to defeat Orion if you can't even find balance within yourselves? You've been here for months and still none of you have bested me! I've been patient long enough! Either rise or fall!"

Titus pulled a sword free from Nico's chest as the old man continued to press his attack, forcing Vinzent and Raito to fight for their lives. Titus's attacks were powerful, quick and precise as they cut through armor, flesh and bone, slowly pushing the Guardians closer to death. He then jumped back to speak briefly.

Titus: "You Guardians are weak and will perish due to your inability to push through your fears and find balance with both Ashla and Bogan. Die!"

The Asronian Emperor dashed towards the Guardians, sword in hand with the intent to kill. He headed straight for Vinzent, but before Titus was able to deal the killing blow, Nico dashed in the way, taking Titus's sword through the torso. Enraged by Nico's interference, Titus pushed the sword deeper into the Elder's torso before pulling the weapon up and out, splitting Nico's chest and neck open. The Elder then fell to the ground as a pool of blood accompanied his defaced body. Titus followed up with several more sword attacks that were blocked by Raito's Prana Energy, but Titus's attacks were too much for the injured Elder and Raito was struck through the leg and stomach before being kicked in the face and into the nearest wall. Vinzent's stress hit an all time high as his yell was heard throughout the entire castle. His eyes glowed with anger, and his hair lifted up like having a fan gently blow one's hair. Suddenly, a blinding flash of light threw Titus off his feet, forcing the old man to tumble against the ground. Titus picked himself up before looking up towards the distraught Guardian with a smile as he commented, "looks like one of them finally accepted Bogan fully. There's hope for them yet Athena." The blinding light dimmed, giving way to a powerful being fuming with Elemental Energy. Due to the Love for his brothers, Vinzent had accepted the cold touch of the Way of Bogan, and his connection to the fundamental purity that was Source Energy that dwelled in all living things. Vinzent, for the first time, had released a **Black Aura** as his command over lightning was strengthened beyond anything he could've achieved beforehand. The Elder's body was covered and submerged with lightning, masked by a combination of his Black and Violet Auras. His white shaded eyes opened, glowing with purpose as the newly formed, *"Guardian of Lightning"*, cocked his head to the side. Feeling the amazing connection, the enlightened Elder looked towards Titus as he levitated effortlessly, ready to beat down the old man for his reckless transgressions...

TEN

RACE

The Hercules, one of the fastest and most sophisticated spacecraft to ever fly, floated patiently on the single-body ocean of Asron. The waves of this water scarred world, brushed against the outer hull of the spacecraft like moving a cup of water side to side. Second-class Elder Guardian Casanova, along with Jasmine, the artificial intelligence, basked in each other's presence while enjoying friendly games of Moxie which was chess and checkers mixed. Jasmine celebrated her ninth win over the frustrated Elder, when suddenly the two picked up an unusually familiar Elemental Energy signature on the Hercules's scanners.

Cass: "Jasmine you reading this? This Energy reading is unlike anything I've seen. Should we fire up the Hercules? It's been four days since we heard anything from them and it doesn't help that we've lost communications with the submarine…"

Jasmine: "You have a point, but I'm sure they're fine."

Cass: "How can you be certain?"

Jasmine: "Because, Nico, Raito and Vinzent are some of the strongest and resilient Guardians throughout the entire Ashura Order, so don't worry so much."

Cass: *sigh* "You're right. I-I guess I'm just jumpy after that Orion encounter..."

Jasmine: "Understandable. Now, King me!"

Cass and Jasmine enjoyed their tenth game of Moxie as Jasmine reassured and reminded her worried companion of the resilience, and strength possessed by Elders Nico, Vinzent and Raito. Cass then turned to look out towards the vast sea as a wave of guilt flooded her thoughts...

Elsewhere deep within the core of the planet, in the large training arena contained within Castle Pandous, the Guardian of Lightning, Elder Vinzent floated effortlessly as he motioned to help Raito to his feet. He looked towards Nico to see the Elder kneeled down while his Healing-Factor worked to regenerate the gaping wound coming from his torso and neck.

Raito: *internal thought* "That Black Aura... It feels the same as Orion's..."

Vinzent: "Can you walk?"

Raito: *grunts* "More or less."

Vinzent: "Nico you good?"

Nico: *grunts* "Y-Yeah, good as new. Thank the creator for the Sun." *sigh of relief*

Vinzent: "Good. Join Raito and find cover."

Nico: "And leave you to deal with— Well, you're definitely looking confident. He's all yours."

Raito's leg injury made it difficult for him to stand, but nonetheless he gave Vinzent a thumbs up as the empowered Elder grabbed and teleported Raito a few meters away, in a streak of lightning. Vinzent then asked Nico to join Raito, telling them to find cover. After a moment of realization, Nico agreed before leaping beside Raito. Following this, Titus stood to his feet, praising Vinzent and his ability to push through his fears, and reconnect with the power gifted by the Way of Bogan.

Titus: "I must say, I was beginning to think you all would die here, but it seems fate has use for you Guardians yet."

Vinzent: "You went too far Titus. If it wasn't for Nico's power, and Raito's reflexes, they would be dead."

Titus: "Yes amazing isn't it? Luckily he had Solar Energy to spare, and I must acknowledge the speed of Raito. However, you think Orion will show mercy? You think he won't go further?! Wake up Guardian."

Vinzent: "That doesn't matter right now. Is this what you wanted? To drag us down here and kill us? You blocked us from the Light to do what, enlighten us by embracing the Darkness we've Guardians fought hard to vanquish? You've done nothing, but threaten our lives and cause an unhealthy amount of stress. What was your purpose?"

Titus: "To show you that you're more than just the Light, and to help you build a true and pure relationship with your inner Darkness. You would've gone to fight Orion, utilizing only the Way of Ashla as merely a weapon to be used, and no knowledge of Bogan which is strength. Though you three seem to be the chosen 'heroes' of this story, tell me, how did your first encounter with Orion go without the teachings of Bogan?"

Vinzent fell speechless after hearing Titus's surprising question.

Titus: "It seems the spirit of truth has left you speechless. I take it you were all beaten and lost your home. That's how it goes in this galaxy when you taste defeat. Because of my teachings, though aggressive, you've been enlightened to the true power that Bogan can provide. Embrace it Guardian, but don't lose yourself."

Vinzent: "Then allow me to properly express my gratitude..."

Vinzent stood several meters away from Titus with enough room to fit a family of elephants between them. The Elder however, made short work of the distance, teleporting directly in front of Titus before generating a fist of black lightning to uppercut the old man in the chin, sending him flying through multiple floors of the castle. Titus then smacked hard against the magical barrier placed by The Nine's ritual. Lightning struck as the empowered Elder appeared next to the falling Emperor in mid-air. Vinzent then grabbed the Emperor's head and threw the old man with unmeasurable force, down back to the training arena with a loud and heavy THOOM. Following this, Titus was slow to move, but suddenly felt something warm on the back of his head. He couldn't see what it was, but he undoubtedly saw the color orange brighten as Vinzent's ball of lightning exploded with an electrifying and deafening ZA-BOOM, filling the training arena with rocks, dust and debris. The blast created a twenty foot crater on the training arena floor, leaving Titus scorched and smoking. Vinzent flew down through the hole in the roof before landing gently next to the beaten Emperor as black lightning crackled from his hands and feet.

Titus: *grunts* "You...you wouldn't kill a defenseless old man *grunts* would you?"

Vinzent: "You're not defenseless, but nonetheless, I am a Guardian of Ashla, and although you have wounded my brothers, they still live, so you shall live too."

Titus sprung up from the ground, and brushed the dust from his shoulder before getting in a deep stretch.

Titus: "That was a test to see if the power gifted by Bogan teachings corrupted your mind, and it hasn't. Though, you couldn't kill me either way. My soul and flesh are forever bound to these castle walls as punishment for the Galactic War. As I mentioned before, I cannot join my wife in the afterlife."

To prove this, Titus took a sword from the ground and pierced himself through the chest. Blood spilled from his opened wound before closing, resembling an improved version of Nico's Healing-Factor. Vinzent witnessed Titus's punishment, but didn't feel sorrow for the Emperor, as he was the man who caused the first Galactic War, and killed trillions.

Titus: "As you've just witnessed, I am free, yet chained."

Vinzent: "Are you surprised?"

Titus: *soft chuckle* "Though a simple question, it speaks louder than the screams of my people. No, I am not."

Vinzent and Titus finished their post-battle conversation before they made their way towards Nico and Raito. Both of the Elders were still shocked by their brother's use of Elemental Energy through Bogan practices, and Black Aura, but before their conversation deepened, Vinzent lost consciousness and collapsed from physical and mental exhaustion. Shortly after, his body reverted back to its normal light-skinned complexion, showing his torn and damaged armor and disheveled curly hair.

Raito: "Vinzent?! What happened? What did you do Titus?!"

Titus: "Relax. He's just unconscious. That's normal when you first awaken spectacular power, something you and Nico will come to experience. Though, I did not expect Vinzent to be able to wield the Black Aura. Be sure to watch over him moving forward. The Way of Bogan only offers the Black Aura to those who house a certain level of malignancy in their heart. Only a chosen few possess such an empowering Aura, but if Vinzent isn't ready, he may lose his way towards the Light. Great power does not come without cost, remember that…"

Both of the Elders nodded as they took Titus's words to heart. The Emperor then gave the Guardians words of harsh truth.

Titus: "Also, for the record, I do not apologize for nearly killing you or Nico, even though you possess a Healing-Factor, Nico, but there's ways around that as you know from your Bogan training. To be blunt, I had every intention of killing you Guardians. Orion won't hesitate."

Nico: "All is well. Though harsh, your honesty is welcoming. I will say, that really hurt, the whole 'open torso and neck' thing, more so than our Bogan training. It actually killed me for a minute. You won't get that lucky again…"

Titus: "I have no regrets. I leave Vinzent to you. Once you've all recovered, we'll continue."

Meanwhile in space, the Orion Crusaders were currently invading another planet, making it the six hundred and sixty sixth planet attacked since laying waste to Journia and its star system. The Obedience embedded its slithering tentacles into the soil, draining the planet of its vital Source Energy, while simultaneously, a ground invasion was led by Orion, Ude: The Arm, and Hando: The Hand. The two warlords commanded forty thousand corrupted soldiers, and six ferocious Walkers, against the local population, and the stationed Guardians of the Paladin and Elite rank. The Orion Crusaders ran through the opposition with complete ease and confidence, with the Walkers using their gravity bombs and sheer force to walk through the planet's ground forces, clearing a path for Ude and Hando to lead their army straight into the planet's capital, slaughtering any who opposed them; Orion floating behind. After taking the capital and enslaving the habitants, Orion commanded his army back to The Obedience before turning to see a little girl with scarlet red eyes. Curious, the false god, in the middle of chaos, floated towards the girl, towering over her as she stood fearlessly. Orion planted his feet, gracing the soil with his touch. He kneeled to one knee and asked the child for her name.

Orion: "What is your name child?"

Little Girl: "Ariel. Ariel Ortega."

Orion: "Ariel Ortega. You are cut from a chosen cloth. When the time comes, lead them to me."

Orion rose to his feet, and gifted the young child with an all black katana before flying to The Obedience, leaving the little girl in the middle of death and madness. Once on board, the giant worldship pulled its tentacles free from the planet, and took off into the planet's outer-orbit. There, Orion commanded his pilots to activate The Black Launcher. Following the command, The Obedience fired a beam of Kinetic Energy at the conquered planet. Moments passed, and the targeted planet began forming cracks of lava all around the surface as if the world were ready to burst apart. Instead, the ransacked planet imploded on itself before being sucked up, disappearing into a violent black hole. The planet was lost to space and time with some evacuation crafts either being destroyed or captured. Aboard The Obedience, any Guardians captured were immediately executed publicly by Ude to lower morale amongst the slaves. Shortly after orchestrating the execution of several Guardians, Orion floated within his personal quarters as he was joined by Elder Luna and The Eye.

Luna: "So much death. So much suffering. And for what? To bring 'peace' to the galaxy?"

Orion: "More so to bring enlightenment with a splash of revenge. We've gone from planet to planet, star system to star system, bringing nothing, but mercy and clemency added with an everlasting Darkness.

I am this galaxy's and all other galaxies last hope for true stability! For true peace."

Luna: "You're insane."

Orion: "I am a liberator and a savior."

Luna: "Why am I still alive? Why haven't I been tortured or turned into one of those grotesque creatures?"

Orion: "Be careful what you wish for Guardian. To answer your curiosity, your use of Cosmic Energy is very…intriguing to say the least. Though, it could prove troublesome, but I believe you're smarter than that."

Luna: "Why don't you just take my Cosmic Energy for yourself then?"

Orion: *laughs* "Where's the fun in that?! Besides, your beauty is unmatched, and we wouldn't want to ruin that soft skin now would we? Now I have a meeting to conduct. Be a good Guardian and stay out of trouble."

After Orion and Luna's brief discussion, Orion flew to meet with The Arm and The Hand, bringing along The Eye, and leaving Elder Luna alone in Orion's personal quarters. Curiosity filled Luna's heart once more as she cautiously pursued Orion and Rose, hoping to gain further insight on Orion's plan or motive. It was an extremely risky venture, but it may prove verifiably beneficial all the same. Orion approached two doors which were covered in bones and gray matter, forcing them to open as he drew near. Inside the room were six chairs around a table, and one larger chair designed for a King. Along the walls stretching far and wide, in suspended animation, were Kings, Queens, Emperors and Religious Leaders from different planets which were attacked by Orion and his forces. The false god called it his "trophy room", and it stood as a testament to Orion's might and further ascension into Godliness. By taking out the leaders of every invaded world, and placing them in suspended animation like a deer head on a wall, Orion had stated without words that he was the one true leader, the one true Creator, and that his will was absolute.

Orion entered into his trophy room before sitting in his throne chair at the head of the table. Luna stationed herself just outside the trophy room with her ear gently pressed against a crack in the wall. Upon sitting, Orion placed The Eye beside him on the right side, while The Arm and The Hand kneeled down before their lord.

Orion: "You may rise and be seated. As you know, I'm going to save Myrmidon and eventually the Universe from its cycle of hate by bringing forth Eternal Darkness across the galaxy, to then build back up in my image. However, during our campaign of saving planets, I realized something...I realized that despite my transformation, life is still... finite, fragile and fleeting. This...is unacceptable, for I am Orion, God of Darkness, and I REFUSE to be bound by anything or anyone... including death."

The room fell quiet with both Ude and Hando hesitant to speak, but Ude found the courage to question his lord.

The Arm: *deep tone* "If I may speak freely my lord..."

Orion: "You may."

The Arm: "Death is the one force that will greet us all, one way or another. Forgive my ignorance, your grace, but how do you escape the inevitable?"

Orion: *pleased chuckle* "Your ignorance is forgiven and your curiosity pleases me. It shows how much you've grown since you crossed my path Ude. My friends, allow me to enlighten you further. The center of this galaxy contains the necessary gravitational force needed to birth Darkness across the galaxy, but I've also found knowledge of a star system, buried deep within Myrmidon's core. And on one of these planets contains a magical tree that gives life to a fruit called, ***God's***

Heart, which when consumed, gives the consumer the power of the Creator."

Ude and Hando, Orion's best fighters, turned towards one another in disbelief as they listened to their lord speak. Rose also perked up in what seemed to be curiosity, and behind the cracked wall, Luna expressed a dismayed demeanor.

Orion: "Now, thanks to our Guardian spy within the Ashura Order, I have the hidden knowledge stolen from The Nine. With its contents, I know which planet contains the tree. I now also know of a few species capable of handling, surviving, and withstanding the backlash granted from the God's Heart fruit…the Infinite Creator himself, a pure blood Asronian, a pure blood Taiyōnian, and a pure blood Sōsunian. Though, I am not familiar with the Sōsunian species."

The Hand: "Then you have won my lord, for you are pure Asronian! Immortality is yours, my master!"

Orion: "Indeed my four armed friend, but you lack vision. We will find the tree housing this power, and I will consume this fruit to which I will obtain Godliness. But once I ascend, I will gain much more than simple immortality. That, my friend will be only but a small gift granted to me, for I, Orion will be the TRUE God, the Creator, and ALL beings of this Universe will see the supremacy and absoluteness of the Asronians! Of me!"

Orion's will was felt throughout the entire ship as Ude, Hando and The Obedience roared with excitement and determination following their lord's true intentions. They all basked in the joy they felt, knowing their lord Orion more or less trusted them with the knowledge of his plan. After these events, Orion commanded his top fighters to prepare for departure towards the center of the galaxy, a journey traveled by very few. The thick collection of stars, asteroids, destroyed ships, and pure Source Energy formed a barrier around all five planets that lay within its borders. The heavy levels of 'space junk' made it unwise to use light speed, and extremely difficult to fly through. This space between the innermost portion of the galaxy, and the outer was called *The Great Divide*. Even for a mighty ship like The Obedience, traveling that fast through that much blockage would certainly spell disaster. This realization angered Orion, but humbled him as well. It seemed the real battle was about to begin.

As Orion finished his business and preparations, Elder Luna rushed back to Orion's room before using the golden opportunity to utilize her Cosmic Energy ability called: *Galactic Reach*, to reach out to Vinzent through their bond. Luna put her long and soft blue hair up in a messy bun before sitting against the floor in a criss-cross formation. She said the words, "Creator, give me strength" before beginning to hum beautifully in different tones. Moments passed and the Elder began to levitate a foot off the ground as her Sunset colored eyes glowed with purpose. Back on Asron, in Castle Pandous, Elders Nico, Vinzent and Raito were resting after their previous encounter with Titus. The Guardians recovered within their individual beds as Vinzent witnessed a vivid dream with him, for the first time, seeing Luna Joyce since her warning to him roughly twelve months ago.

Vinzent: "Luna? W-Wow you are absolutely stunning..."

Luna: "Your compliment is most welcomed, but now isn't the best time for that."

Vinzent: "Of course. Where are you?"

Luna: "I'm aboard Orion's worldship. I can't say that I'm a prisoner, but of course I'm not a welcomed guest either."

Vinzent: *shocked demeanor* "What? Aboard Orion's worldship?! How!?"

Luna: "Story for another time perhaps. Listen, Rachel is here and alive. She's fallen deep into despair and Darkness because she caused Journia's final moments, and assumed you guys went with it. Though, not willingly."

Vinzent: "That was her?…Titus wasn't lying after all."

Luna: "Titus?"

Vinzent: "Story for another time perhaps."

Luna: "Very funny. I knew with even Journia going to shit, you guys would make it out alive. I don't have much time left before Orion returns, so I'm going to establish a telepathic connection of where this ship is currently. Use that waypoint to narrow your search and find this ship. Orion plans to destroy the entire galaxy, and rebuild it under his rule, using the power granted from the center of the galaxy. He also found knowledge of a star system within the galaxy's core, containing a planet with a magical tree, housing a powerful fruit called God's Heart. It's said to give the consumer the power of the Creator, he found this out because of a Guardian spy!"

Vinzent: "You can't be serious…"

Luna: "That's not the worst part. If he gets his hands on this fruit, Orion's power will undoubtedly surpass any being in recorded history, becoming immensely stronger than even the strongest Asronian Emperor."

Vinzent: "In other words, he can't be stopped by any means. If Orion gets his hands on that kind of power, I don't know if we'll be able to stop him, balanced or not."

Luna: "It also seems to me like we're heading towards The Great Divide, hopefully that helps narrow your search. My favor with that monster won't last forever so I give you this intel hoping the One Infinite Creator will see us through. Orion needs to be stopped or else everyone's sacrifice would've been for nothing."

Vinzent: "We can't thank you enough! My comrades and I will save you, Rachel and Myrmidon. You have my word."

Luna: *sigh of relief* "That'll do for now. One other thing."

Vinzent: "Of course…"

Luna: "Rachel is Orion's sister…"

Vinzent: "…But that would mean Orion is… and Titus… Why didn't you lead with that?!"

Luna: "Does that really matter? I have to go. May the One Infinite Creator guide and protect you, in Light and in Love."

Vinzent: "To you as well, in Light and in Love."

The dream ended and Vinzent woke up the next morning with a new flame fueling his motivation and burning his doubt. He woke up the fully recovered Raito and Nico before explaining the conversation between himself and Luna.

Raito: "Rachel is…"

Vinzent: "Precisely."

Nico: "Wouldn't that mean Orion is actually…"

Vinzent: "Theo, Titus's oldest son."

Nico: "This story just keeps on giving."

Raito: "I knew she was alive and I knew she wasn't a bad person."

Vinzent: "Yes, you can rest easy on that my brotha."

Nico: "God's Heart huh? And I thought this story was done with surprises. After the first warning from Luna, I have no doubts. It's incredible how long she's been on his ship. Did she tell you how we could put an end to that monster of a ship?"

Vinzent: "I didn't ask and she didn't say. But now that I think about it, back on Zora, Cass mentioned Kicks found a weakness, deep within the ship. A core? We destroy that, we destroy the ship…I assume."

Nico: "This is the first we're hearing about this, but regardless, you know this could be a trap right?"

Vinzent: "All the more reason for you guys to push past this inner-blockade and open yourselves to Bogan teachings and practices."

Nico: "The Darkness isn't something I wish to revisit. To accept the Way of Bogan within myself means to open old wounds. I just don't know if I can heal from them."

Vinzent: "The Creator will not forsake you if you trust in him, and trust that he has your back. The Darkness is a part of you; it is you. I didn't understand until I felt it's cold black touch. It turned out to be a piece of me I left abandoned. No more. I accept myself fully and unconditionally, both Ashla and Bogan."

Nico: "You make it sound so easy."

Vinzent: "With the Love and Light from the Creator, anything is."

After the Guardians discussed Vinzent's dream/vision, Nico and Raito continued their training with Titus, leaving Vinzent to master his new found Black Aura. After a few more weeks of aggressive combat training and near-death moments, Nico and Raito pushed past their fear of Bogan, reconnecting to their untapped power and strengthening their bond with the Source Energy. Through Titus's Bogan training, Nico found himself to be stronger and his Healing-Factor technique to regenerate with more efficiency without the Sun. The Elder could mutate faster and found that his cells could now hold more passive Solar Energy. Bogan teachings also furthered Nico's understanding of his Solar Mutation ability, as a result, the Taiyōnian learned a new mutation he called: *Yumi*. This mutation allowed Nico to repurpose the muscle-fibers of his arm into a bow, giving the Elder a more efficient way of utilizing his Bakudan ability and/or arrows gifted by Raito's magic. On the other hand, Raito's use of Bogan teachings greatly increased the effect and potency of his Prana Energy, as well as increasing the amount of spells he's able to cast. Elder Raito's stamina had increased exponentially as well, making him much faster with shorter break times between each run, rendering his Stem Shots obsolete. However, they failed to unlock their true potential like Elder Vinzent, due to the priority of Elder Luna's message. Nevertheless, Nico, Raito, and Vinzent were content and humbled with the blessings and experience gained.

On the last night of their journey and training with Emperor Titus, the old man cooked and threw a congratulatory seafood feast to celebrate. The Emperor had everything from crispy crab cakes with tomato butter, to venetian shrimp with polenta, and even cajun seafood boils.

Raito: "Wow, what's all this?"

Titus: "Seeing that this is your Guardian's last night, I thought I'd step in the kitchen to show and give my congratulations to you for surviving Bogan training, as well as accepting the Way of Bogan and controlling it, especially you Vinzent. You Guardians are truly ahead of your time, and would've made honorable Red Nobles. Nico, the Taiyōnians would be proud. Also, I know this won't make up for what I've done, but at least I can offer a moment of peace and rest before your time against Orion. Now, let's enjoy the moment and indulge on some Asronian food."

Nico: "How did you manage all this, you know, with you being a prisoner here?"

Titus: "Though I am bound to these castle walls, my influence and control touches every corner of this planet, plus, the waters are filled with sea life, and it's not hard to influence the sea creatures of Asron."

The Guardians and Titus enjoyed a feast prepared by the old man, in celebration of the Elder's hard work over the last several months. Following the delicious food, Nico reminded Raito that it was story time.

Nico: "So Raito. We're blessed by this moment of peace... enlighten us on your story, the history of Prana Energy and how you became a Guardian."

Raito: "My story huh? Why not... I guess I could start with the history of the first Prana masters, the *Purāna Mages*. Originating thirty years after the first Galactic War, from the planet *Mahō*. Because of the brutal nature of the war, the teachings of Ashla had to be reformed to meet the needs of those who wielded it for battle, thus adding an element of violence to a once peaceful bridge to Source Energy. As a result, the different Energy types were born. One such Energy type being Prana Energy. Thirty years after the war, several Guardians, including a member of The Nine, found their use of Ashla taught Source Energy to be unpredictable and difficult to control due to the constant stress during battle. This realization led these beings to a remote planet called Mahō. There these beings meditated, trained, and found ways to control their Source Energy by infusing the Energy into different objects like staffs, jewelry, and weapons. By this time, many years had passed and Mahō became a paradise for those who found it difficult to control the purity of Source Energy. Schools were formed and temples were built to further the understanding of Source Energy through Prana means. And after a hundred years of research, the *Grimoire* was introduced, enabling the owner to not only filter the chaotic nature of Source Energy into it, but also allowed the keeper to breathe life into whatever spell was written inside. This began the age of Purāna Mages, and the School of Prana."

Titus: "Fascinating. So these Grimoires act as filters?"

Raito: "Yes, and enables the owner to see and use Prana Energy with more clarity and focus."

Titus: "It's humbling to know that the Way of Ashla has an element of chaos, though I hate it was caused because of the war. Please continue."

Raito: "There were two powerful scholars who formed the school, one of which being my great grandfather, Master Felix and the other being a man named Simon Gato. Both didn't always see eye to eye because my great grandfather wanted Prana Energy to be returned back to its gentle nature like Ashla taught Source Energy of old, but Master Simon wanted to increase its power output, and establish a place among the strong. Because of these different perspectives their relationship grew strained, eventually leading Master Simon to conduct his own experiments, some of which involved student test subjects. Because of these experiments, though cruel, Master Simon discovered a powerful new Cosmic Energy type which would be Prana Energy's polar opposite, called *Apana Energy*, and would be fueled by Bogan teachings. When Master Felix caught wind of these horrible acts, he was outraged and confronted Master Simon about these claims. However, when Master Felix entered into Master Simon's quarters, my great grandfather was heartbroken at the sight of mingled bodies, an altar made from stolen Grimoire covers, and jewelry filled with Apana Energy. While investigating, Master Simon returned to his quarters to find Master Felix distraught and devastated. He did not want to believe the rumors, but the evidence was as clear as a glass bottle. An argument ensued which led to the Battle of the Masters."

Titus: "Sounds like Master Simon fell victim to corruption, and power related blindness."

Nico: "You're one to talk..."

Titus: "I take your point. Forgive the interruption."

Raito: "All is well. You've actually given my throat a break. Now, where was I... ah yes. After the Battle of the Masters, Master Simon would be defeated and captured, where he would be put on trial before the court of Purāna Mages. After an open confession, Master Simon would be found guilty, and stripped of his status as Master before having his

Grimoire confiscated. He would also be banished from the School of Prana, and exiled from Mahō, never to be seen again. Afterwards, peace was restored and Master Felix passed away from old age before raising my grandfather, and teaching him all he knew before he raised and taught my father all he knew."

Nico: "So Prana Energy came from the violent aspect of Ashla fueled Source Energy, along with the other Energy types, through war. Moreover, because of the creation of the Grimoire, the birth of the Purāna Mages happened, leading Masters Felix and Simon to create the School of Prana?"

Raito: "Ex-Master Simon, but yes in a nutshell."

Nico: "Though fascinating, it doesn't explain where you got your super speed from. Or how you became a Guardian."

Raito: "I was born with my speed. My mother told me, at a young age, that I was different from the rest of the students in my class, and not because of my speed. Because of my talent and skill with Prana Energy. Because of how fast I could learn a spell, how well I could cast complex spells, and how I was able to conjure weapons of Light like my Light-bow, making me one of the few on Mahō who could achieve such a feat."

Nico: "Briefly going off topic here…"

Raito: "Okay?"

Nico: "You're not from Journia?"

Vinzent: "I thought that's been established…"

Raito: *soft chuckle* "No. Like you, Journia is my adopted home. I am a Mahōnian, born and raised on the rural world of Mahō."

Nico: "So we're a bunch of aliens. Cool. So how did you end up on Journia as a Guardian?"

Raito: "Because of my family's history, it was said I would follow in the footsteps of my father as head Mage for the School of Prana like his father, and his father before him. But I wanted to live my own life and see the galaxy for myself. I thought my father would be disappointed, but instead he, and my mother supported my dream. It had to be fate because after they gave me their blessing, a Ashura Order ship landed, looking for Purāna Mages to join The Order as Guardians and further teach Prana Energy. I saw this as my chance and accepted the call to serve the Creator and bring Light to a Darkened galaxy. Before I left, my father told me one day my gifts would be needed, and to be ready and fearless when that time came, now I see what he meant."

Titus: "A noble reason. Have you achieved your goal?"

Raito: "I've saved countless lives, and achieved the rank of first-class Elder, but it doesn't feel like I've done enough. And how the galaxy is now, it shows. I don't know if it's because I'm not strong enough or what."

Titus: "You've survived against Orion and everything else in your life. Because of your strength, you've made it here and learned how to integrate the Way of Bogan for the sake of that peace. If that isn't true strength then I must be blind."

Raito: "I do greatly appreciate the positive energy, Titus. But yeah, that's my story."

Nico: "Thank you for sharing my friend. I feel a stronger bond with you, Master Raito."

Raito: "I am no Master, though thank you for listening. Speaking of which. Nico, I have a question I forgot to ask while we were on Journia..."

Nico: "Ask away brotha."

Raito: "When a Taiyōnian suffers a fatal injury, where does their consciousness go? When Titus split your chest and neck open, you said it killed you. Where did you go before your wounds regenerated?"

Following Raito's question, both Vinzent and Titus turned towards Nico with childish curiosity.

Nico: "An interesting question. When we suffer a fatal injury, our consciousness goes to the *Realm of Apollo*, which is a place between space, time, and matter. It is a place sacred to a Taiyōnian as it is a realm of spiritual rest, and enables a Taiyōnian to reflect on the actions that caused their death, while also receiving further guidance from the spirit of Surya. Once the body has been healed enough to sustain life once more, their consciousness is pulled back into the body, reviving, and enabling the Taiyōnian to continue onward, thus the Healing-Factor."

Titus: "The Realm of Apollo, so that's where Taiyōnians go after receiving a fatal wound, intriguing. Vinzent you've been pretty quiet so far. Anything to add to this time of peace?"

Vinzent: "Nothing besides a Guardian aboard Orion's ship learned of some disturbing news about Orion."

Titus: "May that news be that Orion is actually Theo, my oldest son."

Raito: "W-What... how did you..."

Titus: "There aren't many Asronians left in the galaxy, let alone one who possesses such potent Cosmic Energy. I saw my wife perish, I saw my second son dead, and Rose was too young, but I didn't see Theo after I was banished. I assumed he died, but after constantly feeling such rage and greed, I knew. Plus, a good father always knows his children."

Vinzent: "Then you know what needs to be done. To Orion and possibly even Rachel, excuse me, Rose?"

Titus: "I've come to peace with this reality, yes. Theo has lost himself to power and vengeance, something I must've brought upon him. But my daughter is kind like her mother, even as an infant. Please save my son and daughter from themselves."

Vinzent: "We will bring them to the Light, one way or another."

The four entities finished their seafood meal and headed to bed for the night. Shortly after, the Sun set, closing the day.

Several hours and a restful night sleep later, the Sun rose on a new day as the Elders packed their things and bid Titus a farewell.

Vinzent: "Despite your past, we can't help but to show you respect and gratitude. We feel forever closer and all the more bonded with the Source Energy coursing through our veins. We learned that this God given power is not to be used as a tool or weapon, but as an extension of ourselves, an extra pair of arms and legs if you will. You helped strengthen our minds, bodies, and spirits, and you showed us that just because we follow the principles and morals of Ashla teachings, it doesn't mean we're automatically altruistic, but moreover by the actions of that individual. We humbly thank you in this life and the next, Emperor Titus."

The Elders bowed in respect to their unexpected teacher.

Titus: "Your respect is most welcoming and warming. It's been a long time since I felt genuinely good about my actions."

Raito: "Athena, Gabriel, and Rose would all be proud."

Titus: *soft grin* "This isn't enough to clear all my sins, but I can safely say I'm on the right track. Do an old father a favor?"

Vinzent: "Of course…"

Titus: "Could you give Rose this necklace, and tell my little girl that her mother and I love her very much. As for my son… save him…"

Nico: "If you don't mind me asking, why the necklace?"

Titus: "My wife made it for her the day she was born. It symbolizes royalty among the Asronian people. But now it represents Love from a mother to her child, and is the only thing worth giving."

Vinzent: "It would be our honor."

Titus gave the red diamond necklace to Vinzent. However, given that Raito was saved by Rachel, and when the time came, he defended her honor among the Guardians, the right was passed to him as Vinzent carefully handed Raito the priceless jewel.

Titus: "You all have shown great courage and valor, so by my right as Emperor of the Asronian race, I make thee honorable and humble members of the Asronian people, and Nobles of the highest standing. I give you three the Mark of Honor, stating that you are to be honored and treated with the utmost respect from everyone familiar with this marking. Though I'm bound to these castle walls, the Asronian race shall find redemption and favor among the One Infinite Creator through your deeds. May your enemies tremble at your wake, may the ground you walk on turn to gold and may the air you breathe be filled with Love and honor."

Each of the three Guardians received a small tattooed marking of a majestic horn on the left side of their neck, which faded into their flesh. Soon after, the Elders made their way to the castle's entrance. They each took one last bow towards Titus with the Emperor bowing in respect to the Guardians as he quietly adds, "looks like the Guardians of this generation do indeed have manners". The Elders made their short journey back to the submarine with Nico taking one last look at the massive castle standing proudly behind them. "Damn" said the impressed Elder as he followed Raito into the water vehicle. Vinzent took control of the vessel with the submarine having no difficulty powering up.

Vinzent: "I guess Titus released the hold on our technology. Everything is practically brand new."

Nico: "Good. Now we can make our way back to Cass and Jazz without interference."

Vinzent dove the submarine into the water as Raito looked out the small window, watching the water fill up the openings.

Raito: "Who would've thought we'd be trained and taught by the man who caused the first Galactic War…"

Vinzent: "The One Infinite Creator works in mysterious ways. You may think you know the way, but the Creator always manages to make you realize that you know nothing."

Nico: "That may be true, but I know one thing…Orion will pay for his transgressions."

Vinzent: "That I believe we all, including the Creator, can agree on."

The Elders continued their journey back to the Hercules as they saw the red colored portal swirling like before. Confident in the relationship established by themselves and Titus, the Guardians openly pushed through the portal. The submarine twisted and flipped before breaking through the ocean's surface, like a whale coming up for air. Conveniently, the sub resurfaced a few meters from the Hercules.

Vinzent: "Sub to Hercules? Do you read me?"

Cass: "Loud and clear Sub. I thought y'all would be gone a little longer than a week."

Vinzent: "A week? We've been down there for roughly seven months…"

Cass: "We counted seven days, three hours and forty-two minutes."

Nico: "Well, this planet just keeps on giving."

Vinzent: "Nonetheless, we have a solid lead on Orion and where he's heading so let's get this show in the air."

Cass: "Copy that. Warming up the engines now. Jasmine, you mind letting in our friends?"

Jasmine: "Sure. It's the least I can do after winning thirty-six times in Moxie. *soft laugh* I commend your persistence though."

Cass grinned and rolled her eyes as Jasmine opened the Hercules's cargo doors which allowed Vinzent to drive, park and secure the sub. Once secured, Cass slowly lifted the ship out of the water before shooting into space like a firework leaving its container.

Jasmine: "So, now that the gangs all back together, where are we heading?"

Vinzent: "This is the waypoint given by Elder Luna. It's the last known location of The Obedience and our only lead on Orion. We'll head there and proceed onward cautiously."

Jasmine: "Roger that. Plotting course and warming up the hyperdrive."

After a beautiful humming sound, the Hercules shot off into deep space as the faction of Elders raced to stop Orion and his goons once and for all.

Cass: "Vinzent, did you say Luna? As in Elder Luna Joyce?"

Vinzent: "I did. You know her well?"

Cass: "I do. We trained together before she was stationed. I trained her on hand-to-hand and sword combat, and she helped me deepen my spiritual life. The report said she was killed in action, but I'm relieved to hear that's false. I hope we're able to save her."

Vinzent: "I'm sure the One Infinite Creator will see us through."

Cass nodded in hopeful approval and walked away to complete a maintenance check on the MT-AT. The door shut behind her as Nico walked up to Vinzent.

Nico: "So…Cass knows Luna?"

Vinzent: "Yeah. They were training partners and friends…why?"

Nico: "…double date?"

Vinzent: *hard laughter* "When this is all over, that's a bet."

Meanwhile in deep space, The Obedience flew at a decent speed towards The Great Divide. Orion and Rose entered into his personal quarters where they saw Elder Luna. He looked over to see Luna sitting in a chair, looking out the window and into the massive wall that was The Great Divide.

Orion: "Have I been deceived? After I've spared your life, and gave you hospitality when I could've let you die alongside your worthless Guardians?!"

Luna: "I don't know what you're talking about."

Orion: "Now you speak to me as if I were a fool!"

Orion commanded The Eye to use her Cosmic Energy to lift and choke the helpless Elder. Luna was then lifted a few feet off the ground as her throat was nearly crushed. She struggled to breathe like a baby turtle struggling to get off its back.

Orion: "Must I remind you, filth, that I have eyes and ears everywhere. You think your eavesdropping and conversation with that Elder Vinzent didn't go unheard or unnoticed?! You think I would be so stupid as to leave you completely unattended?! Have you no respect for your GOD?!"

Orion continued to lecture Luna as the Elder's body fought and fought against Rose's powerful grip, but then Luna went limp as Rose forced the Elder to pass out, almost killing her. Moments passed and The Eye continued to telepathically choke the unconscious Guardian before Orion gave his command to stop.

Orion: "It would seem the Guardian here is unconscious. Drop her then wake her back up. I wish to know exactly the words exchanged between her and the receiver."

After Rose destroyed Journia, Rachel had been subconsciously imprisoned within her own mind. Rachel watched, heard and felt all that was happening, but simply didn't have the will to fight her alter ego. Following this, Rose mindlessly obeyed her brother and master, and woke Luna up with a simple pluck to the forehead. The action jolted Luna awake as she gasped for air.

Orion: "I wasn't going to harm you, but after your disrespect, you need...correcting."

With those words, Orion dragged Luna by the hair and into Makai's old lab. The false god then commanded several corrupted soldiers to tie up the Elder by the feet, wrists and neck.

Orion: "Now. You will show me everything that was said."

Luna stared Orion down as hate and anger flooded her eyes.

Orion: "We'll see how long that flame of yours lasts against my Black Aura."

Orion opened his robe, revealing thousands of black souls imprisoned by him. The souls shot out and flew all around Luna before the door leading to the lab was shut and locked. Horrifying screams from Luna were heard as Orion tortured the Elder harshly and thoroughly, sparing no mercy, for in Orion's eyes, Luna had sinned against him. After a few more minutes of Luna's terrorized scream, the yelling stopped and Orion floated out of the lab as he closed his robe and said to Ude who was guarding the entrance, "I have what I need, she is of no use to me anymore and her beauty is… stained with ugliness. Leave her in there to rot." The door was opened slightly more, giving way to a mentally defeated Luna as she lay across the experimental table, drenched in sweat. Her hair was messy and unkempt, and her once beautiful blue skin was now a dried out light blue, resembling an orange left out in the blazing Sun.

Orion: "Those irritating Elders from before are coming to us. They will undoubtedly reach our position, during that time I leave them to you two. Hando, I'm sure you'll like vengeance on the one called Vinzent, who humiliated you. And Ude, I'm sure that Taiyōnian will come for you for burning his home. You kill those two, you'll have an easier time with the one called Raito. Do not underestimate them. They survived the destruction of their planet and mentioned to push both you Hando and Makai to use the Accelerant."

The two warriors bowed in respect and prepared themselves and Orion's army for battle. As for Rose, she was kept by Orion's side and would be kept in the dark about the Elder's survival from Journia's destruction. If Rose were to find out they survived, it would undoubtedly breed conflict within his Asronian sister, something undesired by Orion. The Obedience sped to reach the center of the galaxy with the faction of Elders hot on their tail in a race to save the galaxy from evil, from Orion…

CHAPTER

ELEVEN

INFILTRATION

Justice, revenge, peace, duty. Different words and valid reasons filled the heads of the faction of Elders present on the Hercules. Regardless of the reason, they knew Orion had to be stopped by all means. Zooming through hyperspace, the Guardians enjoyed this moment of quiet before the storm as Elders Nico and Cass laid together within the crew's quarters, enjoying the combination of colors presented by light speed travel. Elder Vinzent sat in the ship's cargo bay, meditating in order to deepen his focus and mastery over his newly discovered Black Aura. And Elder Raito sat within the cockpit of the Hercules with Rachel's necklace held tightly in his hand. Seeing her comrade perturbed, Jasmine searched for Raito's issue as well as words of blunt reassurance.

Jasmine: "We'll save her Raito."

Raito: *sigh* "Thank you for your concern, Jazz, but that's not what I'm afraid of."

Jasmine: "What do you mean?"

Raito: "Rachel is very much capable of taking care of herself, but with her being a direct descendent of Titus and now corrupted, what if she doesn't want to be saved from the Darkness that clouds her? What if Orion was right about the freedom the Way of Bogan offers?"

Jasmine: "You really care about her don't you?"

Raito: *soft chuckle* "Is it that obvious?"

Jasmine: "I can't speak for Rachel, but I do believe everything happens for a reason. The Love you feel for Rachel is stronger than any freedom Darkness can give. Believe in your heart that regardless there's still good in her, and with such an unshakable faith, you never know what path the Creator will lead her towards."

Raito: "Believe in my heart huh? You know, for an artificial intelligence, you seem to have the biggest heart than any one of us."

Jasmine took Raito's words to heart as she's always wanted to be viewed as an equal amongst her companions and not just as a computer mind. She thanked Raito, and Raito thanked Jazz for her words of clarity and positivity. Soon after, a loud ding was heard throughout the ship as Jasmine spoke through the ship's PA system, informing the faction that they were approaching the location sent by Elder Luna. Reality kicked in as their moment of silence came to an abrupt end. The Elders checked their gear, recovered from any and all injuries, and mentally prepared themselves for the fight ahead. Elder Vinzent called the faction to the ship's war room to discuss their actions upon arrival.

Vinzent: "As you know, we're close to the last known location of The Obedience. Because of The Great Divide, once we're out of hyperspace, we'll have to continue with old fashioned flying."

Raito: "That's not why you called this meeting is it?"

Vinzent: "No. I called this meeting to discuss our plan for when we actually reach The Obedience. We don't have The Order to move in guns blazing, so I was thinking, a stealth mission would be our best bet."

The faction of Elders looked towards each other not believing it was a bad idea, but accepting that they may be on their own entirely.

Vinzent: "We've faced Orion and his goons before, but we have little intel on their ship. I would like Casanova to give us any insight she received from Elder Kicks."

Casanova accepted the request and stepped up, taking the spotlight from Vinzent. The water bender did her best to remember the crucial details provided by Elder Kicks.

Cass: "You guys may already know some of these details, but I'll share my knowledge anyways. Orion's ship, The Obedience, is a massive organic space fortress that utilizes Orion's Black Aura as its main source of fuel, ammunition and propulsion. The ship also uses black hole technology and commands hundreds of small Ryū fighters and landers, as well as The Corrupted army ready for battle. It also possesses the means to grow cannons from its outer-shell at will. With the intel from Kicks, we know The Obedience is alive and very much works collectively with Orion, besides the fact that it has pilots of course. With this realization, we can't necessarily just hop on board or else risk alerting the Orion Crusaders entirely. Kicks was able to infiltrate the ship because of the chaos at the time, and because he took the form of one of the soldiers. None of us can shapeshift besides Nico, but mutations in this case are different. So while you guys were getting beat up by Titus, Jazz and I thought of an idea around that…"

Jasmine: "The ship and its crew, like its captain, are arrogant and would never think they'd be boarded by an unfamiliar entity willingly, despite Kicks doing that very thing. With this fact, why would the pilots need to scan for intruders? Unlike conventional spacecrafts, The Obedience possesses a heart, and thanks to Kicks's intel, we know where the heart is. The idea is to sneak aboard The Obedience, get to the heart and inject it with this toxin. This toxin will temporarily paralyze some of the ship's main functions, but not enough to cause trouble for the Guardians inside, it'll be like a mild heartburn. It should buy you enough time to disable whatever means the ship uses to propel itself forward."

Nico: "Two questions. Firstly, how much time do we have till the toxin wears off? And what will stop the ship from seeing us out right? If Orion's ship is indeed a living organism, wouldn't it detect the foreign biology of those on board without an interior scan? Like how your body detects foreign bacteria?"

Cass: "By Jazz's calculations, you'll have fifteen minutes tops, that is if the ship doesn't clear its system sooner. Oh and as for your cover, you'll drink this..."

Cass held up a bottle with a dark red liquid jiggling inside like jello.

Cass: "This is the blood extracted from one of those corrupted soldiers. Jasmine came up with a solution for the blood to make it edible, but also a biological disguise. If you drink this, theoretically it should make you seem like another one of Orion's lackeys and should last maybe for eight minutes. Jasmine and I advise that you wait to drink it right before you infiltrate the ship for maximum effectiveness."

Raito: "How do you guys know all this?"

Jasmine: "I gathered data from the battle of Zora after Cass informed me. I collected data from our encounters with The Obedience, as well as eye witness reports. I also analyzed the blood from your guy's battle gear right before...Journia was destroyed."

Nico: "Impressive as always Jazz. So, who's going?"

Vinzent: "You and I, my friend."

Nico: "Why am I not surprised."

Vinzent: "You shouldn't be. Your Solar Mutation ability enables you to move more freely."

Nico: "That can't be the only reason…"

Vinzent: "There are other reasons, but partially because I fear Raito's feelings for Rachel would jeopardize this operation–"

Raito: "Hold up now! Don't treat me like a child because I'm showing a little compassion. I understand my feelings for Rachel, but I also understand what's at stake. I am here, in this present moment."

Following Elder Raito's declaration, the Elders aboard the Hercules began to feel warm and heavy. They witnessed a shining light brightening from Raito's eyes. The Elder confirmed his resolve which fired Elder Nico up.

Raito: "I am prepared to do what I must to save Myrmidon."

Nico: "Damn right about that."

Vinzent: "Though I agree with you both, no offense Jazz and Cass, while Nico and I do this, I need you, Raito, in control of the Hercules. I trust no one else."

Elder Raito, though displeased with his role, agreed nonetheless. This led Elder Nico to further his understanding.

Nico: "So I know we're to get aboard the ship, inject the heart and disable its eyes, ears and movement, but what's our endgame goal? What is to be achieved when the time comes to leave The Obedience?"

Vinzent: "To find any survivors, to destroy that monster of a ship, and hopefully take the Orion Crusaders down along with it."

Nico: "That's a tall order for just the two of us."

Vinzent: "We'll do it as quietly as possible. The Hercules will also be in range just in case we need a quick extraction."

Nico: "Enough said, let's hunt!"

With the stage set and the plan established, Elders Nico and Vinzent prepared themselves to infiltrate The Obedience as the Hercules reached the plotted coordinates. Jazz pulled the ship out of hyperspace, and what was seen by the Guardians could only be described as "the work of the devil." There was a star system just outside of The Great Divide that contained eleven planets including its Sun. Yet as the Elders flew by, they saw only shattered planets, destroyed ships and billions of lifeless bodies floating in space. Some Guardians, some men, women and children, others were domesticated animals and wild creatures. The Hercules tried to fly past the bodies, but there were just too many with some empty vessels hitting against the ship's surface, like rain drops hitting against the windshield of a car. Despite all the merciless and pointless killings, the Elders pushed on towards their objective as they simply followed the trail of death and destruction. After cautiously following the path of chaos, passing by several destroyed worlds, the Guardians finally picked up a massive ship on the Hercules's radar, a thousand meters straight ahead. Elders Raito and Cass took command of the Hercules before initiating the ship's cloaking technology.

Nico: *deep breath* "Showtime."

Vinzent: "I forgot to mention, once inside, Nico and I will be going radio silent."

Raito: "How will we know to come get you guys?"

Vinzent: "You'll see the signal, trust me."

Raito: "Roger that. Activating cloak in three...two...one...cloak engaged. Maintain speed and keep her steady. We don't want to draw attention to ourselves."

The faction approached the colossal planet-killer as they couldn't help but to feel a sense of astonishment at the sheer scale of the worldship or of The Great Divide that towered it. The size, power and gravity generated from its thrusters, and from the fear the vessel commanded. This ship was truly Orion's…

Cass: "Four hundred meters and closing. We'll get you guys as close as possible."

The Hercules slowly closed in on its target with The Obedience oblivious to the small threat approaching from the rear. After traveling three hundred and fifty meters, the Hercules and its crew could basically smell the evil pulsating from Orion's ship. It filled their noses and brought tears to their eyes as if they were cutting onions.

Raito: "This is as close as we're gonna get. It's now or never!"

With time of the essence, Nico and Vinzent scurried towards an airlock placed on the side of the Hercules. The two Elders approached the side exit as Cass came to bless their journey with protection and success. Afterwards, Nico and Cass shared a loving embrace before giving them both an oxygen mask, allowing them to survive the journey through space. The Elders put on and activated their oxygen masks, giving Vinzent the green light to shut and lock the hatch behind them. The Hercules then shot a small explosive device against the outer-shell of The Obedience, attaching itself to the surface like glue on paper. A timer began to count down and the lock to the airlock leading to space was opened.

Jasmine: "The explosive is armed and counting down. Nico you'll want to time this perfectly or else it'll be a very short mission."

Nico: "We're ready when you are."

Jasmine: "Roger that."

Raito and Cass steered the Hercules into firing position allowing Jasmine to count down.

Jasmine: "Commencing infiltration in three…two…one…you're clear!"

Without hesitation, Vinzent opened the airlock leading into space as Vinzent grabbed hold of Nico's shoulders. Nico amplified his leg muscles before thrusting both Vinzent and himself out of the Hercules, utilizing the vacuum of space as propulsion. They zoomed at incredible speeds, rapidly closing the fifty meter distance that separated them from their unmissable target. As they zoomed through space, three corrupted soldiers patrolled their section of the massive worldship before stopping to hear a faint beeping noise coming from outside of the ship. The beeping stopped and suddenly an explosion blew a hole in the wall, pulling the three corrupted soldiers violently into the endless void that is space. The hole then began to slowly reconstitute itself, resembling Nico's Healing-Factor. Shortly after, the two Guardians flew through the closing hole and crashed into the nearest wall. Nico and Vinzent stood up and brushed themselves off as Nico added, "I hope nobody heard that." "You and I both", replied Vinzent cautiously. With the first phase completed, the Hercules remained cloaked while maintaining a relatively close proximity as both vessels traveled prudently into The Great Divide. On The Obedience, Vinzent and Nico pulled out and drank their bottle of red blood provided by Cass and Jazz as a way to disguise their unfamiliar biology and Source Energy signatures.

Nico: *disgusted inhale* "It smells like death and feces in here… Now that we're here, any ideas on where the heart is?"

Vinzent: "I have the directions right here, sending you the layout of the ship to your wrist computer now. Keep an eye out for any potential threats."

Nico: "You really gotta tell me that? Says here the heart is above the worm-drive and opposite from the birthing chamber? What in the name of Helios is the birthing chamber?"

Vinzent: "Let's hope we don't find out."

The two Guardians proceeded towards the ship's heart, observing the unique aliveness of The Obedience's interior. The feeling of death surrounded them as the weight of evil was almost too much to bear. The longer they traversed this massive ship of madness, the harder it became to control the Darkness present within. Nico had faced such a challenge before because of the invasion and destruction of his homeworld Taiyō. Moreover, thanks to his mother's loving words and Titus's teachings, he learned to harness his inner-Darkness in a more constructive way. However, due to the Darkness from Vinzent's Black Aura, the Elder's mind slowly unraveled itself as he started to lose control of his emotions, and consequently his powers leading to several bolts of lightning striking uncontrollably.

Nico: "Woah Vinzent! Get it together or this will turn out bad. Do we need to stop?"

Vinzent: *grunts* "N-No. I-I'm fine. Let's continue the mission."

The Guardians continued to make their way towards the ship's heart when suddenly, Vinzent fell to one knee as he struggled to regain emotional stability.

Nico: "Shit. Vinzent! I'm calling the ship... reestablishing radio connecti–"

Vinzent: "No! *grunt* I can do it. How much time do we have left before our disguise fades?"

Nico: *sigh* "Five minutes and forty-eight seconds."

Vinzent: "That's enough time. If we pick up the pace, we'll make it in time."

Vinzent breathed deeply, regaining some emotional strength before being helped up by Nico. The two then continued their journey to The Obedience's heart. As they motioned discreetly through the worldship, they heard multiple footsteps, forcing the Elders to stop and seek refuge. Upon further inspection, the Guardians saw a patrol of five corrupted soldiers moving to investigate the explosion from earlier.

Nico: "Lemme try something. I'll call this attack *Sunshot*."

Nico amplified and mutated his left arm into his newest mutation, Yumi, while forming a solar arrow made from the Bakudan ability. With his arm weaponized, the Elder peeked his head to spot the patrol moving towards them with clear intent and purpose. Nico drew the arrow back, pointed at the patrol before letting it fly against one of the soldiers. With a strong release, the bright orange arrow shot towards its target like a shooting star as the glow stick of death pierced the head of the leading corrupted soldier, killing it instantly. The lifeless soldier fell before the other four corrupted soldiers, causing the rest of the patrol to ready their organic rifles. However, before they were able to move, the arrow began to glow increasingly brighter before exploding, incinerating all four soldiers in a blazing flash of Solar Energy.

Vinzent: "Impressive, but if they didn't know we're here, they know now."

Nico: "That may be true…but I just had to try it out."

With time running short, the Guardians made haste towards The Obedience's heart. While in pursuit of their target, they passed by a room, a disturbing room resembling a laboratory. As Vinzent passed by the opened door, he suddenly stopped because of a familiar flow of Cosmic Energy.

Nico: "This isn't the way and we've only got roughly three minutes left. What are you doing?"

Vinzent didn't answer as he pushed the door open to see Elder Luna laying across a table unconscious. Her once gorgeous appearance was now masked by wrinkles and bruises.

Vinzent: "LUNA!! Luna, can you hear me?!"

The blue skinned woman gradually opened her eyes to see Vinzent hovering over her. He then picked Luna up as she slowly regained consciousness.

Luna: *weakened tone* "V-Vinzent…"

Vinzent: "Shhh. Save your energy. I told you we'd save you."

Luna: *weakened tone* "I-It's…it's a trap…"

With Luna's words of caution, she passed out in Vinzent's arms. Suddenly the door leading out of the laboratory was shut, allowing a heavily scarred eight foot entity with a missing left arm named Ude, a.k.a The Arm, and twenty corrupted soldiers to enter and surround Nico, Vinzent and an unconscious Luna. Knowing their situation was hopeless, Ude spoke briefly to his captives.

The Arm: *sarcastic chuckle* "You Guardians are too predictable. Or maybe my lord is that much smarter. Did you really think you could just walk in and do as you pleased? Despite your little disguises? *maniacal laughter* No. Instead, you both have welcomed yourselves to an early death!"

Seeing The Arm, the murderer who destroyed his adopted home village in front of him, sparked an intense hatred within Nico. His heart rate increased, and his adrenaline flowed like a tsunami. Vinzent could feel the heated rage pulsating from his comrade's very being. The Elder was ready to risk it all to seek emotional revenge for his fallen home of Solla, Journia and all the lives taken by the walking pile of scar tissue.

Vinzent: "Nico, I sense your anger, but think about our situation. We're surrounded, outmanned and deep in the enemy's territory. We should wait and–"

Nico: "ENOUGH! The killer of so many, of Lucas, stands here before us and you want to wait? Wait for what exactly Vinzent? Backup?! We are our own backup! I'm sorry, but I let him go once. I won't make that same mistake…"

With Nico's enraged response, he amplified and mutated both arms into the Ken fists before dashing full speed at The Arm, crashing into him which prevented Ude from drawing his two-handed sword. Soon after, Nico got in a few powered punches which threw Ude forcefully into the wall. The Elder then tackled the eight foot monster as they both smashed through several walls, punching away at each other before gravitating down towards the detention level. With Nico gone, recklessly fighting Ude, Vinzent was left surrounded by twenty corrupted soldiers with weapons trained and aimed at Luna and himself.

Vinzent: "Damn it Nico, maybe I should've brought Raito instead. Elemental Energy: *Lightning Flash*!"

The situation seemed helpless, but Elder Vinzent hadn't given up. He shot a sphere of dark red lightning towards the top of the laboratory that grew in size before flashing, permanently blinding twelve out of the twenty soldiers. The Elder saw his chance and ran through the opening made by Nico; Elder Luna unconscious in his arms. Soon after, blaster bolts flew past the fleeing Guardian as he counterattacked by blasting several streams of black lightning that disintegrated the corrupted soldiers in pursuit. As he fled, ultimately finding cover, the Elder realized that the mission had gone south, in which he decided to reestablish radio communications with the Hercules. At the same time Elder Vinzent peeked over the cover and returned fire, blasting several more of his pursuers with black lightning, but with Elder Luna down, he must practice cautiousness.

Vinzent: "Vinzent to Hercules, come in Hercules!"

Raito: "We're reading you, but it's not a strong signal. What's going on?"

Vinzent: "It was a trap! They used Luna as bait."

Raito: "A trap? But how did they...Okay we're coming–"

Vinzent: NO! No. Listen, currently Nico is engaged against The Arm and I'm pinned down. As it stands, Nico and I will be captured and either killed or tortured then killed."

Raito: "All the more reason to–"

Vinzent: "Raito? Come in Raito... Shit. They must've cut the connection."

Blaster bolts continuously hit and passed by Vinzent as he was crouched behind cover, Luna still injured and unconscious.

Back on the Hercules, Elder Raito tried relentlessly to reestablish radio connection with Elders Vinzent and Nico, but before he could, he and Jasmine were caught off guard by an unlikely enemy... Casanova Meyoki, second-class Elder Guardian, walked out of the ship's engine room before making her way towards the cockpit where Raito sat, attempting to contact Nico and Vinzent. Suddenly, Raito felt a sharp and agonizing pain in his stomach. He looked down and saw a katana blade and a shameful look masking Cass's beauty. Afterwards, Cass pulled the blade from Raito's stomach, forcing the Guardian to fall out of the pilot's seat and onto the ship's floor, coughing up blood.

Jasmine: "Raito!"

Raito: *cough* "W-Why? After all this time. We trusted you *grunts* and you betrayed us. Why?"

Cass: "You think I wanted this! To betray The Order, my family, Nico… Back on Zora, Orion and his goons didn't leave us be. After they killed Rex they let us retreat to the Zoranian capital, but that's what they wanted. We led them straight to their goal. They attacked us again, destroyed the capital and took the Zoranian Chief captive. They would've destroyed the entire planet, but I struck a deal with Orion to save Zora and possibly the rest of the galaxy…"

Raito: *grunts* "Cass… you didn't…"

Cass: "I…I gave Orion information on the DSR, on Bao, The Order HQ and Journia… I was the Guardian spy!"

Jasmine: "How could you Cass?! After everything we've been through…"

Cass: "You don't know what they're capable of! The horror! All the blood… all the death… We are helpless against Orion, Elder or not. I saw first hand what the Orion Crusaders will do to those who oppose them. It was clear Orion's target was the Ashura Order. So I thought if I helped him achieve that very thing, he'd spare the rest of the galaxy…"

Jasmine: "You really think Orion will hold up his end of the deal?! How delusional can you be?!"

Raito: *grunts* "Orion… will destroy everything. Y-You… only helped him destroy… the very force… built to stop him."

Jasmine: "Raito, save your energy."

Raito: "I hope… you're happy Casanova. You've…you've doomed this galaxy…"

Raito passed out because of his injury and loss of blood. Shortly after, Cass walked up to the ship's controls, and pulled out a green worm provided by Orion before laying the worm on the ship's main control panel. The worm slithered its way into the Hercules's hardware, and planted a virus within Jasmine's computer mind, effectively disabling her.

Jasmine: "W-What are you doing?! Stop! If this is about Moxie…you're a sore loser…"

Cass: "Don't fight it. It'll only make the process worse. I'm sorry Jasmine…"

Jasmine: *glitchy tone* "I hooope you've found found peace with thissss…"

With Raito down and Jasmine disabled, Casanova took control of the Hercules, allowing her to fly the vessel towards The Obedience. She sent the "all clear" signal to The Obedience through the implanted worm which allowed her safe passage into the massive worldship. The Obedience formed a giant hole towards the stern of the ship, big enough for the Hercules to fit through as Cass initiated the landing sequence. Upon landing, the traitorous Guardian was met by a hulking four-armed figure named Hando, a.k.a The Hand, and several four-armed Monos. They escorted Casanova to Orion's trophy room, leaving Raito on the Hercules, bleeding to death with Jasmine completely unresponsive. The worm virus implanted by Cass had wiped Jasmine's programming clean, effectively removing the AI's code from the software. Walking through the moist halls of The Obedience, Hando led Cass into the trophy room where Orion, the god of Darkness patiently waited while sitting on his throne.

The Hand: "At your request my lord, Elder Guardian Casanova Meyoki."

Orion: "Very good. Now leave us."

Hando bowed to his master before leaving, shutting the doors behind him.

Orion: "Ahh Elder Casanova, our little spy. It amuses me to see you here standing before me."

Cass: "How so, oh 'mighty' Orion?"

Orion: "Because it further reveals the lie of Love and Light. It shows the corruptive nature of an entity, and how you Guardians are willing to betray or murder your own comrades just to achieve a goal, or as you put it, to 'save the galaxy'. A noble yet foolish notion, you and I have that in common."

Cass: "You and I have NOTHING in common!"

Orion: "Oh? You betrayed your closest allies in hopes of achieving your goal. I did and because of that, here I, Orion, sit before you in all my power and in all my glory. Of course it was for my own goals and ambitions. Nevertheless, you and I have further business to conduct, do we not?"

Cass: "We do. Here is the information The Order has on the star system within The Great Divide. With this, you'll be able to pinpoint which of the five planets has the fruit you seek."

Orion: "Very good. You have done well Guardian."

Cass: "Now you will leave the galaxy in peace?"

Orion: "Oh but of course, after I destroy the current one." *maniacal laughter*

Cass: "We had a deal Orion!"

Orion: "Know your place Guardian. Because of your deeds, you may keep your life. *twisted smile* Be grateful."

Meanwhile, plummeting towards the ship's lower levels, Elder Nico and The Arm continued their brawl as they slammed viciously against the ground. With no clear victor insight, Nico received a brutal kick from Ude and was sent flying through a wall. The force produced from Ude would've shattered the Elder's ribcage, but thanks to Nico's Mamoru shield, he only received a few fractured ribs. After recovering to his feet, Nico regenerated his fractured ribs before wiping the blood from his mouth. Ude drew out his large sword while Nico mutated his arm into the Yumi bow. Tensions between the two warriors were through the roof, but Nico didn't hesitate to let a few solar arrows fly against The Arm. Because of their hastened release, the arrows didn't have the explosive charge from the Bakudan ability. However, they still hit their mark as the arrows pierced The Arm's stomach and knee, but failed to pierce the beast's head because of Ude's instinct to deflect with his sword. Rage and excitement filled The Arm's heart as the eight foot warrior dashed towards the Guardian with sword in hand. Ude was surprisingly light on his feet, but not quick enough to catch Nico off guard as the Elder mutated, using his Jūken blade to counterattack Ude's sword. The two clashed with each other, entering into a deadly sword-duel, constantly swinging, dodging and cutting flesh as blood spilled from both Nico and The Arm. However, Ude managed to deeply cut into Nico's chest, and with a well timed swing, Ude severed Nico's bladed arm, forcing the Elder to stumble backward in pain. With the golden opportunity at hand, The Arm swung his sword and aimed for the Elder's neck, but before receiving the fatal blow, Nico amplified and mutated his good arm into the Mamoru shield and deflected Ude's attack. This gave Elder Nico the necessary time to reconstitute his severed arm to which he quickly mutated both arms, and utilized the Ken fists. Following the quick regeneration and mutation, Nico vigorously uppercutted Ude, breaking his jaw which sent him flying upwards through multiple floors of The Obedience. Nico then mutated his arm into the Hari whip mutation, enabling him to thrust his arm upward as the whip zipped with vengeful speed and power. Shortly after, the small blades at the end of the whip stabbed and caught Ude in mid-air, permitting Elder Nico to pull The Arm back down with immense force and strength. Nico amplified his legs and leaped through the broken holes in the floor and towards the falling warrior. And with impressive velocity the Guardian impaled Ude in the chest with his newly formed Jūken blade. Blood spilled like opening a shaken can of soda as Nico forced the blade free like pulling a cord to a chainsaw. Following the series of fatal blows, Elder Nico ferociously sent Ude back down to the lower levels with a powerful strike from the Ken fists. However despite his bloody chest wound, The Arm managed to block the punch with his one good arm, but crashed down forcibly nonetheless. The bloodied warrior had little time to recover though as Nico landed next to him in a shockwave of dust and rubble. The Elder stood before Ude with his Jūken blade pressed against The Arm's neck.

Nico: "I should kill you right now, but that would make me just as vile as you. So I will grant you the chance to surrender."

The Arm: *laughs maniacally*

Nico: "Did I say something funny?"

The Arm: *deep tone* "In all my years, in all the fights I've experienced, I've only found two worthy warriors such as yourself. My lord Orion, and that Elder on Bao. He took my arm, so I took his life in the name of my lord and in honor of myself."

Nico: "I don't care why or who you took his life for. You will die by my hand for the sake of Lucas and all the good people you snuffed out."

The Arm: "Spoken like a true warrior! YOU ARE INDEED A WORTHY SON OF TAIYŌ!!!"

Ude found a burst of energy, providing him with the means to swiftly and aggressively kick Nico in the torso, which sent the Guardian flying once more through several walls. The Arm then grabbed a small bottle of Orion's blood before drinking the Accelerant. Immediately the blood began to take effect as the eight foot monster grunted with extreme discomfort. His entire body underwent a transformation as his body's muscle mass amplified tenfold. The growth in muscle destroyed his clothes, leaving the now newly formed beast naked, without genitals and armored with gray muscle fibers. His scars healed, and his severed left arm regenerated in a matter of seconds. His body then hardened harder than steel as Ude roared with power and ecstasy. Through the multiple damaged walls, Elder Nico awoke and recovered from Ude's kick. The Taiyōnian used his Healing-Factor to regenerate multiple broken bones and damaged internal organs in a matter of moments.

However, before the Elder could get a clear assessment of his situation, in a flash, The Arm appeared before Nico; a twisted grin showing razor sharp teeth. With lightning speed, Ude energetically struck Nico in the stomach and swiftly grabbed the Guardian, holding and choking the unexpecting Elder.

The Arm: *deep tone* "It seems like the tables have turned, Guardian filth."

With an evil smile, Ude ferociously slammed Nico hard against The Obedience's ground, but Elder Nico was no pushover and quickly recovered to his feet before punching The Arm in the stomach with his Ken fists. The Elder followed the Ken attack with a left jab, right hook, left hook, and finished with a stab to Ude's chest from his Jūken blade. The series of attacks broke Ude's jaw once more, forcing The Arm to stumble backwards, but something was different. Nico felt the incredible power resonating from this beast, but also strangely enough, Ude's newly formed power resonated with Nico's Solar Mutation as well...The Elder thought to himself, "such power, this is no mere man anymore. He's lost all his humanity". Ude spoke out shortly after as if he read Nico's thoughts.

The Arm: "So you noticed? This is the power granted by my lord Orion. Recognize it, Taiyōnian? You should. It came from your species, Solar Mutation I believe it's called."

Nico: "What?! But how?"

The Arm: "Through the insane intellect of Makai, and countless experiments from captured Senshi Warriors. But it was through my lord's blood that gave Makai's experiments merit. Though I cannot form blades like you Senshi Warriors can, I am far stronger than you Guardian. I should thank you! Because of your people's ability, I can spread my wings as wide as I please!"

Nico: "It doesn't matter if you possess a level of the amplification technique. You are undisciplined and untrained. You are unfit for that kind of gift."

The Arm: "Your conclusions have no effect on the outcome of this battle. Now die with honor Taiyōnian filth!"

Shortly after their conversation, The Arm swung his arm in a downward motion against Nico. However, the attack was blocked by Nico's Mamoru shield which was formed by both of the Elder's arms due to Ude's amplified strength. This left Nico's torso wide open as Ude ceased the opportunity and murderously struck the Elder in the stomach once again, shattering Nico's entire rib cage. Ude then grabbed Nico by the leg and slammed him down against the ground several times, deepening the pit of destroyed cement underneath the Guardian. Not finished, Ude picked up his old sword and ruthlessly thrusted the weapon through Nico's chest, pushing it further until the two-handed sword pierced the floor beneath the Elder. Nico reeled in anguish from Ude's attack, but the Elder refused to give up as he generated a massive Bakudan bomb in both hands. Ude could feel the heat coming from these orange spheres of aggressive Solar Energy as they expanded, gaining mass as time flowed onward. Without a second thought, Nico detonated his attack in a huge explosion that destroyed multiple levels within The Obedience. The internal damage forced the massive ship to come to a temporary halt, gaining the attention of Orion who knew Vinzent and Nico were on his ship from the start. However, he decided to allow Ude, Hando and his corrupted army to handle them, but it seemed he needed to step in. The explosion sent Ude flying in the opposite direction as they both received massive physical damage that, at that range, should've killed them both. However Elder Nico's Healing-Factor worked fast and diligently to completely heal his missing limbs and charred flesh. One of the Elder's eyes finished regenerating, allowing him to slowly open the vital organ, but what he saw greatly disturbed him. He witnessed a gray colored monster standing over him, partially healed and burning with the sense of victory and accomplishment.

Nico: *weakened and burned tone* "H-How? That b-blast... should've... killed you..."

The Arm: *spiteful chuckle* "You're not the only one with a Healing-Factor it seems. And it appears mine works faster without a Sun. I envy the power you Taiyōnians possess, but you and your people failed to truly cease the power gifted to you. No matter, thank you, lord Orion, for this amazing gift! Now sleep Guardian..."

Without another word, Ude stomped Nico's face, effectively smashing the Elder's head into a bloodied mess which consequently thrusted Nico's consciousness into the Realm of Apollo. Ude then collected what remained and made haste towards Orion. A few floors above, Vinzent felt the immense shaking generated by Nico's Bakudan bomb ability which threw the corrupted soldiers pursuing him off balance. With this opening, the Elder picked up Luna and made a run for it, sprinting as fast as he could, turning corner after corner until he saw the Hercules parked inside The Obedience.

Vinzent: "What the hell is the Hercules doing here? I thought I told them NOT to come. Vinzent to Hercules, do you read me?... Still nothing. Figures..."

The Elder carefully approached the area containing the spacecraft before seeing two corrupted soldiers guarding the entrance, and seven more patrolling the nearby area. In order to deal with the patrolling soldiers, he'd have to find a safe place for Elder Luna, and to his luck, the Elder found just that. Once achieved, he generated his Red Aura, giving him the means to manifest a lightning bow. Vinzent then equipped himself with a brown colored arrow that had been mixed with his Blue and Orange Auras. The Guardian valiantly took aim and fired, hitting one of the corrupted soldiers between the eyes, killing it instantly. Naturally, the other six soldiers walked towards their dead comrade to check for signs of life, but to their own detriment, the brown arrow exploded while simultaneously melting the minds of five of the six corrupted soldiers patrolling the area. The last one ran towards the other two as they all prepared for battle. Seeing the three from a perfect angle, Vinzent manifested another arrow, but this time, he poured a splash of Violet Aura into it, causing the arrow to glow a beautiful bright Violet. The Guardian released it as the arrow ran through the head of all three soldiers; their lifeless bodies hitting the ground simultaneously. Because of these amazing feats of power and intelligence, the entryway was clear as Vinzent picked Luna up once more and boarded the Hercules. Upon entering the ship, he found it strange that Jasmine was completely unresponsive, but disregarded it and moved towards the ship's medical area to put Luna to rest. Vinzent then walked to the cockpit only to find Raito unconscious, in a pool of blood and on the brink of death. And suspiciously, no Casanova.

Vinzent: "Raito!! Raito, can you hear me?"

Even though Raito lost a lot of blood, he subconsciously fought for life as Vinzent could still feel his pulse. Jasmine still was unresponsive, but Vinzent couldn't worry about that now, he just had to save Raito and Luna. The Elder brought Raito inside the Hercules's medical area, joining Elder Luna before administering first-aid.

Vinzent: "This is harder without Jazz, but nonetheless these Solar Seeds from Nico's extra supplies should help. Looks like you guys owe me one now."

As Vinzent administered first-aid to his gravely injured comrades, the ship's alarms began to blare. The spacecraft defaulted to its generic computer mind to alert Vinzent of the enemies currently shooting at the Hercules. The Elder looked out of the port side window to see about eighty corrupted soldiers outside of the ship, with about twenty of them shooting at the outer-hull of the ship. The lonesome Elder responded by peeking his head out of the ship's emergency airlock to let loose a stream of black lightning that disintegrated four of the twenty currently shooting. The Guardian released another stream of black lightning that scorched six more, but it seemed his efforts were in vain as the number of enemies increased with every passing moment. Vinzent took refuge within the Hercules when suddenly, the shooting abruptly stopped. Curiosity struck the Aura-wielder, so the Guardian looked out the small opening once again to see Orion himself, along with Ude, Hando, four thousand more corrupted soldiers, and Cass. The newly arrived Orion Crusaders surrounded the Hercules as Orion commanded a cease fire to speak with the lone Guardian.

Orion: "We meet again Guardian. I would say it's too soon, but these are times of great joy, for you are in the presence of your Creator."

Vinzent: "I serve only the One true Infinite Creator, not a self-proclaimed imposter such as yourself."

Orion: *soft chuckle* "You Guardians are so defiant. You don't know when to give up, I can respect that."

Vinzent: "We didn't come here for your approval. We came to kill you."

Ude and Hando found Vinzent's words extremely disrespectful as they readied themselves to put an end to the lonesome Guardian once and for all, especially Hando for what Vinzent did to him during the battle of Mos-Dia back on Journia.

Orion: "Relax my friends, all is well. Guardian? You must not know the position you find yourself in. My friend Ude has captured the Taiyōnian. That despicable Elder Luna has seen better days, and the Mahōnian currently fights for his life does he not? I wonder who could've achieved such a task."

Vinzent: *internal thought* "Nico you idiot…"

Orion grabbed Cass by the back of the neck before lifting her up for Vinzent to see as she struggled to free herself.

Orion: "It seems in times of desperation, even your closest allies will betray you." *laughs*

Orion tossed Cass aside as she tumbled away.

Vinzent: *internal thought* "Cass? Did she really do this to Raito? After everything we've all been through?"

Orion: "Be smart about your situation Guardian."

Vinzent: "What are your demands?"

Orion: "My demands? *soft chuckle* I have no demands. I wish to see all of you die an uneventful and gruesome death. But you all have managed to keep me entertained this long, so instead I'll allow you all to witness me become your Creator, and become the first deaths under my rule."

After their discussion, Orion commanded Hando to take one hundred corrupted soldiers to go and "claim" his vengeance. Hando reluctantly obeyed as he and his soldiers stormed the Hercules. Blaster fire and lightning strikes were heard as several corrupted soldiers fell out of the Hercules, scorched and lifeless. Elder Vinzent did his best to defend the ship and his comrades, but the task was too great as The Hand and his men overpowered the lonesome Elder, beating and capturing him, along with Elders Raito and Luna. Hando and his men dragged the Guardians out of the Hercules and, by Orion's order, threw them each in specialized cells. Orion then commanded Ude to throw what was left of Nico in a special prison cell designed for Taiyōnians before commanding Cass to follow him to his personal quarters. Everyone obeyed completely, however, before leaving, Casanova took one last look at Nico as a heavy sense of guilt weighed her down. The traitorous Guardian put her head down, wondering if she even made the right choice. Shortly after, The Obedience continued its journey into The Great Divide, moving evermore closer to Orion's goal...

CHAPTER

TWELVE

SACRIFICE

Violent space storms and unpredictable waves of gravity rocked The Obedience and its crew side to side like a fish boat struggling to survive a hurricane. These were normal conditions given the erratic nature of The Great Divide. Unfortunately for the massive worldship, Orion was well prepared to sacrifice anything and anyone to achieve true Godliness. Sitting in his chair placed above his pilots, the self-proclaimed god grew weary of waiting and left The Obedience's bridge, leaving his pilots to carefully navigate through the nightmarish conditions of The Great Divide. Upon leaving, Orion flew through his father's old worldship, observing the massiveness of the ship's interior. Afterwards, he flew down towards his ship's detention level where Elders Vinzent, Nico, Raito and Luna were each stripped of their gear and gadgets, and were being held prisoner in specialized cells.

Orion first flew to and floated outside of Vinzent's cell, where the Guardian had been placed into a cell called: *Cell of Fear*. It was given that name because of its ability to bring forth the prisoner's deepest fears and darkest realities as tangible and intangible illusions. Knowing that Vinzent was no ordinary Guardian, Orion had also placed several corrupted soldiers in multiple small openings around the cell, and armed with organic stunning rifles with orders to shoot and torture Vinzent. In order to survive his prison, the Elder must come to peace with his shadow-self and enhance his sense of danger to avoid the call of torture provided by the rifle rounds, and to find peace with a horrible reality he had yet to witness. A task rarely achievable even by those with the strongest of wills.

Pleased, Orion flew to Nico's cell as the smell of burning flesh grew ever more potent. Orion reached the cell to see Nico burning alive with several glowing worms connected from the cell to vital-frogs which performed their duties in monitoring the prisoner's vitals. Orion found pride in this cell because it was designed for captured Senshi Warriors, after the implosion of their Suns. The cell was called: *Cell of Honō*, and it was given that name because upon entering, the prisoner was thrown into a cell that was connected to vital-frogs with organic flamethrowers established inside the entire cell. The flamethrowers then activate, burning the entity alive until the vital-frogs flatline, afterwards, the flames cease. However, for a Taiyōnian like Nico, once the vital-frogs picked up signs of life, the flamethrowers would activate once again, burning the imprisoned entity alive until dead, keeping them, or in this case Nico, in a baleful loop of death and rebirth, until he runs out of Solar Energy and perishes, like his ancestors before him.

Pleased once more, Orion moved on to Raito's cell, where the dark lord approached the prison called the *Cell of Pressure*. As the name suggests, upon being locked in the cell, the imprisoned entity is forced to bear the weight of gravity, slowly pressing down with increased levels of artificial gravity before being completely flattened to death like a hydraulic pressing machine. In Orion's eyes, this cell was perfect for a speedster Mahōnian like Raito because the weight of the room drastically slowed the Elder down, preventing any bursts of super speed.

Lastly, Orion flew out of the special cell area and over to Luna's cell which looked fairly normal. The reason for this was Orion was never given the impression that Luna was capable of any worthy physical abilities or strengths besides her unique use of Cosmic Energy. Whether or not she was hiding other abilities did not matter to Orion. With this conclusion, Orion, in other words, tossed Luna aside, deeming the weakened Guardian as "fruitless".

After confirming the security of the Guardians, Orion flew to his personal quarters where his sister Rose was seen in a deep meditative state. Curiosity found Orion as the dark lord attempted to force his way into her subconscious mind, only to be rejected violently like security guards throwing out a thief. But instead of anger consuming Orion, he praised The Eye's strength.

Orion: "Most entities would bend to my mental prowess, but not you Rose. Such power, wasted by The Order and its…Law of One."

Following the attempt, Rose awakened, finding a curious expression for Orion as the false god spoke.

Orion: "I hope I didn't interrupt, but I couldn't help but to see what was in your mind."

Orion spoke to his sister, however the Asronian princess seemed uninterested.

Orion: *frustrated tone* "Why do you not speak? Have you no respect for your future Creator?!"

Following this, three corrupted soldiers approached Orion's quarters as they bravely requested their lord's attention. But as humble as they were, the soldiers couldn't have picked a worse time because upon speaking, Orion released his frustration for Rose upon one of the soldiers killing it with a violent gust of gravity from his Black Aura, leaving the other two soldiers to deliver their important message.

Corrupted soldier #1: "M-My Lord, we're proceeding through The Great Divide…"

Orion: "And?"

Corrupted soldier #2: "D-Due to the size of your ship, we're forced to blast our way through because of how thick and dense the barrier is becoming my lord."

Orion: "Then get it done."

Corrupted soldier #2: "Well you see your grace, with the current power of The Obedience, it'll take us days, maybe weeks to get close to our destination. So—"

Orion: "In other words, you need my power to help speed the process." *sigh*

The dark lord turned back towards Rose as she sat consumed into another session of meditation. The false god turned back towards the two remaining soldiers.

Orion: "Have my station ready by the time I arrive, and bring the traitorous Guardian as well."

Corrupted soldier #1 & #2: "By your decree."

Orion: "And remove this lifeless pile of flesh from my halls before it smells."

Corrupted soldier #1 & #2: *bow in respect* "Yes my lord."

Meanwhile deep within The Obedience's detention level, a lone corrupted soldier approached the Cell of Honō, where he looked to see another soldier behind the flamethrower controls, and two more inside guarding Nico's body from a safe distance. The lone corrupted soldier looked inside the cell, seeing Nico as nothing more than a horribly distorted body of burnt flesh and loose flowing muscle-fibers as the flames continuously kept the Elder in the Realm of Apollo. Disturbed by what took place, the lone soldier gained access to the flamethrower control room by use of a stolen beetle card. Upon entering, the lone soldier stabbed the corrupted soldier in the parietal part of the head, killing it instantly. Next the lone soldier gained control of the flamethrowers before turning them against the two corrupted soldiers guarding Nico's body. They burned to a crisp like putting paper into a fire pit. Afterwards, the lone soldier extinguished the flames and rushed to help the heavily burned Elder. The lone soldier proceeded to implant the Elder with a Solar Seed, allowing Nico's Healing-Factor to take effect faster. A few moments later, Nico's body used the Solar Energy from the seed to prioritize regenerating his heart and lungs, one eye, his mouth, his throat, and left side of his brain in order to communicate properly as best he could despite the burns. With a deep and painful inhale, Nico was alive and furious.

Nico: *burned tone* "I'm gonna…kill you all."

Lone corrupted soldier: "Ooh scary. Is that anyway to say thank you? And here I thought Guardians were peace loving."

Nico's face hadn't fully regenerated, but the expression of confusion was easily noticeable. However, that confusion turned to joy as the lone corrupted soldier's face and body began to shapeshift, showing a black furred, pointy eared and long tailed alien by the name of *Kickatiwa Magana,* otherwise known as *Kicks*; first-class Elder Guardian of The Order with the Cosmic Energy ability called: *Shapeshift*. Nico's right arm partially regenerated as the Elder put out his hand to give a thumbs up, but all Elder Kicks saw was a raised stub and a partially burned smile.

Kicks: "Now look at that million dollar smile…"

Nico: *burned tone* "H-How… are you… alive?"

Kicks: "How am I alive? *chuckles* If you weren't a Taiyōnian I'd ask you the same thing. Right now we need to get you up and find the others. Any ideas?"

Nico shook his head, declining Kicks's question. Kicks let out a deep breath before shapeshifting into a corrupted soldier while giving Nico some spare clothes and his wrist computer he took from the detention's storage room.

Kicks: "Well if you're here then the others must be here on the detention level as well."

The two stumbled out of Nico's cell before making their way down the halls of the detention level. Time passed and Nico's Healing-Factor worked tirelessly to regenerate his body, but due to the lack of Sunlight, the task was moving slower than desired. However, the Elder was now able to speak clearly and walk independently.

Nico: "I can walk now. Thank you my friend."

Kicks: "Can you fight?"

Nico: "Against Orion and The Arm? Absolutely."

Meanwhile towards the bridge of the worldship, Orion poured his dense Black Aura into The Obedience which empowered the massive ship, like giving protein to muscles. The ship's pilots witnessed the Energy levels of the massive vessel increase beyond their normal capacity, enabling The Black Launcher to charge like never before. With a concentrated blast of gravity from the worldship's main cannon, the Orion Crusaders reduced the time it would've taken to venture through The Great Divide as Orion, Rose and all the other Energy sensitive beings began to feel the overwhelming power of Source Energy pulsating from the center of the galaxy. It sent excitement down Orion's spine as he drooled over the idea of his ascension. But the task proved difficult, even for an Asronian like Orion because of the power and density working against him and his ship. It was almost like the Myrmidon galaxy sensed the sinister nature of Orion and worked to protect itself. With this realization, Orion formed a protective bubble around his ship, resembling the one used at the battle of Bao. However, this shield was much weaker due to Orion's focus on pushing through The Great Divide. Following this, The Obedience's pilots warned their master of the several incoming lifeforms speeding towards the ship when suddenly, powerful thuds were heard outside of The Obedience. A loud explosion rocked the ship like a spacecraft breaking through the atmosphere. Several corrupted soldiers with gravity harnesses worked to close the gaping hole from the explosion, but before any work could be completed, multiple seven foot beings of Light, wielding spears and shields called: ***Spirit Defenders,*** invaded the ship. These beings were warrior spirits called upon by the five mysterious planets at the galaxy's center in times of need, and when an entity pushes past a certain point in The Great Divide, resembling a galactic security unit.

These warriors flooded the ship's opening, piercing and bashing with clear intent to protect the galaxy and the star system. Because of the sudden appearance of the Spirit Defenders, the corrupted army was caught off guard as casualties were in the hundreds in mere moments. It was a slaughter, something the Orion Crusaders had never encountered. However, the battle between the two forces shifted in favor of the Orion Crusaders as The Arm and The Hand joined the fight with Rose, a.k.a The Eye, simply watching the chaos unfold…

Down in the detention level, Elders Nico and Kicks were able to move freely, stopping only a few times to allow groups of corrupted soldiers to pass by. As they searched for Elders Vinzent, Raito and Luna, the two Elders heard and felt the chaos taking place multiple levels up, but their focus had not shifted from their current goal. Suddenly, Kicks told Nico to stop as they approached the Cell of Pressure.

Kicks: "Wait, wait. Let me handle this. With everything going on up there, this shouldn't take long."

Nico nodded in agreement and guarded their escape as Kicks shapeshifted into a corrupted soldier and approached the guards protecting Raito's cell.

Kicks: "Hey what's going on my friends. There's some crazy stuff going on upstairs, so I'd be careful if I were YOU!"

Walking up, Kicks sucker punched one of the guards before taking its rifle, and shooting the other corrupted soldier in the face to then turn the rifle on the first corrupted soldier. Kicks then felt the barrel of another rifle against the back of his head as the Elder shapeshifted into his original alien form before dropping the rifle and putting his hands up. However, before the armed corrupted soldier could pull the trigger,

Nico came in from behind and violently suplexed the soldier hard on its neck, producing a small shockwave thus killing the soldier. Soon after, Kicks expressed a sense of gratitude as Nico used his hands to spring himself to his feet.

Nico: "Soldier of the year..."

Kicks: "Good one. Glad to see some things haven't changed after all this time."

Elder Kicks snatched the beetle card from the deceased soldier before entering into the Cell of Pressure's control room. Soon after the Elder deactivated the gravity that pinned Raito to the ground, like having the weight of several elephants lifted from one's shoulders. Raito took a moment to recover before gradually coming to one knee, then to his feet to thank and greet Nico, and the long thought dead shapeshifting Guardian.

Raito: "Nico? Kicks? About time." *sore grunt*

Nico: "Good to see you too my friend."

Kicks: "It's definitely been awhile. Here's your Grimoire, and take this. I only have a few so I'm using them wisely."

Kicks gave Raito his Grimoire and one of Nico's Solar Seeds as a strong flow of Prana Energy flooded the Elder's being. With his Grimoire in hand, the Prana-user casted a spell called *Sunspot*, which created a miniature Sun for Nico's cells to regain some Solar Energy. Thanking his comrade, Nico sat and bathed under the mini-Sun with overflowing confidence and gratitude. He felt the strength of his body returning as he was now able to amplify and mutate his body once again. Following this, Elder Kicks asked Elder Raito if he knew where Vinzent was, to which Raito answered "no". But that wasn't much of a problem now given the Spirit Defenders were keeping the entirety of the Orion Crusaders occupied. This allowed Raito to sprint throughout the entire detention level in order to find Elder Vinzent. After a few swift moments, Raito found Vinzent in a prison called the Cell of Fear. The Elder used a conjured Light sword, and super speed, to sprint around and decapitate all the unexpecting corrupted soldiers ordered to torture Vinzent simultaneously. Raito then swiftly blasted the controls with Prana Energy before going in to check on his comrade, but something was wrong. Vinzent sat rocking back and forth, saying to himself, "the Coin of Life will be flipped… The Kesshō Empire marches near", repeatedly. Knowing time was of the essence, Raito picked up his broken comrade before sprinting back to the others, and once Raito reached Nico and Kicks, they all talked to figure out how to bring Vinzent's mind back from the depths of fear, depression and stress.

Nico: "Vinzent! What the hell happened?"

Kicks: "He must've been put into the Cell of Fear…"

Nico: "The cell of what? How do you know?"

Kicks: "It's a cell that was made to break strong willed individuals. It forces you to relive your worst experiences, and it brings your darkest reality to life through visions. Prolonged exposure can and will drive any entity insane as their will is shattered beyond repair. I've seen it happen too many times…"

Nico: "What are you saying? We just leave Vinzent here to rot away in this hell hole of a ship?!"

Kicks: "I'm saying that he's dead weight, and if we want to survive we need to get off this ship as soon as possible with those who can fight."

Nico and Raito were struck with a sense of disbelief and downheartedness after hearing the unthinkable.

Nico: "You've changed. The Kicks I know would die before abandoning a fellow Guardian."

Kicks: "Being on my own on this ship, hiding amongst the enemy, participating in their genocidal actions just to blend in, just to survive, it tends to change you Nico. It makes you realize that in this galaxy, there are no gray areas. Everything is black or white, where the strong overpower the weak. I survived this long because I chose myself above others. I had to watch innocent kids get turned into mindless murdering machines. I saw strong women forced to give birth against their will Nico, and I couldn't do a damn thing about it. I am a Guardian of Light in service to the One Infinite Creator, and I couldn't do a damn thing for anyone! Do you know what that does to a Guardian Nico? No. I pray you NEVER experienced the horrors I experienced on this ship. At the end of the day, all you have is yourself, other people just get in the way."

Nico: "You don't really believe that, do you Kicks?"

Kicks: "Why wouldn't I? Look around you, The Order is gone and the galaxy is in ruin. If I hadn't rescued you guys then what? Face the reality Nico, it's over."

Nico: "It's not over Kicks, I can't accept that. You freed us, empowered us. The Creator protected you and guarded you for this very moment! Don't you see that? And the Universe has sent us unexpected help in the form of those warriors who fight against the Orion Crusaders as we speak! You say one thing, but yet you went through the trouble of rescuing us, once again bringing hope to the galaxy. We can still do this, we can still stop Orion."

Nico put out his hand towards Kicks.

Nico: "Like old times?"

Kicks's heart began to beat with purpose and confidence as he grabbed Nico's hand, remembering just how strong Guardians are together.

Kicks: "Like old times."

Just as Nico brought Kicks back from the pits of loneliness and separation, Raito sped back to the other Guardians as the Elder explained he found Luna, but his demeanor didn't show signs of further good news. Following his discovery, Raito led Kicks and Nico towards Luna's cell as Nico carried the mentally broken Vinzent on his back. After a short journey through The Obedience's detention level, the Elders came across a normal cell which held a blue skinned entity resembling the Guardian known as Luna Joyce. She was extremely weak and barely clinging on to life as she looked at her comrades with utter joy. However, that joy was quickly masked by worry as she looked and saw Vinzent broken and lost in his thoughts, helplessly drifting through the void of depression, anxiety, and negativity.

Nico: "Luna...we...I-I..."

Luna: *weakened tone* "It's okay, this was out of your control. Thank you for rescuing me. The Ashura Order, you guys, we're my family and I wouldn't change a thing even now."

Luna turned towards the mentally distorted Elder Vinzent before asking Elder Nico to sit him down next to her.

Luna: *weakened tone* "Oh Vinzent, what have they done to you? You and I have had a special connection since the discovery of Orion, and despite the circumstances, I've enjoyed our conversations. I just wish we could spend these last moments together, but I know the others need you. I thought I'd have more time, but it seems the Creator is calling me home. With my remaining vital Source Energy, I'll cleanse your mind, and fix what has been broken..."

Elder Luna turned, facing Elders Nico, Raito and Kicks.

Luna: *weakened tone* "I'm giving Vinzent the rest of my life and vital Source Energy to fix his broken mind."

Raito: "Wait won't that kill you?! There has to be another way."

Nico put his hand on Raito's shoulder before closing his eyes. Right away he knew this was something Luna planned since learning of Vinzent's condition.

Luna: *weakened tone* "Thank you for everything. Knowing that Vinzent will be okay brings me peace and the courage to face the end openly. Vinzent will need time to recover, but when he does, tell him that I love him."

Nico: "I have a feeling you'll be able to tell him yourself. May the Creator guide your path and Apollo light the way."

With Nico's final words to Luna, the Guardian smiled and placed her hand on Vinzent's leg, mentally commanding him to sleep. Despite going to sleep, Vinzent was drowning in deep discomfort as he tossed and turned. Afterwards, she gently laid her hand upon Vinzent's head, pouring her consciousness into his mind. Following this action, Luna, once again looking as beautiful as a humble Sunset, found herself within Vinzent's subconscious mind. She saw nothing, but an endless space of nothingness as huge cracks surrounded her like a heavily cracked glass bottle. The Elder looked off into the distance and saw a young child, crying and afraid as she slowly approached the lost child.

Luna: "Vinzent?"

The young Vinzent anxiously scooted away.

Luna: "It's okay, I'm a friend."

The young child who was crying began to calm himself, wiping away the tears as Luna sat down next to him, gently grabbing his hand added by a loving and trustworthy smile.

Luna: "Doesn't this seem familiar? *chuckles* We always found ourselves in each other's head, talking, joking, planning. For some reason, after we spoke that first time, I couldn't get you out of my mind. I don't know if you felt the same, but…"

The young child who was first seen, now had fully calmed down thanks to Luna's angelic voice. Vinzent was now back to his older and wiser self as he replied to Luna.

Vinzent: "Yes I did. When we spoke the first time, it felt as if I was visited by an angel, and before I knew it, I spent my days wishing to feel your touch, hear your voice, and witness your beauty for the rest of my days. For you Luna, I would leave it all behind."

Luna: *soft smile* "If only we could've had that chance…"

Vinzent: "What do you mean? Where are we?"

Vinzent looked around at the blackness and cracks that made up his subconscious mind.

Luna: "We're in your subconscious mind. You were attacked mentally, but I'm here to save you and bring you back to the Light."

Vinzent: "Thank you Luna, but earlier you said that you wish we could've had our chance? What do you mean?"

Luna smiled again before looking down at her soft blue feet.

Luna: "Let's not ruin this moment with such harsh talk."

Luna stood up before putting out her hand, helping Vinzent to his feet.

Luna: "Come. Let us fix what has been broken."

Following these words, the two Elder ranked Guardians held hands as they both put out their free hand with Luna calling upon the Love and Light of the One Infinite Creator to heal the wounded, to bring together the broken pieces, and to remove the cloud of Darkness that plagued Vinzent's mind. And as Luna called upon the healing hand of the Creator, a bright light was seen by both Luna and Vinzent as it got increasingly brighter. Suddenly the light retracted into itself before bursting free like a star going supernova. The show of colors was magnificent as it left Vinzent stunned and in awe.

Outside of Vinzent's subconscious mind, both Luna and Vinzent's bodies began to levitate as they glowed with a bright white light. However, the light didn't blind Elders Nico, Raito or Kicks, but filled them with a sense of peace and tranquility despite the chaos taking place several levels up.

Back in Vinzent's mind, these beautiful patterns of colors flowed with grace, balance and harmony; a flow only recognized as the Creator's hand. Following this, Luna took Vinzent by both hands as the two looked into each other's eyes, not as Elders or Guardians, but as two entities who loved each other. After a moment of admiration from both of them, they shared a heartfelt kiss as Luna's spirit began to fade into the afterlife.

Vinzent: "Luna! Luna, wait! There's so much more I wish to say and do! Don't leave!"

Luna: "Do not be filled with sorrow, for we will have our time my love, but right now, your friends need you; the galaxy needs you. Don't worry, I will wait for you, and when the time is right, we will meet again, for this is not the end. Now, go. Go forth my love, rejoicing in the Love and in the Light of the One Infinite Creator. Adonai."

Vinzent: *accepting tone* "Adonai..."

Outside of Vinzent's subconscious mind, the surrounding Guardians looked to see as Elder Luna Joyce took her last breath, and that Vinzent's earlier demeanor of discomfort was now masked by peace as his breathing slowed and his heart rate stabilized. They saw a tear fall from Vinzent's face as he awoke. Nico went to help sit up his healed comrade, saying to himself "from Light we are born, to Light we will return. Adonai Luna." Following this, Raito carefully picked up Luna's body as the faction of Guardians motioned out of Luna's cell, and through the detention level in hopes of finding the Hercules and to stop Orion's plan to ascend to Godliness.

Meanwhile in the main area of The Obedience, the battle between the Orion Crusaders and the Spirit Defenders raged on as Ude and Hando utilized their gifts from the Accelerant to keep the intruders at bay. Thanks to Ude's new Healing-Factor and amplified strength, the warrior recklessly charged through the opposition with complete disregard for himself or for the corrupted soldiers killed by his attacks. Thanks to his hulking size, thick skin and four arms, Hando rallied the corrupted army as they pushed against the Spirit Defenders with fury and courage. But before a winner was declared, the Defenders suddenly ceased their attack, allowing the Orion Crusaders to mop the floor with those who remained. Curious, Ude wondered why they stopped fighting.

The Arm: "What is the meaning of this cowardice action?"

The Hand: "Isn't it obvious Ude? Their actions were in vain. Would you continue to fight knowing victory is hopeless?"

The Arm: "You have a point, Hando. However, I do not find honor in hunting easy prey."

As the two warriors boasted about their victory, Orion floated high above his forces as bliss filled his very being. He then addressed the entire ship.

Orion: "My children. Today marks the beginning of a new era. I have found the planet that contains my destiny. As we speak, I move evermore closer to what is rightfully mine. And soon, Myrmidon and the entire Universe will know my name. Now GO! Prepare yourselves, for the Sun sets and Darkness rises."

The entire ship roared with determination and accomplishment as The Obedience moved inevitably closer to the second of five planets, **Exodus**. There lie the God's Heart fruit, and Orion's destiny. Orion flew back up towards the ship's bridge to see his grand prize. This planet was absolutely gorgeous and brimming with Source Energy, like feeling the warmth of the soul. The colors presented were vibrant and pleasing to the eyes, which was added by the beauty of the planet's neighboring siblings and the glorious white Sun. For the first time, Orion felt a sense of guilt for disturbing the natural balance of this star system, but that sensation was quickly and disgustingly discarded as Orion had sacrificed too much, and caused too much death and destruction to reach that moment. Why stop when his goal was literally right in front of his eyes? Orion thought to himself. The dark lord threw away any and all doubt as he manually took control of The Obedience to power through the rest of the way, disregarding the damage it would cause to his ship or its crew. The selfish false god was power hungry, and saw nothing but his prize.

Orion: "I'm coming for you Creator."

A few moments passed and finally after traveling across the galaxy, barely making it through The Great Divide, Orion had arrived at the second planet Exodus, a goal that was two centuries in the making. Orion flew down to deliver his message to his forces, but before he was able, Elder ranked Guardian Vinzent valiantly called out to the false god as Elders Nico, Raito and Kicks stood at his back. But Orion found no interest in them or in the fact that they've escaped from their cells, because in his mind, they couldn't stop him before, and after he gained the power of the Creator, they'd be nothing but dust in the wind. Following this thought, the dark lord motioned for several corrupted soldiers to ready a Ryū lander to minimize wasted time as they sprinted to fulfill Orion's command.

Vinzent: "ORION! You will not escape your fate."

Orion: "You Guardians are too late. Ude, Hando, take the remainder of the corrupted army and finish what you started. Do not come to me until they're dead. Come Rose we have work to accomplish, you too Guardian. You will be used as leverage against them if I deem it necessary."

The Arm and The Hand bowed in respect as they and the remaining corrupted army prepared to fight to the death for their lord. Seeing Cass, Nico called out to her in happiness, but also confusion as she followed the enemy into a Ryū lander.

Nico: "Cass! Cass? What are you..."

Raito: "You didn't know?"

Nico: "Know what?..."

Raito: "She betrayed us Nico. The Order, the faction, you. She's been playing us since Zora. The DSR, Bao, Journia, The Nine, all gone because of the information she gave to Orion."

Nico: "This isn't a good time to lie, Raito..."

Vinzent: "It's true Nico, she was the spy. Why do you think she's following Orion?"

Kicks: "What the hell Cass! I always wondered why Orion left Zora intact. Now I know..."

Nico's heart was struck with disbelief and solicitude. His mind clouded, his heart racing. It was as if he witnessed the destruction of Taiyō all over again. Cass looked back at her lover as despondency filled her eyes. She turned back to follow Orion and Rose off the ship and into the Ryū lander which flew them down to the mysterious world of Exodus. This left Nico confused and hurt as the Elder ranked Guardians of the once powerful Ashura Order readied themselves to battle against the last remains of the Orion Crusaders...

CHAPTER

THIRTEEN

REDEMPTION

The stench of dead vessels and blood filled the air of The Obedience as the Guardians of the Ashura Order were surrounded by what was left of the Orion Crusaders. Elder Guardian Vinzent took a brief moment before the battle to generate his Blue Aura, allowing him to establish a telepathic connection between himself, Nico, Kicks and Raito. With this set in place, the Guardians were able to communicate secretly and with increased efficiency.

Vinzent: "Can y'all hear me?"

Kicks: "Loud and clear."

Raito: "I hear you brotha."

Vinzent: "Nico?... Nico?!"

Nico: "Sorry. Yeah, I can hear you..."

Vinzent: "I get you're confused, but we need you here in the present moment."

Nico: "Y-Yeah… *deep breath* Okay, yeah. I'm here."

Vinzent: "Good. Anyone have any ideas?"

Kicks: "From the looks of it, it seems those intruders cleaned out a good number of them and managed to dispose of a great number of Monos and Walkers, but the corrupted soldiers remain at large, along with The Arm and The Hand."

Vinzent: "In other words, we'll manage. Enough said. This is it Guardians. This is where it all comes to pass. All of our losses, all of our sacrifices, it comes down to what we do in this present moment. Leave all fear and doubt behind, for today…we hunt."

Vinzent's words sparked a flame inside the heart of his fellow Guardians as they fought to save the galaxy from Orion. Raito used his Grimoire to cast a spell called: ***Blinding Mist,*** which sent thick smoke bursting fifty meters in every direction. Following the distraction, Nico and Vinzent tossed several orange colored bombs both to the left and right which resulted in the incineration of several pockets of corrupted soldiers. The Orion Crusaders retaliated by firing blindly into the mist, hoping to hit something, but their efforts were in vain as Elder Nico charged out of the smoke like a glowing bull as his Mamoru shield performed its duty. He then leaped high above the battlefield as Elder Kicks held onto his shoulders. Afterwards, Nico launched Kicks with great velocity towards The Hand, leading to Kicks shapeshifting into The Hand before crashing viciously into Hando. The two identical behemoths punched away at one another as they tumbled across the battlefield. While in mid-air, Nico mutated his appendage into the Yumi bow, allowing him to rain down explosive Bakudan arrows upon the enemy. After clearing a place for him to land, Nico showcased the deadly nature of his dual Jūken blades by slicing all who stood in his way. Several meters away, Elder Raito utilized his inherent power of super speed to create a raging tornado. Elder Vinzent added to Raito's effort by coating the swirling gust of wind in lightning, resulting in the creation of a windstorm that swept away corrupted soldiers, Monos, and Walkers alike. While dueling against three Monos, Nico felt the extreme wind produced from Raito and Vinzent's windstorm as his dreadlocks flowed with the harsh wind. After disposing of the attacking Monos, Nico amplified the muscles of his legs to leap high into the air once more. The Elder then mutated his arm into the Hari whip mutation before latching onto the ceiling that covered the battlefield. With a mighty push from his strengthened legs, Nico shot down like a cannonball towards a large group of corrupted soldiers and a Walker. Just before impact, the Elder mutated his arms into the Ken fists which, on impact, created a massive shockwave that decimated all corrupted soldiers within a twenty meter radius, while also gravely injuring the Walker. The shockwave sent a ripple throughout the entire ship, adding on to the long list of damages sustained. The Orion Crusaders didn't give up though as The Arm came in hard and fast, punching Vinzent into a nearby wall, and grabbing Raito, effectively stopping the windstorm. Ude then slammed Raito onto the ground, but before The Arm could strike the Guardian, Nico dashed in and sliced off Ude's arm with the Jūken blade. The Taiyōnian followed his assault by drop kicking The Arm in the chest, sending him flying a few meters away. Afterwards, Nico put out his unmutated hand to help his comrade up.

Nico: "You okay brotha?"

Raito: *grunts* "Never better. I appreciate the save."

Nico: "Call it even?"

Raito went to answer Nico's mid-battle question, but before he could, The Arm returned Nico's attack by punching Raito away, to which the attack was blocked by Raito's Prana Energy shield. Ude then swiftly struck Nico in the torso and grabbed him to slam the Elder viciously through multiple levels. The Arm jumped down after his prey, hungry to finish what they started. Following the attack, Nico got up and used his Healing-Factor to swiftly fix what was broken, and to ready himself for a final confrontation with the monster that was The Arm. Seeing that he had seconds to spare, Nico looked around, forming a plan to which the Elder noticed the level he was on. Upon realizing, a confident smile showed up on Nico's face as an idea ringed in his mind, nonetheless answering the call of genius. Ude, Orion's top fighter and general, came down through the opening he created with purpose and excitement. Upon landing, The Arm searched for his prey as he taunted the Elder.

The Arm: *deep monstrous tone* "Guardian! What happened to that fiery spirit I saw before huh?! Do you hide because you are weak? Or because you know you are hopeless? And here I called you worthy...HA! Solla was your home correct, Guardian!? Beautiful, shame I burned it to the ground. I would've loved to hear those screams again. *maniacal laughter* Come out Guardian, your comrades need you."

The Arm spared nothing as he broke through doors and walls alike to find his prey. Nico however, felt peace within his being, and shunned the evil from which Ude brought to the surface. With a clear head, Nico planted multiple Bakudan bombs along the floor before mutating his arms into his Ken fists. Following this, the Elder clashed his fists together as a loud thud filled the halls of the detention level. Ude's transformation, and level of Solar Mutation granted the warrior immense power, but dulled his intelligence as upon hearing his prey, the beast recklessly charged for the sound, and after bursting through a few walls, The Arm found his target.

The Arm: "At last Taiyōnian. Let us shed blood not for our masters, but for the joy of battle!"

With these battle-ready words, Ude's animal instincts took over, suppressing all rational thoughts as the unexpecting warrior ran straight for Nico. Ude attacked the Elder with a few beastly swings that were easily dodged and blocked because of Nico's calmed composure. This however, enraged The Arm as he felt as if the Guardian toyed with him. Thinking this, Ude roared with anger as his attacks became increasingly violent with every swing sending a small shockwave in its wake. Nico however, wasn't on the defensive for no reason, for with every step backward, the two moved closer and closer to Nico's trap. Ude continued his endless barrage of attacks, when suddenly, Nico made his move. The Elder mutated both arms into his dual Jūken blades before cutting deep into the knees of Ude, to which the beast fell to his hands. Afterwards, Nico flipped over The Arm while simultaneously detonating the Bakudan bombs he had placed earlier. The bombs exploded in Ude's face, destroying the beast's arms and chest as The Arm laid there temporarily helpless. Nico then mutated his arms, using his Ken fists to pick up and forcefully throw Ude into the Cell of Honō, locking The Arm inside. Because of Ude's artificial Solar Mutation, he would surely break free, so before Ude's wounds healed completely, Nico activated the flamethrowers then sliced the control panel in fours, using his dual Jūken blades. The Elder watched as Ude burned alive, being trapped in a state of constant death as the beast cried out screaming in agony as the flames torched his flesh.

Nico: "Look, people of Solla, of Taiyō. No more will this monster hurt anyone else, for he will repay his sins in fire."

After taking a moment to ask the Creator for forgiveness and to catch his breath from all the constant amplifying, mutating and healing, Nico sprinted through the detention level's halls as fast as he could. He needed to get back in order to help his comrades defend against the Orion Crusaders, and to defeat Orion once and for all. As the Elder ran back to help fight, he picked up a familiar frequency on his wrist computer.

Meanwhile, Elder Kicks, shapeshifted as The Hand, went toe-to-toe with the real Hando as the two behemoths traded blow for blow. But despite looking the same, Kicks did not share the same strength and was eventually overpowered and stabbed through the stomach by a torn off horn from a deceased Walker. Kicks shifted back to his normal alien complexion before coughing up blue blood. Following the fatal blow, Hando saw the golden opportunity and stepped on Kicks's legs, shattering them to dust. However, before Hando had a chance to finish the Guardian, Vinzent blasted Hando in the chest with a strong stream of Violet lightning that sent the titan flying into a nearby wall. The Elder then ran, killing several other corrupted soldiers along the way before reaching and picking up his injured companion. With Kicks over his shoulder, Vinzent turned to find cover, but instead was met by more corrupted soldiers who would sacrifice life and limb for Orion.

Vinzent: *heavy panting* "Shit...there's no end to these guys."

Vinzent refused to give up though as the Guardian generated his Red Aura to manifest a lightning sword. The Elder dripped a dab of his Orange Aura to give the sword explosive properties. This combination proved extremely fruitful because the sword not only cut through soldier after soldier, but also added the bonus of small explosions that cleared out surrounding corrupted soldiers. A few meters away, Elder Raito recovered from Hando's attack, and sent several corrupted soldiers to the afterlife with well placed arrows from his Light-bow spell. Time slowed down for the Elder as he took a moment to witness the situation deteriorate exponentially. He saw Elder Vinzent fighting for his life while protecting Elder Kicks, and knew Elder Nico was fighting alone against The Arm. In need of divine guidance and a power boost, Raito searched deep within himself for a solution. The words of the Asronian Emperor, Titus Ronan, "Build a true and pure relationship with the Source Energy by embracing the Darkness within", flooded the Guardian's mind. Soon after, half of Raito's Grimoire began to glow in a white light as the other half turned black as charcoal before swirling together. The Guardian could hear his spell book calling to him as if he heard a familiar voice. Raito held his spell book with both hands before instinctively bringing the glowing book into his chest as it dissolved into his physical being, and into his spirit like snow under the Sun. Afterwards, a burst of Ashla and Bogan fueled Prana Energy shot from Raito, and out through the top of The Obedience like shooting a powerful flare gun into the night sky. The blast pushed all the surrounding corrupted soldiers away from Raito as the Guardian stood on air effortlessly. Vinzent felt the immense power pulsating from his comrade as he looked to see not Raito, but a being purely composed of Prana Energy, shining brighter than a full moon. The Elder's hands, feet and dreadlocks changed into a beautiful golden yellow; his eyes matching. Soon after, the symbols engraved on his Grimoire were copied all over his torso and arms in black writing like majestic tattoos.

Vinzent: "You've fully embraced Bogan teachings and found your way to enlightenment, huh Raito? Welcome brotha."

Following Raito's balanced enlightenment, The Hand commanded all of the forces present to open fire on the strange being. Without hesitation, all remaining corrupted soldiers turned and fired their organic rifles, and launched explosive slugs towards Elder Raito. Vinzent used the distraction to find cover for himself and Kicks. Following the barrage of rifle shots and exploding slugs, the corrupted army forces did nothing, but waste ammo and resources as Raito stopped all the attacks as if he pressed pause on the speeding bolts of death. Seeing that their efforts were wasted, the Orion Crusaders ceased fire, to which the empowered Guardian looked down upon the enemy before turning the paused blaster bolts against the enemy, killing those closest to himself and Vinzent. Next Raito demonstrated his use of Ashla and Bogan teachings by putting out his hand to freeze time within the walls of The Obedience. Raito, the *Master of Prana Energy*, flew down towards the ground, observing the frozen corrupted soldiers as they stood as still as freshly designed statues. The Elder then found Vinzent before moving into the Guardian's subconscious mind to speak to him.

Raito: "Vinzent?"

Vinzent: "W-What the...Raito?!"

Seeing Raito inside his subconscious mind gave Vinzent the uneasy feeling that his mind was yet again damaged or worse, but Raito reassured his perturbed comrade that he wasn't dead or broken, and showed Vinzent the astonishing power of true Prana Energy. Raito allowed Vinzent to see what had transpired only moments ago.

Vinzent: "I'm guessing you did this…So this is the true potential of fully realized Prana Energy when infused with both Ashla and Bogan teachings. You can stop time…wow. How do you feel?"

Raito: "I feel…empowered. It feels like I've connected with the Creator, and the Creator connected with me. I understand what Titus meant now, about the purity of Source Energy."

Vinzent: "You have found your way to enlightenment my friend."

Raito: "Yes. This is different from any spell or incantation. I asked the Creator for a way out, and he has provided to say the least. This… gift, *Empowerment* seems like the correct name, for our Creator has empowered me with Love and Light to serve those in need, both in Light and in Darkness."

Vinzent: "Well said brotha. The galaxy will know peace once again. Given that you've put the battlefield on ice, are you able to attack these hopeless fools?"

Raito: "For some reason no. I'm only able to move to and from the subconscious mind, at least when time stops like this."

Vinzent: *chuckle* "I guess that would be too easy. So what now?"

Raito: "Stay here in cover. Let me handle the rest."

Vinzent reluctantly agreed as Raito exited from Vinzent's subconscious mind. Raito then snapped his fingers, unfreezing the entire battlefield as chaos resumed like unpausing a movie. Corrupted soldiers lost their lives because of the redirected blaster bolts from Raito, forcing Vinzent to take cover once again. The Hand felt a weird sensation as if he's lost time, but he shook it off and continued the assault against the being of Light and Darkness floating above. Corrupted soldiers continuously fired upon Raito as the empowered Guardian shielded himself from all attacks effortlessly. He then flew down a few meters from the ground, enabling most of the corrupted soldiers to charge the Guardian. But despite vastly outnumbering Elder Raito, those who pursued him welcomed themselves to a hastened death. The Master of Prana used his empowered super speed to eliminate vast groups of the enemy with the speed of light. Seeing nothing but a white blur, followed by dead soldiers filled Hando with utter dread. Raito then suddenly appeared in front of Hando before slapping the ten foot titan into a wall. Shortly after, Elder Raito appeared in front of a batch of soldiers and swiped his hand like swatting a fly away. Following this act of Prana Energy, the soldier's eyes and mouths glowed as each entity burst into millions of tiny white particles which floated up, and faded out into the air. The remaining corrupted soldiers, plus Hando who pulled himself out of the wall, hesitated to press on, but their fear of Orion outweighed their fear of death as The Hand commanded more corrupted soldiers to eliminate Elder Raito, totally overlooking Elder Vinzent who worked tirelessly to stabilize Elder Kicks's fatal wound, via his Green Aura. All of the surviving soldiers surrounded the Guardian as Raito swiped his golden yellow hand against the besieging enemy, erasing their very being from existence, not even leaving the bones; the feat even frightened Vinzent. Shortly after, the battlefield grew quiet as tiny white particles faded into the atmosphere like water turning into vapor. The Hand, who was the lone survivor, backed away in utter fear as he only witnessed Orion and Rose achieve such feats of power. However, that fear inevitably began to disperse as Raito's body of pure Prana Energy flickered like a damaged light bulb. Vinzent's worry skyrocketed as Raito's Empowerment ability wore off. And just like that, the Prana-user reverted to his normal form and fell to his hands and knees, completely exhausted. Seeing this, Hando smiled and walked up boasting about his luck.

The Hand: "It seems Orion's favor falls to me. *deep laughter* I will be honest, you Guardians possess such amazing power...a shame you all must die. You would've made perfect slaves."

Hando picked up the fatigued and powerless Guardian by the head, squeezing it like a stress ball. Raito grunted out in torment as blood ran from his nose and head, but before Hando could kill the first-class Elder, a concentrated blast of blue lightning struck The Hand, mentally stunting the titan as he dropped Raito. Adding to his attack, Vinzent generated his Red Aura and manifested a sword before adding a drop of his Black Aura. With a shockwave of Energy, Elder Vinzent's sword crackled with power and lightning, added by noticeable weight. Vinzent then dashed for Hando in a flash of lightning before cutting The Hand's arms completely off. Hando roared in agony and annoyance as he found himself constantly losing limbs. Following the attack, Hando unexpectedly found his movement restricted as Nico, who just returned, used his Hari whip mutation to wrap the ten foot behemoth by the legs and neck, leading to the small blades from the whips to dig into Hando's flesh. The two struggled as one worked to hold, and the other worked to break free as The Hand jumped, jerked and swung Nico into walls to free himself. Vinzent witnessed Nico struggling and knew he had to lend a hand. With that conclusion in mind, Elder Vinzent manifested a red bow and arrow. The Guardian then dripped his Black Aura into the manifested arrow, blessing it with the power to achieve victory. Soon after, with a strong release and laser focus, Vinzent fired the arrow against Hando. Because of Nico's amplified strength, the Taiyōnian slammed Hando against the ground to tighten his hold on the armless foe. Nico then saw the black arrow speeding towards them, so the Elder swiftly released The Hand and mutated his arm into the Jūken blade. Shortly after, Nico hastily sliced deep into Hando's achilles heel, forcing the behemoth to one knee. This steadied The Hand, enabling the arrow to meet its target and puncture Hando between the eyes. Because of the power granted from Vinzent's Black Aura, the arrow melted straight through The Hand's head, carving a hole big enough for all to see the internal nature of his brain. Moreover, the black arrow didn't just carve a hole a foot wide into Hando's head, it also blew a giant hole in one of The Obedience's engine rooms, ultimately crippling the box-shaped worldship. Besides the damage to The Obedience, Elder Vinzent recovered to his feet before checking on Raito, leaving Nico to check on The Hand who finally lay dead, never to harm another soul again.

Raito: "I see you're getting acclimated to your Black Aura."

Vinzent: "I still have a ways to go, but this Aura is unlike anything I've ever felt. That aside, are you alright?"

Raito: "I'm fine, thank the Creator. I see what Titus was talking about now. The exhaustion after awakening such power."

Vinzent: "Yes, but it's a small price to pay for such Energy. I wonder if every entity in the galaxy can achieve such power?"

Following Vinzent and Raito's post-battle discussion, the two were forced to regain their balance after feeling The Obedience slowly breaking apart. As the two Elders began assessing the situation, their wrist computers informed them that the Hercules was in close proximity and that the ship's systems were coming online. These facts bred suspicion within those who confirmed the notifications, but the Elder's doubts were abolished by a familiar artificial intelligence.

Vinzent: "This ship won't last much longer. We need to gather everyone and find the Hercules."

Raito: "Agreed... Wait, Vinzent you seeing this? Someone is activating the Hercules's systems..."

Jasmine: "That would be me."

Raito: "Jasmine! You're okay?! But how?"

Jasmine: "After Cass stabbed you and infected me with that worm virus, I was forced to disperse all my data and memories before any permanent damage was caused. After I regrouped myself, I found the heart of the virus. I burned its code with several firewalls, effectively cleansing myself. As a result, I was forced to commence a hard system reset that took longer than expected, but nonetheless, I'm back and ready to help."

Raito: "Sounds like quite the digital adventure."

Vinzent: "I'm glad you're back Jazz."

Following Jasmine's return, Nico called Vinzent and Raito over. Once they got there, their hearts were struck with more grief as Kicks laid down, blue blood pouring from his fatal wound caused by The Hand. Nico kneeled down beside his dying friend as sadness and anger masked his tone.

Nico: "Kicks, I'm sorry. I should've fought harder. And now... and now..."

Kicks: *weakened tone* "There's no need...for sadness. Death...is not the...end...remember?"

Nico: "Take this Solar Seed. There should be one left..."

Nico pulled out the last Solar Seed for Kicks, but the dying Elder closed his hand back as Nico gave a confused reaction.

Kicks: *weakened tone* "Save it...you guys *cough* will need it..."*cough*

Nico: "We're gonna need you too Kicks! You can't die, you just got here..."

Kicks: *weakened chuckle* "You have...all you need...right... beside you."

Nico turned to face Elder Vinzent then Elder Raito, then back to Elder Kicks.

Kicks: *weakened tone* "This...is as it should be...Listen to me...I've been on this ship...for a while...and I've done...some horrible things..."

Nico: "But that wasn't your fault."

Kicks: *weakened tone* "Let me...finish. My soul is...tainted with the sins of the...Orion...Crusaders. *grunts* There is...no place for entities...like me. Despite that...you three have given me...purpose again...and I can't thank you enough. That being said..."

Kicks reached into his bloodied satchel to pull out a remote for explosives.

Kicks: *weakened tone* "I've...planted several bombs...in key places... throughout the entire ship, but because...of the ship's size... It wouldn't... have been enough... to destroy this ship. But, thanks... to your reckless Bakudan bomb... Nico *painful chuckle* And... Vinzent's arrow... conveniently hitting one of the... engine rooms... these bombs should... finish the job. *grunts* I want...you all to leave...this ship... Leave it behind...in thought...and in spirit."

Nico: "You know I can't do that Kicks. We don't leave Guardians behind..."

Kicks: *weakened tone* "This isn't the time for that Nico! Take this... and GO! Let me...pay for my sins...the only way I can..."

Kicks ripped his family necklace from his neck before giving it to Nico for safe keeping. Elders Vinzent, Raito and Nico then headed towards the Hercules as Nico looked back at his long time friend for the last time. Nico was the last to enter the door leading towards the Hercules before it was closed and locked. Raito and Vinzent rushed to the cockpit of their ship before they both jumped in the pilot seats. Vinzent went to start the engines, but was filled with worry and confusion because of the Hercules's failure to start. Both Raito and Vinzent tried the engines once more, but only heard the stalling of the thrusters, and scraping of the ship's outer-hull from external damages. Following this, Vinzent asked for a status report.

Vinzent: "Jasmine, status report. Why can't we get this show in the air?"

Jasmine: "It seems the main thrusters and the vertical thrusters were damaged by extensive external damage. There also seems to be pieces of The Obedience that collapsed on the port side of the ship. Because of the damaged thrusters and debris from The Obedience's interior foundation, we don't have enough thrust to lift off. By my calculations, we'll need a push to free us from the debris, and to lighten up the ship if we wish to go anywhere."

Nico: "I'll handle it."

Nico found the airlock towards the top of the Hercules as the Elder leaped out and made his way towards the back of the spacecraft. He then amplified the muscles in his legs and arms to the extreme, pushing past his normal limits. As a result, several muscle-fibers originated from his pores, wrapping and overlapping his arms, chest and legs. This gave the Elder the strength and means to slowly push the spacecraft, freeing it from the debris that weighed down upon it. Nico pushed and pushed, struggling to free the Hercules as the spacecraft was no lightweight object. After pushing with all his might, the craft gained the necessary conditions to commence the take-off procedure. Soon after, Nico leaped onto the Hercules and climbed inside through the airlock before locking it shut.

Raito: "Good stuff Nico! Now let's get out of here."

Nico: *heavy panting* "Yeah… no doubt…"

Kicks, barely able to stay alive, saw the galaxy's last hope leaving before saying, "forgive me Creator", as the shapeshifting Elder pushed the button, causing a chain of explosions that was heard and felt throughout The Obedience. Following this, Vinzent and Raito focused sharply, flying the Hercules through the massive worldship, blasting down walls and dodging falling pieces of The Obedience's interior. Finally the faction of Guardians found an opening out of the exploding vessel, but, upon seeing their escape, the pilot's of the huge worldship began to slowly close the opening. Seeing this, Vinzent asked Nico to take control of the Hercules as he channeled his Violet Aura. Vinzent's eyes began to glow as Violet lightning crackled from his body, and with a thrust of his hands upwards, the entire outer-hull of the Hercules was covered and shielded by Vinzent's Violet lightning. The Hercules burst through the closed door of The Obedience in a brutal strike of lightning. Afterwards, The Obedience exploded, piece by piece with one of its pieces colliding against the already damaged Hercules spacecraft. Because of Elder Kicks's well placed bombs, Nico's huge Bakudan explosions, and Vinzent's arrow carving a hole into one of the worldship's engine rooms, the massive vessel lost its thrusters, its entire port side, as well as its ability to stabilize its flight capabilities. Following these serious damages, the stern end of The Obedience exploded in an enormous explosion that sent small and large pieces of itself far into The Great Divide, adding to the sea of destroyed ships. The shockwave from the blast shoved the damaged Hercules as the spacecraft flipped and was tossed around like a tornado carrying a car. After a few moments, the mutilated Hercules shot out of the thick smoke and fire, and towards the second planet of Exodus. However, because of the gravitational force of Exodus, both the gravely mangled enemy ship and the Hercules were pulled uncontrollably into the planet's orbit then atmosphere. The Guardians worked vigorously to steer the Hercules away from where The Obedience would make its crash landing, which the Elders managed to do so. Due to this feat, the Hercules succumbed to engine and thruster failure which left the spacecraft and its Elder crew at the mercy of Exodus's gravity. The feeling of despair filled the small spaceship as emergency alarms blared uncontrollably.

Jasmine: "We have engine failure! We've lost thrusters one and three. I suggest you Guardians get seated, we're coming in too hot!…"

Elders Raito, Vinzent and Nico took the AI's words to heart as the Hercules broke the sound barrier upon entering the atmosphere of Exodus; a trail of smoke and fire tailing the defaced ship. Knowing they were about to crash land, Raito casted two smaller Prana Energy shields around himself and Vinzent, given Nico's Healing-Factor. Raito did this to increase the strength of both shields. Nico initiated the emergency landing protocols, but like before, the vertical thrusters were offline, giving the Guardians no way to slow down. And with a heavy THOOM, tumble, and slide, the Hercules violently crashed on the planet Exodus. The Obedience off in the distance, crashed soon after the Hercules, leveling the surrounding area like dropping a nuke. Following the crash, Vinzent woke up and found himself still strapped to his seat, but as he looked around, he saw pieces of the Hercules scattered across the ground like broken glass. Upon coming to realize his situation, Vinzent found nothing more than gratitude for the Creator, thanking the Creator for his survival. But after looking at just how bad the crash was, could he say the same for Raito and Nico? He unstrapped himself and fell to the ground with dizziness filling his mind as his body worked to adapt to the strangeness, and powerful nature of the planet. The Order's records on the planet Exodus, or any of the five planets, were almost nonexistent, other than the fact this planet contained a powerful fruit, and possessed a special connection to pure Source Energy unlike anything anyone had experienced. Vinzent was left in awe as he felt the purity of Love and Light from the Creator, but also a sense of Darkness from the planet. Nevertheless, despite the pure nature and beauty of this new magical world, Vinzent knew he had to find Elders Raito and Nico, and stop Orion from destroying Myrmidon, or risk losing such a blessed system of planets to the hands of evil and Darkness...

FOURTEEN

EXODUS

False god, lord, master, Asronian. Orion held many titles, and was feared throughout Myrmidon. Besides avenging the Asronian race, one fact brought absolute disgust to Orion's mind, and that was the existence of beings more powerful than him.

Orion floated slowly through this mysterious land of Exodus, along with Rose and Elder Casanova. He felt the weight of danger on his shoulders as if the planet itself fought against him. He found overflowing interest in the planet however, because of how intricately connected everything was, not just with every living animal, plant, molecule, and bacteria, but with the star system and Universe itself. Furthermore, Orion found astonishment in how the planet reacted to Rose's presence. The flowers flourished with colors, the animals sung and danced with harmonious intent, and the wind blew with grace and compassion. Following these events, the native animals that surrounded Rose, suddenly fled in fear because of Orion's wicked Aura, and hunger for power. These animals, blessed with Exodus as their home, sensed and knew why such a being was here, and what his intentions were. Their animal instincts led them to hide in caves and holes, fearing for their lives, however, Orion had no interest in such creatures and simply motioned past them. Realizing that the planet was reacting to Rose, Orion, calmed his hunger for power and allowed a cool mind to prevail.

Orion: "It would seem this planet has a special connection to you my sister. The animals stop at your feet, the wind kisses your skin, and the flowers come alive as your eyes gaze upon their beauty. Surely you must know where to find the God's Heart fruit?"

Rose considered her brother's words, allowing curiosity to flood her mind. Following a short moment of silence, the Asronian princess sat on the soft grass of the planet to meditate, deepening her connection to the planet and Source Energy around her. As she sat meditating, Rose began to hear a soft voice call to her, guiding her to what she thought was the God's Heart fruit. But from Casanova's perspective, the Asronian was simply stalling.

Cass: "Why is she stalling? Must we delay further?"

Orion: "Your mind cannot comprehend what takes place currently. Quiet Guardian or risk overstepping your boundary, forcing me to reconsider why you're even still alive."

Cass: "With all due respect Orion, I really don't think–"

Orion swiftly grabbed Casanova by the mouth. He then proceeded to ignite black flames from his free hand, putting it closely against Cass's stomach. The flames melted Cass's armor and burned her flesh as Casanova yelled in grimming pain, but her screams were muffled because of Orion's cold hand squeezing it shut. The false god then warned the disrespectful Guardian.

Orion: "Listen to me carefully, Guardian. Your input is not wanted or welcomed. You will do as you are told and nothing else."

Finished, Orion tossed Cass to the side as the Guardian hit the ground tumbling. She then got up, gathering herself while administering first-aid to herself by using her Elemental Energy to cool her burn.

Orion: "Now, *sigh* let's not have anymore altercations like this, or else that will be the end of you. Do I make myself clear?"

Cass: *grunts* "Yes, my Lord."

Meanwhile at the crash site of the Hercules, Nico awakened with an agonizing pain in his abdomen. Looking down, the Elder found a piece of the broken ship lodged deep in his stomach. Nico tried to grab the penetrating piece of metal, but found that he was missing an arm as well. The Elder quietly said, "here we go", before pulling the piece of metal free from his body, allowing a continuous flow of blood to pour freely. Afterwards he fell against the ground and took several painful inhales, allowing his Healing-Factor to stop the bleeding, and regenerate the wound, broken bones, and missing arm completely. Soon after, Nico slowed his breathing and attempted to contact his comrades using his wrist computer, but just like on Zora, all he received was static. The Elder ranked Guardian then made a different attempt, contacting Jasmine to help assess the current situation, but there seemed to be interference from the planet's magnetic Energy making it difficult to communicate.

Nico: "Jasmine? Jazz you there?"

Jasmine: "I'm... hav– ...difficulty...you. Find...oth– finish this!"

Nico barely understood Jasmine, but after hearing "finish this", the message was clear. That led to the Guardian finding a new sense of duty that fueled his inner flame. Checking his regenerated wounds, he looked around at the strange new world, its luscious forests and its strange mythical creatures with a sense of astonishment. However, the urgency of his task outweighed any desire to sightsee. With this in mind, the Elder amplified his leg's muscle-fibers, allowing him to leap through the tree line to which he spotted a suspicious stream of smoke. He gained a sense of direction and utilized that advantage to motion towards the smoke, swinging and somersaulting through the forest. Occasionally, Nico would leap above the tree line which gave him a great view to keep a lookout for Orion, Rose or Cass. With a final swing and soft landing, Nico quietly approached the smoking area with his Jūken blade formed. Instead, the Elder was relieved to see Elder Raito who was busy using his super speed and technical skills to repair what was left of the Hercules; his amazing speed and precision unmatched. Nico looked in wonderment given Raito's progress. After the crash, the Hercules was completely obliterated and yet, the Prana-user managed to rebuild the ship's structural integrity and bring power back to the defaced vessel. Elder Raito suddenly came to a stop after feeling the presence of another, but found it to be his Taiyōnian comrade.

Raito: "Nico. Good to see you're up and moving. Not to say you couldn't recover regardless."

Nico: "Good to see you too my friend. I guess I was flung from the ship? I swear, my Solar Mutation techniques have saved me more times than I'd like to admit."

Raito: "They've saved us as well."

Nico: "I give all the credit to the Creator, Lotus and the Three Suns of Taiyō. But that aside, any ideas on where to find Vinzent?"

Raito: "I thought he was with you. After we crashed, my shield broke and I was knocked out by the aftershock of holding those shields through the crash. When I woke up, I saw these three strange six armed beings gathering pieces of the ship. They disappeared before I could free myself. Thieving animals."

Nico: "Maybe they were curious. We are, after all, aliens trespassing on their world."

Raito: "I guess you have a point. Still doesn't make it right to take what doesn't belong to you."

Nico: "On that, you are right my brotha. Despite the damage, you've made some amazing progress in this short amount of time Raito."

Raito: *sigh* "I don't know if I'd call it progress…"

They both looked in the direction of their destroyed spacecraft.

Raito: "We don't have flight capabilities whatsoever, the weapon systems have gone to shit, and the outer-hull has completely lost its integrity. The only thing I managed to do was bring power to the ship's core, rebuild the foundation and activate the windshield wipers."

Nico: "In other words, it can't be fixed."

Raito: "It can be fixed, but we'd need to be at some kind of spacecraft repair shop or something of that nature. And I highly doubt this planet has such a place."

The Guardians found acceptance given their situation, but that calmness was quickly dissolved after sensing a new presence approaching at high speed. With the unknown land surrounding them and Orion on the same planet, Raito impulsively conjured a Light-bow, and Nico instinctively formed his Jūken blade, readying themselves for a fight. But their tense attitudes were suddenly washed away as Vinzent glided through the sky on a manifested board of red lightning. With a sigh of relief, Nico and Raito relaxed and lowered their guard.

Nico: "Glad to see you in one piece. How did you find us?"

Vinzent: "And you as well brotha, but I followed the thick stream of smoke."

Raito: "You think the enemy would search this area as well?"

Vinzent: "I don't think so. They would've by now if they were going to."

Nico: "Plus you both saw and felt the hunger for power coming from Orion. His senses are strictly focused on his goal. That, we have in common."

Raito: "You guys are right. I've done all I can for the Hercules given the lack of equipment. Nothing more to do now besides save the galaxy from Orion. Any ideas on where to look first?"

Nico: "I think I have an idea…If Casanova is with Orion and on this planet, I'll be able to feel her Source Energy, and she'll lead us straight to him."

Raito: "How? That doesn't seem like something your Solar Mutation ability can do."

Nico: "Cass and I share a rather… intimate bond which makes it possible."

Raito: "Enough said."

Both Raito and Vinzent agreed to Nico's plan as the Elder sat on the ground before closing his eyes, repeating his mantra, and deepening his focus. In a gradual flow of Solar Energy, Nico's consciousness zoomed throughout the entire planet as he searched for Cass's Source Energy signature. The Elder's consciousness ran through trees, animals, and plants before finding the spirit of an entity, blue in coloration, along with a dense and heavy blackish-red spirit, and a reddish-black spirit. Afterwards, Nico's consciousness zipped back to his body as the Elder let out a deep breath.

Nico: "I found her. She's accompanied by two others, one I recognize as Orion's Black Aura and another I don't recognize. Maybe it's Rachel?"

Vinzent: "Where?"

Nico: "A hundred and forty-four miles Northwest."

With the general direction declared, Raito ceased the opportunity and ran off in a burst of super speed towards the location, leaving Nico and Vinzent to catch-up. Following this, Vinzent generated his

Red Aura before manifesting a longer red lightning board, fit for two passengers. The two Elders then hopped on, allowing Vinzent to zip off towards Cass's location at slower speeds then that of Elder Raito, who was the fastest Guardian to breathe air.

Vinzent: "Can you feel it Nico? The Source Energy of this planet is strong with the power of the Creator."

Nico: "Yes I do. My wounds regenerate faster, and I feel stronger and more connected to the Creator than ever before. You know what also comes with that don't you?"

Vinzent: "Yes. Orion will feel the same boost of power, for the Creator does not discriminate, but only works to keep the balance between good and evil, Light and Darkness, Ashla and Bogan."

Nico: "Everything that's happened, all the people and Guardians lost, has led the three of us to this very moment. Let's not let the lives lost be in vain."

Vinzent and Nico followed the trail leading to Cass, with Raito fastly approaching the spot as the galaxy's last hope raced to stop Orion, and bring balance back to the scarred remains of the known galaxy.

Meanwhile in a field filled with beautiful flowers and clean air, Rose floated criss-cross as she meditated to find the God's Heart fruit. Rose's eyes began to glow, and her hair stood tall then suddenly, a mysterious voice was heard only by Rose.

Unknown voice: *softly* "Choose wisely my dear…"

With this brief and strange message, the glow in Rose's eyes quickly dimmed as she simultaneously unfolded her legs. The Asronian then flew away at incredible speeds with her instincts pointing her in a direction she felt was right. Following the Asronian's sudden enthusiastic nature, Orion formed a box around Cass that lifted her up because Casanova's speed did not and could not compare to the two power houses she followed. With Cass inside Orion's magical box, the self-proclaimed god was able to pick up the pace, as he, after an increase in speed, was able to catch and follow close behind Rose. The speed at which Rose and Orion flew shoved Casanova back against the inner-rear wall of the small box. She then was suddenly thrown against the floor of the box as if Orion slammed on the breaks. Cass got up and rubbed her head as she complained about the lack of light. But before the Guardian could speak further, the walls of the box split open, setting Cass free. The Elder was about to show a sense of gratitude, but was stopped as amazement filled her eyes. For the first time since being consumed by her inner-Darkness, Rose spoke.

Rose: "We are here… The *Tree of Power*."

The Guardian was left speechless as she was towered by what she thought was the biggest tree in the known Universe. Standing at five hundred and thirty-three feet, and over seventy-five feet in diameter, this mighty piece of life brought amazement to even Orion. But the moment of humbleness was quickly masked by greed as Orion's hunger for power consumed him once more. The false god was so close to his prize that his excitement ran rampant, alerting the tree's guard. Two places on the tree opened, allowing two twenty foot, four armed guards, with coarse-like skin and tattoos to emerge. They both held a large two-handed sword, leaving the other two hands free. As they walked from the tree, one of the titans suddenly spoke.

Goliath #1: *deep tone* "We are the *Goliath*, caretakers of the Tree of Power and protectors of God's Heart. Why have you come?"

Orion saw his chance to gain favor from what he thought were his new chosen guards. Upon this thought he flew up to the speaking Goliath's face before conversing with the titan.

Orion: "Goliath! As the guards of the Tree of Power, you carry wisdom and knowledge. You know exactly who I am and what I've come to claim."

The first Goliath paused for a moment before speaking once more.

Goliath #1: "We know who you are, Theo Ronan, son of Titus and Athena Ronan. And we know what you seek…However, there is much blood and life lost due to your efforts, and your heart is unbalanced. As a result you are unworthy, thus forbidden from God's Heart, and are banished from this star system. Leave this planet or risk judgment by the will of the Creator."

After the first Goliath finished its warning, the two massive titans retreated back into the Tree of Power, but just before they're fully submerged within the tree's trunk, Orion's anger reached a new high as he blasted the closest one with a powerful blast from his Black Aura. The blast stunned the giant which caused it to crash to one knee.

Orion: *furious tone* "I am Orion, God of Darkness! You, nor anyone else will deny me my right as the ONE…TRUE…CREATOR!!!"

With this, Orion unleashed his Black Aura and attacked the two Goliaths for their disrespect. But Rose, his sister, stood there and simply watched Orion fight the first Goliath. However, Rose was forced to defend herself against the sword of the second Goliath as the giant swung his sword against The Eye. The shockwave from the attack was so great, the force generated threw Cass to the side as she tumbled away. This was a needed reality check for Casanova as she knew this fight, and these beings, were out of her league entirely. Following the second Goliath's sword swing, the Asronian princess instinctively blocked with an Cosmic Energy shield, then counterattacked by forming an identical Goliath, red in coloration, that attacked the second Goliath. Over by Rose, Orion's lust for power blinded him from the present moment, to which the first Goliath caught the Asronian prince with its sword, which sent Orion crashing hard onto the ground below. In a flood of rage, Orion shot up towards the sky, leaving behind a shockwave as he took off. The dark lord blasted the first Goliath in the face with more of his Black Aura, stunning it once more. He then grabbed the titan by the horn and flew upward, taking the titan with him. Soon after, Orion broke off the Goliath's horn, causing the giant to plummet down towards the ground as it grunted in extreme discomfort. Following a loud and thundering crash from the first Goliath, Orion threw the broken horn at his target before tacking on more of his Black Aura behind it, which increased its velocity. A few moments later, the sharp object pierced the first Goliath, threw the chest and heart, allowing a fountain of glowing yellow blood to pour from its wound. Orion flew down and landed on the dying Goliath's chest as a sign of contempt towards the Creator.

Orion: "The mighty protectors of the land died by my hands, and when I consume your precious fruit, your Creator is next."

And with Orion's disdain, the first Goliath's glowing eyes faded to blackness as the titan lay dead by Orion's might. Afterwards, Orion looked to check on The Eye, but upon looking, he simply chuckled as Rose's red Goliath stood with one foot on the second Goliath's decapitated head.

Orion: "Soon I will possess power even greater than our father. Come, let us finish this at once."

Rose and Cass followed Orion into the Tree of Power. They journeyed through the giant opening which led into the tree's inner-trunk, but nothing happened. No lights flashing, no doorways opening, and they could no longer feel the power pulsating from the God's Heart. But that's when Orion was given the idea to allow Rose to take the lead, given that the planet reacted to her presence earlier, and Orion couldn't have been more correct. Rose stepped forward past Orion, and the tree opened up to her as if she owned the towering piece of life itself. The inner walls of the tree shifted and changed as doorways were made, which made a straight line leading to two wooden doors with the saying:

"The fruit of the Spirit wasn't intended to be a list of goals for us to produce, but it is the Holy Spirit through us who produces fruit." As Rose read the saying, and dripped a drop of her pure Asronian blood on the wooden doors, they opened, showing an altar with the God's Heart fruit in all its power and glory. The two approached the fruit as Cass stood near the chamber's entryway. Upon further inspection, Orion was surprised to realize the fruit really was a fruit, a red apple even. However, this was no ordinary apple. The core elements of fire, earth, water, air, and ether, all circulated the apple in complete and unified harmony. It pulsated with fluidity and dominance, and with every palpitation, a wave of Source Energy was felt. Even as they drew near, they felt pressure on their chest and the overwhelming sense of absoluteness. Orion, Rose and Cass all felt the power the apple possessed, and unsurprisingly, Orion did nothing but savor the moment and give praise.

Orion: "My time has come at last! It is more than I could've ever hoped for. You have done your master a great service Rose, and when I become your Creator, I will bless you as my right hand, and we will rule over all! Now...take the fruit from the tree, and let us ascend."

Orion was power hungry and ruthless, but he was no fool. Despite all of his power, even he knew what sat before him was pure untamed Source Energy. This fact humbled him, so he commanded Rose to pick up the Apple and hand it to him. Following Orion's command, Rose hesitated before she grabbed the apple from the rough and deeply grooved altar. The apple was heavy, and forced Rose to carry it with two hands. The pulsating red fruit palpitated gracefully, and with strength. She looked into the Apple and saw her reflection, along with the corruption that had consumed her. She wondered for a minute if what she was doing was the right thing, handing her brother the God's Heart Apple. That moment of self-doubt however, was quickly dismantled because of the manipulation put in her subconscious mind by Orion's Black Aura. Rose, Orion's puppet, came back to reality and motioned to give Orion the apple, but unexpectedly, the apple flashed with a sudden burst of pure Source Energy. The shockwave shoved Cass against a wall, knocking her unconscious, and forced Orion to protect himself with a shield of Black Aura. The Asronian princess screamed as the Apple's Energy lifted her body from the ground, and tossed her eyes as they rolled to the back of her head. Following the overwhelming power of the God's Heart Apple from just holding it, Rose released the apple as it levitated a foot off the ground. She then dropped and fell down to the ground unconscious. Orion's demeanor suddenly changed as disappointment, followed by disbelief and opportunity, filled the very bones of his body.

Orion: "Was the apple too much for even a pure Asronian? Have I been betrayed? Nonsense. I trust no one to be betrayed in the first place. This is just a test of my resolve. Rose was too weak, but my will is absolute."

With Orion in great distress, he worked to wake The Eye from her unconscious state, but his efforts were in vain as the angered false god yelled in fury. Following this, Rose, now in the form of her old self, found herself within her subconscious mind as an unfamiliar soul, with glossy red skin and dressed in all white, walked up to her and began to speak with a familiar tone...

Mysterious soul: "Oh how much you've grown, and how beautiful you are!"

Rachel: "W-What...Where am I? Who are you?"

Mysterious soul: "My name is Athena Ronan, and you my dear, are in your subconscious mind. Might I ask your name?"

Rachel: "R-Rachel. Rachel Rose."

Athena's soul: "Ah! What a beautiful name. Titus would love it..."

Rachel: "Who?"

Athena's soul: "Nevermind that dear. I've been keeping an eye on you for quite some time now. The blood of the Asronian race flows strong within you. And it seems fate has led you to the one known as Orion, and now the God's Heart Apple lies before you, but yet, I've sensed great distress within you. What's wrong my dear? Are you not happy with your choices thus far?"

Rachel: *sigh* "My choices haven't been my own. I feel as if I've...been the passenger of my own life. This power I was given, it's taken on a life of its own and was called Rose by Orion who claims to be my brother. If this is my power, why does it feel like it's someone else's?"

Athena's soul: "Did he now? Interesting. Nonetheless, being Asronian royalty isn't always the best for those who wish to live a normal life. With that horn and the blood that flows through you, you'll always have a target on your back."

Rachel: "Royalty? What do you mean?"

Athena's soul: "You come from a long history of Asronian Emperors and Empresses. Unfortunately they haven't always used their power for good, but through you my dear, that can change. Right now you have the choice to follow the path of your destructive ancestors, or create a path of renewed glory for us all."

Rachel: "How can I create a new path when I can't even take hold of my own power...my own life...? You all put so much faith in me, but I'm nothing but a mass murderer who killed their friends..."

Athena grabbed hold of her daughter, embracing her with a Loving and forgiving hug.

Athena's soul: "Do not fear my dear, for you ARE loved, and more powerful than you realize. There are times in one's life when they fail to make the right choice, but during that moment of failure, a different choice is presented. The choice to lay down and give up, or the choice to stand tall and grow from one's failure. The comrades that fight by your side are strong and resilient, and even now they refuse to give up. The Creator is with you my dear. Stand, and reclaim your life."

Rachel's face expressed a sense of relief, but also a surprising sense of calmness as she somehow knew her Elder comrades survived the destruction of Journia. The Elder felt an overdue sense of peace, Love and Light wash over her as, for the first time, Rachel Rose smiled allowing tears to roll down her face.

Rachel: "Thank you Athena. Your Love has brought me back to the Light, and I have found redemption with the One Infinite Creator. How can I repay you?"

Athena's soul: "You need not worry about such things. You have already blessed me with your presence, and have made me the happiest mother in all of existence. I only ask that you forgive your father, and survive, for yourself, and for all Asronians before and after you. And save your brother from himself. He has fallen from what is good, and it's time for him to join his ancestors in the afterlife. I give you this spell, *Soul Tether*. Use it to send your brother's soul to the afterlife."

Rachel: "I will survive, and I will save my brother. You have my word… Wait …MOTHER?!"

And with that, the soul of Athena faded back into Rachel's subconscious mind. Out in reality, the Guardian's eyes opened wide, not as Rose, but as the third-class Elder Guardian, Rachel Rose. Orion saw his sister had awoken, but something was different. He could no longer sense the hold on Rachel he once held, and this angered him greatly. Disgusted and disappointed, Orion swiftly grabbed Rachel by the throat and drained the renewed Guardian of all the power gained from touching the God's Heart Apple. Rachel screamed in agony as she felt her lifeforce being drained as if someone were ripping flesh from her bones. Cass regained consciousness after being knocked into the wall, and saw that Rachel was back and close to death from Orion's Dorein ability. Rachel's screams were unbearable as they continuously grew louder and louder, but before Orion could drain her completely, Casanova found her resolve and purpose once again as an Elder Guardian of the Way of Ashla. She subconsciously knew Orion could not obtain such power. So she used her Elemental Energy of water to increase her blood flow, which in turn, increased her body's strength and agility beyond her normal limitations. This ability was called: ***Shark's Might***. Following the utilization of Shark's Might, the Guardian drew her katana with every intent to attack Orion as she powered her weapon, and dashed towards Orion and Rachel with magnificent speed and courage. She formed a shark with her katana, with the ability being called: ***Shark's Bite***. Orion, however, was so blinded by his hunger for power, and his rage towards Rachel's betrayal, he failed to see or sense the bloodlust coming from Casanova's attack. As a result, Cass's attack made a clean and direct hit against the false god, cutting deep into both arms of Orion that held Rachel. Cass then followed up with a clean slash to Orion's torso, which forced the false god to stumble backwards as black blood spilled. The Guardian saw her chance to kill Orion as she swung her katana towards his neck, but Cass was a fool to believe he would fall so easily. Before her sword could connect, Orion flared his sinister Black Aura which caused Cass a split second of unbalance, during which, the false god swung his leg hard and fast against Casanova. Due to Cass's ability, Shark's Might, the Elder was able to pull free her second sword, "Sword of the Fearless", that she received from the people of Zora. She used both weapons and her increased strength to block Orion's ferocious attack, but the force still proved too great as the strike threw her hard against another wall, while simultaneously shattering her sword from the Zoranians, and cracking her own katana. The Elder Guardian Casanova was slow to her feet as she held her side and coughed up blood. Orion dashed for Cass and grabbed her by the face with his bleeding arm. This enabled him to strike her six times in the stomach as more blood spilled from Cass's mouth with every strike. He dropped her as she folded in absolute pain. Unfinished, Orion picked up Cass's cracked katana before kicking her side, causing the Elder to flip on her back. And with devilish intent, Orion thrusted Cass's katana through her chest before completely breaking it off, leaving it like a stick in the mud. Rachel, drained and extremely weakened, grunted in pain as Cass laid bleeding out with her own weapon broken off in her chest.

Orion: *grunts* "I never trusted you Guardian, but I will acknowledge you for landing a blow on me. So as a reward, I will keep you alive long enough so you may witness my ascension. Don't die on me Guardian. However you Rose. *sigh* I expected more from you sister. Though, it proves you are unfit for the power you possess, and that I must and will walk this path alone."

Orion approached Rachel and picked her up by her hair as she struggled to gain freedom. The false god punched Rachel several times, and continued to drain Rachel of any and all of her blood and Source Energy, thus furthering his ascension into lone Godliness. The Guardian struggled and struggled, but after a while, Rachel's body went limp and her skin shriveled up, losing its precious red complexion. Orion saw the loss of strength within Rachel, so he simply tossed her aside like a dirty sock. He then motioned towards and grabbed the God's Heart Apple with it being noticeably heavy for even himself. The power flowed through him and sent waves of Source Energy, but unlike Elder Rachel, Orion was strong enough to handle the initial shock of the divine fruit. As the false god held and admired the Apple, Rachel was simultaneously thrown to the side, but before she hit the ground, the Elder ranked Guardian Raito appeared like lightning and caught the falling Asronian. Soon after, the Elder ranked Guardian Nico appeared, calling out to Orion with the Elder ranked Guardian Vinzent at his back. They all knew what had to be done, and were fully prepared to lay down their lives to achieve it.

Nico: "Orion!! Your time has come once again. And this time, the full might of Ashla and Bogan stands against you. You will not be shown mercy."

Orion: "You? Show me mercy? *laughs* Oh? I see you bear the Asronian Mark of Honor on your necks. My father is the only one who possesses the means to produce such a mark, which means he lives... *chuckle* No matter, the God's Heart Apple is in my possession, and I've already tasted some of its power as I hold it even now. You Guardians have no idea what true power is, nor does she. She was too weak for the Apple, and for the life she was given."

Orion pointed towards Rachel as she lay barely conscious in Raito's arms.

Raito: "Rachel!…"

Rachel: "R-Raito… you came…"

Rachel fainted from exhaustion because of her loss of vital Source Energy from Orion's draining Cosmic Energy ability; Dorein.

Orion: *chuckles* "Though she struck me, it seems the Elder called Casanova didn't fare well against my power. She lays there clinging to life…pathetic. Because I am merciful, I will allow you to tend to her, though she is beyond saving."

Following Orion's words, both Nico and Vinzent looked over to see a pool of blood, and a wounded Guardian with a sword protruding from her chest. Realizing the wounded Guardian was Cass, Nico immediately ran over pulling the katana free from her chest while Vinzent administered his Green healing Aura to her wounds. Nico's worst fear came to fruition as his lover lay dying in his arms. And all he could do was spend the last moments she had laying with her, comforting her.

Nico: "CASS!"

Cass: *coughs* "M-My love…what a terrible way…to see me."

Nico: "You look as beautiful as ever."

Cass: *painful chuckle* "I'm…sorry Nico…I never…meant to betray… you … the faction… or The Order. I-I was just… scared… of what… Orion would do…"

Nico: "It's okay now. I am here and will handle the rest. Go, join the Creator and find peace in the afterlife..."

Cass smiled brightly for the last time as her joyous demeanor faded ever so gently. Nico felt her soul leave her body and join the Creator in the afterlife. And in that moment Nico understood what he had to do. He did not feel sorrow, he did not feel grief, but aggressive clarity as he allowed the wound of Bogan within him to not consume, but to bring balance, allowing a controlled rage to fuel his resolve. Nico kissed Cass on her forehead for the last time before he got up with her in his arms, and laid her corpse next to Rachel. Nico stood to his feet, and looked at Vinzent, then towards Raito as they stood against the embodiment of evil and Darkness. Orion smiled boorishly at his opponents with complete confidence in his ability; in his power. The false god sensed the teachings of Ashla and of Bogan flowing within each Guardian. However it mattered none, for his will was unshakable, his power unmeasurable, his revenge undeniable. He was Orion, God of Darkness, and the galaxy was his for the taking...

FIFTEEN

RISE

Hope and despair, trust and disloyalty, Love and hate. These emotions; these paths to and from the soul go hand in hand, existing only because of its counterpart. They cannot exist without the other, just as Ashla cannot exist without Bogan, and Bogan without Ashla. It is a battle all entities must face, and was a battle won by Nico, Vinzent and Raito, first-class Elder Guardians from the Ashura Order. Every action taken, every word spoken, every life stolen, had led the Guardians to that very moment. They stood against Orion, false god of Darkness with courage and valor. They did not buckle in the face of great power; they did not show fear or concern for their own safety. But rather a sense of honor and duty for in that present moment, nothing else mattered.

The air within the Tree of Power was heavy and filled with tension, like two entities experiencing the spirit of awkwardness. Orion, self-proclaimed god of Darkness, stood against Elders Vinzent, Raito and Nico with the God's Heart Apple in his hand, and blood running down his arms and torso from Cass's assault. The fight for the galaxy began after Orion made the first move and swiftly blasted the Guardians with a wide dose of gravity from his Black Aura. Nico and Vinzent were struck and sent flying violently out of the magical tree. Raito saw the black field of energy hurtling towards him which pushed the Elder to use his super speed. He then dodged the attack before bravely running up to

Orion to forcibly snatch the God's Heart Apple from the Asronian. This enraged the false god, causing him to flare his dense Black Aura which produced a sizable shockwave. Elder Raito, Elder Rachel, and Elder Cass's body were all ejected from the Tree of Power, but before they hit the ground, Raito casted a spell called: *Gummy Hand*, which he used to catch Rachel and Cass with before landing on his feet, joining Nico and Vinzent outside. The Prana-user placed Rachel and Cass in cover, and granted them protection with a Prana shield over them before zipping off to hide the Apple. Soon after, Raito joined Nico and Vinzent as they prepared for their final confrontation with Orion.

Raito: "I've placed Rachel and Cass away from the battlefield. They should be safe for now. I also took the liberty of hiding the Apple, though I don't know how long we have till he senses its potent Source Energy."

Vinzent: "It'll have to do for now, but at least we can go all out. That frees us up to finish this once and for all."

Nico: "Good, let's hunt."

Orion: "I see now why you three have survived to this very moment… You three are my final test. A test I intend to pass."

With these words, Orion dashed for Raito and struck him into a tree with a palm from his Black Aura. The Guardian tumbled away, forcing Vinzent and Nico to go on the offensive. Nico amplified and mutated, firing several explosive arrows towards Orion from his Yumi bow. Orion flawlessly evaded all of the arrows sent as they zoomed past him, exploding in violent blasts of Solar Energy. The last arrow followed shortly after, but was caught and sent back towards Nico with even greater velocity. Nico blocked the counterattack, but was sent crashing into a nearby bolder from the arrow's explosive properties. Following the counter, Orion was put on the defensive, gracefully dodging several bolts of lightning from Vinzent. The Elder continued his attack and created several lightning clones, of Red and Blue Aura, that attacked Orion, but were easily defeated by the false god's combat prowess.

Orion: *laughter* "Is that all you're capable of Guardians? Maybe you aren't worthy of being my honored guards afterall."

Orion laughed in the face of Nico and Vinzent's weak attacks, but his disrespect was premature. Those clones of lightning from Vinzent were merely a distraction, a way to redirect Orion's attention away from the sky, which gave the Elder the appropriate time to make his next move.

Vinzent: "Your underestimation of us is welcoming, but you are too easily distracted Orion. Those clones were a warm-up. Elemental Energy: *Raging Dragon!*"

Vinzent's plan was a success as the false god looked up with childish amusement. The sky above Orion darkened as a huge lightning dragon, made from Violet, Blue and Red Aura, burst through the stormy clouds and roared viciously as it descended upon Orion. The false god had little to no time to defend himself as the dragon of Vinzent's power mercilessly crashed head first onto Orion, striking the false god with a quick and enormous bolt of lightning. Following Vinzent's attack, the Elder checked to see if his efforts silenced the false god. The dust settled and Orion was seen standing within the two mile crater with strength and pride. Steam rolled from his body like fresh hot coffee. His black robe was now torn and scorched from the heat of Vinzent's Elemental Energy. With his robe burned, Orion ripped the ruinous fabric from his upper body, showing a muscular physique masking his dark red skin.

Vinzent: "There's no holding back with you Orion. So for the sake of the galaxy, I will give my all!"

Orion: "Yes! Show me the fruits of your Bogan teachings Guardian, and I will repay you with death for ruining my robe."

The two beings of power clashed in a show of tremendous power from both sides. The two traded blows, sending both Energy blasts and fists. However, despite Vinzent's use of Bogan teachings, to Orion, he was nothing more than a novice fighting against a master. It wasn't long until the Elder was forced to manifest a shield of red lightning to block a continuous wave of gravity that grew in power and size.

Orion: "Do you really think you can win!? My power has no bound! Even without the God's Heart Apple, I am invincible!!" *maniacal laughter*

Vinzent struggled under the weight of Orion's mastery of the Way of Bogan, and after a moment of constant struggle, the Guardian's shield shattered, leading to Vinzent taking the full force of Orion's power. The Elder was sent crashing into a mountain, creating a large shockwave as the rocky structure crumbled on top of the Guardian. The false god flew over and pulled Vinzent's unconscious body free from the rocks, while possessing a sphere of densely formed gravity. Orion pointed his hand towards Vinzent, but before he could take the life of the Guardian, Nico rushed in and went to kick Orion away, but missed due to Orion's quick reflexes.

Orion: "Back so soon, Senshi Warrior?"

Nico: "I would ask how you know of the Senshi Warriors, but you are an Asronian…"

Orion: "You think I don't remember the Senshi Warriors of Taiyō. That was what the proud Taiyōnians who fully mastered their Solar Mutation, called themselves right? Come. Show me just how powerful a Senshi Warrior is with Bogan fueled Solar Energy."

Feeling the Solar Energy from Exodus's white Sun, Elder Nico charged towards Orion with his Ken fists formed and fuming with power. Orion could tell the Way of Bogan had indeed strengthened the Taiyōnian, but worried not for he was Orion. The two clashed as Orion's

Black Aura met the heated force of pure Solar Energy. Because of the injuries sustained from the Goliath, Elder Cass and Elder Vinzent, Elder Nico, through the teachings and strength provided by Bogan, was able to push Orion into a corner. With a well timed Ken strike to the abdomen, Orion tumbled against the ground for several meters before coming to his feet. However, he wasn't quick enough because when he looked up, Orion saw a sphere of Solar Energy hurtling towards him. Mistaking it for the Sun, Orion quickly realized this sphere of heat resembled Nico's Bakudan bomb ability. The explosive approached Orion as he stopped the burning Solar-bomb with his bleeding arms. It scorched Orion's flesh and caught his robe on fire, forcing the Asronian into a situation he hasn't dealt with since his life as Theo. Suddenly, the false god felt the weight of the Bakudan bomb he previously stopped greatly increase, as if another sphere of Solar Energy was placed on top of the first one. The weight was too much for the injured false god, and after struggling for a second, the weight crushed Orion before exploding in a loud and colossal KA-BOOOOM! The shockwave from the blast shook the nearby area, tossing trees and flattening the surrounding area. When the dust settled a crater, a mile wide and a mile deep was born. Nico, who protected himself with the Mamoru shield, leaped down into the crater to see if his Bakudan bombs finished the job, but the Elder did not see Orion's body which put the empowered Taiyōnian on the defensive. Nico searched and searched, until he felt the ground beneath his feet rumble. Suddenly, Orion burst from the ground beneath Nico with power and vengeance. The false god upper cutted the Elder, then blasted him with his Black Aura. The Guardian recovered which enabled him to mutate and utilize his Jūken blade. Seeing his enemy close in rapidly, Orion countered the incoming Guardian with two more blasts of dense gravity, but his attacks were annoyingly deflected by a shield of muscle-fibers. Orion was then forced to defend against a barrage of blade swings. The false god, for the first time, was at a disadvantage due to his accumulating injuries, and could not escape the weaknesses of flesh and blood. But that's when it clicked…he would need to consume the rest of the God's Heart Apple in order to fully become a God, but how could he escape the Elders long enough to find the Apple? Orion pondered this question while defending against Elder Nico. Following

Orion's brainstorming, Nico caught and slashed once more into Orion's body; black blood covered the Guardian's elongated blade as he stood before the false god. Once feared throughout the galaxy, Orion now stood a bloodied mess. The false god spat on the ground before the Taiyōnian as black blood ran down Orion's body. He questioned Nico, hoping to stall and recover some used Source Energy.

Orion: "My, my. *coughs* Such power, such rage. Feels good doesn't it? *grunts* *painful chuckle* Feels good to have the power to decide who lives and who dies huh?"

Nico: "You take, enslave and murder without ANY disregard for those who it may affect. You've brought about the second Galactic War, killed trillions and for what? Power? Control?"

Orion: "To reveal the hypocrisy within the teachings of Ashla. Have you ever wondered why things are the way they are? Why despite the 'Love' and the 'Light' of your Creator, suffering and death are still constant? Whether you kill me or not, suffering is inevitable. There will ALWAYS be someone like me to take my place, and do you know why? Because Darkness lives within us all. You cannot escape from the hatred you feel which is why you possess the power you do now. The hate fuels you… empowers you."

Nico: "You're right. I can't escape from the Darkness or the hatred that plagues my heart, but I can embrace it, accept it, Love it and use it to rid the galaxy of entities like you. No matter how powerful or how many of you there are. The Love and the Light of the One Infinite Creator will ALWAYS prevail."

Orion: "You Guardians are all the same, betting everything on the Creator. How can you, a Taiyōnian, who's lost his native home embrace the Way of Bogan yet practice Ashla teachings? How has the hand of Darkness not offered itself to you? Are you not angry over the destruction of Taiyō, of your blood family?"

Nico: "I still deal with my demons. I still question the Creator everyday, and wonder why after hundreds of years of suffering from Taiyō's Suns, did he still feel the need to use your people to destroy Taiyō anyways. It took me a long time to accept my reality and face my demons, not as an evil that needed to be destroyed, but as a part of myself. I embrace the Darkness, yet follow the Light because that's where truth, Love, and self worth lies. And where forgiveness has a chance to show you a greater, more powerful version of yourself."

Orion: "You are naïve Guardian. My people destroyed your homeworld yet you forgive. I, Orion, erased the Ashura Order yet you forgive. I destroyed Journia yet you forgive. I killed your beloved, yet you forgive. Do those losses mean nothing to you? Are you to do nothing to avenge your loved ones?"

Nico: "Yes you and your people have taken a lot from me and my comrades, but that doesn't mean we can't work together to end this cycle of hatred. I know The Order took everything from you, but there's still hope in the Love and Light from the Creator."

Nico witnessed the confliction upon Orion's face, and saw an opportunity to make peace with the false god. The Elder foolishly lowered his guard, deforming his Jūken blade before offering his hand to Orion. The false god paused and pondered Nico's words and actions, for he too wished to end the cycle of hatred. However, Orion's methods of achieving peace were different. He could not bring himself to follow blindly behind the Light, behind the lie of Love, behind the Creator. Nor did he feel obligated to share the throne with anyone besides himself. Seeing his chance, Orion, with speed and precision, ran his Black Aura covered arm through Nico's chest. Following this, Nico quickly amplified his arm, mutated and swung his Jūken blade to create space between them.

Orion: "I'll acknowledge your power and resolve Taiyōnian, and you're correct. This cycle of hatred must and will end, however not in the way you think. With a strong Light comes an ever stronger Darkness! And the Way of Ashla is nothing more than a weakness I will exploit!"

Nico: *grunts* "You fool!"

After Elder Nico failed to persuade Orion, Nico unsteadily swung his Jūken blade in order to decapitate the head of Orion, but before the Guardian was able to save the galaxy, Orion did what he said and exploited the Light and Darkness within Nico's heart. The false god looked into the Elder's heart and flooded the Guardian's mind with memories of his blood family and the destruction of Taiyō, emotionally stunting Nico for a brief moment, but it was more than enough time for Orion. The false god exploited Nico's moment of emotional instability, and attacked the Elder directly in the face with a full blast of concentrated gravity. The blast was so powerful that it, at that range, disintegrated the top half of the Elder's body, and carved a giant hole through a mountain. Nothing was spared besides Nico's waist and legs. Seeing the troublesome Guardian vulnerable, why wouldn't Orion take it upon himself to finish the job? With that realization, Orion used his Black Aura to form a dense field of gravity which flattened Nico's remains in a splash of blood, like pressing an iron against wrinkled clothes. During which, the false god thought to himself, "not even the most seasoned Senshi Warrior could heal from such an injury." Said the false god spitefully. Orion knew however, he needed the God's Heart Apple because of the amount of damage taken from fighting the Goliath, Casanova and now three Bogan wielding Elders. So after annihilating Nico's body, thrusting him deep into the Realm of Apollo, leaving only Nico's legs and a large puddle of his blood under Exodus's white Sun, Orion took to the sky as he struggled to find the God's Heart Apple. His search was unsurprisingly interrupted by a blast of Prana Energy, which he blocked with his Black Aura. Afterwards, Orion blasted several more waves of gravity, but inevitably missed due to Raito's super speed. The false god continued to search for the majestic Apple, however he could not focus as he was, yet again, threatened by Raito's power. Seeing a fight against the Prana-user was inevitable, Orion flew down towards Raito to face him.

Orion: "Ah yes. The spell caster. It would seem your use of Bogan taught Prana Energy will be another test of my resolve. One I will surely pass…"

Raito: "I do not intend to fall so easily Orion."

Orion: *chuckle* "Good. Wouldn't be a challenge if so. Now, show me your strength Guardian!"

Raito: "With pleasure. Prana Energy: *One Thousand Stars!*"

Five hundred tiny spheres of Ashla fueled Prana Energy, and five hundred tiny spheres of Bogan fueled Prana Energy, six inches across, appeared then began circulating around Raito. The Elder motioned his hand forward as the spheres of Light and Dark shot off towards Orion like shooting stars, hence the name. A few spheres made contact with Orion's dark red flesh, burning and bruising his skin on impact. Instead of succumbing to the Source Energy of Elder Raito's Prana style magic, the false god focused his mind and zeroed in on the swift movements and pattern of Raito's spell.

Orion: *internal thought* "Focus. Read the movement. See the pattern…This is no more than child's play. I will show this fool the fluidity of a God."

The false god elegantly evaded Raito's spheres of empowered Prana Energy, twisting, bending and ducking in ways that captivated Raito. However, this was no time to admire the movement, for this was in fact Orion. Raito witnessed the majority of his attacks fail to reach their target, so he took it upon himself. The Elder bolted towards Orion with super speed that even the false god couldn't follow. Raito appeared in front of Orion, and made a ruthless punch to the cheek then to the liver, which sent Orion flying upward. The series of attacks prevented Orion from attacking as Raito finished his assault with a powerful arrow of Prana Energy. The attack again put Orion on the defensive as he blocked the strike with an Black Aura fueled shield, but was pushed further into the sky. Following Raito's arrow, Orion felt the threat of another pending attack, but his reaction was a split second too late as Elder Vinzent appeared, and struck Orion to the ground with a hefty bolt of Violet lightning. The false god aggressively crashed into the ground as steam and lightning rolled and crackled from his body. He was slow to get up, and felt the warm blood of his vessel run down his body as if he were in a warm shower. Suffering injuries from the Goliath, Elder Casanova, and now Elders Vinzent, Nico, and Raito, left Orion bloodied and bruised, but not defeated; his will would not allow it. Breathing heavily, the Asronian searched tirelessly for an immediate answer to victory, and that's when he suddenly felt it... The sensation and pure Source Energy of the God's Heart Apple, as if the fruit awakened. Orion knew if he felt it, then the Guardians before him felt the Source Energy as well, though it mattered none. Elders Vinzent and Raito stood before their great enemy with a Light bow and arrow, and a hand crackling with lightning empowered by Violet Aura, aimed towards Orion; their intent clear as a calm sea.

Vinzent: "You've lost Orion. Surrender and keep your life."

Though in a weakened state, Orion was still as powerful as his father before him, and he demonstrated this fact by flaring his Black Aura which threw Vinzent and Raito off balance. Seizing the opportunity, Orion quickly and savagely blasted Vinzent into a nearby forest with gravity. He then proceeded to use his Black Aura to manipulate the gravity of the surrounding area, making it difficult for Raito to utilize his super speed. With his movement restricted, Orion struck Raito with several well placed punches, knocking him into the ground and out cold. The false god saw another opportunity to lessen his workload, however, before he could kill another Elder Guardian, he was halted by a bolt of lightning from Vinzent, who was seen speeding towards the false god. Seeing his only way to victory was through the Apple, Orion flew away towards the beacon of Source Energy with Elder Vinzent following close behind on a manifested board of red lightning.

Meanwhile within the large crater formed from Nico's Bakudan bombs, a pair of flattened chocolate brown legs, covered by loose-fitting black pants, bathed in a pulsating pool of red blood as Exodus's exalted white Sun shined above. Diving into the pool of blood, Nico opened his eyes frantically before looking around at his surroundings. Upon further investigation, the Elder realized he was within the Realm of Apollo. This was confirmed by the soft warm sand placed within the realm, added by a hulking pyramid, three rotating Suns and three powerful spirits; Helios, Surya and Apollo. Nico looked from the eyes of his soul as the Father Sun, Helios, shined his Light on what appeared to be a body made of Solar Energy. Within the spot where Nico was killed, the pool of blood began to sway and jump like an angry ocean. As a result, Nico's Healing-Factor began to regenerate his body, forming everything from his circulatory system, to his muscular system, to even his nervous system. During the healing process, within the Realm of Apollo, the spirit of Surya motioned forward as a goldish-white figure with four arms, and spoke with the Taiyōnian…

Spirit of Surya: "Sun-child, why have you returned to the Realm of Apollo? And with such a complete injury as this?"

Nico: "Forgive me, Mother Surya. I have fallen victim to trickery and deception. I have lowered my guard in hopes of achieving the impossible…"

Spirit of Surya: "Hmmm. Though troubling, your heart was in the right place, Sun-child. Do not place hope in those who have shown you who they are, but rather approach every situation with an open mind. The enemy you face will not spare a drop of power to achieve his goal, neither shall you."

Nico: "What do you mean Mother Surya?"

Spirit of Surya: "You are the first Taiyōnian to open thyself to the Way of Bogan. Use its gifts and show your enemies the power of the Suns."

Nico: "With your, Father Helios, and Spirit Apollo's guidance, I will not fail."

Spirit of Surya: "Be warned Sun-child, because of the severity of this injury, *Saibo Shi* has entered into its beginning stages. Proceed with courage and valor, but with caution and vigilance from here on out."

Nico: "Yes Mother Surya. Thank you, Father Helios, Spirit Apollo, Prophet Lotus, and the Creator for the Love and Light I'm blessed to receive. We will emerge victorious."

Spirit of Surya: "Very good. Now rise, Senshi Warrior, and go forth, rejoicing in the Sun and in the protection of the One Infinite Creator. Adonai."

Nico: "Adonai."

Following Mother Surya's blessing, Nico's consciousness was pulled from the Realm of Apollo and back into his fully regenerated body on Exodus. The Elder opened his eyes, giving them time to adjust to the bright Sun above him. Afterwards, Nico realized where he was and why he was there. Upon this realization, he stood to his feet and remembered what Mother Surya said about the teachings of Bogan, and how he should use its gifts fully and openly. So after demolishing the fear that gated his full command over the Source Energy within, the Elder felt a surge of power he hadn't felt since escaping Taiyō's demise. Following Nico's full release of the Way of Bogan, the Elder's eyes and mutated markings began to glow increasingly brighter as his Solar Mutation entered into an overcharged mode, causing his entire body to amplify to a level it never had before. The Elder's muscle-fibers freed themselves from his pores, resembling the beginning of a mutation, however, this was quite different. The loose flowing fibers turned from a reddish-pink, to a black as dark as coal. These black fibers wrapped, not just around Nico's arms, but around his entire body, head and dreadlocks included. This new Bogan fueled technique of Muscular Amplification acted as a type of muscle body armor; hardening like steel. As the newly formed black fibers covered Nico's face, the small area formed an extremely dense skull that shielded his face; his eyes glowing with Solar Energy. Shortly after, Elder Nico looked down at his hands and witnessed the mutated markings of his Solar Mutation appear, then cover his body like before. The explosion of Solar Energy, through the Way of Bogan, could only be regarded as a ***Supernova*** and was the name given to Nico's new super mutation. With Supernova active, the Elder forcefully propelled himself out of the crater, and towards his struggling companions.

Meanwhile zooming through a forest of trees, Vinzent chased Orion on his board of lightning while throwing several explosive lightning bolts. Orion flew flawlessly through the forest in desperation because of the growing presence of the Apple's Energy, but had a laborious time finding the fruit. However in Elder Vinzent's case, Orion's distracted demeanor made him a relatively elementary target. Because of this, Vinzent struck the fleeting false god with a hefty dose of Violet lightning which electrocuted, and threw Orion into a group of innocent rocks. The Asronian was pinned between a rock in a hard place once again, but just when his hope seemed to reach its end, there it was, the God's Heart Apple in all its power and glory, levitating gracefully by a collection of bushes and tree branches. Orion used his Black Aura to brutally shoved Vinzent into several trees before he motioned to pick up the majestic fruit of the Creator.

Orion: "At last. *deep breath* The cycle of hatred will end, and this galaxy will fall and rise as me as its lord and savior."

Vinzent recovered from Orion's swift attack and saw the false god in possession of the Apple. Thinking of the worst case scenario, the Elder hastily dashed for Orion, in a flash of lightning, as time seemingly slowed down for them at that moment. Orion held, then quickly consumed the God's Heart Apple with one bite, just as Vinzent stabbed Orion through the throat and chest, hoping to keep Orion's body from digesting the Apple and to kill him for good. In that moment, time regained its normality which saw the greatly injured false god fall, face first into the dirt of Exodus. Afterwards, Vinzent cautiously approached Orion's body to check for vital signs, but that's when the Elder sensed something odd. The Guardian flipped Orion on his back, and noticed a strange steady glow originating from Orion's stomach. The Elder's instincts kicked in however, and he went to stab the glowing spot coming from the false god. But before his blade made contact, a loud heartbeat flooded the ears of every entity present on Exodus, quickly followed by a random, yet ferocious wave of Source Energy that sent Vinzent, and the entire surrounding area flying like a tornado blowing away paper. The Aura-user tumbled against the ground then recovered before feeling uneasy due to the devilish Energy coming from above. He looked up in utter distress at the newly revived Orion, his body white as snow with black veins running visibly through his body. His hands, feet and neck were pitch black like the deep void of space. Three black horns, all a foot in length, protruded from his head and resembled Asronian royalty; greater than Emperor Titus in his prime. The empowered Asronian turned and faced Vinzent as the Elder witnessed a strange symbol form on Orion's chest which translated to one word, "Power". Orion, in all his newly obtained Source Energy and might, levitated high above his opposition with words of discouragement.

Orion: *laughs maniacally* "When will you Guardians learn, the Light is an embarrassment to life itself. It is a lie for there is only true strength in DARKNESS!! I, Orion, God of Darkness, have achieved my right as the ONE TRUE CREATOR! Rejoice! For you Guardians will have the pleasure of witnessing my ascension, and becoming the first to perish by my Holy hands... Source Energy: *Sinful Bite*!"

Following this, Orion put out his hand toward the Guardians as he charged up a blast from his newly obtained Godly Source Energy. The wind picked up and the clouds darkened, covering the white Sun as Orion let loose the charged attack in the form of a snake, but before it could make contact, Elder Guardian Nico jumped in the way and blocked the powerful attack with his Mamoru shield, empowered and reinforced by his Supernova mutation. The explosion was massive and sent both Elders tumbling for several meters. As the two tumbled against the dirt and rocks, they both were caught and stopped by Elder Raito's super speed, enabling them to gather themselves.

Nico: "Appreciate the save Raito."

Raito: "Thank me after we save Myrmidon."

Orion: *sigh* "If we hadn't killed off the Taiyōnians ourselves, I might've believed you were immortal, but we all know that's not true. *laughter* Your kind were all so… exasperating. Regardless if there are three of you or three hundred. I am Orion, and who are you to an Asronian God!?"

Vinzent: "Let's find out…"

CHAPTER

SIXTEEN

FALL

The defiant Guardians angered Orion, but also amused him as he could sense Ashla, and Bogan fueled Source Energy rising from all three Elders. Nico, with the power from Exodus's white Sun, however now covered, stood strong and ready with his new Supernova mutation active. Vinzent, in all his power, fully released his Black Aura which transformed him into the Guardian of Lightning. And Raito embodied the purity of Prana Energy, which enabled the Elder to cast his special spell called: Empowerment. Together, the Trio of Light and Dark stood face to face against the self-proclaimed god that was Orion, focused, and determined to free the galaxy once and for all. With synchronized attacks, Elder Nico attacked Orion with the Ken fists, Elder Raito with a Prana bow and arrows, and Vinzent with a fist of black lightning. Although they were enlightened to the Way of Bogan, Orion easily blocked all attempts on his life with an Source Energy shield; silver in coloration. The false god laughed in the faces of the Guardians before him.

Orion: *maniacal laughter* "Yes! YES! Cling to what little hope you have left and watch as I shatter your dreams and burn your hopes! Source Energy: *Sinful Explosion!*"

Orion jumped back before forming a tiny white sphere of Source Energy from his hand before it expanded to the size of an inflated hot air balloon. The false god threw the giant explosive towards Nico with unmatched velocity and power, forcing the Elder to reinforce his Mamoru shield with both arms, but it proved ineffective as Orion's bomb crashed and blew up the Elder in a humongous explosion of Source Energy, which leveled the surrounding area, and sent Raito and Vinzent flying once more. Orion flew down to the two mile crater produced, and to his amazement, Nico was seen partially standing as the Guardian's Supernova mutation worked to repair his damaged muscle armor. Orion then formed a black staff and stabbed the Elder through the exposed part of his body. Nico reeled back in pain, but found enough in himself to snap the rod in half with one Ken fist and swing against Orion with the other. The attack however, was effortlessly blocked by Orion. The false god returned the favor and expeditiously uppercutted Nico in the chin which cracked his freshly mutated face armor, and sent him flying high above the darkened clouds.

Orion: "This Energy is incredible! Who can stand against the mighty ORION!!"

Orion burst with more Source Energy from the Apple, as he praised and found new joy in himself, but that moment of bliss was interrupted by the Elder Guardian Raito. Using his empowered super speed from his Empowerment ability, Raito sprinted after Orion, zipping towards the false god with unfollowable speed. Raito reached his target and attacked with a fist of Prana Energy that managed to cause Orion a noticeable amount of pain, and sent the false god crashing into a mountain. This was due to Prana Energy being the fundamental enemy of Bogan teachings due to its Ashla nature. The false god burst free from the distorted mountain with a roar of fury, but that burning anger was extinguished by several bolts of black lightning, forcing Orion to deflect with a Source Energy shield. However, the Asronian underestimated the power of Vinzent's Black Aura, as a result, a bolt of black lightning struck and threw Orion into the ground below. The false god then recovered to his feet and fired a hefty dose of Source Energy, knocking

Vinzent away. Soon after, Orion found his movement restricted by a giant hand of Prana Energy. Raito, with Orion in hand, tightened his grip before throwing him up high and into the clouds. Orion felt the pending attack of another approach from up above before looking to see Elder Nico, diving down due to his mighty punch moments ago. The Guardian mutated his arm, and used his Ken fists to strike Orion back down to the ground with immense force and power. Nico quickly mutated again and used his Hari whip as a grappling hook to hook into the ground. With the whip secured, Nico pulled and flung himself at marvelous speeds towards the false god, while also simultaneously mutating the other arm to use his deadly Jūken blade. Following the hard landing from Nico's Ken attack, Orion quickly recovered to his feet, and looked toward the sky to see a figure speeding towards him with a double-ended blade pointed straight for him.

Nico: "Thanks for the assistance Raito! Solar Energy: *Blazing Bullet!*"

Orion took the time to swiftly form a black spear of pure Source Energy right before Nico came crashing against him. The force from the collision caused the ground around them to crack and buckle as the two entered into a blade-to-spear duel; Raito adding arrows from his Light-bow when he could.

Orion: "This new mutation of yours is quite an impressive gift, Taiyōnian. But we both know without your Solar Mutation, you and your Senshi brethren were and are nothing. And as for you, Prana-user, let the sea be your tomb, as it was for my people."

After a few moments of intense dueling, Orion gained the upper hand and broke Nico's mutated arm then thrusted his spear towards the Guardian's chest. Fortunately this time, Nico's black armor, from his Supernova mutation, completely covered his body and held strong, protecting his body from Orion's assault. Following this, Orion ruthlessly struck Nico on the side of the head with his spear then blasted the Elder into a nearby forest with a focused dose of Source Energy. The blast caused Nico to crash into several trees and rocks before being stopped by a boulder. Orion proceeded to duel against Elder Raito and was, for a time, outmatched by Raito's empowered super speed. However despite the speed at which Raito now commanded, Orion's timing was perfect as he blasted the Mahōnian far out and into the sea. Quickly following this, Vinzent recovered and appeared in a flash of lightning before Orion. Without hesitation, the false god thrusted his spear as he aimed for Vinzent's throat, but the Elder elegantly bent backwards to dodge as he simultaneously kicked Orion's spear free from his hands. Vinzent then used his hands to propel himself upward towards the spinning spear before he kicked it back towards Orion with great force. The false god went to catch the fastly approaching spear, but was suddenly pierced in the back by Raito's Prana arrow. This surprised and threw Orion off balance which enabled Vinzent's previous attack to hit its mark as Orion's own spear pierced his shoulder. Afterwards, Elder Vinzent landed a few meters from Orion, putting his hands on the ground to send a stream of Violet lightning running through the earth, and up the spear that connected the false god to the dirt of the planet. The lightning ran through the Asronian's body like blood running through veins, and lit up the area like a lightning storm at night. Vinzent's empowered Elemental Energy consumed Orion as the false god roared with more annoyance than pain, due to his inability to move freely. Afterwards, Vinzent stopped the flow of lightning as Orion stood there steaming with his spear protruding from his shoulder.

Orion: "Very good. Very good!! More, MORE!! Show me how desperately you wish to save this galaxy."

Thanks to the Supernova mutation empowering his Healing-Factor, Nico swiftly recovered as his afflicted injuries completely regenerated. The Guardian then got up and took to the skies, leaping several meters towards the fight. He looked and saw Orion temporarily immobilized, so with his broken arm freshly regenerated, the Elder landed then leaped up and constructed his Ken fists. The Guardian dove for the false god and crashed into Orion, creating a large shockwave, and temporality stunning the Asronian. Following this, Raito casted a spell called: **Binding Light**, which formed a sphere of Prana Energy that encircled and imprisoned Orion, placing the false god in a temporary state of confinement. The Guardians then cautiously jumped back and surrounded the Binding Light spell as they held a triangular shape around the false god. Shortly after, they saw the burning hatred coming from Orion's blood red eyes, added by a twisted smile; they knew the fight was far from over.

Orion: "You think your soft punches, weak lightning and distasteful Prana bubble can stop ME!? *amused chuckle* Allow me to show you the Source Energy I now command!"

Lightning struck and the ground began to shake as the binding spell that held Orion captive, began to crack and break. Orion's thick Black Aura, different from Vinzent's, visible to the naked eye and toxic to the lungs, was seen pouring from above the cell like smoke from a burning building. The Guardians readied themselves for whatever evil awaited them. They were confident in their power found from the Bogan lessons taught by Titus, as well as each other, but would it be enough to stop Orion's might? This thought briefly crossed Raito's mind as he witnessed his spell being broken out of with somewhat of ease. The Aura of Orion grew denser and heavier with every passing moment, and finally, with a roar and thrust of power, Orion shattered Raito's binding spell, effectively freeing himself. The shockwave produced blew the Guardians away as the force felt like being pulled into the vacuum of space. It blew everything away and produced mass deforestation that stretched for miles. Despite their teachings in both Ashla and Bogan, the Guardians struggled to hold their positions as the force from Orion proved greater than previously anticipated. Finally however, the force produced from Orion ceased, and the Guardians were able to gain their footing once more. After recovering, the Elders saw and felt Orion once more in all his power as he floated gracefully. The Elders found a sense of discouragement after witnessing the false god cast a spell on himself that resembled a greater version of Nico's Healing-Factor, called: *Sinful Recovery*, which healed his wounds completely and fueled his sinful resolve.

Orion: "You have seen and felt a drop of the power I possess, yet you still fight against me...Why?"

Vinzent: "Because it is the right thing to do. Because everything you've done and everything our comrades have sacrificed has led to this very moment. Lucas, Matt, Rex, Luna, Kicks, Rachel, Cass, and all the lives you've taken. Their sacrifice will not be in vain! So here we stand against you, and we will NOT fail!"

Orion: "And here I thought you three would become my new personal Guardians. *sigh* No matter, your deaths were all but assured the moment you stepped foot on this planet. Now, tremble before your Creator!"

Orion released his latent Godly Source Energy, provided by the Apple, and transformed himself into a true demon. The transformation consumed his body in Black Aura as he formed two extra arms and a third eye. His horns grew a few inches taller and thicker, and his body grew in size and strength. With revolting Source Energy coming from all four hands, Orion taunted his prey.

Orion: *deeper tone* "You wish to hasten your deaths!? Come!"

Following Orion's taunt, Nico remembered again the wise words of his mother. He wondered why his mother's words poured into his mind at a time like this, but nonetheless, the Elder gave thanks and was fueled by his resolve and duty to the galaxy; to his family.

Nico: "Sometimes the Creator puts us through hard times to show us our true potential. Sometimes we must realize that we are sinners in need of forgiveness, of redemption, of guidance. We must own our sins. We must close our mouths and open our hearts to the Source Energy; to the Creator. Only then will we see just how powerful we truly are. Let us finish this!"

Nico relayed his mental message to Vinzent and Raito, which fueled their resolve, and strengthened their willpower, pushing them beyond their limits. Together they roared and exploded with Solar, Elemental, and Prana Energy with Orion even noticing their power increase. Soon after bursting with Energy, the Guardians clashed against the demon Orion like swords of Light and Dark meeting against a battleaxe of pure Darkness. Their battle intensified, reshaping Exodus's landscape itself which caused natural disasters across the planet. Their punches caused mountains to crumble like a stack of cards, oceans to split from their blasts of Energy, and forests to be swept away from their combined speed. It was the battle for Myrmidon and ultimately the Universe.

The Guardians pushed their attack relentlessly, matching each other in power, strength and agility; the perfect trio. However, despite their flawless teamwork, and three-on-one matchup, Orion, in all his might, was still able to not only defend against all three Elders, but eventually the false god followed, learned and countered their attacks, sometimes going on the offensive. The battle raged on for what seemed like eternity as the Guardians began to notice the decrease in their physical stamina and Energies. They knew the power granted by the Way of Ashla and the Way of Bogan would not last much longer, and the only reason they were able to keep up with Orion thus far was due to their own special abilities, willpower, and the majestic Mark of Honor from Titus, which provided them with a miniature boost in Bogan fueled Source Energy. Orion noticed this and pushed his attack even further without regard for what the Creator's God's Heart Apple might do to his mortal body.

Orion: "It seems your Light and even the Dark has begun to leave you stranded while I grow STRONGER!" *laughs*

Orion released a burst of Source Energy that shoved all three Guardians away, causing them to tumble against the ground. They were slow to their feet as Vinzent agreed with Orion.

Vinzent: *heavy panting* "I hate to admit it, but he's right. Nico, your mutations are getting slower, and your armor's integrity is beginning to give. Raito, your Empowerment ability is beginning to flicker, and

I can tell your speed is decreasing. And I can feel my Aura Conversion concentration slipping, and my body overheating. All the while Orion's strength somehow grows. We can't afford to draw this out, we need to finish this. Let's try that…"

Nico & Raito: *heavy panting* "Agreed."

Following their reality check, Nico and Raito both sprinted off in opposite directions, leaving Vinzent to the side. Elder Nico charged in first with his dual Jūken blades mutated on both arms, followed by Elder Raito who casted his Light Bow spell and took to the skies. Together they formed the ultimate combination of close and long ranged attacks. Raito was also seen chanting syllables that haven't been heard since the end of the first Galactic War. However, Orion didn't notice because of the consistency of Nico's blades and Raito's arrows. After a few more bladed and arrowed attacks, Nico formed a small Bakudan bomb before throwing the pile of unstable Solar Energy towards Orion. Instinctively, the Asronian demon blocked the attack with a Source Energy shield, but as the smoke cleared, Nico swiftly leaped through the smoke and behind Orion, thus leading to the Elder grabbing the false god by the arms and chest. He then yelled for Raito as the Prana-user threw several white and gold chains towards the two. Orion countered by forming several tangible blades of Source Energy, which broke through and pierced Nico's body. The Elder coughed up blood as Orion's blades traveled deeper into his neck, chest and shoulders. However, despite the injuries, Nico held on to Orion as firmly as his body allowed. Orion began annoyed at how close the Elder got to him, he found it disrespectful and unmannerly. Upon this conclusion, Orion went to remove himself from Nico's mutated clutches, but soon noticed his movement was gravely restricted. Upon further inspection, the demon Orion realized Raito was not only shooting arrows of Prana Energy, but also was forming chains empowered by the Way of Ashla which were hidden by Nico's constant attacks, and Raito's muffled chanting.

Orion: "Again! Do you think you Guardians can hold me–… What is this? I can't break free!"

Elders Raito and Nico both smiled as the plan became reality. Raito, along with firing Prana Energy arrows, also chanted and casted another binding spell called: **Holy Chains**, a binding spell used to hold powerful Bogan practitioners, and was used to capture Emperor Titus Ronan and Theo Ronan during the first Galactic War. The greater the level of Bogan mastery by the captured entity, the stronger the chains. However, the spell could only be used effectively when Raito had Empowerment active, due to the Energy required. Fortunately for Elder Raito, the Mark of Honor offered a boost in Bogan fueled Source Energy to the Guardians. This meant Raito, despite now reverting to his original form, could keep the spell active for a short while longer.

Nico concentrated all of his Solar Energy to hold Orion still as the two Elders created the galaxy's strongest binding attack. Orion struggled and yelled in fury as his body burst in black flames. The flames scorched Nico vigorously, and at a distance of several feet, slowly burned Raito as well. Elder Nico began to grunt in extreme discomfort as his armor slowly chipped and burned away due to Orion's intensified black flames, but nonetheless Nico held strong as he knew letting go wasn't an option. The Taiyōnian put all of his remaining Solar Energy into his Healing-Factor to compensate for the constant burning. As a result, Nico did not have enough spare Solar Energy to keep up his body armor, and was forced to release his Supernova mutation. Following Orion's burst of black flames, his anger was suddenly masked by worry as he felt a powerful concentration of Energy, pure Source Energy in origin, several meters ahead. The false god looked and saw Elder Vinzent, squatting with a three foot lightning bolt crackling in his hand. Multi-colored lightning struck from the bolt with a sense of ferociousness and wildness. The colors inside, red, orange, yellow, green, blue, violet, and indigo, circled in and around each other before harmonizing together to form a dense flow of black Energy; lightning flashed inside like a thunderstorm. The bolt of Source Energy was beautiful and extraordinary, as if the Creator handed it to Vinzent himself. Orion looked further behind Vinzent and saw the souls of Guardians killed by his hand, including, Elder Luna, Elder Cass, Elder Matthew, as well as The Nine. And as each entity touched Vinzent's back, the bolt of black Source Energy grew in size and power.

Vinzent: "You have hurt, and killed, and enslaved long enough, Orion! The power from the Source, and those fueled by it stand against you! Now rest in Eternal Darkness! Elemental Energy: *Cosmic Bolt!*"

Vinzent grunted in pain as the pure nature of the lightning bolt charred his arm. But despite the pain, the Elder threw the bolt with boundless strength as the rushing blast of Elemental Energy took the form of a multi-colored Lion against Orion as Nico and Raito's Holy Chains held the demon still. Even Orion knew this assault was extremely problematic, an assault he didn't know if he could survive, so in a desperate act, the false god gave out a deafening roar, added by an extraordinary flare of Black Aura. The wave of Energy shattered Raito's Holy Chains and broke Nico's mutated grip. Fear ran through all three Guardians which forced Raito to do the unthinkable... He rushed in the path of the Cosmic Bolt, and stabbed Orion with a Prana Energy knife in order to keep the false god from escaping his fate. Nico, despite his burns and wounds, worked to keep Raito from being directly hit, but he was too late and couldn't fully protect Raito... And in a loud and bone crashing clap, a gargantuan explosion engulfed the battlefield, consuming Nico, Raito, and Orion in a blaze of blinding Elemental Cosmic Energy and lightning strikes, while shoving Vinzent several meters away. The Guardian tumbled against the ground before manifesting a red lightning sword to slow himself down. However, due to all the fighting, Vinzent found himself completely exhausted, and felt the loss of his Black Aura as he reverted to his original form, thus allowing blood to drip from his wounds and burned arm; his curly hair becoming completely disheveled. He slowly recovered to his feet and began to limp through the dust and towards the explosion. The dust subsided, enabling him to look out into the distance, but what he saw shook him. Raito, back in his normal form, laid across the dirt, unconscious and missing both legs; blood continuously pouring from his wounds. And Nico was exhausted and left with little to no Solar Energy, leaving him with only enough to prevent a true death. To add insult to injury, Nico couldn't heal himself as the entire right side of his body was caught in the blast and torn away. The remaining parts of Nico's body were burned by Orion's black flames. Orion however, stood bloodied and with his left arm torn away from Vinzent's Cosmic Bolt. Orion roared in absolute torment as he fell to one knee and held the large wound that bled constantly.

Vinzent: *exhausted tone* "How could this be? W-We used everything we had, but it still wasn't enough to kill him? Did the God's Heart Apple really give Orion the power of the Creator?"

Orion took the moment from Vinzent's hesitation and jumped a few feet away; a distorted bloodied mess yet again. He showed his appreciation for the Guardians before healing his wounds with Sinful Recovery.

Orion: *grunts* "My, my. Thanks to your friends there for taking the initial blast. I don't know what that was, but I must applaud you Guardians for pushing me this far. *painful chuckle* This has surely been a pronounced test for me, but now the Way of Ashla and Bogan of the Creator has left you and you shall perish…"

Orion geared up for his last attack against the exhausted Guardians. Out of options and Elemental Energy, Vinzent raised his burnt fists and prepared to fight his last fight. But just when all hope seemed lost, Orion coughed into his hand and saw black blood dripping from it. Moments later, the false god grabbed his chest and was brought to one knee, then to his hands and knees. The Asronian coughed up more blood as he and Vinzent were left in utter confusion.

Orion: "W-What is happening to me!? I am a GOD!! *coughs* How could I be brought to such a point as THIS?! *grunt* I will achieve victory, it is my right…it is my DESTINY–……"

Vinzent looked amazed as he witnessed the Source Energy from the God's Heart Apple leave Orion's body, and ascend towards the sky, reverting the false god back to his original form. It was as if the Apple ultimately rejected Orion's soul and slowly stole the lifeforce from the Asronian rather than grant him the power of the Creator.

Some of that stolen Source Energy absorbed back into Rachel's soul as her skin recovered its beautiful red complexion, enabling her to regain consciousness. When the dust settled, and the blinding light from the Creator's Source Energy faded, Vinzent did not see the almighty Orion that plunged the galaxy into a second Galactic War, but rather a weak and shriveled entity, barely clinging to life. The Guardian hardly sensed any Source Energy coming from Orion, as if he was an infant fresh from his mother's womb. Vinzent looked back towards his injured comrades, Raito's breathing was faint and lite, and Nico barely able to inhale. He then looked back towards Orion as he approached the unrecognizable demon of darkness.

Orion: *weakened tone* "This can't be. This can't be! I have been forsaken. The galaxy *coughs* is mine. I am a god... You, Guardian... What have you done to me?...

Rachel: "They have done nothing but protect the galaxy long enough for the God's Heart Apple to reject you."

Orion: *weakened tone* "What?..."

Rachel: "Did you really think that after everything you've done. After everything you put this galaxy through, you'd come out on top?"

Orion: *weakened tone* "It is my right... My... destiny... I will avenge my people... I will... become ruler over all!..."

Rachel: "It was said that only the chosen species, as well as the Creator himself may reap the benefits from consuming the God's Heart Apple. Though you are pure Asronian, your heart is tainted with evil, greed, vengeance and pure Darkness. In other words, you were unbalanced, thus unworthy, like the Goliath said. And you were judged by the will of the Creator."

The wind of Exodus blew as Orion was left speechless and demoralized. Rachel then tried to show her brother the Light.

Rachel: "There's still hope brother. Come to the Light, we can still have peace and rebuild the Asronian race, the right way."

Orion: *weakened tone* "Hope? Peace? The Light? *raspy breathing* Do not be fooled by such lies. There is no such thing as peace or hope or the Light. *raspy breathing* There is only chaos, despair, and Darkness. There will always be only Darkness."

Rachel: "What happened to you? How did you become so lost?"

Orion: *weakened laughter* "Lost? No my sister, I was the only one who was found. While our father and mother were blinded by the Ashla teachings of those Guardians, only I saw the deception behind those smiles, and it was only a matter of time before they feared the level of Source Energy granted from the Way of Bogan and struck against us. *raspy breathing* Father would not listen to my plea to destroy the lie of Light, so I gave him motivation…"

Rachel: "W-What are you talking about?"

Vinzent: "You didn't…"

Orion: "Yes! I used what little power I acquired from the Way of Ashla and killed our brother Gabriel, effectively framing the Guardians!" *coughs*

Vinzent: "Because of you, countless lives were lost!!" *grunts*

Orion: *weakened tone* "A small price to pay to rid the galaxy of the lie of Ashla before they rid the galaxy of Bogan practitioners; of those of great power."

Rachel: "Why Orion? Why trick our father, hurt our family and doom Asron?"

Orion: *weakened tone* "Same reason why you Guardians stood against me. To rid the galaxy of the Light. Those who follow the Way of Ashla do not know power. You all do not know that in this galaxy, Love and Light will not help you survive. They only fill one with false hope and dull one's senses. How can you Ashla followers pour all your Energy into the Creator? A silent God?"

Rachel: "A galaxy full of Darkness will not have a chance to experience unconditional Love or even the Light to reveal one's strength or achievements. Father must've known that our people could learn what the Way of Ashla had to teach, and further pushed a relationship with those who taught it, not because he was blinded, but because he and mother knew just how powerful the Creator's Love really is. Don't you see that? Our parents wanted to end the dark history of the Asronians, but because of your obsession with destroying those who chose Love over conquest, you stripped away what could've been a loving future for the Asronians."

Orion: *injured chuckle* "You think I feel sorrow or grief? Only I realized how blinding the Light really is; how weak it makes an entity. The Way of Ashla will not provide you with the means to protect yourselves when the Empire comes for Myrmidon."

Vinzent: "Empire?"

Orion: *weakened tone* "You all will find out soon enough. The teachings from Ashla will not save you from them, and you all will perish. The Light will not shine this time, Guardians…"

Rachel: "There truly is no saving you… goodbye, Orion."

Elder Rachel turned away in sadness before walking to tend to Nico, as well as to provide Raito with Kicks's last Solar Seed. As she motioned past the exhausted Aura-user, she presented Vinzent the honor of killing her lost brother once and for all.

Rachel: "The power is in your hands now Vinzent. There is only one thing left to do…Kill him, get revenge for those who fell to Orion's sword. I don't know what happened to him, nor do I know anything about this… Empire, but he is no longer my brother."

Elder Guardian Vinzent stood there for a moment, contemplating the right path. Every bone in his body told him to listen to Elder Rachel and decapitate the murderer right then and there, but then he heard a whisper; a familiar voice. The voice of Ra.

Ra's whisper: "There is a better way… Show him the Love and the Light of the One Infinite Creator… Show him the Law of One."

Vinzent looked towards the sky. He saw the clouds recovering from the storm made from their battle. He felt the wind calmly brushing through his messy hair. Vinzent let out a deep painful breath before he turned his attention to Orion.

Vinzent: "I understand now what Ra meant. Death is mercy and is less than what you deserve, but revenge is not mine to give, never was. I… forgive you for what you've done Orion, because the Creator teaches us forgiveness in all living beings, so maybe you can be forgiven too. However, once this is done, you will live out the rest of your days as a prisoner. Maybe then you'll see the foolishness of your actions like your father."

Elder Vinzent turned his back and motioned toward Elders Rachel, Raito and Nico, leaving the false god to ponder Vinzent's words. But instead of peace and acceptance for his upcoming reality, Orion's anger grew even more than before. The false god refused the Way of Ashla and cursed the Creator. Because of his anger, Orion found the resolve and strength to stand to his feet, shaking and grunting as if standing in freezing temperatures.

Orion: *weakened tone* "Who do you think you are? *raspy breathing* You think I'm in need of your pitiful Light?! Of your forgiveness? Of your silent Creator?! *raspy breathing* I…I am Orion, God of Darkness! I am inevitable!!"

Orion charged up the last bit of his vital Source Energy against Vinzent as the unstable Energy grew larger and larger, eventually towering over Vinzent as it stood as a testament to Orion's internal fury. The Elder couldn't believe Orion possessed that much strength after the beating he took. Exhausted and depleted of all Elemental Energy, Elder Vinzent fell on his butt and put his burned hand on his head before saying "well shit," to the sight of the enormous pile of Source Energy set before him. Orion held the sphere of Energy up high, but suddenly the Energy dispersed and faded into nothingness. Elder Vinzent found himself to be utterly perplexed by this action, and wondered if Orion hopefully had a change of heart. However, the reality that was present before him told a different story.

Rachel: *exhale* "Rest now Orion. You are released from your pain… In Light, and in Love, Adonai. Cosmic Energy: *Soul Tether*."

Orion had succumbed to his injuries, as well as the backlash from being rejected by the Creator's fruit. As a result, his body hardly possessed any Source Energy which gave Elder Rachel the golden opportunity to rush her brother and place one hand on his chest, and one finger between his eyebrows. Orion's eyes rolled backwards as Rachel performed a tethering spell on the false god. A burst of Cosmic Energy forced Vinzent to shield his eyes as the shockwave produced slid him backwards. When the light faded, enabling the Elder to regain his footing, Vinzent, at first, was left completely speechless, but later found the words to question Rachel who was seen panting.

Vinzent: "Wha… What did you do?"

Rachel: *panting* "I…I tethered his soul to the spiritual realm and forced his soul to roam aimlessly within that realm for eternity. But his will was too strong to tether his soul directly to the afterlife, and I didn't have enough Source Energy to send both his soul and body, but without his soul, Orion is dead."

Following Elder Rachel's Soul Tether ritual, Orion's soulless body fell backwards as black blood covered the ground beneath him. His battle wounded body relaxed as his soul was forced out. Rachel and Vinzent could feel the coldness and vile nature of Orion's soul as it passed by them. Unlike most entities, Orion's will was far stronger than most even after death. Because of Orion's unwillingness to let go of the physical world, and of his desires, his soul manifested itself as a shadowy field of Black Aura, visible only to those who've experienced the Way of Bogan. The Elders paused nervously as Orion's soul left a chilling message.

Orion's Soul: *deep raspy tone* "With a strong Light, comes an even stronger Darkness... There will be a time when the Coin of Life is flipped once again... And there will be a time when Darkness is the side that is flipped, for the Empire approaches... You will not escape this cycle...for it is necessary..."

Shortly after the chilling message from Orion's soul, the Black Aura vanished from sight, leaving Rachel to wonder if simply removing Orion's soul from his body was enough. However, she looked over and saw Orion, the self-proclaimed god of Darkness, dead and soulless on the surface of Exodus. Afterwards, Vinzent suddenly collapsed next to a defaced Taiyōnian and a leg-less Mahōnian, leaving Rachel to give out an irritated, yet relieved sigh.

A few hours passed since the death of Myrmidon's destroyer. The second planet, Exodus, which had been turned into a battleground, was utterly devastated. The once gorgeous world was now covered in craters, crumbled mountains and angry seas. Elder Rachel flew away from Orion's grave as she used her flight capabilities to carry Elders Raito, Nico and Vinzent, with Cass's body along with them. On Orion's grave lie three red flowers with the engraving, "Theo Ronan. Beloved first son of Titus and Athena Ronan."

Rachel flew a dozen more miles before she saw what seemed to be the Hercules, and upon a closer look it was. The Asronian flew down and witnessed a group of six armed creatures repairing the destroyed ship. However the ship seemed different, it seemed more organic than machine. This was because the creatures used pieces from The Obedience to repair the vessel, giving the craft the means to repair itself, kind of like a self-heal system. As Rachel landed, and the creatures finished their repairs, the Asronian Elder brought the unconscious Guardians aboard the Hercules before placing them in the crew's quarters, which had been redesigned with organic technology. Following this, Jasmine found joy in Rachel's return but also a level of fear.

Jasmine: "R-Rachel… are you…"

Rachel: *chuckles* "Yes, I'm me again."

Jasmine: "Does that mean…"

Rachel: "Yes. Orion is dead, it's over."

Jasmine: *sigh of relief* "Holy shit, you guys really did it?!"

Rachel: "By the grace of the Creator, they did. However, not without sacrifice…"

Rachel showed Raito's life threatening injuries, Nico's destroyed and charred body, and Cass's corpse. Vinzent was lucky enough to receive a few broken bones and second degree burns from his last major blast of Elemental Energy. But after seeing Casanova soulless, Jasmine was relieved about her friend finding her way back to the Light, but the AI also registered a level of grief for what it cost.

Jasmine: "Oh Cass. It seems she found her way back to the Creator, but had to repay her deeds with her life. As for everyone else, I'm able to stabilize them. Raito however, is in bad shape, but once we find a proper hospital, everyone should make a full recovery, Elder Raito included. It's a good thing you gave him a Solar Seed."

Rachel: "Best news I've heard in a long time."

Jasmine: "I'm finally glad it's over."

Rachel: "Indeed."

Jasmine: "...Are you sure you're okay? We literally just won the war, though short, we won! Everyone's sacrifices were not in vain! But you seem distant from that joy..."

Rachel: "Forgive me Jasmine. I know I should be glad this nightmare is finally over, but a lot has happened, and right now I just don't have the energy."

Jasmine: "That's completely reasonable. We've all been through a lot. That aside, what are those creatures that fixed the ship?"

Rachel: "I have no idea. But, their technical skills are impressive despite having no technology on the planet."

Jasmine: "You're right about that. Well, whatever they are, they have some amazing skills. Not only did they completely rebuild the Hercules, but they upgraded it beyond anything I or Raito could've done. They've successfully infused parts of The Obedience with the Hercules, incredible. Can you feel it?"

Rachel: "Feel what?"

Jasmine: "The Source Energy from the ship. It almost feels alive."

Shortly after their conversation, Jazz took control of the Hercules and powered up its engine. The ship hummed alive like it never had before which filled Jasmine with excitement. The AI thanked the alien engineers responsible as the aliens waved goodbye in delight. Afterward, the Hercules lifted above them and shot off into the sky then into space, and towards the barrier that guarded the planet Exodus, its four siblings, and white Sun. As Jasmine flew the Hercules through the temporary tunnel formed from Orion and his ship, a being of Light, resembling a Spirit Defender, appeared before Elder Rachel and Jazz with a message.

Spirit Defender: "Greetings children of the One Infinite Creator. I appear before you not as a warrior, but as a messenger for the Creator. Because of the valorous deeds committed by Raito the Mahōnian, Vinzent the Sōsunian, and Nico the Taiyōnian, they will be granted uncontested and protected entry through The Great Divide, thus allowing access two the five planets: *Genesis*, Exodus, *Leviticus*, *Numbers*, and *Deuteronomy*. No being throughout Myrmidon's history has been gifted with such an honor. Be sure to enter into this sacred space with peace, Love and Light. Adonai."

After the Spirit Defender's message, Jasmine continued through the closing tunnel of The Great Divide. Rachel and the AI found a sense of astonishment after witnessing the Spirit Defenders surround and guide the Hercules out of the TGD. They then bangged their swords against their shields, praising the unconscious Guardians, Raito, Vinzent and Nico, for their bravery and heroism. Afterwards with nowhere left to go, Jasmine plotted a course to Journia, or what was left of it. The Hercules's hyperdrive hummed with Source Energy before blasting into hyperspace, leaving Exodus' star system and everything in it behind for good...

CHAPTER

SEVENTEEN

HOPE

The third-class Elder and pureblood Asronian, Rachel Rose, sat within the cockpit of the Hercules while looking out into space to observe the dazzling colors of hyperspace travel. The Elder didn't know how to feel about everything that transpired on Exodus. The conversation with her mother, the ritual which banished Orion's soul, or the fact Orion murdered Gabriel and indirectly started the first Galactic War. Her mind was clouded and overwrought, however she knew one thing was clear, and that was the galaxy was finally free from Orion's tierney. This thought temporarily brought a sense of relaxation to her body, but not her mind. Rachel's thoughts were steered away by the voice of the faction's artificial intelligence named Jasmine.

Jasmine: "We're coming out of hyperspace and... strange."

Rachel: "What is it Jasmine?"

Jasmine: "I'm picking up a signal from outside of Journia's orbit?"

Suddenly a request to communicate with the Hercules was shown on the ship's dashboard. Rachel was hesitant to answer, but nonetheless did so.

Rachel: "This is Elder Rachel Rose. I read you loud and clear."

Elite Guardian: "An Elder, thank the Creator! This is first-class Elite Jackie, commander of the civilian evacuation fleet. I thought all the Elders were killed."

Rachel: "Most were killed, unfortunately, however some of us still stand. That aside, I'm relieved to hear some people… survived the attack on Journia. What's the situation?"

Jackie: "We have thirty-two civilian crafts low on fuel and several more in need of repairs. We've traveled through the local galactic area of Journia, but all the habitable planets have been destroyed. As it stands now, we won't last much longer."

Elite Jackie remained calm for the most part, but Rachel could feel the nervousness creeping behind her strong tone. Following Jackie's distress call, Rachel shifted her mind to finding a planet for the surviving Journia population to seek refuge, however, none came to mind. Shortly after, the Hercules popped out of hyperspace, appearing directly in front of Elite Jackie's battleship and her fleet of citizen and Guardian spacecraft. The fleet was composed of smaller starfighter carriers and decommissioned battleships, but because of the Orion Crusaders, some of the battleships were gravely damaged and in need of extensive repairs. Elder Rachel noticed a particular battleship exploding piece by piece. This caused Rachel to question Elite Jackie.

Rachel: "Jackie, what's the status on that damaged battleship to your left?"

Jackie: "Battleship number five, status report…"

Acolyte Guardian: *hastened tone* "Commander. We're having issues with the ship's engine. It's been destabilized from the Orion Crusaders. I don't know how much longer we have till it explodes. We also have children aboard this vessel."

Jackie: "Start the emergency protocol, women and children first. Have the men help with the evacuation, and any Guardians help to minimize further damages."

Acolyte Guardian: "By your request commander."

Shortly after giving out her commands, Elite Jackie announced the situation to the rest of the citizen fleet and their assigned Guardians. The other spacecraft prepared smaller lander vessels that were used to pick up the citizens aboard the dying battleship. But suddenly, things took a turn for the worse. The stern and port side of the damaged battleship exploded, inevitably shoving the ship towards the rest of the fleet. Fortunately, the citizens still aboard were pointed towards the starboard side of the ship, and were generally unharmed by the explosions. However, that was no time to relax as the damaged vessel was still due to explode at any given moment. Seeing this, Elder Rachel knew that saving who she could after throwing Journia into a sea of destruction, could be a way to show Myrmidon the goodness in the Asronians. So after receiving the go-ahead from Jasmine, the Asronian Elder sprung into action. Rachel journeyed to one of the Hercules's airlocks, leaving Jazz to fly and land the beige vessel inside of Jackie's battleship. Upon their arrival, several Guardians were seen running towards the Hercules, leading Rachel to redirect them towards Vinzent and the others. After securing Myrmidon's heroes and carting them to the fleet's lead doctor, Sarah McCorvin, Elder Rachel flared her Cosmic Energy and obtained what little Energy she had left from Rose; her alter ego. Guardians and civilians within the immediate area felt a gust of wind rush past them with a sense of confusion, given the metallic walls of the battleship surrounding them. The Asronian Elder glistened with the power of her ancestors before creating a red shield around herself which granted her the means to fly out into space. The Guardians and civilians were perplexed by the feat committed because they never saw someone survive the lifelessness of outer space, despite Rachel doing that very thing. She flew towards the battleship, dodging space debris and pieces of the damaged vessel as she drew near. The Asronian arrived at the scene and quickly realized how grave the situation was.

Rachel: "Jackie, I've arrived at the battleship and it doesn't look good. Have the Guardians completed the evacuation protocol?"

Jackie: "The last ship should be passing you now."

Following Elite Jackie's confirmation, the battleship completely exploded, engulfing the surrounding area in a blazing flash of heat. Everyone within the fleet shielded themselves and prepared for death, but as the light dimmed and faded nothing happened… Upon further inspection, the civilians and Guardians saw a red transparent bubble of Cosmic Energy, surrounding the massive explosion. Elder Rachel formed a protective bubble around the vessel right before it exploded to contain the blast, effectively preventing the destruction of Journia's last pocket of survivors. Shortly after, the Elder flew back to Elite Jackie's battleship as they all thanked Elder Rachel, and continued their search for a habitable planet. The first-class Elite named Jackie, was a tall four armed alien woman, with short violet colored hair, scarred purple skin added by a scarred right eye. The Guardian utilized Elemental Energy with an adept command over the earth element, and was the first to thank and greet Elder Rachel.

Jackie: "I've seen some powerful Guardians in my time, Vinzent, Lucas, Nico, Raito, hell even Matt and his big brain; rest in peace. But I've never seen a Guardian survive the lifeless conditions of raw outer space, let alone protect an entire fleet of ships. You Elders never cease to impress."

Rachel: "I give all the credit to the Creator and his Love and Light."

Jackie: "As humble as ever."

After Elder Rachel's brave venture into space and safe return to the civilian fleet, she, along with Elite Jackie, and several other Elite ranking Guardians discussed their next move to ensure the people's safety.

Jackie: "Thanks to Elder Rachel, the fleet is free from the previous issue. However, we're still in dire need of a habitable planet, and fast."

Elite Guardian #1: "We've exhausted much of our fuel and energy searching for one and still nothing."

Elite Guardian #2: "The people are starting to grow worried, especially with the past battleship scare."

Jackie: "Yes. I am aware of the situation and stress of the people, but we must not lose heart and faith in the Creator. He will provide."

The commanding Guardians went back and forth, reviewing the facts and current situation. It seemed the fleet was doomed to perish by the hands of space and time, but their fear and doubt were erased by renewed hope and confidence. Jasmine, who was tapped into the fleet's software, cleared her digital throat and grabbed the attention of everyone present within the walls of the conference room.

Jasmine: "Ahem. If I may. Have you all searched the outer portion of the galaxy?"

Jackie: "Given that the Orion Crusaders' killing spree was done mostly within the galaxy's middle and inner portion. That was the first area we checked. We either found inhabitable or destroyed worlds. Why do you ask?"

Jasmine: "There's a planet by the name of Zora inside the outer portion of the galaxy. My faction and I… had a mission there. It's a sand covered world, ruled by giant worms who attack and destroy any and all things electrical, however the planet is habitable nonetheless."

Jackie: "And the local population?"

Jasmine: "More or less friendly."

Jackie: "Hmmm… It'll have to do, beats wasting any more resources otherwise. I hope you're right about this. We only have enough fuel for one more hyperspace jump."

Elite Jackie activated the public announcement system, enabling the Guardian to give out her command to the civilian fleet simultaneously.

Jackie: "All pilots, plot in the designated coordinates and prepare for light speed travel."

The Guardian pilots did as they were commanded and planned a course for Zora. It did not take long for each vessel to shoot off into hyperspace, leaving the broken pieces of the destroyed battleship forever floating in space.

Meanwhile inside the spacecraft hanger of Elite Jackie's battleship, Elder Rachel entered into the Hercules before making a short walk towards the crew's quarters. She walked through the newly revived spaceship, noticing the fluctuating parts, smooth walls, and pulsating nature as if the ship were breathing. Rachel was impressed all over again by the technical skills possessed by those six armed beings on Exodus, but soon returned to reality as she checked on the recovery process of Raito and Nico before motioning towards Vinzent, who was seen resting peacefully. Later Rachel traveled towards the Hercules's cockpit where she and Jazz reviewed the Elder's progress.

Rachel: "I see Elders Raito and Nico are still holding strong, but still need a proper hospital. What is their status?"

Jasmine: "Correct. Raito lost a lot of blood due to his injuries. His legs can be replaced, but I doubt the Zoranians have the technology to achieve such a feat right now. Like I said before, it's a good thing you gave him a Solar Seed. And Nico's Healing-Factor is extremely slow and in a weakened state to which I've never seen, but nonetheless it's active. I don't know what kind of black flames Orion produced, but Nico is having a difficult time healing his wounds. His fatigued state could also be a byproduct of his Supernova mutation. Nonetheless, he will need an extended time under direct Sunlight if he is to recover completely. There is good news though."

Rachel: "That's refreshing."

Jasmine: "Indeed. Elder Vinzent only received several broken bones and second degree burns on his right arm. He'll make a full recovery and should awaken within the next few days."

Rachel: "That is good news. And what about you Jazz? Are you feeling one hundred?"

Jasmine: "I appreciate your concern. I'm still recovering lost data from that worm virus Cass infected me with, but luckily I was able to pull all the important information before any real damage was done. What about you?"

Rachel: *sigh* "Orion's soul was banished, but for some reason, I fear that this isn't over..."

Jasmine: "Meaning that Orion's soul could return and bring him back?!"

Rachel: "Not on its own no. To untether his soul from the spiritual realm and reconnect back to his body would require a Prana Energy master, and I doubt Raito or anyone from Mahō would commit such an odious action. It's just... something Orion said that's been bothering me. 'With a strong Light, comes an even stronger Darkness.' And the mentioning of an 'Empire'. Do you think he met me? Or maybe the coming of a greater evil?"

Jasmine: "I see your worry, but I also see your strength. You had the chance to join Orion, but instead, you fought against him when you were able. That's all the proof I need. Orion was right, a strong Light does cast a stronger shadow or Darkness. However, the Light and Love of the Creator flows through you, no matter if you practice your style of Source Energy through Ashla or Bogan teachings. To me, you'll always be a Guardian of the Ashura Order. And if there is a greater evil lurking in the shadows, with you, Nico, Vinzent, and Raito, we'll be ready."

Rachel: "Thank you Jazz. The best thing for me to do right now is to keep moving forward, and to be ready if or when that evil reveals itself."

As Rachel and Jasmine finished their conversation, Elite Jackie was heard on the PA system as she announced the fleet's arrival to Zora's star system. One by one, each spacecraft apart of the civilian fleet popped out of hyperspace as they descended down into Zora's orbit then atmosphere. Upon flying through the clouds, several civilians and Guardians saw the remains of giant worms. This bred a sense of mystery within Jazz's computer mind as the AI remembered the fierce nature and close call from the first encounter with them. The fleet flew for several more miles until they saw what seemed to be a village built primarily with the bones and scales of the slain worms. With no fuel left, several battleships made an emergency landing in front of the Zoranian village. Following this, a group of Zoranian guards, including the Zora elected Chief, cautiously walked from their village gate with weapons trained towards Jackie and the Guardians behind her as they exited their exhausted spacecraft.

Zoranian Chief: "Por qué has venido? Sus máquinas atraerán los gusanos hacia nosotros. Vte!"

Jackie: "Jasmine, any ideas?"

Rachel: "Allow me. Cosmic Energy: *Universal Tongue*."

Zoranian Chief: "You must leave this place and take your machines with you."

Jackie: "I can understand you… can you understand me?"

Zoranian Chief: "Y-Yes… you speak our language?"

Rachel: "No, but thanks to the Creator's Light, we share the same vocabulary."

Zoranian Chief: "Your ships, your teachings. You are Guardians of the Ashura Order, yes?

Jackie: "Yes, and we need your help…"

The Chief thought it over for a moment before turning towards his village and motioning his hand to follow.

Zoranian Chief: "You and the red skinned Guardian may enter. The rest must stay here with their machines turned off."

Elite Jackie turned to the other Guardians and gave them the command. Following their commander's order, the civilian fleet powered down its ships and machines. Shortly after, Elite Jackie and Elder Rachel followed behind the Chief into the village. Several four armed Zoranians approached Jackie and pointed at her four arms with a sense of comfortability. Wanting to form an authentic relationship with the Zoranians, Jackie displayed her use of Elemental Energy by forming a massive rocky structure for the children, both from the civilian fleet and Zoranian people, to bond and have fun. Soon after, Elite Jackie waved goodbye before catching up with Rachel and the Chief. They then entered into a large tent where a table and chairs were set up. Jackie and the Zoranian Chief sat across from each other to discuss the fleet's fate.

Zoranian Chief: "You Guardian's use of the Creator's Light is astounding, but nonetheless, we have business to discuss, yes? My name is Kwame, Chief of Zora. Why have you all come here?"

Jackie: "Chief Kwame, I am Elite Guardian Jackie and this here is Elder Guardian Rachel. We seek a new world to call home and to reestablish the Ashura Order."

Chief Kwame: "And what of the planet of Journia?"

Rachel looked away in regret.

Jackie: "It was… destroyed by the Orion Crusaders."

Chief Kwame: "When they attacked Zora, I lost my father and many brothers and sisters. It seems they have taken a piece from everyone, yes?"

Jackie: "To say the least."

Chief Kwame: "Not so long ago, the Ashura Order helped protect this world from complete destruction, now we will return the favor. It would be our honor to welcome the Guardians of the Ashura Order to Zora! Though, because of the worms, the endless seas of sand are what dominates the land."

Jackie: "We Guardians humbly thank you for your generosity. And don't worry about Zora's vegetation. We will bring life and health back to this scarred planet."

Chief Kwame: "Then let this be the beginning of a new era!"

Elite Jackie and Chief Kwame shook hands, solidifying the alliance between the Zoranians and the Guardians. Afterwards, the Zoranian population welcomed the rest of the Guardians and Journia civilians into their village with open arms and warm hearts. The Zora people also prepared a special tent for those who were injured, including Elders Raito and Nico. It was truly a moment of happiness and reassurance.

Two years had passed since the civilian fleet arrived on Zora. Within those two years, The Order and Zoranian people worked tirelessly to heal and rebuild Zora's forests, oceans and to wipe the giant worms from the face of the planet completely. Together, with the help from the power and knowledge possessed by the Guardians, they rebuilt schools, hospitals, spaceports, and took back lost land from the once dominant worm species. They eventually turned the sand covered world into a second Journia, overflowing with an abundance of life, Love, and Light under the Law of One. With the worms gone, technology flourished, and before long, starships were back in the skies, and the primitive life once lived was nothing more than a distant memory. The Ashura Order rebuilt its HQ, and formed a special area of the building called: ***Hall of the Fallen***, for those who died fighting within the second Galactic War. Among those specially honored were Elder Casanova Meyoki, Elder Lucas King, Elder Matthew McCorvin, Elder Luna Joyce, Elder Rex Caldwell, and Elder Kicks Magana. Standing in the Hall of the Fallen were Elders Nico and Vinzent who were now fully recovered. They were joined by Elder Raito who continuously worked to get acclimated to his new artificially cloned legs.

Raito: "Do you think they're at peace?"

Nico: "Without a doubt. From what Vinzent told us, Orion's soul is gone and The Order, though crippled, stands strong. Ironic that Cass did what she did to save this planet, because here we are now, flourishing on the very planet she saved all those years ago."

Raito: "Indeed brotha. What do we do now?"

Vinzent: "We continue to honor those fallen. We continue to rebuild this world. We gather our strength and prepare ourselves for whatever monster lurks in the shadows next. And we teach the next generation of Guardian to accept and master both Ashla and Bogan teachings. The next time an entity threatens Myrmidon, the Ashura Order will be ready."

Elders Nico, Vinzent and Raito all walked from the Hall of the Fallen and out of the newly built Ashura Order HQ to see a sea of civilians, Guardians and Zoranians. The three Elders were surprised and wondered what the celebration was for.

Raito: "What's going on?"

Rachel: "I told everyone about your guy's heroism and bravery against Orion."

Nico: "We only did what needed to be done. Any Guardian would've done the same."

Chief Kwame: "Nonetheless, we're all here to honor you three, and to ask you three to lead the newly formed Ashura Order from this day forward as the *Trio of Light and Dark*."

All three Guardians were perplexed by the request, but nonetheless accepted such a humbling role. Together, Elder Nico, Elder Vinzent, and Elder Raito officially formed and established the new Ashura Order, becoming the Trio of Light and Dark; the three strongest Guardians in Myrmidon history. A few hours later, after the setting of the Sun, the Zoranian population, the Guardians and the Journia survivors, honored the Trio with a huge festival, which included a feast, fireworks and several different activities; this day would later be named the Day of Libertad. The world of Zora, now home to the Ashura Order, was filled with confidence, strength, and peace as they celebrated their victory over Orion and the galaxy's new found peace. Everyone danced, laughed, sung, ate and enjoyed the present moment, a moment that was thought to be never again. Everyone gave thanks to the One Infinite Creator and continued to celebrate like never before. Following this, Elder Raito walked up to Elder Rachel and asked her to join him for a walk to the beach. She agreed and hopped on Raito's back to which the Elder found contentment for his new legs and zipped away using his super speed; not much of a walk. The two traveled through the luscious forest before arriving at one of Zora's majestic oceans. The way the night sky reflected off of the water caught Rachel off guard. For a moment, she completely forgot about the heavy negative thoughts that still flooded her mind two years later.

Raito: "Beautiful, isn't it?"

Rachel: "Absolutely! It's amazing how an entire planet which was once covered in sand, now is filled with forests, animals, and even these gorgeous oceans. It shows the stubbornness of life, Love, and Light of the Creator."

Raito: "Yes it does."

Rachel: "But I have a feeling you didn't bring me out here just to view the ocean."

Raito: "No. Rachel, you are such an extraordinary and beautiful person, and the spirit you possess is captivating. The first time I saw you, I was struck with such courage, not only to save the galaxy, but to save you, and to fight for you against impossible odds. Because of your strength, I found power and peace within myself."

Rachel: "What are you trying to say Raito?"

Raito: "You bring me peace. A peace that no one has ever brought to my heart before. Runaway with me... let's begin a new life, together. You and I, and the vast new galaxy."

Rachel got up from the sand and turned her back towards Raito. The Asronian thought about leaving it all behind. Her responsibilities, her mission as the last Asronian, but she knew she couldn't.

Rachel: *sigh* "Raito... I-I can't... You can't either."

Raito: "What do you mean? Do you not feel the same?"

Rachel: "I do Raito, honestly I do, and it would be a blessing to build a life with you. But you and I have responsibilities that only you and I are capable of completing. You, Vinzent and Nico must train the next generation of Guardians. You three must lead this new Ashura Order and establish order to a broken galaxy."

Raito looked out towards the ocean, the waves flowing gracefully as sea animals leaped from the ocean's surface. The Elder saw the truth behind Rachel's words, but still disappointment flooded his mind.

Raito: "I see. And what about you?"

Rachel: "I have to fix what Orion did. I have to show the galaxy that the Asronian people can contribute to the galaxy's well-being, and not just its downfall. I must redeem my people."

Raito: "Sounds like a tall order for one Asronian."

Rachel: "The Creator will guide me through."

Raito: "In that case... here."

Raito pulled out the red diamond necklace given to him by Titus.

Rachel: "It's beautiful Raito! Where did you find such a priceless jewel?"

Raito: "It was given to me by your father and made by your mother. They love you very much Rachel. Don't forget that."

Rachel's eyes began to water as she gave Raito a loving hug.

Rachel: "Thank you Raito. I-I don't know what to say..."

Raito: "Just be careful on your journey, and don't hesitate to call me if you need help. Guardians are stronger together."

Rachel nodded her head and smiled before leaning in to kiss Raito just as a huge firework lit up the sky above them. Shortly after, Raito and Rachel returned to Zora's newly built capital, Journia City, where the celebration over the Day of Libertad continued like rushing water.

Vinzent: "Raito! Rachel! Where have you two been? Nico was just about to tell us the history of his people."

Raito: "We're coming..."

As Nico told the history of Taiyō, Rachel turned away and looked towards the color filled sky while grabbing her necklace. She whispered, "thank you mother, thank you father. I love and forgive you, now and forever", before turning back to lay her head on Raito's shoulder. They enjoyed Nico's story, and the peace, Love, and Light that came with such a glorious time.

Elsewhere deep within the planet of Asron, Titus walked the halls of his castle when suddenly he saw Athena and his son Gabriel dressed in white and with their hands out. Titus's heart was filled with joy, but then masked by despair as he knew he couldn't leave the castle walls. But that's when his despair was demolished by his wife's words.

Titus: "M-My wife, my son… What is this?... Why are you here?

Athena: "To bring you home my love."

Titus: "But I… I can't leave these walls. I am a prisoner here for eternity because of my selfish and heinous actions against the galaxy. Because of my actions against you…"

Athena: "Was it not your teachings that ultimately saved the galaxy, my dear? Though you have caused a lot, the galaxy, and our daughter lives because of your actions. You have found peace and balance within yourself, and have repaid the Darkness you caused with Love and understanding. You have found forgiveness in the eyes of our daughter, in the eyes of the Creator, and so you are forgiven."

Gabriel: "Come now father, let us go home."

Titus reached up and grabbed his wife's hand, a soft and loving feeling he thought he'd never experience again. Soon after, the Emperor's soul left his scarred and aged body as he regained his younger complexion. His soul was then dressed in all white to match his wife and second son as they ascended towards the sky, breaking through the magical barrier to join the Creator in Love and in Light. Shortly after, the sky upon Castle Pandous cracked and broke, allowing the ocean world above to completely flood the entire area. Asron was now a completely water filled world, through-n-through…

The Myrmidon galaxy, light years away from the present day Milky Way galaxy, was battle scarred and ransacked by Orion, the self-proclaimed god of Darkness. He sought revenge over everyone and everything for the destruction of his homeworld, but lost himself to his own Darkness and greed in the process. The Ashura Order, formed by The Nine, fought and protected the galaxy from that Darkness, but lost brave men and women in the process. Over fourteen million Guardians stood against Orion at the start of the year long war, now only roughly two thousand Guardians remain scattered across the recovering galaxy. However, despite the life changing losses, the Ashura Order still stands strong, and works to not only bring peace and order back **Among The Stars**, but Love, Light, and balance through the teachings and guidance from the One Infinite Creator...

VENGEANCE

Towards the center of the galaxy, on the second planet, Exodus. The Obedience, a destroyed vessel, laid broken and buried under trees, rocks, and nature. Curious about the technology aboard the vessel once again, several six armed entities, who repaired the Hercules two years ago, entered back into the worldship. The smell was horrible as hundreds of dead bodies, including Hando's body lay dead, rotten and decomposed. The beings traversed deeper within The Obedience's lower levels, and down towards the specialized detention level where they saw, to their surprise, an entity engulfed in black flames. Unsure as to what or who it was, the curious beings found a way to power down the flamethrowers and extinguish the black flames. They mistakenly moved closer to the burned entity, but before they could do anything else, one by one they were ruthlessly slaughtered in cold blood by none other than Ude, a.k.a The Arm. The beast managed to regenerate portions of his body, due to Sunlight piercing through the cracks, before bursting through the walls and out into the open world of Exodus. He wandered for hours until he found his master's grave, allowing utter disbelief to fill every corner of his soul. Ude dug up Orion's soulless body and carried it into the Tree of Power several miles South of his location. As Ude traveled to the tree, he noticed the destruction from Orion's battle. The massive deforestation, the ginormous craters, the shattered mountains. He wondered how in the world Guardians could defeat his lord, but the thought was discarded and mattered none as Ude had one task; one goal. And that was to protect his lord's vessel until the day his chosen one comes to reunite Orion's soul with his body, and to once and for all, show the galaxy the strength in Eternal Darkness…

www.ingramcontent.com/pod-product-compliance
Lightning Source LLC
Chambersburg PA
CBHW031150020726
47499CB00002B/306